VOICES FROM THE PAST

A Quintet:

SAPPHO'S JOURNAL
CHRIST'S JOURNAL
LEONARDO DA VINCI'S JOURNAL
SHAKESPEARE'S JOURNAL
LINCOLN'S JOURNAL

Books by

PAUL ALEXANDER BARTLETT

Novels

Voices from the Past:
Sappho's Journal • *Christ's Journal* • *Leonardo da Vinci's Journal*
Shakespeare's Journal • *Lincoln's Journal*

When the Owl Cries

Adiós Mi México

Forward, Children!

Poetry

Wherehill

Spokes for Memory

Nonfiction

The Haciendas of Mexico: An Artist's Record

VOICES FROM THE PAST

A Quintet:

SAPPHO'S JOURNAL
CHRIST'S JOURNAL
LEONARDO DA VINCI'S JOURNAL
SHAKESPEARE'S JOURNAL
LINCOLN'S JOURNAL

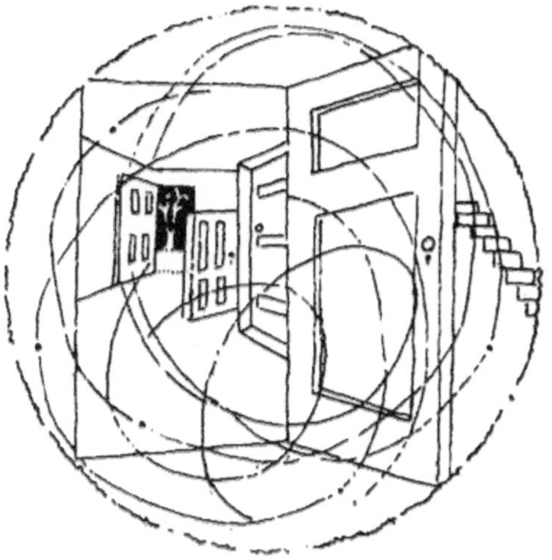

by
PAUL ALEXANDER BARTLETT
and
Illustrated by the Author

Edited by
STEVEN JAMES BARTLETT

AUTOGRAPH EDITIONS
Salem, Oregon

AUTOGRAPH EDITIONS
P. O. Box 6141 · Salem, Oregon 97304

Established 1975

First Edition

ISBN 978-0-6151-4120-6

Library of Congress Catalog Card Number: 2006030830

Printed in the United States of America

Library of Congress Cataloguing-in-Publication Data

Bartlett, Paul Alexander.

Voices from the past : a quintet : Sappho's journal, Christ's journal, Leonardo da Vinci's journal, Shakespeare's journal, Lincoln's journal / by Paul Alexander Bartlett and illustrated by the author ; edited by Steven James Bartlett. -- 1st ed.

p. cm.

Summary: "A collection of five historical novels written in the form of journals by the Greek poet Sappho of Lesbos, Christ, Leonardo da Vinci, Shakespeare, and Lincoln, integrating their thought, writings, and the testimony of others"--Provided by publisher.

ISBN 978-0-6151-4120-6

1. Sappho--Diaries--Fiction. 2. Jesus Christ--Diaries--Fiction. 3. Leonardo, da Vinci, 1452-1519--Diaries--Fiction. 4. Shakespeare, William, 1564-1616--Diaries--Fiction. 5. Lincoln, Abraham, 1809-1865--Diaries--Fiction. I. Bartlett, Steven J. II. Title.

PS3602.A8396V65 2006
813'.6--dc22

2006030830

VOICES FROM THE PAST

CONTENTS

PREFACE

Steven James Bartlett

Senior Research Professor of Philosophy, Oregon State University
and
Visiting Scholar in Psychology & Philosophy, Willamette University

Voices from the Past is a quintet of novels that describe the inner lives of five extraordinary people. Progressing through time from the most distant to the most recent they are: Sappho of Lesbos, the famous Greek poet; Jesus; Leonardo da Vinci; Shakespeare; and Abraham Lincoln. For the most part, little is known about the inward realities of these people, about their personal thoughts, reflections, and the quality and nature of their feelings. For this reason they have become no more than voices from the past: The contributions they have left us remain, but little remains of each person, of his or her personality, of the loves, fears, pleasures, hatreds, beliefs, and thoughts each had.

Voices from the Past was written by Paul Alexander Bartlett over a period of several decades. After his death in an automobile accident in 1990, the manuscripts of the five novels were discovered among his as yet unpublished papers. He had been at work adding the finishing touches to the manuscripts. Now, more than a decade and a half after his death, the publication of *Voices from the Past* is overdue.

Bartlett is known for his fiction, including *When the Owl Cries* and *Adiós Mi México*, historical novels set during the Mexican Revolution of 1910 and descriptive of hacienda life, *Forward, Children!*, a powerful antiwar novel, and numerous short stories. He was also the author of books of poetry, including *Spokes for Memory* and *Wherehill*, the nonfiction work, *The Haciendas of Mexico: An Artist's Record*, the first extensive artistic and photographic study of haciendas throughout Mexico, and numerous articles about the Mexican haciendas. Bartlett was also an artist whose paintings, illustrations, and drawings have been exhibited in more than 40 one-man shows in leading museums in the U.S. and Mexico. Archives of his work and literary correspondence have now been established at the American Heritage Center of the University of Wyoming, the Nettie Lee Benson Latin American Collection of the University of Texas, and the Rare Books Collection of the University of California, Los Angeles.

Paul Alexander Bartlett's life was lived with a single value always central: a sustained dedication to beauty, which he believed was the most vital value of living and his reason for his life as a writer and an artist. *Voices from the Past* reflects this commitment, for he believed that these five voices, in their different ways, express a passion for life, for the creative spirit, and ultimately for beauty in a variety of its forms—poetic and natural (Sappho), spiritual (Jesus), scientific and artistic (da Vinci), literary (Shakespeare), and humanitarian (Lincoln). In this work, he has sought, as faithfully as possible, to relay across time a renewed lyrical meaning of these remarkable individuals, lending them his own voice, with a mood, simplicity, depth of feeling, and love of beauty that were his, and, he believed, also theirs.

The journal form has been used only rarely in works of fiction. Bartlett believed that as a form of literature the journal offers the most effective way to bring back to life the life-worlds of significant, unique, highly individual, and important creators. In each of the novels that make up *Voices from the Past,* his interest is to portray the inner experience of exceptional and special people, about whom there is scant knowledge on this level. During the many years of research he devoted to a study of the lives and thoughts of Sappho, Jesus, Leonardo, Shakespeare, and Lincoln, he sought to base the journals on what is known and what can be surmised about the person behind each voice, and he wove into each journal passages from their writings and the substance of the testimony of others. Yet the five novels are fiction: They re-express in an author's creation lives now buried by the passage of centuries.

I am deeply grateful to my wife, Karen Bartlett, for her faithful, patient, and perceptive help with this long project.

✧

For my father,
Paul Alexander Bartlett,
whose kindness, love of beauty and of place
will always be greatly missed.

SAPPHO'S JOURNAL

"Violet-haired, pure
honey-smiling Sappho"
– Alcaeus

FOREWORD

Willis Barnstone

Distinguished Professor Emeritus of Comparative Literature
Indiana University

Paul Alexander Bartlett's journal of Sappho is a masterful work. I had recently completed a translation of the extant lines of Sappho and am familiar with his problems. He was faced with the almost impossible task of reconstructing the personality of Sappho and her background in ancient Lesbos. To my happy surprise he did so, in a work which is at once poetic, dramatic and powerful. In *Sappho's Journal* he does more than create a vague illusion of the past. He conveys the character of real people, their interior life and outer world. A mature artist, he writes with ease and taste.

Sappho's poetry, quoted in this novel, is included with the translator's permission. The poems appeared in *Sappho, Lyrics in the Original Greek*, with translations by Willis Barnstone, Anchor Books, Doubleday, 1965.

For clarity, the calendar used by Sappho has been translated into our modern calendar.

Sappho's Journal

Sappho, walking on her island beach,
pauses by a broken amphora:
With one foot, she nudges the terra cotta and black jar,
its painted chariot, charioteer and horses:
The charioteer wears a laurel wreath.
Sappho, about 30 years old,
her hair braided around her head,
naked, sandaled, saunters along the Mediterranean,
gulls and pelicans flying, surf and gull sounds in early morning yellow.

Villa Poseidon, Mytilene
642 B.C.

The great storm beats across the island, rattling the olive and the cypress, piling the surf on the beach, hissing the rain across my roof. It is cold and the light of my terra cotta lamp is cold. Some say that a storm will wash away our island, but I do not believe it. Our island will be here long after I have gone, and so will our town, my dear Mytilene, so wrong, so right.

Alcaeus would revel in this gale and go out in it and let the rain lash him and then he would come and take me in his arms.

The storm will rage all night and the gutters spew, and I will rage at my solitude, a solitude that grows and grows.

Growl on, spew on, beat and tramp—tomorrow's sun will return and the sea's eye will glitter and I will gaze across the bay—and Alcaeus will not be here.

My feet are cold and the lamp is weak and the wax hard, and I must go to bed.

Yesterday, the wine workers gathered at a nearby vineyard, old men and girls, in tattered clothes, some lazy, some hard-working, pressing the grapes, many of them my friends. Spade-bearded Niko directed the pressing, sitting at the base of an oak, wearing a stained robe, his voice low. Women carried hampers of grapes loaded with purple clusters, the women's skirts wet with dew, the grapes mottled with damp. Clouds made the day cool. Someone toyed with a flute, the men treading, emptying husks over sandy soil, now and then pausing to talk under the oak, the circular press letting out its red, everyone tasting. Many amphorae were broken, before they were finally filled and capped.

I wanted to help. How sweet the smell flooding my nose.

Atthis has been my girl-child today and we have strolled together up the long, long path to the outcrop, beyond the temple. Atthis and tall white marble columns, with their busy apricot-breasted swallows, have assuaged my loneliness. How lonely we become, as we grow older, even when there is someone to share. The key to self gets lost; self-assurance diminishes. Once, it was only necessary to dash around the garden or throw back one's head and laugh...

Yellow-headed Atthis, lazy-eyed, sitting on the steps of the temple ruin, wove a flower wreath for me and I wove one for her. Then, returning home, we bathed at our fountain, splashing each other, the sun on us and the slippery marble. Afterwards, we lay down and slept, and I dreamed of a ship at sea, her mast broken, her tangled sail and rigging dragging.

Will the war never end?

Fog, as grey as a shepherd's cloak, ruffled the bay for a day and a night. Then, stabbing us, came clarity, and inside that clarity, centered in it, a brown intaglio, a small wooden carving, first one ship and then another. Our fleet had sailed back to us! I watched from the terrace, unable to speak. Atthis ran up to me. Anaktoria came. Gyrinno came. Boys yelled. Old men rushed past the house. Dogs barked. Someone banged a drum. Such clamoring!

But was it joyous news, I asked myself? Why were the women in a knot at the corner? Why hadn't fast rowers raced to tell us? Had the fog tricked the fleet?

Changing my clothes, putting on new sandals, I walked to the pier and the seagulls screamed and we waited and waited. People surged all about, saying wild things, shrieking—then, ominously, fell silent. Their shouts were better than their silence. The ocean seemed too calm, as if it had been smothered by the fog or dreaded the arrival of our fleet.

I had pictured the ships as fast moving, bright on bright water.

As the first one approached, I saw no happy faces, no lifted hands, no raised shields, no plumed helmets at the rail, no flags.

I heard an oar drag and in that sound I heard the rasp of death. If Alcaeus is dead, I will take poison—and I saw myself going to Xerxes, our Persian chemist, and asking for the powder. We had agreed, years back, during another crisis, that he would allow me this gift to free myself, if I must. His yellow face vanished, as

I watched an anchor plunge slowly and saw the sail topple into the water and heard a man cry some name.

Shouts went up.

A chorus began.

Voices caught our song, way out at sea, assuring us that these were not phantoms.

Alcaeus?

Ten years ago, almost ten—ten years ago, he had left Mytilene, the wars sweeping him away. Ten years we had lived with fear creeping about our island. Ten years—how my fingers trembled. I saw those years, there on the wharf, saw them in the gulls' wings, in the distraught faces about me, my girls', my friends', my neighbors'. We had all waited for this homecoming. And now, now our fleet was gliding toward us, grey-hulked, no flags raised, oars shuffling like sick crabs.

Was it defeat or half-victory? Who, among our men, was lost, dead, or wounded? Gull on the masthead, apple at the end of the bough, what can you tell us at such crucial times? For an infinitude, the oars paced, a boat swung, another boat anchoring alongside, the armor on deck flashing, the waves gulping at the gulls.

I turned away, moved back.

And then I saw someone helping Alcaeus ashore—wounded or ill—and old, old, I thought.

Beauty said to me: This is only change.

And I said: But what is change?

And I slipped away, not daring to meet him, hoping someone would shout a name and confirm that this was another, not Alcaeus. But no, I knew. A woman knows a man she has loved, however battered he may be. I turned to watch his blundering progress.

The chorus had dwindled—only those at sea, the far off crews, still carried the hymn. I could not remain any longer. I hurried home, past his house to mine, wondering what kind of haven it could be, wondering what people would say at my flight. Yet this was not flight; it was merely a postponement, waiting for a sign, a chance to prepare myself. Alcaeus...must I send someone to him? What must I do? Go to his home? Shall I be there for him when he arrives?

At my door I turned and retraced my steps to his house, the laces of my sandals making a sound I had never heard before, the gulls wailing, the sounds from the wharf intermingling and incomprehensible.

And I was there when he came with his servant, an ugly Parthian, helping him. Yes, I was there and put out my hand to touch him, hearing his troubled breathing, seeing his torn and disheveled clothes, his rank beard, and knowing he was ill. I remembered the dream, the ship with its broken sail. And I remembered our love and I said to him:

"Alcaeus...it is I, Sappho..."

He squared his shoulders, his cloak slipping away. His arms went out to me, then dropped to his side.

His eyes had the marble core of nothingness in them.

Appalled, I could scarcely stand. O God, what is this that can happen to a man? Why has it happened? His arms in bandages, his eyes forever bandaged by the dark.

"Alcaeus..."

He heard my whisper and shuffled backwards, bumping his servant; he moved forward then and gripped me hard, twisting my flesh, his great muscles rising in his hands.

"Take me to my room... You haven't forgotten the way, have you?"

I took his arm and the Parthian opened the door and servants bowed about us; yes, I took his arm and silently we climbed the stairs to his room, his clothes rough against me, his sea smell around me. We passed his library that held the books he had loved. We passed his mother's room, where she had died. We passed where light fell around us, though no light entered his eyes.

"You are in your room," I said.

"Where?"

"Beside your Egyptian chair."

"Can I sit down on it?"

"Yes, it's ready for you."

Grasping the heavy frame, he lowered himself and the taut leather squeaked. I placed a pillow behind him and drew a fur across his knees, then sat next to him. The door had shut itself and we were alone. We listened to each other's breathing and his hand sought mine and climbed my robe to my face and the coarse fingers felt my cheek and I felt them reach my heart, with the past roaring around me like the recent storm.

I couldn't speak. I felt that the war was forever between us and I hated those years, those battles, the lines on his face. My hate was there, between us. Then, then, tears came to his eyes. Silently, he wept. And I drew him to me.

I heard the wind cross over his house.

Voices shuffled below us in the courtyard, the excited voices of the caretakers, the idle, the hangers-on. I could imagine their leers, their whispers. I lifted his face toward mine and kissed him, his heavy beard sticking my mouth.

There was a sob—a broken gasp. How ill he looked, how tired...

"You must lie down, Alcaeus. Come, I'll help you."

And when he was settled, I brought him water.

"Water...there hasn't been much water these last few days at sea..."

So he had come home, "homeward from earth's far end," on the shield of blindness. I saw him next day and the next, but he seemed strange, withdrawn. I found two of his servants but he wasn't interested.

I thought of him as old. But was he old? Age was in his scars, in his streaked hair and beard, the hands lifting and settling awkwardly.

Warm under the stars, the daphne fragrant, his sea terrace tiles smooth underneath our feet, we sat alone, some rooster vaguely saluting the night, the movement of the surf faint, almost lost. I crushed some daphne in my palm, remembering their four-pronged flowers, remembering—remembering Alcaeus after his field games, his javelin and discus throwing, his flushed face, his eyes lit, his mouth hungry for mine. Remembering—was he remembering, too?

"There was no daphne where I was," he said, his voice sullen. "It would have been better to have died there, than come home like this."

"It's spring, Alcaeus, don't talk like that," I said, and wondered what spring might signify to him.

He did not speak for a while, then quietly, as though to himself, or from another world, he repeated lines we had loved:

"The gods held me in Egypt, longing to sail for home, for I had failed to seek their blessing with an offering..."

His voice had not changed, I realized with a start. Surcharged with new meaning, it entered my being, as he went on about the galleys and the old men "deep in the sea's abyss."

The phrase haunted me because it was he who lived in an abyss.

As days passed, defeat was all that we heard in our town, not outright defeat, but capitulation—retreat combined with truce, truce necessitated by deception. Or was it confusion? The soldiers I met, after their drunken reunions, spoke of the war with bitterness. Ten years, they said. Ten years, for what? And how many of us came back? Those who had been away longest considered themselves outcasts and those who had returned during the war complained, unable to recognize their families.

Standing on the wharf, I familiarized myself with the fleet, its remnants, anchored forlornly in the bay, boys swimming around the hulls, the decks bone dry, hawsers trailing, a door off its hinges, the cordage so rotten a gull might topple a spar. Disgust in my mouth, I tasted the waste of life, Alcaeus', my own, my friends'.

What is life for, but love?

And love sent Atthis and me along the beach, stretching our legs, running, dashing in and out of shallows, finding periwinkles, the day even-tempered, goats nibbling at wild celery, their bells lazy, a fisherman waving at us as he cast his net, clouds over the mountain. I noticed Atthis against the luminous water, her fragile face trusting life. Her yellow ringlets in my lap, she sang to me and then, eyes shut, fingers in the sand, she seemed to steal away.

"What are you thinking about, darling?"

"You..."

"What about?"

"You and Alcaeus—you are so troubled for him."

"Then you have seen him?"

"Yesterday. And I'm afraid."

"Why?"

"Because what is there left for him—and you?"

"I can't answer you, Atthis. Time answers such questions."

I sense my old loneliness, a loneliness that was distorted like a ship's rib, tossed on the beach, warped because of bad luck.

"His arms have been injured, too," Atthis said.

"They will get better, in time..." And I heard time in the receding wave and felt it in her ringlets and in her hands.

"You're so sweet," she said and I saw myself mirrored in her eyes. And it occurred to me that Alcaeus and I would never again be able to exchange notes, those hasty, affectionate scribbles. Would he ever again dictate his bawdy poems, lampoon dictators and brag about war? Had pen and desk become his enemies?

Many things occurred to me, there on the sand, as Atthis and I talked softly.

Sappho's garden, terraces of roses, shrubbery and cypress,
has the ocean below: moonlit, she stands white-robed
close to marble statuary:
a nude Hermes, *a bust of Aphrodite,*
a niobe, an athlete from Delphi.
Sappho sits down on a bench and fingers a lyre.

Tonight, I have returned to my poetry, for the solace and sound of my pen. Here in my library, time will be defeated for a moment, at least. The sun's last rays stream in, so yellow, they might be made of acacia. The cooling light covers my desk and bookshelves and relinquishes its hold of my vase. A fragment clings to the amphora Alcaeus gave me long ago. Its dancing, singing men seem somehow out of focus; yet it seems I hear the flute and lyre of the ceramic players.

I dreamed I talked with Cyprus-born...

No, that is a poor line.

Maybe this is a better theme for tonight:

But I, I love delicate living, and for me,
richness and beauty belong to the sun...

There was a symposium and Gyrinno danced for the guests and afterwards brought me news about Alcaeus, how he left the party and wandered to the beach. There he quarreled with Charaxos, both armed with sticks and staggering drunk. At first, Gyrinno garbled the news, mixing it with the symposium's talk of war, the defeat, the hatreds of many kinds, including punishment and forfeit. It must have been a sorry meeting, this reunion of our warriors. Gyrinno reached me drenched with wine the men hard thrown on her. Other girls had been treated the same.

Welcome home—men!

When I had soothed Gyrinno and bathed and perfumed and powdered her, I went to the beach, thinking I might find them. Yes, they were there, quarreling on the sand, my lover and my brother, kicking their naked shins on driftwood, their servants standing by, only half interested and half awake.

"Charaxos," I began.

"Ah...I rather expected you."

"Sappho?" called Alcaeus.

"Get up, both of you." I moved past the servants indignantly.

"Just leave us alone," growled Charaxos.

"Leave a blind man with you, when it is you who is really blind?"

"Let's not resume our quarrel," said Charaxos.

"When have we stopped?"

"Please go away," said Alcaeus, "I can take care of him, myself."

"I'll not go! I intend to see you home!" And I ordered the servants to separate them and leave me with Alcaeus.

Mumbling, he followed along the shore, walking uncertainly, but keeping out of the way of the inrushing water. Where rocks littered the beach, he allowed me to help him, and was soon apologizing.

"I haven't been home a month and already I act the fool. What right have I to criticize anybody? So he brought home a slave woman. Haven't I had my share?"

I did not interrupt, preoccupied as I was with guiding him. Besides, my anger with Charaxos was too old, too deep-seated, too complex. It was not a subject to pursue on the beach, with the wind carrying our words and the breakers drowning them. This was, I preferred, a private quarrel.

With Charaxos and his men following a distance apart, we made a pretty picture, hiccoughing through Mytilene! Its silent streets were topped by a new moon; Venus seemed swallowed by a single window. Why were we in such contrast?

Laughter and outworn songs...swaying and shuffling...until the shutting of my door.

Alone, I sit beside my lamp to consider its flame, the why and wherefore of its integrity, fragility. Shadows are commonplace when we ignite a lamp. Yet, without a light, there are profounder shadows.

I hear that Alcaeus goes out alone, forbidding his servants to follow. Everyone has become uneasy.

Today, he dismissed his secretary. So poor Gogu has sought me out to explain what happened.

"Someday he will do me in. He has threatened this often enough!" He was trembling so hard, he could hardly speak. It is no wonder Alcaeus calls him a "stick of driftwood." He has an abandoned air that begs to be found and picked up.

"The least word, the least word upsets him. And you know how Alcaeus can rant!"

"Yes, well..."

"He says our great fight at Sigeum was lost through sheer carelessness. Of course, he blames the other officers..."

But then, Gogu has never held anyone's interest or respect for long. Who but Alcaeus would have hired an epileptic, in the first place? Almost everyone has rescued Gogu, at one time or another, from the surf, the wine shop, the brothel or the forum. How does this knobby skeleton manage to survive and endure?

"You will speak to Alcaeus? You promise?"

I promised. The dread of having Gogu permanently abandoned is worse than imploring Alcaeus to take him back. Besides, his scholarship is often surprising, and Alcaeus can use his help.

So later, I invited Alcaeus and some friends to supper. We sat around the courtyard fountain and listened to the harpists playing under the burning lamps. Libus, Nanno, Suidas—they are good company for Alcaeus. He seemed more like himself again, joking and talking. Again he lampooned Mimnermos and mimicked "that strange-smelling country poet from Smyrna." But I detected a morbid note, a self-hostility that cut him more than it did those he scorned.

Will he ever write again?

He left early, insisting he would find his way home by himself. A soldier, reduced to being treated like an irresponsible infant—of course he resented it. But I know he did not return home. Instead, he has rambled into the hills again.

Now the others are gone. And I wonder, looking towards the slope, what it is that Alcaeus hopes to find, a new life?

I shall not be able to sleep indoors tonight. My bed will have to be under the trees. Perhaps the wind can bring me some special message.

The banquet honoring the warriors was held last night.

Alcaeus had his collection of war shields displayed on his dining room walls. Of hide and metal, in various shapes, they united the room and its glazing lamps and candles. I felt myself the focal point of a painted eye on a circular hide, as I sat by him. I could not recall such an assembly in years: Scythian, Etruscan,

Turkish, Negro. Bowls of incense sent threads to the ceiling. Wisps floated in front of me where a man in Egyptian clothes, headband studded with rubies, sat beside his courtesan.

Alcaeus made his way to the dais, when everyone was seated, about fifty of us. Hands resting on a table, arms healed and ringed with copper bands, he leaned forward, waiting for silence. His hair had been freshly curled, and his beard trimmed and brushed with oil. I was troubled, thinking he might be impudent or truculent. Instead he spoke gravely and it was difficult to believe he could not see us. I thought he glanced straight at me.

"Tonight, friends, there will be no tirade, no poetry. I wish to pay my respects, and offer my thanks for our return to our island. I know how beautiful it is..."

There was a murmur of appreciation.

"Soldiers have a way of talking out of turn," he went on, reminding them of the gossip that had come to his ears, shameful talk that made faces blush with guilt and anger.

"It's time for me, as their commander, to speak. Very well, I will!" And his voice thundered across the room, to make sure that none would miss or mistake its message. Was this the Alcaeus who had joked and sported and sung ribald songs, as the popular friend of young men who were proud, rich, playful and naive? Here was someone speaking out of experience...

"I assure you the truce was an honorable truce—and will be respected." An older, solemn Alcaeus...who reviewed the war with wisdom.

"And now let us forget fear and enjoy life and see that our people prosper." It was an impressive speech, one they would long remember.

Our personal servants, assisted by the usual naked boys, waited on us, pouring the Chian wine. Gradually, people began to move about, to talk and drink together. Men long absent from such gatherings moved nervously or waited glumly—alone or in knots of two or three, feeling separate. How does one forget the battlefield? I heard the burr of ancient Egyptian. Persian was spoken by men from Ablas. Women gathered about the newly returned; some were excited, some were beautifully dressed, their hair piled in curls, their shoulders bare, wearing gold sandals.

As the evening wore on, the old familiar sense of freedom returned. Restraint dropped away. Voices and laughter increased. Then applause broke out as a Negro entertainer entered, carrying a smoking torch.

Under the edge of the portico, he freed a basket of birds and juggled several wicker balls. I had never seen this gaunt, ribbed giant, beautifully naked; some said he had come on a wine ship as a crewman. He spun the cages higher and higher and as they whirled in the torch light, he tore open first one and then anther, to liberate the birds. A magnificent performance.

The suggestion worried Pittakos and he pushed through the crowd to take the floor. Pittakos, with his rasping tongue and fish eyes—was there a more dishonest ruler? How ironical that he should represent us! As he kept folding and unfolding his robe, he spoke about our fleet, how he would have the ships repaired and converted into fishing boats for the use of the community...never mentioning that our fleet was rotted!

Presently, the musicians and dancers wandered among us and the party went on. After many songs and a lot of wine, Alcaeus slipped his arm through mine and suggested we go upstairs. It was all very obvious, of course—that he was drunk and I unwilling, that times had changed and everything with it. When was it we had dashed, hand in hand, up his staircase, giggling and pushing one another? How many years ago?

Ah, deception and illusion, do we dare recreate the past and its former happiness? Only in memory is it done successfully. Yet, here we were in his room.

Life is for love!

In the old days, when we had made love, we had closed our eyes, to intensify sensations. Now he would not need to shut his eyes. And his arms, hands, fingers—once young and sure—what could they remember?

I could not keep back tears, tears he would never know, as he stumbled, laughed, then sprawled over the fur covering of his bed. While the music filtered in to us, I cushioned him in my lap and wiped the perspiration from his face, hating the war and the years behind us. After mumbling a few words, he turned over and fell into profound sleep.

So, that was the resumption of our love...and, as I leaned against a hillside olive, the salt air fresh about me, I accepted defeat, aware that my loneliness would appear again and again. There, on the hill, gazing seaward, where fishing smacks moved, I rubbed the horny bark, envying the tree's longevity and its years ahead. Would I trade places, to brood over Mytilene, for centuries?

Alone?

Then Atthis circled me in her arms, creeping up behind me and cupping my eyes. I recognized her by her laughter and perfume.

"Atthis..."

Alcaeus' home is much older than mine, with patina walls, Parian marble floors, and a collection of rare Athenian busts. His library has a Corinthian copy of Homer and a collection of Periander's maxims, while I have been contented with some papyri, of choral lyrics and dithyrambs.

As I stretch out in a leather chair in his library and read to him, the honeysuckle makes its fragrance outside, surely a woman's flower, so fecund. I try to keep my voice and thoughts within the room, beyond the reach of its fragrance. The honeysuckle does not suit us or the room. And Alcaeus knows this, too. His impassive features grow stern, as though to reprimand me. Insatiable Sappho! Yet how can I help it? I must love and be loved.

Laying down the book, I kneel and place my cheek against his knee. His hands, gliding over my hair and neck, are dead. His voice, out of its black, reproaches me.

I want to cry: but I didn't blind you!

The other day in the library, he said:

"I wanted to write something great... During the war, I conceived of a series of island poems, bucolic, legendary, praise of this life." And he motioned toward the ocean and our island.

"Dictate to me," I said, hoping to rouse his impulse.

His silence, at first natural enough, went on, and I became embarrassed by his stare at the bookshelves.

"I want to help you, Alcaeus."

Again the silence. How was I to get through it?

Taking a volume of his poems, I read aloud several of his favorites. Slowly, his face relaxed and he settled deeper in his chair. After a while, he said:

"Read some of yours, Sappho."

I opened a book, one of my earliest ones, and read several passages. But I could not continue; I felt my mind wrapped in fog; my hands became icy. I shut my eyes and said to myself: See, this is what it's like to be blind. You're blind,

blind to love and life...

As I kissed him good-bye, I longed for our youth, its freedom, its daring, its quarrels and fun.

Walking home, I told myself I should never return to his house.

In looking back over the pages of my journal, I am alarmed by the passage of time. When I was young, I thought time was a philanthropist.

I remember so well that day mama took me to the ocean, and the rain fell unexpectedly, lashing and soaking us. We finally discovered a shepherd's hut, but I got colder and colder in its windowless gloom. Lying on the floor, among stiff hides, with the rain sounding loud and the hides smelling strong, I thought the storm would never end. Toward dusk, a shepherd and his boy came, dripping with wet and shivering, and my mother dried the boy and made him lie down with me under the hides. Were we seven or eight? Together, our bodies grew warm and we lay still, listening to the wind and the rain thud across the green roof, while the shepherd went about building a fire and preparing supper. I have forgotten the boy's name, but not his face. Forever after, I thought of him as my first lover. I doubt whether we spoke a word all that delicious evening.

Now I find it hard to renew ties with the past. Not only Alcaeus...but Dioscurides...Pylades...Milo...the very names make me unhappy. All destroyed by war. What special stupidity do men possess that they must involve themselves in such a gamble, with loss inevitable, anyhow?

The columns of the temple of Zeus, in Athens,
stand white against the moonlit sky.
A woman walks among columnar cypress,
her sandals scraping sand and gravel.
A hawk wheels above.

The masks I have on my bedroom walls seem less clever than they appeared years ago. Our theatre, too, has changed through the years, become more mediocre.

Yesterday, at the play, I sat closer than usual and was delighted by the comic faces, so new and frightful that children screamed and squealed. Good, I thought. Perhaps the play may take on life.

...A man with a tambourine strutted about...an old beggar, pack on back, pulled at his beard and mimicked words sung by the chorus. He seemed to be one of us or a Chian, maybe. It was pleasant enough to soak myself in comedy for a while, for right after the play, Charaxos found me and suggested we stroll in private. Obviously, he had something on his mind!

He began by offering me an exquisite scarab, saying he had purchased it for me, from a sailor who had touched port.

"For me?" I became suspicious! I fingered the beetle-shaped oval, unlike any I had seen. An amethyst was set in the center with characters engraved around it.

"An Etruscan scarab should make a pretty keepsake," he said.

"Then I think you should keep it."

"Why? Are you afraid?" he asked.

"Of what?"

"That it might bring bad luck."

He laughed ironically, as he flipped and caught the scarab, with a flick of his wrist.

"What is it you want?" I asked, coming directly to the point.

"To be treated with respect, Rhodopis and I—not criticized."

"Do I say too much?"

"I don't like your tongue." He was scowling now.

"Nor I your woman's!"

"Leave her out! I warn you—she's no longer a slave!"

"It wasn't that she was a slave that bothered me."

"A courtesan, then!"

"No, you should know better than that. Oh, no...it was your assumption that our family funds could be lifted, without my consent and without my knowledge. Taken to buy Rhodopis. You sold three or four wine ships to pay her price, along with the money taken from me."

"Can't you forget..."

"Not conveniently. Nobody enjoys being robbed."

"I have said I would repay you."

"But that was nearly two years ago. And you go right on selling wine and buying equipment. I have heard that you added a ship last month. Wasn't it convenient to pay me then?"

His fist tightened over the scarab, and he bowed and turned away, rejoining his wife who was strolling behind us with her friends and servants.

Theatre!

Villa Poseidon

Atthis, Gyrinno, Anaktoria and I went swimming in the bay by the driftwood tree. It was late, the sun misty, its eye sleepy, pelicans roosting, a dolphin or two frolicking close to shore. I had been unable to forget my meeting with Charaxos, until Anaktoria, who is the best swimmer among us, grabbed me by the heels as I floated by, and towed me to the bottom. That ended my anger and irritation. I lit after her, snatching for her long hair. Arms around her, I forced her to tow me toward shore, making myself as heavy as possible.

As the four of us played on the beach, I thought: When will this happen again? Something about the late afternoon—its hammered out sun, its tempered air, its windlessness, its smell of spring—seemed unreal even as it happened. We tossed our blankets on the sand, dashed back and forth to the water's edge, splashed each other, then arranged ourselves in a circle and began combing each other's hair. We sang and laughed, comparing, whose was finest, whose was thickest.

Atthis, whose hair was shortest, bragged she could swim the farthest. That started an argument.

"Who swam halfway round the island last year?" demanded Gyrinno.

"Who was born at sea?" said Anaktoria.

"You can tell the best swimmer by the shape of her buttocks," said Atthis. "Look at mine, how flat they are." She jumped up, to show us.

"A boy's buttocks," laughed Gyrinno.

"Here. Measure. Mine are smaller," said Anaktoria.

So we measured, laughing, fussing, pushing, our hair streaming around us—a gull on the shore padding back and forth, scolding. Atthis won, but Anaktoria had the loveliest breasts, so round, almost transparent in that evening light. I have rarely seen a girl of such grace, not the childish grace of some, but the accomplished grace of true femininity. As the others became aware of my admiration, they became jealous and peevish, and tried to shift the praise.

They talked about my smallness, my violet hair... "your deep blue eyes"... "your melodious voice..."

But this was Anaktoria's hour. She had been away, visiting in Samnos, staying with her family, and I was eager to hear the news.

"I thought I was homesick... But it is Mytilene I love best... My brother has a girl now. He goes to her house whenever he is not working. I saw very little of him... Life there was very dull. Family visits from door to door. The same cup of wine, the same paste of nuts and fruit, the same questions, answers, family anecdotes and jokes... How lonesome I was!"

Growing quiet, all of us responded to the evening, the lingering sea-light, the arrival of the stars, the whispering shingle, the breeze, carrying the scents and sounds from Mytilene.

Anaktoria and I walked home together, feeling our bond closer, stronger than before. I had missed her more than I thought: I had missed her a dozen times a day.

I have been sick today and to amuse myself I have made some jottings about my girls:

Atthis—lover of yellow ribbons, scared of the dark. To avoid going out, will invent a headache, a toothache or a stomachache. An orphan, she gets homesick for the home she never had. Prefers women to men. Tells amusing jokes and stories. Loves laughter. Mimics. Is made jealous easily. Speaks slowly...ivory-skinned.

Gyrinno—the daughter of a wine merchant, can outdrink most men. Worries about her figure, eats next to nothing. Uses violet perfume. Our best dancer. Otherwise, is lazy, careless of dress and makeup. Never reads. Wants to marry someone wealthy and entertain lavishly. Snores.

Anaktoria—hair yellower than torchlight, soft-girl, dabbler in poetry, dreamer, lovely singer. Plays lyre and flute equally well. Adores games, trees, flowers, swimming, archery. Wants to travel, be a priestess.

Then there are the new girls: Heptha, with copper hair... Myra, who is Turkish... Helen, a scatterbrained darling... Ah, but each is exquisite in her own way. No two are alike. I love them all.

And yet, I am grieved, since my own daughter is jealous of them. Dear, foolish Kleis, who pretends she has never been a child and is yet so far from being a woman.

I have spent weeks over a poem, revising, revising.

I do my best writing in the morning, when the sea light is sparking my room. How important the harmony is to me: harmony in my house, on the island, in my heart.

Sometimes, I call my girls to let them hear what I have written. Sometimes, in the evenings, I recite my poems for friends. Sometimes, I go days, unable to write a word. They are cold days.

Shall I use eleven syllables?

A poem does not grow like a leaf, but has to be shaped. I often think of a lyric as an amphora; little by little I must mold its lines on the wheel of my mind. It is the structure, containing the song. It must be graceful, strong, so that the words and the music can flow...

The wings of the swans have drawn you toward the dark ground,
with yoke chariot bearing down from heaven...
Come to me...free me from trouble...

Today I received a letter from Aesop, written at Adelphi. It is a joy to hear from him. I thought he had forgotten me. What a good companion he was, all those days in Corinth... Companion? He was more like a father!

His handwriting is the most perfect I have ever seen. Each letter formed so patiently, each thought expressed so beautifully. Does he strive for perfection because be cannot forget his deformity?

I remember his eyes used to transfix me with their brown hypnosis.

He must be fifty, I think.

He had his beard trimmed and his hair curled, every morning. His robes, so elegant, so clean, were always perfumed. I seldom saw him without his doll, that bull-leaping doll of Cretan ivory, brightly painted! But his apartment was simple, tastefully furnished, elegant as his clothes. Each bath towel, I recall, bore a brilliant red octopus.

When he looked after Alcaeus and me, we ate with him every day at least one meal. Through all the years of our exile, he remained our most faithful friend. His friends were our friends. His house was ours. His servants. He treated everyone with equal respect.

"I never forget that I was a slave," he often said.

He was much sought after, not only for his humor, but for his wisdom. His reddish whiskers and black brows gave him a comic look. But he sensed his profundity, as he guided me about Corinth and sat beside me at the temple of Apollo, watching the people and the boats and the sea birds, and hearing the choral virgins sing.

Evenings, he would lay aside his doll and tell me fables. He had learned many from his father, a Persian, and he was constantly visiting orientals to pick up their stories and jokes. I hear his smooth, somnolent voice...an effortless storyteller!

"I will certainly come and visit you," he writes. "I am tired of Adelphi. The people make me uncomfortable. I want to roam over Lesbos, to be with you and Alcaeus. I want to see your home."

Will he come? I hope he can. His letter has taken weeks to reach me. I suppose he could be on his way, by this time.

It must have been almost dawn, when Alcaeus and a group of revelers came banging at my door, shouting, laughing. We let them in and they demanded breakfast, some of the more intoxicated trying to seduce my girls, who were quite amused.

When the others were gone, Alcaeus drew me aside to speak in earnest.

"Do you know that Kleis goes to Charaxos' house?"

"What do you mean by that?"

"That she visits your brother's house frequently."

"Do you know this...or is it gossip?"

"We just went by his place. She's there now. I would know her voice anywhere."

"Yes, of course..."

"I don't like his slaves, as you know, and I don't think they are fit company for Kleis."

"No, no, certainly, I shall speak to her..."

"It will take more than that, I'm afraid."

"Why, Alcaeus, she's a mere child..."

"Oh come now, Kleis must be fourteen or more. If she were my daughter, a pretty girl..." He held up a warning finger, then left.

Fourteen? No doubt he meant well, was sincere, but I resented the implication.

Have I really been lax? Is my little girl in need of direction? It seems she was ten or eleven only yesterday. Fourteen, indeed!

Kleis never knew her father. He is one of a thousand dead, because of the wars. If he were here, she would not think of slipping off at night. She looks much like him. I remember his face, the candid eyes and lips.

I remember the ivory gleam of his body. Ah, if he were here...

How am I to forbid Kleis?

Where is my frivolity? Where is my enthusiasm?

The sun's color whitened my shutters and I threw them open on the sea and the light burnished the tiles and splashed the masks and my bed and I stared into its eye, to surprise its oracle.

I am criticized for my simple dress, my tastes. The townspeople say I should not be aloof. They say I am too aristocratic. They say my parties are too gay and exclusive. They say my wealth is insufficient. They say...Yes, I could go on with this pettiness. But why should I?

I have my work and I must live to see beyond the moment, below the surface; I must interpret the whole heart. For I know too well the inexorability of time, the disappointments that nibble one's heels. I must offset the pain, the loss. There is no one to take my arm, there is no one to lean on. There is only my work—and my girls.

All day in the fragrant lemon forest, fallen fruit underneath the trees...all day alone. I have hated loneliness and yet I must be able to rest and get away from responsibilities, to welcome the gods of trees and ocean and those long dead, whose marble shrines dot a corner of this wood. There are so many dead. However, life must be better than death or the gods would have chosen to die. Life must be day-by-day and hour-by-hour. And I talk to myself and totally convince myself and then the mew of a gull shatters my conviction.

Our spring revel saw us high on the mountain, the ocean misty blue, our erotic flutes wailing the dawn. Kleis and I danced together, my girls joining us one by one, the deepest notes growing in volume, the slight notes dropping away. How the wet grass slid our feet!

I closed my eyes, remembering nothing, letting the song have me; then, eyes open, I went on forgetting, forgetting where I was, what this was: I was simply dancing, flashing with someone, alone, dancing for myself and the oncoming sun, dancing because I love to dance, dancing because I love life and time is dead. Yes, time is dead at our spring festival and the flowers never spill from our hair.

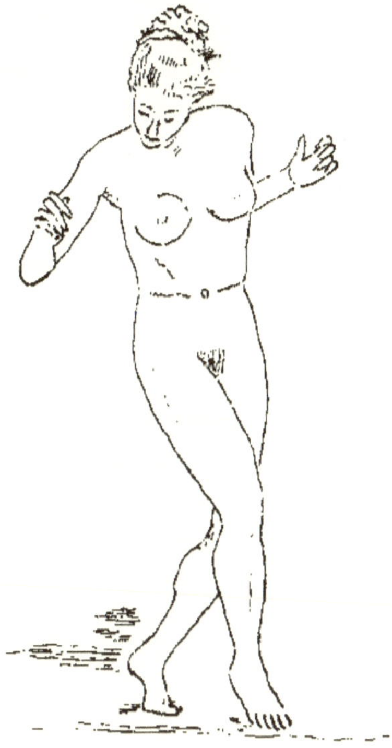

Girls bared their breasts and arms to the light. Men clapped in unison. The music sped up and the faster pace widened our circle of dancers. Our bare feet kicked blossoms thrown by boys. We ate and danced, drank and danced again. Kleis, it seemed to me, danced more beautifully than anyone.

Beauty, I said: We are here again, help

us to find life's meaning.

Beauty said: There is always meaning, look for it.

The step and re-step, circle and re-circle, gulp of air, ache of chest, ache of legs and arms, sullen eyes, eyes longing for embrace...longing... longing...isn't that what life is?

Our tumbled-down temple rose behind us, whitish pillars, roofless phalli, our gowns, arms and faces, circling.

Through my blur of happiness, I saw Anaktoria, Libus, Gorgo, Nano, old friends, fishermen, villagers. Old women went about hawking oranges. Old men drank and talked.

In the afternoon, resting under trees, I became aware that the crowd had scattered into small groups. How hungry we were! How thirsty! Then more dancing and, with tiny fires in the twilight, food cooking, pots bubbling, love-making, songs. It was the dusk I love. And it was easy to grow sentimental, to talk of Alcaeus and miss him, to remember our fun at other festivals. Crickets bubbled like little pots. Frogs burped. A bat fluttered over our fires. Below, somewhere on the bay, a ship winked and made me feel that the sky had gotten below us.

A warm wind and some scarves, that was all I needed to sleep, a sleep somewhat troubled because Kleis was not with me. But during the night she appeared and slipped into my arms, where she began to cry. I comforted her and slept and thought no more about her girlish tears till morning, when she whispered about Charaxos, his heavy drinking, then the darkness and torches, the wild games and dances higher up the mountain...

"I shouldn't have gone with him! I should have stayed with the other boys and girls right here. This time, he has changed me. I'll never be the same! And I can't bear the sight of him!"

...A journal is for solace, for strength.

I write in my library, the rain falling, Kleis in her room, asleep. How sad when youth is tricked! One speaks of treachery, stupidity, ugliness. One thinks of family honor. And then I realize that Charaxos has no sense of honor, that my code is incomprehensible to him. So, I'll not show my distress—our distress.

Life is for the strong, they say.

How strong must a person be?

I feel like dry smoke. And smoke twists and turns inside, not knowing which way to go. Nothing is hotter than the heat of anger.

Charaxos—how the name burns my tongue, sears my tablet. It is impossible to concentrate!

It wasn't enough for us to quarrel over money! You, with your scarab, your Egyptian clothes, your obelisks, your slaves, your woman!

Perhaps Kleis is mistaken. Children are given to exaggeration.

I don't know what to believe.

Today, an earthquake shook our island, sloshing water from our courtyard fountain, making birds cry out. As the walls of the house trembled, I shut my eyes, thinking: No, not yet...there's still so much.

And I made up my mind to go out more, to get about more. With Kleis. We need more time together.

How tall she is! With golden hair and mint eyes, she grows more like her father each day. I detect a restlessness in her nature. Is it because of what happened, or because she is with me? Or do I imagine it?

Her shoulders stoop, her face is sad. When I speak to her about it, she straightens and gazes far off, her eyes worried. Perhaps we make a strange pair.

Gems:
A horseman on a gold agate,
a Nike on chalcedony,
a nude girl on jasper,
a fighting lion on rock crystal...
Sappho is enjoying her collection:
the sun, in her bedroom, is all white.
She is all white.
The gems flash:
We see Sappho's face in her hand mirror,
the faces of her girls around her,
girls singing.

One of my girls has had a birthday. It should have been a happy day. There were garlands, songs, dances... Then, someone came to me, brimming with the amusing story: Kleis has been heard to say that she doesn't know how old she is!

"I've had so many double birthdays, I've lost count," were the words repeated to me.

Why do we wish to be older, younger, always in protest? Why are we never satisfied?

I wish there were no birthdays.

For several days, Kleis and I have sailed, our boat a good fishing boat, captained by a young man named Phaon.

It was our first excursion around the whole island, in years. We sailed past Malea Point to Eresos, to Antiss, then Methymn, and round our island, back to Mytilene. I have never seen the water so calm. Probably because of the recent hot spell, the captain said.

What a peaceful island, our Lesbos... We saw Mt. Ida, olive groves, cypress, temples, bouldered shores, goatherds, date palms, sailboats, dolphins... We thought of Odysseus, trying to identify ourselves with that heroic past, we—only islanders enjoying a holiday!

A striped awning sheltered us during the hot hours of the day. Nights were cool and comfortable. Our handsome captain was attentive. I thought he was particularly agreeable. Our food was tasty. How time drifted along.

Of course it was our being together, lulled by the sea, that made the trip so happy for Kleis and me. It was our shared regrets, our resolve for the future, that brought us close. It was the little things we did for one another, the sleeping together...the voiceless communication.

How wonderful it is to get out of bed and stand by the window and take in the sea and breathe deeply.

How good it is to dream a little.

Phaeon...it is such a beautiful name.

There are days when my girls seem utterly listless. Their activities have no meaning to them. Nothing pleases them. I hear them arguing among themselves, apart. It is as though a stranger had come to be with them.

And Kleis seems more withdrawn. Does she resent the others or do they resent her? A curious unease creeps about the place.

Sometimes, I wonder whether it is I who lacks.

I do not feel well.

Time is slipping by...

I don't know what to do about Kleis: she goes off by herself, and does not tell me where she goes. I can't very well send someone to check on her. That's an ugly thing to do.

I think she isn't visiting Charaxos' house, because he has sailed for Egypt on one of his wine ships. Of course she could be seeing someone else.

Is it possible that she is interested in Phaon...how shall I find out?

I met him on the pier, the wind blowing, the water choppy under grey skies. He left off caulking his boat with a cheery "Hello" and climbed onto the pier. How pleased he was to see me! Was I planning another trip?

Sitting on piles of rope, he told me of an underwater city he had seen, with a great bronze statue of Poseidon by a temple...

"The water was like glass, not a seaweed moving, not a current..." His hand swept sideways, spread flat. "Oh yes, coral...and plenty of fish, big ones. I swam halfway down to the city, but there was no air in me to swim deeper. A fish watched me, from one side of Poseidon, its body curving behind the statue. Poseidon's eyes were made of jewels..."

Phaon is a handsome young man: I think a man is a man when he is handsome all over. I measured him with my eyes, as he talked to me. I measured his feet, hands, thighs, shoulders—the symmetry is unusual. His skin is the color of oakum and his muscles glide perceptibly under his skin. He smells of the sea.

I stayed a long while, talking on the piles of rope, exciting talk. What would it be like to swim with him? To dive deep with him?

We talked and talked. He never mentioned Kleis. And I forgot why I came.

I went to Alcaeus, to tell him about the submerged city.

"You mean Helike?" he asked. "A quake tore apart the coast and it went under," he said, and described something of what I had heard.

"Phaon says the city is visible when the water's clear, and still," I said.

"Phaon?"

"Yes, you remember, the captain who took me on a trip around the island..."

"He fixed his sightless eyes on me and I felt stunned, as one hypnotized. I trembled. Then his expression altered and he changed the subject as quickly as a man might draw a sword during battle.

"I never thought I'd be blind. I never memorized any faces. My home, our bay, the ships—I can't recall things at will, with certainty. There's so little difference now between sleeping and waking. Anything may come to mind.

"A soldier stares at his hand, slashed by a spear. He can't believe he's wounded. It's not his blood spattering the rocks...

"A man lies beside his shield, a hole in his side. He can't believe he sees what he sees..."

Mytilene

For several days, I have been working with Alcaeus in his library. He has taken heart, at last, and is pouring out words, political invective. I sit, amazed. Even his dead eyes have gathered light. He jabs out phrase after phrase, juggling his agate paperweight from hand to hand, steadily, slowly. I barely have time to write. He breathes deeply, his voice sonorous.

Facing the sea, afternoon light on his face, he could be my old Alcaeus.

Thasos brought us wine.

And we worked still late, our lamps guttering in the wind, the air rough from the mainland, tasting of salt. Shutters groaned.

"To strike a balance between common sense and law, this is the cause to which we must pledge ourselves. Our local tyrants must go. They realize there isn't enough corn. Poverty, we must grind against poverty. If our established life and prosperity can't be made to serve, they, too, will go..."

Walking home, I was hardly aware that a gale had sprung up. Exekias, carrying my cloak, seemed surprised at my singing.

A note from Rhodopis—naturally, I was astonished. Her note concerned Kleis: could we talk together?

It was hard to order my thoughts. Rhodopis writing to me, especially with Charaxos gone...

I fixed an hour and we met at a discreet distance from the square, a bench in the rear of a small temple.

Despite the extravagant clothes, the careful makeup, how hard the eyes, the mouth. And I wondered how I looked to her, in my simple dress. But Rhodopis knows the sister of Charaxos is not naive.

It was a brief meeting, cold, the matter quickly attended to.

After waving her servants to stand apart, she faced me with unveiled scorn:

"You daughter's visits are making my household a difficult one," she said.

I flushed.

"So the plaintiff has become the accused? An interesting reversal," I murmured.

"I will expect thanks," she said, with a mocking smile, twisting her parasol into the sand, "for sparing you public embarrassment."

I knew she was sharpening her wits, and paused. She lifted a scented handkerchief to her mouth and took a slow breath.

"I have waited a long time for this, but I'm more charitable than you think. I won't keep you waiting. It is Mallia—a servant boy, who has caught Kleis' fancy..."

Vaguely, I had the flash of an image: a fair, slim, country boy, not one of the slaves.

"And what is it you want?" I said, in the same level voice.

The parasol twirled.

"Oh, things could be arranged..."

I did not doubt this. But not knowing the relationship between Kleis and Mallia, remained silent. My silence seemed to exasperate Rhodopis.

"Of course, you could send Kleis to a *thiase* in Andros," she exclaimed. I refused to flinch. Sending one's daughter to school elsewhere was to admit one's own school had failed. Rhodopis knew this, as well as I.

"Or, I could dismiss Mallia, but then, where would the lovers meet? And if he took her home with him..."

I still waited. Somewhere there was a trap. Rhodopis had not written, then met me, without a purpose.

"Perhaps you have given too much thought to family honor, Sappho. So critical of Charaxos...of me." Her voice had grown confidential.

"If Kleis has done anything foolish, I am willing to accept the responsibility," I said.

"And the consequence, too...with my husband?"

I stood up, brushing off the bench dust.

The interview was over: obviously, further discussion was useless. Why let Rhodopis press her advantage? I nodded and left, with the sound of her laughter behind me.

Why?

It is a question I must answer: it is a multiple question.

Has Rhodopis done this to spite me, wound me, shame me?

Is Kleis doing this to assert herself, to prove that she is not a child? In protest, against me, my house? To estrange us farther?

Did Kleis tell the whole truth about that day at the spring-revel? If I knew what happened...

She seemed so happy on our ocean trip. Or was it I who was happy? Perhaps I teased her too much before Phaon. Did she think I had no right to be attracted to him? Do I make her out to be more sensitive than she really is?

Love is a jealous companion.

Right now, all I can see clearly is that perfumed handkerchief and twirling parasol.

I have never been afraid of consequences attached to my own actions. Must one learn to be braver than that? Or is this a matter of impersonal wisdom?

I have sent for Kleis...

It is true she is fond of Mallia, the boy acting as guardian to her in the house of Charaxos, protecting her from Charaxos.

It was Mallia who served as wine boy at the spring festival.

Curiously, it is Rhodopis who has sided with them in opposing and blocking Charaxos. Yet, that is not so curious, either.

"You're wrong to distrust Rhodopis," says Kleis.

But my doubts persist and I consider her a foolish child. For why would she make a confidante of Rhodopis?

"I wish you could be happier with me," I said.

Our talk seemed to unlock her heart and she burst into tears and I learned how much of a child she is. For it is still filial jealousy that makes her difficult. She cannot bear to share me with my girls, my friends, even my work.

Poor, darling Kleis, how hard it is for some of us to grow up, to learn to walk gracefully alone. I kissed and comforted her as best I could, assuring her of my love.

"There's a place for you here, Kleis. Please try to find it. I know the girls are eager to help you, if you'll let them."

She promised, but the far-away look remained in her eyes.

A *thiase* in Andros—the thought saddens me, for then she would be far away.

I have hurled myself into work. During long silences, while I am thinking, composing, I hear the water clock outside my door. Drop after drop, it fastens itself to my memory.

The wind has continued for days on end, the sun hazy, the surf magnificent in its wildness, all craft beached, no gulls anywhere, a sense of abandonment throughout our town, people scurrying to get indoors.

Only in the garden is there shelter, near the fountain. An angle of the house shuts off the strongest blasts.

I have ordered everyone to work. At least they appear busy.

While the wind howled, a tempest rose in me.

I woke during the night to fight it. Yet, there it was, that perfect symmetry, stripped to the waist, brown caulking material in his hands. I did not need to light a lamp. I had memorized his body. We were moving toward the submerged city; I saw myself swimming beside him; in the water, he was above me, then below me; then we were one, diving together.

I have fought other storms in my blood, and yet this one, with the wind howling, the surf beating, threatens to overcome me. I have never felt more deserted. Death and blindness have made my bed sterile.

Beauty, stay with me! I said.

Beauty said: Don't be afraid.

How shall I cope with this whirlwind? What does it know of surfeit, satiety?

I'm too old, compared to his twenty or twenty-two. He may have a woman of his own, a country girl, a young, simple, laughing slip of a thing who satisfies him.

In my dream I saw him at the prow of his boat, talking with Kleis.

I should send her to Andros.

I need to go to Andros, myself!

I must seek Alcaeus...he must help me...

I see Phaon in his bed, his young arms, his young legs, his close-cropped hair, blue eyes, smooth face.

Like a storm punishing the olives, love shakes me.

I must go to sleep.

Forget!

Another letter has reached me from Aesop. Still in Adelphi, he writes he has been sick with fever.

"My consolation is that I am sick for good reasons. I am sick of men being mistreated. I am sick of injustice.

"As you know, I have been more than a fly on a chariot wheel. I have spoken out publicly and this has raised dust and stones. People stare at me on the streets.

"I am sick of the aristocrats. I am sick of prejudice and ignorance. There must be a better life.

"A free society...this is the most fabulous joke of all time. The ones who rant loudest about it would run the farthest, were it to happen.

"I may have to flee soon, back to Corinth, it seems. These rulers here have friends. They know how to apply pressure.

"Write me, Sappho. I need your sense of the gracious. Beauty foremost—I wish I could think as you think.

"Tell Alcaeus I send him my best, that I miss him..."

I took my letter to Alcaeus and read it aloud in his library.

"I'm afraid it is serious this time," I said.

"It is always serious, when we speak out," said Alcaeus, laying his palms flat on the desk.

"He says it is dangerous for him to come here."

"He must learn restraint!"

"And you, Alcaeus, do you think you have learned restraint?"

There was silence and then he said:

"Those of us who are free must speak, or there will be no freedom, no free men left to restrain those who think in terms of chains."

Sitting in the square the other day, I listened to Alcaeus speaking, excited because he had taken cudgel in hand. Blind though he is, he strikes an imposing figure, even majestic. Leaning on his cane, staring over the townsmen who crowd the forum, he looks a pillar, his head shaggy, beard glistening with oil, clothes immaculate.

Something about the day had a timeless quality, as though none of it was old, the exorbitant taxes, the stringent laws, the situation of the veteran—and the sea rolling, the gulls crying, the sun shining.

Pittakos has not shown any noticeable objection. Perhaps he remembers the youthful champion, before the exile. Then, it was not easy to ignore the charges against those in office, the outcries against "drunkards, thieves, bastards!" Now Pittakos nods and walks on his way, aware that a blind man may be an excellent orator but no longer a soldier.

And recalling the years in exile, I knew how bitter Alcaeus was. If there is less vehemence in his voice than before, there is also greater conviction.

Aegean shells, beach shells,
shells in a woman's hands,
shells in a child's hands.
Underwater, fish glide
through a sunken ship,
passing huge wine jars,
a young Hermes,
sponges...coral...kelp...sharks.

Alcaeus has taken back his former secretary. I am glad for all our sakes: Alcaeus', Gogu's, mine. I hear they are working hard. Now, when Thasos inquires at my door, I make excuses. They can get along without me.

I keep hoping and waiting someone else will come to inquire, will bring a message. Since he never looks for me, I must not look for him.

I will walk by the sea until I am too tired to move.

My pretty Gyrinno is sick with too much sun and too much swimming so I go about pampering her and nothing pleases her more.

It has been some time since I brought her a tray, one I fixed especially for her. I combed her hair tonight, cooled her skin with ointment, and teased her till she made me promise a gift, a silver mirror from Serfo's shop, one with suitably naughty figures on the back and handle: "the convivialists," Serfo has named it.

To help pamper Gyrinno, we had musicians in the courtyard. The air was so warm, so languid, nobody wished to go to sleep. These were wandering musicians, from neighboring islands, and their songs were mostly new to us. They repeated the ones we liked best, tender mountain airs.

Kleis, who has a phenomenal memory, was able to join them the second or third time, harpist and flutist accompany. It was an intimate evening, ending with a tale by one of the wanderers, of Pegasus winging over the ocean on an errand of mercy for a lost lover.

Toward dawn, I woke to find Atthis with me, her cheek against mine. More aware of my inner needs than others, she had come to comfort me, alleviate my longing. Her perfume, kisses and caresses were not the crude, male love I wanted. However, I was half in my dreams and I remembered the music and the tale and the moonlight, our songs and voices, and everything blended into a pattern of peace and goodness.

There are times when our hearts are particularly open to beauty: this was one of those times. Everything, at this moment, assumed perfection. And because we recognize its illusory quality it is the more precious.

Out of the night comes the word someone has tried to communicate, that we are plural, not single...not forgotten. Here, in this comparison, are strength and courage.

Yes, there are times when our hearts open.

There is more to life than wandering over an island. There is more to life than happiness. There is more to life than work. There is more to life than hope. What is it?

Under a cypress, above the sea, facing the sea, I asked myself this question and found this answer:

Certainly, the living is all: there is no life after death: and since there is no other chance than this chance, it must be enough to have beauty and kindness and time to enjoy them.

Here, on this slope, earth's form assures me this is true. And at home, among my girls, I can find it so, each girl an affirmation.

Why is Kleis involved in spats with Gyrinno, Helen, Myra? Why are the girls put out with her? Why can't they agree to do the same thing at the same time?

Why is there so much unrest and dissatisfaction everywhere? Corinth, Sparta, Argos, Sicyon...the news reaches us by boat.

Why is Phaon far at sea, headed for Byzantium?

It seems to be a world of questions.

When I think how many gods exist, I am shocked by man's confusion and gullibility.

"Man is like a cricket. He sees the cricket's limitations but not his own. The cricket can't read or write or think scientifically. He can't sail a boat or build a house. He potters away in his clod or field. What can a cricket know about god?"

That's what man says, unable to see beyond his own clod. He scoffs and sneers but what is he but a two-legged cricket, brown, yellow or black? I'm sure the cricket has his illusions, some of them as pat as ours.

Charaxos has returned to Mytilene.

Our meeting was unavoidable, of course. He had on the commonplace mask of the man in the street and talked about his trip, the grinding poverty in Egypt, the bad state of our mercenaries there...

No mention of settling his debts! Not a word about Rhodopis! Evidently Kleis does not exist.

"All of us are well, thank you," I said. "Nothing has changed for us here."

What is there between us? It is something deeper than ourselves. When I walked away, my eyes burned and my cheeks felt hot.

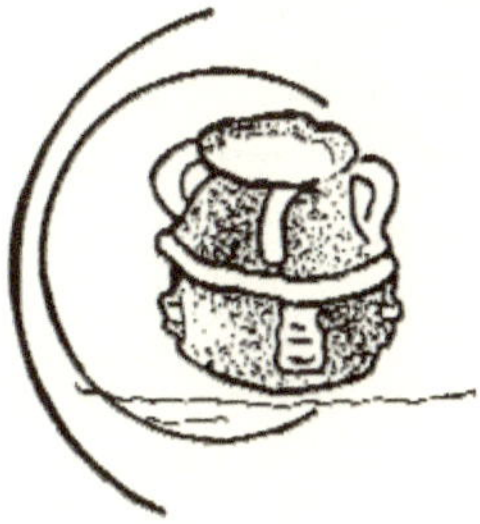

Here is a passage from my first journal, written in childish hand:

Today is my birthday and mother gave me earrings and papa gave me a brooch with a carnelian stone. We had a party on the beach and papa burnt his fingers in the fire as we cooked the mutton meat. I don't like mutton meat. I don't like smoky fires. Papa sings badly. My dog got sick.

I suppose all that was very important to me.

Is our life important to anyone else?

No word from Aesop.

Sometimes I have to get away from everything and everyone, myself as well.

I went to a nearby fishing village. Necessity can be ingenious. The fishermen have managed to build good boats out of the battered wrecks that littered our shores. They tell me that the exporting of sponges has become extensive.

I wish I could sail with a sponge crew. I went with a crew once. Glued inside my decorum, I can't believe I was free...wild...bold...headstrong...long ago.

Yes, I would like to cruise into deep blue water and stare down, then to the sponge shallows and swim down, down.

My new book is ready.

It was interesting to visit the Kamen house and check the copies.

I stopped for a moment in the alley to gaze at the sun symbol painted over the house door. More and more, geometric designs are giving way to more plastic ideas in decorating. Polychrome painting seems to grow more imaginative. Our ceramics are becoming more forceful. I thought of these things as I looked at the sun symbol, done in blue and gold.

The Kamen brothers were, as always, mysterious, stiff, like Egyptian clay long dried by the sun. It is too bad they can't apply some of their art to themselves. They are such emaciated creatures, I wonder what they eat?

Each waits for the other to speak; each scrapes, bows, tries to efface himself. Tall, nut brown, with hair tied behind their necks, deer skin aprons over faded clothes, they make me feel like an intruder.

As for my book, it is excellently made. The brothers are perfectionists in their craft. To them, poetry is nothing. Do they read it at all? However, the libraries will be pleased to receive these copies.

I am sure this is my best work.

Thousands of white herons flew over our island this morning, making the sky a sky of motion. They flew almost all morning, flying toward the mainland. I watched them from a bridge in town, leaning against the cool stone rail, Anaktoria watching with me, perplexed. Not a bird faltered. What directed them? Not a sound, as they flew. Some of the townsmen gathered to stare, dead silent. In tens and twenties, they flew over and onward, apparently at the same speed. Twice the flocks covered the sun and our town darkened, tiled roofs turning grey.

There were murmurs...

I remembered the herons as I tried to rest, wings and more wings, bearing me away.

Sometimes, we troop to our old theatre, lost in its bowl of cypress and overgrown with grass and weeds, seats and benches crumbled. Laying aside our clothes, we toss rover reeds, have a try at archery, play catch. Or we race or go in for leap-frog or tug-of-war.

Little boys like to pester us and poke fun. Little boys—how delightful they can be.

If the day is sultry, we loll. Usually, the complaint is "too much sun." I used to think we needed lots of sun and exercise but now I'm not sure.

Lying on a moss-topped stone, time seemed to pause: I think there is trouble brewing. I don't put it past Rhodopis to concoct something. Even Kleis has been too alarmed to return to Charaxos' house. Mallia has told her to wait.

There has been a to-do because the "right" people did not attend the homecoming party for Charaxos. What a pity! I know of no changes in the life of Mytilene that required a unanimous celebration.

"Why must there be bad feelings between their house and ours?" Kleis has asked. "Of course I hate him for what he did to me."

My knees trembled.

How explain life to one who has not lived it!

"You could help me, if you wanted to," she said.

Just like that!

I believe we only know what life gives us: can sound be described to the deaf?

"After all, Charaxos is your brother," she reminded me.

I wanted to say: He was, before all, not after all.

I can barely check my anger, angers, one on top the other, too many for me to consider and come through sane.

As I went home, I saw a man beating his slave. The slave, who has had everything taken from him, is being punished publicly for an insignificant theft!

The situation is becoming impossible: Why has Charaxos dragged Alcaeus into our quarrel?

I found them hurling insults at one another, Alcaeus' house and servants in an uproar. I hurried into the library and had to pound on the door.

"I can thank you for this!" shouted Charaxos, the moment he saw me.

"Leave, Sappho. I asked him to come and now I'll have him thrown out," Alcaeus bawled, lunging across the table.

"Our hero!" snorted Charaxos.

"Enough. Get out!"

"Suppose you and I have a private word elsewhere," said Charaxos to me, bitterly. "As for you, old battle ax, I'll settle with you another time. I'm sick of your trouble-making. Maybe one exile was not enough..."

Quick as a flash, I slapped him. He eyed me grimly, then turned and left.

Naturally, Alcaeus refused to tell me what the visit was about.

All this is contemptible.

I can not forget the scene of the angry men, the threat.

Perhaps the next move had better be mine? Before my opponent makes it a "check" from which I can't escape...as they say in the new Persian game.

My girls sense that I am troubled and try to distract me.

"No work today!" cries Gyrinno.

"Let's hunt flowers in the woods."

Heptha bothers the cook to prepare me special delights.

Anaktoria dresses up a song, Helen and Gyrinno dance, Atthis tries a musty joke.

It is a healing tempo...I am grateful...

These are lazy, summer days, the hammocks full, doves cooing in the olives. I send my thoughts on a long trip: may they find Phaon and bring him back to me.

This is theatre season and the talk is of actors and acting. I like to familiarize myself with a play before attending its performance because I can appreciate it much more. I never miss a play if I can help it, whether comedy or tragedy, though I prefer comedy. But I think the "offstage" is interesting, too—that is, if one can remain a spectator there. It is when we become involved that we lose our theatre perspective.

Neglates, who used to be a leading actor in Athens, likes to sit with me. He is our best critic. He is always urging me to write a play, "something about us," he says.

"The theatre needs you. Why don't you try? We need new blood."

I suppose he is right. If we rely on the old writers altogether, the stage will become stale. Perhaps I can think of something for the religious festivals next year.

Theatre means meeting people I seldom see anywhere else. I like the contacts.

People feel sorry for Scandia because he is the father of such a charming, marriageable daughter. White-faced, pinch-eyed, his neck twisted by a boyhood accident, one arm dangling—would they feel less sorry for him, if his daughter were ugly?

Andros is the next thing to a dwarf in size. He has the face of a twenty-year-old, although he must be well over fifty. He needs no one's pity—only some money! He is the best mask-maker our theatre has ever had.

Moonlight: Hand in hand,
Sappho and her daughter, Kleis,
walk along a path through hillside
olive groves, the ocean white below,
the murmur of waves part of their leisure and
sad conversation about Aesop.

Mytilene
642 B.C.

My heart is heavy... Aesop, my friend, is dead.

He could have had a kinder messenger—it was Pittakos who brought me the news.

"The mob killed him for causing trouble in Adelphi," he said, his eyes cruelly cold. He had met me on the street, after a performance of "The Martyrs."

Did he think this the right time to let me know? Was it a warning?

I stared at him, as he shambled beside me. Then, before my face could reveal too much, I lowered my veil and walked away, trembling, my eyes unseeing.

I did not go home for a long time. I walked by the shore until the ball of fire sank wearily into the dark water. The hills had a beaten look, the sea an oppressive flatness. A gull's cry wept in me. Alone...alone... I was much more alone.

Alone in my library, I opened the box Aesop had given me and removed his fox, lion, donkey, raven and frog. He had moulded them for me. Two were made of light-colored clay, others of dark. They were as highly glazed as scarabs. I arranged them on a shelf above my desk and could feel my friend's presence, as though he were beside me.

But there would be no more letters.

No visit!

Lighting my lamp, I began my ode to "The Friend of Man."

I knew Alcaeus would be as disturbed as I.

I expected him to roar, "The mob!" Instead, he bowed his head, his hands on his lap, and remained silent. Slowly, he clenched his fists and gouged them into his thighs. Muscles corded his arms and swelled as he stood.

"He should have come here, to us!"

"He was sick, Alcaeus."

"Then I should have gone to him! Why was I doubly blind? I knew he was under attack for opposing the aristocrats."

Round and round, back and forth, we talked: what might have been, what should have been:

"If he had gone to Athens, he would have been safe with Solon."

"If only he could have stayed in Corinth..."

And remembering what a friend Aesop had been to us, he said:

"He knew I liked bread from that oven of Stexos... He was always bringing me my favorite wine."

"He couldn't do enough, that time I got so sick. The best doctors, he..."

"Wild boar, to help you get strong."

We recounted the fables, their Persian origin, the circumstances of their telling. How he loved travelers, especially from the East.

I see Aesop on his balcony, the wind making him blink his eyes; he has on dark blue trousers, yellow sash and gold blouse and carries his doll and is smiling and nodding.

Was it his profound understanding of life that made such a difference? He showed breadth of mind at all times. Revealing human character through animal traits, he taught us the comedy of our faults and aspirations.

Alcaeus has begun writing letters, to protest against this outrage in Adelphi, to alert friends, to cry out.

High on a hill, I sit and stare at my bare feet and try to guess how many steps they have taken.

I peer at my legs and consider the color and texture of my skin. I rub my hands over my knees and ankles.

What of Phaon's feet, the rigging they have climbed and the decks they have walked?

Storms have crashed over him. He has held his ship to sun and stars, legs spread wide, feet on the planking.

Does the sea mean so much to him? Is it his woman?

As I watch the arrival of boats in the bay, the unloading at the dock, I keep remembering his brown face.

The rains have begun.

They flood across the mosaic floor of the courtyard, draining noisily.

I am weaving a scarf, very white, light in weight, my seat a strip of rawhide on four pegs.

Around me the girls sit and chatter. Heptha and Myra weave together, working at one loom, whispering. The rain and wind come together over the house. Laughing secretly, Atthis and Gyrinno dash off, padding through the rain, across the court.

Kleis unwinds my ball of thread and keeps paying it out slowly, rhythmically, her hands in time to a song she is humming to herself.

The white wool is restful. I can weave nothingness or I can weave in my whole past, the sea, my house, the cliffs, the trees.

My fingers are Phaon's.

I have not changed my mother's house since she died because change is no friend of mine. Occasionally, I have had to repair or refinish a table, and a chair or picture, but were mama to return tomorrow she would feel at home.

I often think that I will meet her, as I go from one room to another, mama gliding softly, smiling, holding out her warm hands to me...we would sit and weave by the window, the sea beyond, our voices low. With our terra-cotta lamps gleaming, we would talk until late, too sleepy to chat any longer.

I can't remember my father, he died so young. His lineage, extending to Agamemnon, frightens me: That inheritance must carry into these thick walls and the glazed tiles—a strong house.

Mama gave me his royal flute, said to be carved from a bull's leg, but it has been years since I have taken it from its silk-lined box. Its sickly color never pleased me.

Its music comes to me sometimes: mountain vagaries, war music, sea songs, fragments of a day I can never know.

A bat coasts through my open windows.

Is there a better hour than dusk?

I feel that life is infinitely precious at such an hour, that sordidness and decay are lies. It is the hour when we cross the threshold of starlight.

Sometimes, before dropping asleep, I long to see Olympus, as part of this general dream:

Never is it swept by the winds nor touched by snow,
a purer air surrounds it, a white clarity envelops it,
and the gods there taste of happiness that lasts forever...

It has been a dreadful ordeal. I can hardly describe the events of this past fortnight.

I had barely recovered from the shock of Aesop's death, when word came that Alcaeus had been attacked.

I had gone to a friend's home and we had been chatting on the sea-terrace, when children burst in with the alarming news. I hurried with them to Alcaeus, the boys distressing me with their fantasies.

I found Alcaeus in bed, severely bruised and cut, with Thasos in attendance.

"It was Charaxos," Thasos said, quietly.

I must have gasped. I could not speak.

"I was alone...wandering," Alcaeus explained, then turned his face to the wall.

And I dared to hope that Charaxos would come to his senses! I pressed my lips to Alcaeus' hand.

"I'll get Libus," I said.

"Someone has already gone for him," said Thasos.

Libus, too, was shocked: he ordered the servants to bring Theodorus, another doctor.

As the news spread through town, people gathered in the street in front of Alcaeus' house, angry townsmen, yelling about Charaxos, calling on Pittakos for justice.

During the night, a mob threatened Charaxos' home, and in the morning, they stoned the place, battering shutters, screaming and demanding justice.

Pittakos sent soldiers to maintain order but the soldiers sided with the mob, forcing the doors, smashing furniture and chasing away the servants.

Sometime during the day, Charaxos and Rhodopis fled in one of their wine boats, heading for the mainland. I understand there was a fracas in the square, some wanting to overtake the ship.

For two days, I did not leave Alcaeus' home, taking turns at his side. In that circle of close friends, death pushed us hard, trying to break through.

Finally, Libus, more lean-faced and pallid than usual, from his sleepless nights and responsibility, drew me aside:

"He's going to pull through. You can go home and rest. Trust me..."

I slept and dreamed and came back and the days went like that before Alcaeus was out of danger, and we cheered him on the road to recovery.

Pittakos and some of his officials visited him, expressing their regrets, saying a committee had called, demanding Charaxos' punishment. I kept out of the room, leaving Alcaeus and Libus to handle the situation.

"Our tyrant sides with me!" Alcaeus chortled after they had gone. "I've won!"

It is a poor victory: we have not won back our years of exile. But, for the citizenry, this is something on the side of justice and worth talking about.

For my part, I suspect that Charaxos will return presently, unmolested. He is too important to our local welfare, employing too many, to be brushed aside. When his boat anchors, Pittakos will fine him lightly. By then, sentiment will have cooled.

Justice is rightly placed among the stars.

On my next visit to Alcaeus, I took my clay animals and placed them in his hands, describing each, one by one. He felt them carefully—too slowly—a sad expression on his face.

"So Aesop made them?" he said. "It's good you have them...proof that his world is still here. I wish I could remember his...his faith..."

Taking the figures from Alcaeus, I put them on a table between us: we three had sat at a table like this, in exile, planning, planning: those worries swept back again, distorted. Confused, I could feel myself trapped. I knew that in those eyes opposite me, death sat there, at least a part of death, the same death that was in those clay animals.

Our hands met across the table.

Villa Poseidon

It is useless to cross-examine Alcaeus. He will not discuss Charaxos.

"Here, do me a favor, read me something from Hesiod," he says, and hands me the poet's advice to his brother.

How history repeats itself! Family problems haven't changed: this is an earlier Charaxos, who bribed judges to deprive Hesiod of his inheritance.

If I did not know better, I could almost believe Charaxos had used this story for his model.

As time goes on, I feel the stigma of our relationship more and more. How can I be his sister?

Despite the liberality of our views, I am astonished that Alcaeus respects and trusts me. I can't shake my guilt: the fact that Charaxos has cheated and betrayed me does not exonerate me of blame. I am tired of all this. It is a confusion I can't accept indefinitely.

Phaon's ship has anchored in the harbor.

I have remained in my room throughout the day.

I have enjoyed the detail from my fresco—Etruscan girl strewing flowers, hair streaming over her shoulders, face filled with joy, arms outspread.

I am like that girl.

I took Exekias. As oldest member of my household, I feel she is the best chaperone. In her crumpled face there is more than Assyrian placidity: she has known me longest and is sympathetic and discreet: she says things the way my mother said them, so warmly I can't forget.

We left the house early, our scarves about our heads, women sweeping doorways and steps, sprinkling the dusty street, cleaning where horses and cattle had passed. Birds sickled from the eaves, dogs and horses drank at a watering trough, nuzzling moss, rubbing gnats, their hairy comradeship obvious in roll of eyes.

We had not been in the market long when I saw him, alongside a stall with a sailor, both drinking coconuts, shaking them, holding them up, tipping them, draining the juice, laughing. They had on shorts and were brown, incredible ocean brown.

Then Phaon saw me. Hurriedly, he set down the coconut and left the stall and came toward me, smiling, wiping his fingers on his shorts. In the way he spoke, in the way he stood, I sensed how he had missed me, other tell-tales in his voice and hands. And I knew, as we talked, that he sensed my longing as well: it brought us closer that we made no secret of our feelings.

A parrot jabbered atop its cage and a monkey squealed and battered at its bronze ring, until its owner brought bananas. People crowded us, elbowing with baskets of fruit and shrimp. Phaon and I walked under palm-ceilinged aisles, dust sifting around us, light finning through stalls, over herbs, nuts, wines and cheeses...the smells made me hungry. Together we ate Cappian cheese, tangy to tongue and nose.

"It never tasted better out at sea," he said.

"I hope everything tastes better now."

"It does...yes, I'm home again!"

Exekias ghosted behind me, face alert, her hands pushing me along; so we moved, past the pottery lads, one of them glazing a bowl between his calloused knees, the color as bright as the sliced oranges beside him ready for eating.

"Do you suppose you and I can sail again?" he asked, as we watched, seeing ourselves instead of the pottery boys. "There should be time...soon...when I'm unloaded."

I caught his half question, half statement.

"If I were invited, I'd consider."

My teasing brought a flash from him and laughter and he moved back a little, nodding agreeably.

As I walked home, I felt that my mind had been invaded by everything around me. I tried to hurry, thinking I'd remember all, the prices of the traders, the baskets of starfish, the white parrot; I'll remember his voice, his feet in the dust, his smiles.

Exekias babbled dully about food and flagrant cheating, her basket bumping my hip. I wondered how I could wait, through the days ahead, how could I occupy myself, until Phaon and I sailed? It was a question for water clocks and gulls, spindrift and wind, thought unfolding in my room, scudding across the floor to the window, stopping there, leaping out, to other lands, other times, backlashing with the net that contains yesterday...flames in a cruse...Atthis, slipping her perfumed hands over my eyes...

My lips burn, my hands are moist, I feel faint... Is that my voice, the sound of my laughter? Am I walking over these tiles?

Did I have supper last night? Drink? Rehearse a song?

My girls realize I am lost—wandering. I can't look into their eyes for long. When I see Kleis cross the room a trickle of ice slips down my back.

What if he finds me too old, what if my love doesn't please him...if he mocks me, or stands in awe, or wants to amuse himself?

Phaon...

I see you against every wall, against the sky, in the dark, in the sun under the trees. My flesh aches, my arms melt. Never has passion fermented so strongly in me.

Yet no messenger comes.

I can't bear the nights, to lie alone, to feel my breath on my pillow, feel the cool sheet.

In the morning, I ask Exekias questions, just to hear her voice, not listening, for how can she know whether he has forgotten me or is afraid or sick?

He is busy with his boat and port affairs. He has gone to visit his sister, with no thought of returning soon. He has sailed. He talks with his men—coarse talks. He eats, drinks, works, sleeps, snores.

No—he is fixing our boat for our trip.

No, he has many sweethearts, dark, tall, frivolous, lusty, daring—all young.

Why do I punish myself?

I hurt with weariness and desire. I will simply face the bedroom wall and shut out the light. No, I will concentrate on my work. What shall I write about?

Where is the sea that we sailed?

Was it a long trip?

Was our sail grey or brown?

Was the water rough?

The answers mean so little. Born of the sea, where is love more beautiful than on the sea? Like water, light, warm, swaying, the indispensable ingredient, the transformations, the necessities, the luxury, with the whites of the waves whiter than salt, with gulls flashing in the sun, with the bow of the boat swinging.

We swam, dove, played, laughed. There was bread soaked in honey and nuts dipped in wine and fruit, whose peelings we tossed to the birds. There was the creaking of the sail for our silences, the long brown tiller arm reaching to the sun, his hands on my shoulders.

He padded the bottom of the boat and we lay there, the wind heeling us briefly, the water sucking and his mouth sucking mine and the hunger of his body—the hunger I knew no sea could satisfy. Cradled, we talked softly:

"Was your trip good?"

"We had good weather for several days, then storms... It's like that, you know, most every trip. I try to keep far away from the coast, to avoid shifting winds. I keep farther away than most sailors. It shortens the trip..."

"You're not afraid?"

"No."

"When will you be leaving?"

"I have no cargo."

"Stay...Phaon..."

We had supper and I hated the food that kept us from our love-making.

A sponge lay on the floor and he dipped water over me as the sun washed over us, sinking rapidly. Why couldn't it stay for us? I saw him as Cretan, as Babylonian, as Persian, inventing his lineage. His atavistic hands moved certainly, oarsman's hands, netman's hands, the sea's...mine.

Nothing's more rhythmic than love with waves for bed, rocking, sucking, soothing. I lay there in his arms, thinking of the plants below, the glassy window of the water, the fish, coral, ruined cities...the lovers of other days, the mother of us all, love, pulsing in the rigging, in the pull of his legs, the hasp of his fingers. The rollers were kind to us, never too violent yet tingling the blood. The backs of waves looked at us. The spray spilled salt on our skin, gulls screaming.

We made love again, better than before, this time under the moon, our bodies wet from swimming, the summer night blowing over us, bringing us closer to shore where the surf boomed. Moonlight ignited inside the water and phosphorescence added to the brilliance. Flying fish sprang free. His body was so dark, mine so white...la, the rough of him!

Were any other lovers as happy that day?

As we stretched side by side, he said, with sleepy tongue:

"I remember an evening like this, a night of phosphorescence. I was lying on the deck, almost asleep. A flash tore the sky, silver light...it came streaking nearer and nearer. I woke some of my sailors. My helmsman shouted. We pointed and argued. The light hit the water and sent up boiling steam. We smelled something. Stripping, I swam where the light had hit the water. We were becalmed and I thought I had seen something white but found only dead fish, their bellies shining. The largest one filled my arms and I swam back to the boat and hauled it aboard. It had a brand across one side. We argued, and threw it back."

"What was it that fell?" I asked.

"Some said it was a star," he said.

"I was born in Pyrgos," Phaon tells me, his head on my lap. "I was born in a terrible thunderstorm, in my father's hut. He was a very clever fisherman but there were times when we got very hungry and on one of those times we waded out to sea, he and I, to throw a net...we were hungry. I wasn't helping much but I was there, small, perhaps learning something. Ah, that little island was barren and poor. And there I was in the water, the sun coming out of the sea, blinding me. And then my father screamed and I saw him fall. I tried to reach him. I splashed. I ran. I fell. I shouted. We were alone, we two. My father was thrashing about. It seems he had fallen into a pool, a rock pool, you know what they are. Maybe he forgot it was there, or didn't know. I can't say. But he had been hit by a shark and was bleeding. So I helped him, as best I could, both of us splashing, falling, the surf rising around us, big. He fell on the beach and I ran for help but before I could find help and come to him he had bled to death, on the sand, his hands on his wound, the wound from the shark."

We went up the mountain, to the outcrop and the temple, spent all day alone, the sheep tinkling their bells, the heat steady. He knew of a spring unknown to me and a hollow olive where bees had a hive. Only deep in the olive grove was it cooler and we buried ourselves under the trees.

The watery brown of his body was mine. I found his voice deeper than I had thought. I found his mouth. Discoveries went on, nothing repetitive, the wind, no, the olive shade, or the moss and mushrooms. Crushing a mushroom he rubbed it against his thighs. The smell of mushroom in the cool, dark place! His smell and mine; the smell of earth: life was a vortex of fragrances, peace on the fringes, then a shepherd's bell!

"I've wanted to be a shepherd," I said.

"It would be too lonely for me," he said. "It's lonely enough at sea. I look for a sign of land, a strip of floating bark, land bird or turtle. I look...there at the bow I'm always looking...now it will be you, ahead, in the sea. At sea I have my crew...no, I couldn't be a shepherd. But you?"

"For me, I'd have more time to think, to write, to gather the world of stillness. I could weave it into a pattern we'd recognize as important: succor, inspiration, hope. There is a cliff...you know it... the Leucadian cliff... I'd go there with my flock and dream as they fed about me, the sea below us, the murmur of antiquity around us.

It wasn't easy to visit Alcaeus and hear him talk, as he reclined at supper, his hands close to a lighted lamp, restless fingers, perturbed in a blunted way: the tensility of the battlefield gone from them: moving, they move in on themselves.

"Sometimes, I want to see a face...your face, Sappho. I want to see many faces, the faces of my men. I'd like to see a helmet and plume, the scarlet horse-hair plume...color...what a great thing...

"My house has no window or door. Who wants a house that way?

"What of other blind men and their darkness! What good can that darkness do them?

"When my father was small he was scared of the dark. I never was. But this dark has become fear...words can't break it. Only sleep breaks it. When I'm lying in bed, on the verge of waking, I think, remembering the old light, I think, the sun's up. But where's the sun!"

Someone had dusted his shields and spears on the wall: I noticed the black point of an Egyptian lance, the cold grey pennons on a Persian hide: perhaps they had decorated the sand outside his tent.

This contrast troubled me and yet I longed to share my happiness: the child in me wanted to discountenance reason: the brown shoulders and rolling sea never left me as we talked and I tried to comfort, reminding him of days when it was fun to climb the hills and explore the beaches, fun all day: he admitted there had been time without pain and wondered why we were eventually cheated?

Fog leaned against the house and I described it and he asked me to walk with him. As we followed the shore, he talked of warriors he had know, "strategists," he called them; he boomed his words, excited by memories and the walk and the fog, which he could feel on his face and hands. His cane cracked against driftwood and I restrained him, to find his hands trembling.

The blue of the Aegean is reflected
in the faces of the 50 rowers of the trireme
as they chant and pull;
the blue is reflected on the ship's hull
and the banks of oars.

Phaon and I were offshore in his rowboat, the small sail furled, the surf near by, doubling into smooth green, sunset brazing the horizon. We had been gay, drifting, oar dragging, taking chances with the surf. Upright at the stern, Phaon looked about idly: we had been talking about going for a swim. Suddenly, he faced me and shouted:

"Over there...see them...pirate boats!"

"What?"

"Over there, the other way...those three boats...see the red shields at the bow...Turkish pirates...they're attacking Mytilene. I'll row for the beach. Hang on."

His oar splashed and the boat pitched; pulling with all his strength, he drove us toward the shore, the surf rising, the bow high. I thought we would capsize but before I could make out the pirate ships he beached us and we scrambled ashore, drenched and shoeless. Together, we raced for the square, shouting at everyone we met. Together, we dashed for Alcaeus' house, and threw open his door.

Men in gold, red and blue uniforms stormed our dock and invaded the town. I hung on, behind shutters, unable to tear myself away as the armed gang rushed past the house, forty or more, most of them yelling, one of them, in silver turban, whistling through his fingers, brandishing a scimitar. My mother had described such an attack...I could hear her and see her pained face...a terrible story I had never quite believed.

Phaon yanked shields and spears off the wall and armed Thasos and another man I scarcely knew, a visitor. Women and children hollered and scuttled inside, making for the rear of the house. Something crashed against our street door and men bellowed wildly at us. I saw wood rip the door. Thasos moved in front of me, urging me to hide. Phaon, with shield and sword, his clothes still sopping, threw open the door and beat off a Turkish spear. Catching two men by surprise, he wounded one in the neck and both fled, the uninjured man, a youngster, helping the other one, his shoulder turning red, their short swords rapping their legs as they ran. The injured man lost his turban as they rounded a corner...

"What happened...What's going on?" bellowed Alcaeus, behind Thasos.

"Turks," Phaon shouted, checking the damage to the door, swinging it on its hinges, his hairy shield high on his arm.

Long after dusk, men scouted the streets, all the Turkish boats at sea: the town buzzed with shouts and whistles: a drum throbbed: the raiders had killed two and injured several and plundered a winery and mill, removing flour and filling goat skins with fresh water at several fountains. I piloted Alcaeus about for a while, until my girls discovered me and begged me home, dreading a repetition, though by now armed soldiers had set up guards.

Stars shone brilliantly.

The bay, mirror-smooth, seemed utterly innocent of piracy and death. It accused us of our own folly.

Alone in my room, I reviewed the raid, our floundering ashore, our dash to Alcaeus' house, the brilliant uniforms, wild faces, wild cries, Phaon at the door, Thasos wanting me to hide, children whimpering.

The drummers were signaling each other, the surf sullen, the wind rising.

In a room near me, someone was sobbing. Peace would not return to my house or Mytilene for a while: how long, I wondered? Peace, how frail it is, how carefully it must be protected.

I realized I should comfort my girls and not sit and watch the ocean. It was hard to go to them, harder still to listen to their fears and accusations. When they questioned me I felt that what I described had never happened or happened to someone else. Atthis, holding a puppy in her arms, said she wanted someone to protect her and burst into tears, realizing how unprotected she had been.

Why hadn't I come with Phaon? What if the Turks had climbed the hill?

"You forgot all about us, you just left us here! Oh, Sappho!"

Next day, with my house quieted, I had time to write:

Accomplishments require sacrifice of mind and body; for some, accomplishment will be slow as the sea eating sand. I prefer the swift attainment—it is most inspiring. Death, because it is an incessant threat, retards progress, inhibiting our will to succeed, seeping under us at unexpected moments.

Surely, if we are to conspire against death, if we are to get the most of life, we must be clever, relying on intuition and knowledge, to reach any goal. Surely, the most important element in life is the humane, the kindly, the uncorrupted, tying together little things into something worth while, that will have significance now and later.

Poseidon
641 B.C.

Then, what is love? Isn't it sharing a personality never encountered before? I think it is this kind of interchange and it is exploring someone's thinking, with and without words. With Phaon, it is sharing the sea, the oarsman's hands, the swimmer's legs, yarns on the beach in the firelight. With Alcaeus, it has been our friends, our families, our town, our writing, our exile—years of knowing each other. The differences between Phaon and Alcaeus are so many it would be foolish to try to list them. Comparison gets me nowhere.

I suspect that love is too subtle for any analysis: love is so subtle it escapes while we look. Being in love is rather like being someone else, laughing someone's laughter, tasting someone's wine, dreaming someone's dreams. I feel that close to Phaon. Together, we share the fire, the fire that wakes us in the night, that flies into our eyes, the fire that makes my mouth tremble, that makes me laugh in my mirror, that makes me test my perfume bottles and sends my girls for new powder.

I steal to him—with dignity. I crush him to me, dignity gone. I lose, I gain. I cringe, I lunge. Phaon, you are my body, in me, wanting you, wanting... We are the wanters, haters of nights that keep us apart, haters of time.

Its roaring deafens me: I, I didn't hear you. I, I was wrapped in thought. I was making love...I was reliving the sea, I was in the boat. I was planning our next meeting...I was singing... Darling, I was saying.

Riding donkeys, Phaon and I set out across the island, to visit his sister, riding all day in slow stages, to reach her hut and sleep there. I thought we would never find it, but that was my thinking. Phaon led us through a jumble of hillside rocks, through little valleys, right to her door, a hut of rocks and straw, her shepherd's crook beside the door.

Kleis is so unlike my Kleis.

She seems able to speak without words, perhaps because words are not very useful to her since she lives alone. She nods and smiles, her smile serene. Small, dark, light-boned, she appears out of the past, no sister of Phaon, unrelated to our island. I had not expected her to be so unlike us. Using her particular mystery, she made us comfortable, made us feel at home, a gesture now and then, a word, some roasted seeds, another word, as we talked. Her delight in having us was obvious, coming from deep inside. She has wonderful wind-swept sight, from the rapture of lonely skies, her communions. She is priestess of self-contained youth. She shared her food and we shared things we had brought. Phaon talked of his sea trip, the Mytilene raid, his voice in accord with her quality.

As our relationship deepens, I am more and more aware of his quality. It is best seen in his slow, slow gesture. Or in a spontaneous grin ending in a chuckle. It is in his carriage—his calculating look. His qualities are older than mine, seasoned by the primordial: his speech is older, in vocabulary, accent, intonation.

Kleis and I sang after supper, the supper fire burning.

Her sheep were near us, muffled, shuffling contentedly.

Venus hung over us.

How unlike my Kleis, in her singing and her songs: her songs are songs mother knew: they made me tremble and I wanted to clasp her to me: Phaon had forgotten most of them but joined us sometimes. We sang of lovers and wanderers.

She, the daily wanderer, was less a wanderer than any of us: her natural resources were always at her spiritual command.

Kissing me good night, she said:

"I love you for coming."

Going back home, we poked along, talking and resting at likely places. We stopped in an orange grove to eat, water rippling by us in an irrigation ditch. Cross-legged we ate cheese and dates and drank wine Kleis had given us, the summer smells around us, flowers, so many kinds of flowers in this place. Lying beside me, Phaon told me more about his life:

"...We met a storm off the Egyptian coast, the wind rushing us, tearing our sail. I was at the rudder when the sail split. I ordered my men to huddle in the lee and mend the sail. How we shipped water. The bow crashed. All of us thought we'd go down but they kept on with the mending, folding the fabric, squeezing out the water, wiping rain and spray from their faces. I've never heard a fiercer wind, raging off starboard...

"When we had the sail mended I had someone take the rudder and helped hoist. A wave bowled us over. It was nearly dark and the rain slanted toward me. Out of the side of my eyes, I thought I saw something on the sea, a man, a tall man. I said nothing but worked hard: I couldn't talk or yell in that sea. Part way up the mast, I looked down. Nothing. In spite of wind and rain, we hung our sail and swung out of the troughs. Back at the rudder, I saw him, saw him moving, white, tall, through the whipped tops of the rollers."

Villa Poseidon
641 B.C.

My girls still carry on about the pirate raid.

Gyrinno found a short sword and brought it to me.

"Look, I showed it to Archidemus and he says it's from the Turks. Those are rubies on the hilt, he says. Feel them. See...see..."

Her fingers tremble with excitement.

Her breath catches:

"What if they'd broken into our house? It would have been awful. Aren't you proud of Phaon?"

The whole misadventure leaves me cold. I think of the burial of our dead. I see the blood rushing down the neck of the wounded man. There was blood on Phaon's sword. He and Alcaeus had bellowed over their victory. Victory?

I pushed away the pirate's sword, and said: "It would be better if there were no pirates."

Gyrinno is disgusted.

What is wrong with man? Is man's piratical weakness an instinct? Women don't go in for piracy. We know the value of living and appreciate life's perilousness. We give birth to kindness...each baby is kindness itself.

I have forbidden Gyrinno to keep the sword: she must get rid of it, give it away, throw it away, I don't care.

Rain, rain, rain.

The girls appreciate my happiness since a sense of grace envelops me.

We weave and the rain falls, so gently, our looms fronting the windows and sea. I am weaving a white scarf, quite blemishless.

Weaving has always been the most delightful pastime: I sit and weave and the wool goes in and out: I can see nothing in front of me or I can see my whole past, or tomorrow, or Phaon, the ocean, my house, the faces of my girls...

I work silently sometimes, planning, composing. The art of weaving thoughts must have begun with the loom. The rain falls, and weaves its sounds. Atthis and Anaktoria sit on either side of me, Anaktoria singing to herself. She is dressed in white and Atthis wears blue.

Across the sea a wedge of rain scuds, slowly approaching our island. Shepherds are in their huts. Seamen are ashore. It is a time for all to rest.

At the bridge in town where I had watched the migratory flight of herons, I met Alcaeus. He was perched on the rail, cane crossed over his legs, waiting for Thasos. Glad to see me, he pulled his beard, fragrant and carefully oiled. I found him cheerful. He talked about a Carthaginian ship, in harbor because of broken oars, after sideswiping another boat in a thick fog. As I listened his face altered: it was as if he were in pain or remembered something tragic. Interrupting my comment, he asked:

"What's he like? Is he tall, this Phaon?"

I described him, touching his arm to lessen his resentment.

"So...he's not the soldier type!"

"Must he be?"

"No...a sailor, then!"

"Alcaeus!"

"I know...I know...the changes that have overcome me. I know them better than you."

"And I know my changes."

"Must our friendship end?"

"Alcaeus, let's not go on like this. We understand each other."

"Yes...yes...of course. I apologize... I should have scorned the war. Why was I bellicose?

"I could have kept to my books. I understand it takes infinite time to probe, time to evaluate, time to mature. I have always wanted skill—like yours, working, as you work, through intuition and knowledge of the past. By probing I could have come closer to freedom."

"You have found your freedom," I said.

"Where?"

"Attacking Pittakos, and his sort."

"That's another kind."

"I realize that."

As we strolled home, Thasos with us, he kept thinking, elaborating. Something hurt in me. Wasn't I deluding him? Was there freedom? When he stumbled, I stumbled.

He had been my Phaon. I thought of his encouragement, years ago, when each of us was desperate. That encouragement, that will to help, buoyed me and, talking swiftly, I promised him help, promised closer friendship.

Standing at his door, leaning on his cane, eyelids closed, he recited something heroic and it was my turn to change: my expression must have altered as quickly as his: his sincerity was an answer to mine: I knew he could not see and yet hid my face in my arm. Walking on, I felt he was still in his doorway, trying to see me, trying to understand.

A boy, with a yo-yo, asked me to stop and watch him perform tricks:

"Sappho...I can make it do things," he cried, dangling his yo-yo over my sandal, climbing it up my robe.

Sparkling eyes laughed and I bent and kissed him.

Yesterday, Anaktoria and I walked to a vineyard above the bay, a yard of crumbling walls, twisted, neglected vines, where bees hummed and swallows flicked apricot bellies. It was unduly warm and we threw off our clothes and lay on old leaves, in the shadow of a wall, the waves grumbling behind the stones, coming up, as it were, through masonry and ground.

I noticed her hand in the grass. I noticed my own. It seemed another's hand. The grass altered its identity. I felt my naked knee, pressing a stone: it seemed another knee although I felt the stone. I thought: nature tries to claim us before we are aware, before we are willing to let her. Swift, she likes to confuse, preparatory to that eternal grasp of hers.

Crickets piped under the wall, asking for cooler weather. Abruptly, they stopped, perhaps to listen to Anaktoria's singing. She sang until I fell asleep, to wake and find her sleeping, hands cupped over her breasts, afraid the bees might sting them. The wall's shadow had lengthened and birds were quarreling. Summer's integrity stretched from vineyard to horizon.

I thought about the two of us, our fragility, neither of us marred: sometimes, when someone is loving me, I am especially glad I have an unblemished body: I know my lover will have something to remember.

The ring Libus gave her glistens on her little finger.

Deeper, deeper—our love goes deeper, taking us completely; the early lamps sputter out; the stars gleam in the windows; there is talk of leaving, another trip to sea. But we shake off impending loss with each other's hunger; he says, your perfume stays on me; I say, the smell of you stays on me. He says, come closer, farther under. I say, I can't, I'm stifled, I'm submerged. Oh, impetuous lips. The depth of having someone your own, the depth of being the heart for someone. Phaon...the name, the body, the breath on my neck, special ways, his weight underneath me, supporting me, the sea coming through the windows.

There is nothing better than love.

O Beauty, you know I love him because he is the way I want him to be, you know he is kind...care for him!

A man speaks before the Acropolis in the moonlight:
"Stranger, you have come to the most beautiful place on earth,
the land of swift horses, where the nightingale sings
its melodies among the sacred foliage,
sheltered from the sun's fire and the winter's cold.
Here Bacchus wanders with his nymphs, his divine maidens;
and under the heavenly dew forever flourishes the narcissus,
the crown of great goddesses..."

I have not seen Phaon for days and I feel eaten by rust, the rust that consumes bronze. I feel myself flake between my own fingers. Nothing distracts me. I tell myself I have no right to such feelings; it is wrong: be aware of the beauty around you, I say.

I have always believed that those who live beside the ocean should know more about beauty than others. Their minds should be richer, their faces kinder, their stride freer. Rhythm should be their secret.

I know this is false but I must evoke beauty. I must capture the magnificence of the sea and use its power. I must trap changes and repetitions, the storm's core and summer's laziness. There is superiority in these things, to help us through life.

But, with Phaon away, few things come alive: I am seaweed after the gale. Husk, why trouble others? So, I sulk. Or, when my girls insist, I revive briefly.

When will the atavistic fingers come and when will I smell the cabin's wick and the nets? Oh, drown me, Egyptian lion, Etruscan charioteer, lunge and shield: yours is the tyranny.

Surely feminine love is kinder, less responsible, graced with evasions. Masculine love is a beginning, an intensity that goes on. Masculine love pushes into the future, asking roots, a thread of continuity.

. . .

Last night, Phaon took me among terra-cotta lamps, their wicks flaming coldly. Perspiration glowed on our bodies. A cat jumped on our bed and Phaon pushed it away: wind rustled: leaves shook: flames swayed: this was the love I had wanted and I accepted it and made it live: no little girl's love, mine was glorious, damning all loneliness, knowing he would be gone again.

A dried flying fish revolved on a string above Phaon's cabin door. His boat rose on a gradual swell, seemed unwilling to glide down.

"Let me sail with you when you sail next time," I said.

"How could I take care of you?"

"Right in this cabin."

"Would you sleep on the floor?"

"Why not?"

"What about food? Food goes bad...our cheese spoils...our meat...our water. Sometimes we can't land a fish."

A smile wrinkled his face, as he hulked against the cabin wall, his smile vaguely reassuring.

"What about the heat and cold?" he went on.

"I was hungry and cold in exile."

"That was...years ago."

The flying fish spun, and I thought about time. Had so many years lapsed? I said no more. He had silenced me effectively for I could not endure those prolonged trials and no doubt the sea voyage was impossible: luxury had softened me. The spinning fish would have horrified Atthis. And was I very different?

But we sailed along our coast, hugging it, unloading fruit, getting away from the windless heat of Mytilene, selling dates, lemons and limes. As we sailed in a faint wind, the crew sang. Lolling under an awning, I heard stories of catches at the deeps just beyond us, deeps where the water shimmered flatly, as if of rock. One crewman, not much bigger than a monkey, dove for shells while we crept through shallows. Pink shell in hand, treading a wave nakedly, he offered me his prize, as I leaned over the side. Kelp floated around him and tiny blue fish darted in and out, under his legs and arms, angel fish lower down, perhaps frightened.

While the monkey-man dove for shells, youngsters swam from small boats, hailing us, boarding us, some bringing fish as gifts. A blond, husky body, his shoulders thickly oiled, shared an orange with a girl who had his oval face and fair skin: twins, I thought, and went to the stern to talk to them, comparing their arms and legs, their features and hair. The flock of youngsters cluttering our desk found us amusing and laughed at us.

The twins talked about a wrecked ship, "from a strange land...you can see her at dawn, when the water's quiet...she has a sunken deck, a huge rudder turned by chains. A great red and gold beast is carved over the stern..."

As we shared our oranges, juice trickled between her breasts.

Someone shouted and there was more laughter, and, as if prearranged, the youngsters abandoned us, dove overboard and swam shoreward, splashing, calling, wishing us luck.

I wish I were that young, I told myself.

That night, heat lightning brushed the sky, forming kelp-shaped ropes of yellow. Huge clouds massed about a thin moon and Phaon prophesied rain.

My head on his lap, we drifted, watching, listening to a singer, invisible man at the bow. His words made me uneasy as he sang of lovers lost at sea. Our sail had enough wind to fill it and yet we appeared immobile.

I drew Phaon's face to mine and his mouth tasted of oranges.

Above us, behind us, his flying fish rocked.

The lightning played among the stars and wet the sail and our helmsman bent sleepily over the rudder: it was a night for love and when the cabin had cooled, Phaon and I sought each other: he placed an orange in my hand, the singing went on, the sea sobbed, the orange fell.

"Phaon?"

"What is it?"

Keep me, wait, go on, love me, don't...I wanted to say so much.

I caressed him, breathed him in, the sanctity, the favor, the graciousness, the ephemeral. I wandered through caves. I dove to the wreck of the red-gold ship. I...

Later, we divided the orange and its sweet dribbled over us and he pressed his mouth there and we laughed, thinking with body.

I woke to see the moon sink below the ocean, to see how beautiful he was, his ship and fish swaying as a fresh wind clattered the sail.

Noon found us back in Mytilene.

Phaon

He is god in my eyes...
my tongue is broken;
a thin flame runs under
my skin; seeing nothing,
hearing only my own ears
drumming, I drip with sweat;
trembling shakes my body
and I turn paler than
dry grass. At such times
death isn't far off.

Anaktoria's flesh seems almost transparent—a sensuous softness coming from inside. When my girls are dancing on the terrace or in the garden, I wonder who is most beautiful.

Kleis spins. Atthis bends, arms upflung. I see a grape-tinted breast, fragile ankles. Yellow hair flies over shoulders. Gyrinno's throat is perfect. Malva's thighs. Look, Atthis and Anaktoria are dancing together. For an instant, their lips meet.

Tiles are blue underfoot.

Our wonderful harpist, an old woman, watches with burning, lidless eyes, remembering her naked days, playing them back again.

Cypress are drenched with sun.

Winter has come and Alcaeus has changed.

Winter—Libus and Alcaeus sit in my cold room, waiting. They have been waiting a long time for me; they were here when I returned from my birthday trip.

Alcaeus' face is deeper lined: it has been lined for years but something has happened abruptly, pain has pinched the flesh into new, tiny, angry wrinkles.

Friends have reported that he is drinking again and yet this is more than drink because I realize it is inner debauchery: the eyes cannot confess: instead, the voice tells.

We huddle in our warm robes, the wind howling, and he says, in this new voice:

"What has kept you? We've been waiting a long time."

Libus says:

"We haven't forgotten."

"Or isn't this the day?" Alcaeus asks peevishly.

"Of course it's her day," Libus says.

Alcaeus chuckles.

When was it, I kissed that face, admiring its masculinity? His hands never trembled.

Wind shakes the house.

Mind travels to other days when we struggled in exile, when Alcaeus, badly dressed, kept us in food, stealing, conniving. Often there seemed no way to get by. I sat, waiting, blind to life. That sort of blindness was weakness on my part, or acceptance or hope. Listening, while we drank, I asked what hope he had? He was deriving some satisfaction from his relationship with Libus. There seemed nothing else. Little by little, he forgot why he had come to see me: happy birthday became grimaces, guffawing, vituperations over battles. He and Libus grew excited, enacting scenes with their hands, shuffling their feet.

"This is how I beat off his genitals..."

Alcaeus roared, hand on his beard.

"I beat open his helmet..."

Yes, the war...

And in my room, I found relief listening to the wind, remembering the boat's passage to Limnos, my friends there, the festival in the vineyard, flute and drum, carom of bodies, laughter: Was it Felerian who laughed that low pitched melodious laugh? Was it Marcus who hurled his spear through the target? I erased Alcaeus: so much of life demands voluntary forgetfulness!

My girls had clambered about me at the dock, detaining me. Why does their love soften me? So often there are petty squabbles but, at reunions, they dissolve: the moment becomes a moment of accord, making life worthier: Gyrinno insists on carrying my basket, another smooths my scarf, another offers flowers. Kisses. They buzz into a flurry of plans.

"Tomorrow, we'll go up the mountain..."

"Tomorrow, we'll..."

Ah-hah-who, ah hah-who, the quails cry, as night comes.

I light mama's lamp, so smooth to the fingers after all these years, like alabaster. The wick struggles into flame, as if reluctant to leave the past.

My Etruscan wall girl comes alive.

"Ah-hah-who."

I take off my chain and pearl cluster and lay them in their scented box, pausing, sensing, dreaming.

Perhaps Phaon will be back soon—unexpectedly. I could not remain longer in Limnos, thinking he might return—tonight. I long for his mouth, the jerk of his legs, his *obelisko's* tyranny.

Hunger—let me sleep tonight, tired after the voyage.

No sooner have I returned than I am upset. Life is constricted... I stand among Charaxos' Egyptian treasures, confronting him: a twisted, gilded serpent god sneers at me: fragments of gold leaf blink: mellow gold is underfoot: I sway, as I talk, my parasol clenched across my belly.

"Now, I know," I say to him.

"You know what?"

"That you schemed with Pittakos, to have me exiled, with Alcaeus."

"What?"

"After all these years I've found out. Stop lying. You tried to get our home, that's why you wanted me exiled. What a brother you've been! What a fool I've been!"

For once he shut his mouth.

"During the war years you made many trips, to sell your wines...refusing to help me financially...yours is a debt you won't pay...and you don't care. I've dedicated my life to writing...I live no lie. I work to make life significant.

"And now, why have I come? To quarrel? No, to tell you the truth. I've nothing more to say. I want you to know that I know. It's a satisfaction..."

I could have talked on, but I left, snapping open my parasol, clutching Ezekias' arm, walking swiftly, curbing my pulse, hearing a seagull, the wind icy at the corners of the town, dogs sleeping in the sun, carts passing.

I tried to believe something was settled, that life was worth more for having told the truth. Yet, I wanted to return to Charaxos, demand apologies and restitution, apologies for impertinent, biased criticisms, as if apology, like a brand, could stamp out wrong, as if there were restitution for my cheated years.

Somehow, as I walked, as Ezekias chattered, Aesop commiserated: his hunchback shoulders squared my shoulders: his doll had the dignity of a scepter to prod my spirit.

A tow-headed youth greeted us and I thought: I wish I could have a son. Yes, to give birth again. That glory cancels many defeats.

In Libus' house, I turned to him and said:

"I told Charaxos what you told me weeks ago."

"But I shouldn't have told you, Sappho."

"It was time I knew the truth."

"And now you have an enemy," he said.

"He has been my enemy all the time, Libus."

We sat on his veranda, an agnus-castus sheltering us from the wind. His boy brought us drinks.

"Are we better friends?" he asked.

"I trust you more."

Tree shadows moved across his mouth and chin.

"Trust is not always friendship. I shouldn't have informed. How shallow we are, the best of us. We bungle. Friendship, yours and mine, it's hard to measure, perhaps we shouldn't try: isn't it better left alone? Friendship, that's what we've had all these years...I overstepped propriety."

How pale Libus was, in his grey robe, shadows ridging the fabric, chalking his face, thickening his lips, greying his hair. His sandals moved nervously yet he never moved his hands: they remained weighted to his lap.

I ate supper there, lingering with the ancientness of his rooms, dark mosaics, the crowning of a king behind him, Libus' chair of white leather, the king in the mosaic studying his crown, his jewels flashing red, a hint of Corinth and a hint of Crete.

Remembering my shepherd visit, I wrote this:

EVENING STAR

Hesperus, you bring
Homeward all that
Dawn's light disperses,

Bring home sheep,
Bring home goats,
Bring children home
To their mothers.

What is it urges the mind to seek beauty? What is the challenge? Why go where there are no charts?

Beauty says it is a kind of love.

So, I make love, in my quiet room, the word symbolic of man, life's continuity, my paper taken from reeds and trees. I write of birth, love, marriage and death, sensing that the unrecorded is vaster than the recorded. I sense the stumbling: the past could be a gigantic storm, fog obliterating at moment of revelation, fog fumbling from man to man, saying come, saying stop. The past is a wave through which no swimmer passes. As surf it inundates, then vanishes. On windy nights, it moans at my window, beautiful and hideous. I struggle on.

I quote from my journal kept in exile:

> *For three days we have had little to eat, days of quarrels, bitterness and savagery.*
>
> *I gave myself to a merchant and he has returned the favor by feeding Alcaeus and me. We ate in the kitchen, glad to find considerate slaves. We can remain long enough to recover our strength, if not our hopes.*
>
> *How I long for home and my servants, fish as Exekias can prepare it, onions in Chian wine, olives from Patmos. It helps to list the good things. Surely they are not lost.*
>
> *How wretched to cheat myself to keep alive, to cheat the face, the mooning eyes, the stupid mouth, the odor of flagrancy, the disbelief...chattel, cringe, lie still, perform.*

Copying those lines I remembered things I have never recorded, our filthy clothes, windowless room, flies, thirst, sickness...Alcaeus in jail... I was fined...authorities jeered at us...no sympathy, no luck until Aesop, his fox, raven and rooster.

I never thought him brilliant but he was always entertaining, agreeable about the smallest problem. Nuances come to me, as he told of a turtle that ferried a small turtle and then, at the end of the pleasant ride, said:

"Little turtle, you must pay."

"How can I pay?" asked the little turtle.

"By doing me a favor."

"Well, what can I do?"

"Hump along the beach and snatch me a fly."

"I'll do my best," said the little turtle.

After humping and snapping till almost noon, the little turtle brought a fly to the big turtle. Finding the big fellow asleep, the little one had to cuff him.

"Here," said the turtle, between closed lips.

"Ah," exclaimed the big turtle, swallowing the fly, tasting it with care. "Umm, that's the first fly I ever ate! You see a little fellow like you can do things a big fellow can't."

During the night an earthquake woke me and I wandered through the bedrooms, to see about my girls. Atthis needed covering and as I arranged her covers she murmured, "Mama, mama." Before I could slip away, she grasped my hand.

"Are you homesick, darling?"

When I kissed her, I found her face wet with tears. "Why don't you go home for a few weeks?" I whispered. "You were calling your mama in your sleep. If you're homesick, you must go home. Let's talk about it tomorrow. Do you want me to sleep with you?"

So we cuddled together and almost at once she relaxed and, after a few endearments, slept with her head on my shoulder, her violet fragrance around me. I held her fingers a long time. Drowsily, I asked: where do we go...why can't we remain young...happy? The last thing I recalled was the sweetness of her perfume.

The earthquake had been forgotten.

Alcaeus sat on his leather stool, his dog at his feet, sunlight behind him; elbows on his knees, he said:

"...I prefer that hymn. There's really no finer. In spite of time it's full of force, spring's arrival, the brevity of summer, the dying year. It has the shepherd's power, the forest's—passion tamed and sanctified. Another one I like is...

The woods decay, the woods decay and fall...

Libus, sitting near Alcaeus, quoted his favorite, huddling in his robe, his face averted:

Alone, in sea-circled Delos, while round on beach and cove,
before the piping sea wind the dark blue storm waves drove...

"Why do you break off?" I asked.

He did not answer but said:

"They knew, those ancients, how to supplicate the lowliest...they preferred the virginal...snowy peaks...whispering groves...the hunting cry..."

Warming my feet on a warming stone, I said I preferred the golden hymn and repeated fragments...

Long are their ways of living, honey in their bread,
and in their dances their footsteps twirl, twirling light...

Fragment of talk:

"We can't marry, unless we have a child...you'll be twenty-three soon...it must be like that...my house is a house of women..."

I thought of those words as I passed Phaon's house, beyond the wharf, isolated. As I passed, waves climbed its base, licking at boulders. Its walls are thicker than most, cracked and mottled. I used to be afraid of that house as a girl and as I passed these thoughts brought back some of that apprehension. I glanced at the seaward balcony, tottering on wasted beams, painted years ago. Seagulls squatted on the flat roof, as they have day in and day out. There are five rooms underneath those tiles and his mother and uncle lived and died there, a harsh struggle in rooms of simple furnishings, coils of rope, nets, brass fittings and bronze anchors.

Phaon lives there with two men, their servants and a hanger-on. Kleis visits occasionally. A parrot, some say nearly two hundred years old, gabbles sayings and fills the sea-sopped silences.

Yes, his house troubles me—its darkness, its evocation of poverty and my own exile.

While I was ill, Libus cared for me, the mastery of his hands relieving pain. By my bed, talking soothing talk, he brought gradual relief, just as two years ago. His hands are more than hands, it seems. Magical masseur, he explores yet never gropes: his fingers, padded at the tips, press, release, wait. Our friendship, with all its confidences, in spite of differences, weathers the years and is stronger at such a time, under his mastery. As he obliterates pain, he blinks absently or smiles his pale smile, withdrawn yet assuring. He learned his art from a young Alexandrian, a man he met while studying in Athens, who spoke many desert languages.

"I'd like to see him again. I've learned something through my own experiments; we would share. Of course, he's a great man."

And when I asked Libus about my illness, he said:

"Too much work, too much rich food, too much concern. You haven't been using common sense."

I didn't care for this and said:

"I know from what Alcaeus says, you help him more than anyone. You can help me."

"I'm not able to help him all the time."

"You mean his drinking?"

He shrugged.

"Let's call it something else. He does nothing so much of the time. That's where the trouble lies. He's not thinking...doesn't care."

"He wouldn't let me in when I went last. Thasos had to turn me away."

"The great soldier...drunk."

"What can I do?"

"Try again, Sappho. You and I know what he is—and was. You used to understand him better than anyone. Now, well, I do what I can. He's growing worse...have you heard him bellow at me or Thasos, as if he were commanding officer? No doubt you have...and more..."

Libus' hands pushed and then, feather-weight, stroked upward, over and over, inducing me to breathe steadily: his hands brought warmth, my thinking became clearer. As he pressed, the weight on my heart lessened; as his fingers covered my stomach, rotating their tips, I felt bitter anguish might not come again.

Lecturing me, he cautioned me about food and advised less exercise: rest, let the days flow by.

So, I sail with my girls, lie in the sun, walk, poke along lazy trails, fuss in my garden. Winter is hard on me. Chills come, leaving my stomach knotted, my eyes afire.

Phaon has returned.

Phaon and Sappho kneel in a grove,
a cithara beside them:
age-old trees shade the lovers:
the age of a ruined temple is part of
the timelessness of the grove:
bronze Phaon and white Sappho,
dusk takes over their whispers,
their motions, the wind in the olives.

Under the olive trees we faced each other, alone, the sun coloring the ground, patching yellow and brown. A butterfly circled, as if considering us. Tenderly, Phaon fitted his hands over my breasts and I held him in my arms; swaying, we kissed: we had not talked much and we knew talk could come later: his legs crowded mine: his hand undid my hair, spilling it over my shoulders: confirmation was in that undisturbed place and accord burned our mouths and throats. Encystment was the slipping down of robes, our knees touching, the feeling, self, and underneath self, the ground, our earth: yet we were not aware, only before and later: the consummation dragged at the trees: I forced him to me, forcing back his face, his mouth: how warm his stamina: tenderly, we rose, to fall back: tenderness, how it becomes ash, taking us by surprise: I couldn't stop quivering till his hands stopped me: his voice was real so all was real: then, he was home and this was not a lie: I knew it on the slope of hills sloping to the ocean: I knew it in the boat, far at sea.

When we learned of a terrible earthquake at Chios, we loaded Libus' boat with food, wine and water and set out, before dawn, across choppy water, Phaon and I at the stern, under blankets, Libus managing the sail. We were part of a small fleet but I couldn't discern another boat. Spray swished overhead and fog, ahead and astern, seemed ready to pincer us. Under our hull the water flooded ominously; the sky, without its stars, might have been the ocean.

Our hard trip brought us into Chios tired and hungry; we had been unable to look after ourselves but, without eating, we began to distribute food and wine.

Chios—happy town—lay broken. I walked about, remembering, stopping here and there: all the central part, shops and temple, were dismembered, had windy dust blowing across it, greyish dust that seemed mortuary. Yet, I saw no dead, only the injured: Libus helped them, bandaging, talking: I gave wine and water, afraid: he was annoyed by my fear: I could not find Phaon and that worried me. Wine, and water, dribbling them, my hamper shaking, the wind icy and dust in my mouth, I felt sick again. A child raced to me, wailing: crouching down, I mothered her, fed her a little bread: as we crouched, a slab of building fell, tottered forward and disappeared in a wave of dust.

"The quake came and came and then came again," an injured woman said, accepting dates and cheese.

By now, I saw others from Mytilene and their hearty faces cheered me. But how the gulls screamed. Flocks wheeled and screamed.

On the beach we lit fires and cooked our suppers, wind and dust still bothering us: Phaon and I ate with people from home, our fire put together from the prow of an old boat, the talk about Chios and the injured, their lack of food and care. We slept in beached boats, the surf snarling, stars breaking through fast clouds: I remembered the big dipper and frightened people... Libus woke us early and we did our best to help, using splints, caring for a head wound, bandaging a boy's chest... Libus scarcely allowed himself time to eat.

The wind had subsided, and I felt less fear and went about with my basket of food and wine. In the afternoon, we welcomed other boats from Lesbos and after a second night on the beach—this one calm, all the stars awake—we sailed for home, three of us leaving at the same time, our boats so many grey corks on a line.

As I stared back at the stricken town, I heard the gulls. "Phaon, it was bad," I said.

"Yes, very bad, though I've seen worse."

"I hope I never do."

"These people had help...sometimes there is nobody to help."

"We're in the lead," Libus cried. "We'll be the first ones home. Now for some sleep."

Today, I had a letter from Solon: he discussed politics and his immediate intentions and then went on to consider my poetry, praising it for its lyrical quality, refreshing themes, compassion and sense of beauty.

I respect his judgment and his quotations sent me to my books, to reconsider and evaluate. For a while, I sat at my desk, thinking over passages, contemplating the ocean, serenely blue as usual. Life, for the moment, was balanced: it had acquired profundity and calm: here was my reward since I believed his assessments just: for once, I needed no one to share: I needed nothing.

But I picked up Aesop's clay fox and recognized my need: the bite of yesterday cornered me.

Kleis has fallen in love—this time with a cousin of Pittakos. I am amused, and have done all I dare to make the pair happy, picnicking and boating.

I have seen him at play on the field, built well, long of leg, with a homely, genial face and grin that consistently makes up for mediocrity. Like his cousin, I could add. But that's unfair. When I see him screw up his mouth in front of Kleis, I sag. The next moment he brightens and seems about to say something intelligent. Then, the cycle resumes. Love, I remind myself, with inward nod, can be curious.

Well, I am playing the game—if it is a game—circumspectly, knowing winds can be fickle. I gather news from my girls who too often babble.

"See, how she conducts herself! She's grown up!"

"My, they're serious!"

I am aware of her airs.

Am I to forget her clandestine meetings of a few months ago and expect her golden head to settle down?

She confides in me and I conceal my smiles.

However, doubts from deep inside prompt me to accept and not go in for ridicule: where is another daughter, where is the boy suited to your taste? Is she to fall in love your way? Deeper, I discern the sacredness of life, elements of faith and love.

Thinking these things, I go where the hills plunge to the bay: I listen, under my parasol: there is much more than sound or silence: I am confronted by yesterday, in the gulls: I squint, and there, on milky horizon, I glimpse the spirit of man, blundering, a plant in his hand, a rope dragging behind him, a dog by his side: what is the rope for?

I think of my school and how taxing it is to teach kindness, moderation and beauty: yet, I am confident, teaching is worth while and living worth while: good meals, laughter, music, dancing, love: they are there with him and his dog and the rope, in sound or silence.

Kleis, may you find a good way, all the way.

For my part, my relationship with Phaon affords discovery, Sumerian lassitude, great rivers and forests, prowling sand, the bay and its currents, the hull dipping, the rower heaving his arms, groaning.

Illusion, deceit, whatever it is, this is the happiest period of my life.

As I walked by the columns of my garden, I recognized that never have I accomplished so much. I have unlocked doors. I see my esthetic way: my personal recollections have pulled out of ruts. I have uncovered uniqueness, sensibility... I have seen what it has cost man to survive: dunes against dunes, lack of water, perilous heat: I have weighed his potential, his grace, his beauty. I have sensed that appalling black that existed before the coming of books. I have heard torn sail and smashed rudder. I have felt the foundering.

That darkness must not come again!

We must see to that!

I walked among my statuary and benches, absorbing the difference in roses: home and happiness were secure in me: my writing must be a part of this place: marble benches, a face augustly seaward, lichened with green: another face turned toward the sun, his enigma personal, his serpent's head prowling through a disc.

I found this in my journal, written more than fifteen years ago:

> *Yesterday, Cercolas and I spent the day in an olive grove where men were knocking olives off the trees...we walked far.*

That is all I wrote and yet that was one of the most joyous days. What kept me from describing our happiness? Was I too close to it? Or was the next day one of those hurried days and I thought I would write about our day later on? Later?

A year later Cercolas was dead at war.

And what made those hours precious? It was our accord, the day itself and everything we saw and did. I realize this now. His arms were around me, or mine curled about his waist. His mouth went to mine, many times. Mine to his. I wish I could remember what we said but I remember his smiles and I remember his coarse brown Andrian robe and I remember how we looked at this and that, making each thing ours.

Cercolas...your name is euphonious...your fingers reach out of death...I glimpse your smile.

But is this all that remains when we are gone?
Is this the answer?

I have often relived the experience of giving birth. Had Cercolas lived, there would have been other children. Kleis was born on a summer's day, the ocean lapping after a windy night, a dragonfly in my room, clicking its wings over my bed. Mama saw it and murmured:

"There...see it above you. Now, I know you'll have a girl!"

Shortly afterward, Kleis was born, the dragonfly still there: how blurred, it seemed, and how the ocean faded and reappeared as I fought. I felt I would drown in sweat, drops pouring down my neck. Mama wiped my face and hands, her voice soothing, as she cooled me. I wasn't afraid: no, a new happiness surged through me, even while my wrists were breaking and my knees afire. Even while the pain tore me, I was aware of this happiness: I was bringing life, defeating death, adding to our world. My heart sang, though sweat drenched me, and the dragonfly, clicking its green wings, seemed a ragged dot or great bird.

I was glad Cercolas wasn't there: I tried to remember his love-making but all I could remember was pain and mother's voice and the chatter of Exekias and the sound of the sea. When Kleis had come, I thought: my wrists are broken and my knees burn but I'm glad, glad...and mother kissed me and said: Go to sleep, darling.

When I woke, the top of the ocean had become pink and pink webbed the sky: it seemed I was staring through woven stuff, skeins in rows, with wool dropped and tumbled between: the pink darkened nearest the water and stars were visible—a sunset like many others and yet different because Kleis was here: this was her first sunset.

During exile, when Alcaeus and I had the same room and bed, he tried to make me feel our bad luck couldn't last. He would roar against it. He might begin the bleakest day with a song.

"Hungry—let's go beg!

"Thirsty—let's find a fountain. There's cool water in the shade of a carob."

Our feet grew blistered. Days I lay on my mat, too sick to move, he brought me bread or a flower. Kneeling by me, smelling of the streets, he'd rub my hands...

"We'll find a way."

When we shared the big bed at Aesop's, its sides painted with flowers, Alcaeus cheered, reminding me of our luck.

"Remember those candle stubs I found?" he laughed. "Remember the roast lamb I stole—how the guy rushed after me, jabbing the air with a knife. Remember..."

I remember my gratitude to Alcaeus and Aesop must not end. Without their help I would have died.

I dreamed the other night that Alcaeus and I were exiled again, that Alcaeus came to me, as I lay between heaps of dung: he crawled toward me, clothes in rags, exhausted, blind. I opened my cloak and offered my breast—wanting to suckle him.

Waking, I realized how late it was.

Four of us, with Libus as guest, had supper at a table on the porch, a reception to honor Anaktoria's return...*bourekakia* and stuffed grape leaves, Anaktoria serving, maturer with that overnight bloom, that overnight assurance.

"Do you like *bourekakia*?" she asked Libus, too obviously thinking of him, offering him stuffed leaves instead of *bourekakia*, offering herself, at least for the night, something in that spirit, making fun of Telesippa, her newcomer rival, who was also interested in Libus, diverted, momentarily by someone's comment about my harp, a point to bandy for effect: how charming they were, bathed and perfumed, Telesippa in her city clothes, Anaktoria in her Cretan style, Gyrinno's jewels amusing us, the topaz swallowing her throat.

"You see Sappho's harp has twenty strings and is for Mixolydian songs."

The topaz tinkled and a smile went round, coaxing us to feel better.

I told them about the harp I had invented, admiring them as I talked, hair, shoulders, arms...enjoying each girl. I realized they were especially mine. No one else would have such an opportunity to influence them.

We listened while Anaktoria described her visit, her baby sister, the sailor who died on the wharf, the arrival of an Ethiopian girl, slave for a merchant. She talked as I had taught her, gestures well timed, head poised. She has lost her island mannerisms, such as gulping impulsively and biting off chunks of food.

Brushing aside her shoulder-length hair, blue eyes a little wild, Telesippa gossiped about her dressmaker, "the best in Athens," whose "tattling is incessant."

Libus steered the conversation to something sound and Atthis carried on: yes, no doubt, teaching helps.

Later, we sat on our terrace and passed around sweets and nuts and Libus joked, sultry jokes of the last generation, wanting to impress the girls.

Old tiles underfoot...youth around me...the thick walls of my house above the sea... I relaxed until someone mentioned Phaon and I saw him working on his boat, hands stained with oakum, knees rough from the planking.

"Phaon—I say good night to my girls. You'll be with me, soon. Soon, I'll be buried under your mouth."

Tomorrow, we meet after the games on the field.

I'll see him there, legs flashing, discus flying, his spear digging its hole. I'll see him rock with laughter and splash himself clean.

Alone, I rubbed my hands over my body, thighs, breasts, ankles, wrists and shoulders: my flesh is firm: I know, as I sense my own integrity, that before long I must lie in death.

No waking touch on my belly and knees, no chance to comb and dress my hair at leisure, no mirror for dawdling, no winging of gulls.

Poseidon

Of the poems I have written recently, I like these most:

Love, bittersweet, irrepressible,
Loosens my legs and I tremble.

I could not hope
To touch the sky
With my two arms...

·

The sun sprays the earth
With straight-falling flames...

·

O, Gongyla, my darling rose,
Put on your milkwhite gown...

·

When seastorms scream across the water,
The sailor, fearing these wild blasts,
Spills his cargo overboard...

·

The night closed their eyes,
And then night poured down
Black sleep upon their lids.

Alcaeus prefers the last two.

In a vase, on my table, a white rose opens and I see the face of Anaktoria. The rose is the most perfect flower, some say. Of the two kinds, the garden and the rambler, I prefer the rambler, climbing through the night, bringing its fragrance into my room, white in the starlight, ivory in the moonlight.

The sea and its waves are something we never forget yet never remember: how the surf leaps and splits into foam, how the foam cascades into white and divides into blue. From shore to sky there is blue, in patches like marble, areas like grey and porous granite, ribbons of blue that submerge in whorls.

How quiet the blue, how serene where afternoon sun polishes a path aimed for the shore, Cretan, Ethiopian, Etruscan, where men and ships have sailed—their hieroglyphs ruddered by chance. The ocean is always chance, yet it is subdued, finally modulated by place and time. Wherever we travel, there is the element of chance, rain, storm, heat, cold, before us, deceptive, feminine, wrapping us in fog, cities, deserts, islands, birds, starry decks and windless watches.

We never remember the sea because it alters momentarily, making rainbows, spreading colonies of butterflies, floating celery stalks, turtles, heaving shells and driftwood—beaching itself with footprints that fill with seepage or disappear underneath the wave.

Cercolas and I had such fun, when we were newly married and rode our white mares, across the island and along the shore, sometimes swimming them. When the oldest became sick, I put a pillow under her head and tended her until she died, on the beach, beneath the thatch of her stable.

Cercolas took the other mare, to die with him at war, I suppose it was. How can I know?

Our horses have gone, six or seven at a time, until there are only colts and old ones—I see them on deck and in holds, their white faces peering, yellow manes shining: white, in memory of our mares, white as gulls. I wish I could hear their whinnying across the fields, as they race toward me.

Warriors brag about their fearless horses but I prefer mares that nip my hands and tug my clothes.

Music is a tree, a cave with sea water sloshing, a shell to the ear, a baby's laughter, the lover's "yes." I suppose it came from the flint, the arrow. Cercolas was music. Mother was music. The loom and harp are music. I have heard music in my dreams. I dream many kinds of music when I play the harp.

I like music best at night, under the stars; I like it when I lie down in the afternoon, aware, yet not truly aware; I like it when I am up the mountain, the wind harsh; I like it when I am on the shore, the beach fire low, sparks rising, the sea almost at rest.

I like music when I eat, when I am at the theatre, or alone. Lonely music is marrow-wise, aware of secrets, revelatory in surprising ways, prying, blurring—

altogether deceitful. I like the harp better than the horns. Drums frighten. The voice is best: its story is man's, the sea's, the mountain's, and the sky's.

How I used to laugh at rimes Alcaeus wrote against Pittakos:

Old Pitt, we found your cloak
Among the fish and fisherfolk;
We saw your mouth gape and perk
Whenever a blouse made something jerk.

I suppose Pittakos paid many a visit to the fisherfolk—he was young enough then. And Alcaeus was clever enough to wring every drop of satire out of P's doings. His foolery endangered many of us. What a disgrace Pittakos remains in office. How fine it would be if Libus were empowered.

Libus says:

"There aren't enough of us to overthrow this man...he's entrenched till he dies. It's better to wait. Look at Alcaeus, what has his fight gotten him? Part of his tragedy comes from his inability to overthrow this man."

Yesterday, when I visited Alcaeus, I shivered and pulled back. Alcaeus stepped forward and grabbed my hand.

"Come, darling, we're having a drink. Join us."

Libus signaled me to sit down: their dining room was full of phantoms; shields glared; pennons dragged at me. With an apish grin, Alcaeus reeled across the room to bump against a table and chirp a drunken song.

It was rainy and dark and the melancholy afternoon and room closed in. You must pretend, I said to myself. Pretend he can see. Pretend there's nothing wrong...imagine...

As the three of us drank together, a scrawny, red-fleshed boy served us, downcast, looking as if recently beaten.

As we drank, the melancholy of Alcaeus' soul spread, seeping through taut throat muscles: intelligent things said with difficulty, good things said badly, reminiscences slightly distorted. What is more dismal than a damaged life, damaged beyond alteration, no matter how much we care? What more futile than communication at such a time?

I could not look at him but looked at Libus instead, his ephemeral face growing more ephemeral as he continued drinking, wrestling with his dogged silence.

Drink could not help... I fled home.

Mytilene
641

Three soldiers have been washed up on a raft, scarcely alive: all of them were taken to Alcaeus' house to recover, if that is possible. Libus wanted them there, to care for them. They are islanders and had been imprisoned over a year. For days they had been adrift, paddling, foodless except for fish and birds. I hear from Thasos that one of them, not much older than Phaon, throws himself against walls and stalks about babbling to himself, begging for water.

Alcaeus is in his element, determined to help these derelicts: he's captain again, in command: he's kinder and more resolute with this trio, which he believes he understands: oh, I sympathize with these sun-blackened wanderers, these lovers of freedom who defied jailers. I, too, know what it is to defy, and what it costs.

I sent them food but I could not go to them.

Later, I changed my mind; I wanted to see them, to see what their failure had done to them, what their fight had cost. I decided I might be able to encourage them, so I brought Atthis and we asked Libus to let us in and we talked to two of them, giving them food and helping them eat and drink, and everything went well till the mad fellow heard us and hurled himself against the bedroom door and burst in, to collapse in a heap, jabbering, writhing, eyes rolled back.

Atthis jumped from her chair and cried:

"Uh...how terrible...like a worm!"

Libus knelt by the young man and his hands quieted him. Not a word was said: then he turned to Atthis:

"He's been through a lot. Exposure...heat...no food... We can help him. He'll be all right, in time."

With a few reassuring words, he got the fellow up and led him away.

Later, I learned that one of the older men is a cousin of Phaon's. Phaon has heard the details of their days on the raft, and I am pleased by his kindness, the hours he gives to stay with the pair.

He and Libus are restoring them: food and encouragement are cancelling horror. Even the mad fellow is mending, eating and drinking normally, talking rationally much of the time. Phaon's cousin claims he fought with Alcaeus, but Alcaeus can't identify his bearded soldier: is it lapse of memory?

Or was it, as the cousin says, the period when Alcaeus lay injured, the spear wound in his skull healing, those weeks of pain that brought about his blindness?

Sappho and Phaon, in a small boat,
drift seaward, oars dragging:
shimmering light seems to tow the boat seaward.
Stripping, bronze, Phaon dives
expertly and brings Sappho a handsome conch:
listening to the shell they lie in the boat
and begin to make love,
a bronze gull sculptured on the sky,
the sound of waves.

Phaon's crew is loading his ship with pottery for Byzantium, a cargo that has to be delivered soon. This realization sharpens our love, though he thinks too little of distant voyages and I trouble him too much with warnings.

Summer is upon us and I accept the lethargy of eating, sleeping, dreaming. He likes summer heat, our damp bodies, my sticky perfume and sticky fingers... cool drinks. He enjoys fruit mixed with coconut and has had my girl prepare mixed salads...

"Fruit. In hot weather, nothing's so good. And there's never any fruit at sea."

"Not for long."

"You know...when I come back, Kleis may be married. Your family will be bigger, you know." He talked languidly, with his cheek against mine, as we sat on the beach.

"I hadn't thought of that."

The thought troubled me—fixing time around me: Kleis could not be this old!

Baskets and dishes cluttered the sand around us, wind puffing, light ebbing to lavender, fog on the water, floating above the surface, a boat creeping, its mast slicing misty layers, moving between floors.

What shall I give him for luck—a charm? A coin?

Why not my mother's drachma? She was lucky: there was no war in her time: she had lovers and then a husband to whom she was faithful. She did not have to endure an island without young men and know what it was to live among women for ten years.

Yes, the old initialed drachma of hers...

The loading of the amphorae was delayed and we sailed in his smaller boat, with a crew of three, to the bay where the wreck lies, our sailing so smooth the hem of my skirt hardly swayed. Phaon equipped us for diving and since the ocean lay incredibly calm, we located the wreck easily by tacking in circles. Kelp had snared the masts—giant legs of brown. Her masts struck fists against us, as greenish fish crossed and recrossed her deck. Splinters of light sank straws, fidgeting straws that reached the dragon's gold and red.

I worried, afraid of kelp and fish.

Phaon disappeared beyond our bow: his brown arms yanked at the kelp; he bobbed and swam toward me, treading water, puffing.

"Let me help you."

"No. It's too deep," I refused.

He and his crewmen dove by holding rocks meshed in pieces of net; they coaxed me until I had to try, sliding down rapidly, too fast for me: I knew I could let go of the rock or jerk the line attached to it and be towed upward; I wanted to be brave and gulped and oozed out bubbles, peering up. I wanted to put my feet on the wreck but I never reached her. Lungs bursting, I swam upward, soared, unable to see clearly. My lungs hurt a long time afterward, as I lay on deck, amazed at the crew's folly and strength: there was no end to their enthusiasm, their plunges from deck and rigging: by sunset, they had hacked through the wreck, entering the dead cabin: when we raised anchor and swung for shore I was glad, and hungry.

That night, I dreamed of gaping fish that carried coral fans: our sail became a net that filled with fish of reddish hue, then sank, to be towed to sea: all night a gentle sea rocked us, the dipper above our rocky shore.

In the morning, while the bay lay limpid, before I could finish eating, our men dove and chopped. As I lazed, birds spiraling, someone hollered and floundered toward our boat and I rushed to the side to see a sailor with a green cup, treading water, offering me his prize.

So the men had not been excited for nothing.

Phaon was as pleased as his men. Hunkered on the deck beside me, he nicked the green of the cup's rim and uncovered gold, the gold gleaming. I'll remember his hands as he passed the cup to me.

Who made it, how old is it, how long was it below? we asked each other, as I held the cup, our deck swaying.

The crew's crazy conjectures and laughter went on, as they went on diving.

It was hard for them to give up and sail for home: stars pegged our rigging and flipped over glassy combers: fish leaped: we watched as great white crests rose: we slept and woke, our deck slanting, boom groaning.

Phaon woke and we talked, of our separation and reunion.

"You will be gone a long time!"

"Perhaps my trip won't be so long."

"Let's come back to the old wreck."

"Will you dive?"

"I tried..."

We whispered and saw the dawn, a dawn that had streamers of rain splotching the horizon, pelicans one after the other in long files, our island in the offing, quite black.

I was sleepless most of the night, getting out of bed, restless because of the warmth, standing by my window, waiting for a breeze, the stars out, Mercury but no moon, the stars and the crickets and a nightingale and the sea, and someone, somewhere in the house, moving, then silence. I was thinking of him, wanting him, and I began a poem, changed it, rephrased it, thinking, my body needing his body:

Slick with slime to satiety he shoots forward
playing such music upon those strings,
wearing a phallus of leather,
such a thing as this enviously,
twirls, quivering masterfully,
and has for odor the hollow mysteries,
orgies for leaving, orgies for coming;
the oracle comes, comes with companions,
comes with mysteries, lover of mine,
displays this randy madness I joyfully proclaim.

I started the poem once more...such a thing as this enviously, that's suitable... twirls, quivering masterfully...hollow mysteries...there are good things...

Dawn came and there were the sounds of pigeons, gulls, servants coming and going, girls whispering...the laughter of girls.

The bay lay almost black and Phaon's ship was quiet, its mahogany rails shining, someone leaning over, utterly motionless. I looked about for a moving bird or a boat. Huddled on the wharf near me, a man slept, toothless mouth open, nets over his legs and thighs. A similar mesh covered the water, as far as I could see.

Wanting to say good-bye, I stood to one side beside Atthis and Gyrinno, chilled, afraid. The slow unwrapping of the clouds irked me: a number of men arrived and carried bundles aboard, their motions slow, their laughter irritating. Was man always oblivious?

Then, from at sea, voices came, shifting uneasily, an oar creaking between unintelligible words, a dog whining, a girl coughing. Loneliness filtered from the sky and depths.

The man still leaned over the rail...

"Off with the ropes."

"Everyone's aboard."

"Let's sail."

It was Phaon's voice: "let's sail": and he called to me, called to all of us: I heard Libus and Alcaeus: I heard the oars: as the ship headed seaward, Atthis hugged me and my loss was in that receding figure at the stern, sail climbing the mast behind him: had I shouted good-bye?

Bitterness struck me: again I knew I had no right to such a mood. Better to have a fling at Charaxos, there on the wharf, in his white clothes, sullen, bellicose, his friends snubbing me as we walked past.

Home seemed meaningless.

Had Alcaeus felt this way, on his return?

I knew he had and knew he had had ample reason and threw back my head, as I opened my door, and walked to my room alone, determined to think clearly: but it was no more than a resolve and the loneliness of those sea voices came and that voice, saying: "Let's sail."

My ocean window called me.

Was that his ship, that mere dot, that point of wood under banks of cloud?

I couldn't keep back my tears: what was it, his spirit, his dignity, his thoroughbred body? No, it was the conjunction of these and the very thought, this summary, increased my sense of loss. He was warmth, impulse, reason for living. Words! And he was more than words!

By now the dot had disappeared and against the clouds, birds wheeled and drifted and scattered raindrops fell, scenting the air. I went out and let them wet my face and take away the sting and then closed the shutters of my room and lay down.

Rain has such music.

I let it lull me to sleep, sleep, in the morning, warm, in my bed, a day or a year...sleep...was it from the depth of the sea?

That night a storm engulfed us, ransacking our trees, banging our shutters, moaning over the roof until Atthis got into bed with me, thoroughly scared.

"Don't be afraid, darling."

"I am...I am...Aren't you?"

"No...maybe a little."

"What about Phaon?"

"He's far at sea by this time."

"But isn't that bad, to be far at sea?"

"I don't know...hush."

I resented her pliant body and scented arms and hair: yes, at sea, Phaon must be battling gigantic combers: his cargo might shift...his sail might... When Atthis hugged me, I felt stifled and yet, as she quieted and the storm continued, I was grateful I could comfort her. If I could not have Phaon, I, at least, had someone who loved and needed me.

Rain and wind knocked open the shutters and I rose and closed them and dried my feet and got into bed again.

Floor tiles had chilled me.

Rain cuffed roof and sides of the house... I heard the surf growing wilder, sloshing over rocks, climbing the lower cliffs, rising and falling onto itself with a hiss.

I straightened my hair on my pillow, knowing I had hours to wait: I said, you've seen a lot of storms, sleep. Your island isn't in danger. But, nothing could keep me from thinking of his boat and its struggle. I named off members of his crew. I named their families.

Phaon's cousin was with him—a wretched re-initiation, after those hideous days on the raft.

I heard Anaktoria and Gyrinno talking in the next room.

I thought of the madman, living with Alcaeus, walking about with him: I'll make something of him, Alcaeus had said to me, the face revealing that his madness had not left him.

Joy and exaltation are the triumphs...
today is the imminence...
even shadows have their fire...
the stars burn...
O, sea rover, fight...

The storm split roofs and hurled boats ashore, uprooting trees, damaging walls.

Slowly, the old town pulls itself together.

Old town—you have seen many storms during your centuries. Is it true, you let this one slip past you and sent it to sea? You should have kept it! You can withstand battering better than a small ship! Is it true, what the fishermen say, that many were drowned?

Men and boys go about town, picking up tiles to load their baskets.

Driftwood clutters the beach.

Men were hurling stones, grabbing them off the beach and throwing them. I heard them hit Pittakos and saw him stagger, his flapping rags jerking, his arm flung over his eyes. Silent, feet wide apart, he stayed his ground.

Alcaeus, facing the sea, lidless-eyed, roared and lunged about, arms extended, yelling:

"Kill him...kill him...let me wring his neck!"

Beside him, the madman off the raft, howled and hurled stones.

About a dozen men were circling Pittakos, most of them blabbing defiance, closing in.

I rushed to Alcaeus and squeezed past him, to cry out... I told them to stop, asking them to stop in the name of our island, our town.

"Get back," Alcaeus warned.

I faced them, feeling their hate: it bubbled through me, seemed to ooze from the sand, from the sea, from antiquity: the hates of my ancestors, hatred of tyranny and unfairness.

No one threw: they watched me, as I walked toward Pittakos: maybe they thought I had a stone.

"You get back," I cried. "Go home, before they kill you, Pittakos. Get back everyone...go home."

Nervously folding and unfolding his robe, Pittakos backed away. A hand went to a spot where a stone must have struck. I felt no pity but stepped closer.

"I don't know what caused these men to turn on you... I don't want to know...go home, before it's too late."

Without replying, he shuffled away, a sandal off.

"Is he going?" asked Alcaeus, finding me, hand on my shoulder.

"Let him go," I said, facing the others.

Grasping Alcaeus, I forced him to walk with me, muttering to him, seeing Thasos, dropping his stones with a guilty grin.

I wanted to forget the faces but I knew most of the men: young, bearded faces, most of them friends of Alcaeus, some of them his soldiers.

"Don't lead me," Alcaeus protested.

"You need to be led."

"You came at the wrong time."

"What's to become of you?"

"Let me go," he said.

"I'll see you home. Here, Thasos, take his arm. Thasos, were you mad?"

"We should have stoned him."

"Why?"

"He quarreled with Alcaeus—spat on him."

Alcaeus leaned on me and I sensed his weariness as if it were mine: he was breathing hard and had to rest, stopping again and again. Behind us, his madman wandered, his Pamphilus.

"I'm too old for this kind of horseplay, it seems."

Thasos and I were saddened by his tragic features; we frowned; minute wrinkles had enlarged and deepened; his hands trembled; his mouth was open. He seemed in the past, with his men, galled, waiting: What is memory for, I asked myself, to crucify? Shut off from the day, is this the best memory can do?

When I sat with him at home, I said:

"What was the quarrel about?"

"First, some water."

Thasos brought us water. The cool of his gourd helped.

"Pittakos has stolen from the city...again...I came at him with the facts...I know the truth...many of us know."

We remained silent a while, my hand in his.

"It's an old truth—for us," I said.

"Very old," he said.

Presently, the madman entered, carrying himself stiffly, chalk faced, chastised.

Oblivious of us, appearing more normal than any time I had seen him, he talked with Thasos, regretting the incident.

Soft-talking men, inside an inner room, brought home to me the innocence of our own lives, how based on impulse, how like kelp, twisting, sinking, headed for shore, dragged to sea: we are mad, we are sane, or between: we exert ourselves and the world seeks revenge; we accept and earn ridicule and belittlement: we affirm ourselves and alter our lives and the lives of others: war is such an affirmation.

Innocence? Why not call all life innocent because dependability can not be assured. And, if life is innocent, then what is there but compassion and patience and kindness and beauty and love?

"It would have been better if they had killed him," Alcaeus said, rubbing his hands over his face.

I said nothing.

"I could have him murdered," he said.

"Alcaeus...wait..."

"Wait? How much longer must we wait?"

"He's old."

"Are we children?"

"He knows what's happening."

"No—not even yet."

"That couldn't be."

I saw Pittakos by the sea, spray dampening his clothes, his mouth to the gulls: I saw him, hand over eyes, legs spread; I heard stones hitting him... I could take no more and saying good-bye to Alcaeus, I walked home, eager to be alone, for now the town seemed withdrawn, callous, incomplete, a failure. I touched a hollow in a wall and picked a leaf and, where a street opened on the bay, looked and looked: the sea's salty taste acted as a philter and years of contentment and ease surged about me, trying to reinstate themselves: my girls met me and we went home together, sharing our innocence.

Just the other day, I dreamed of Serfo's place, his fabrics around me, things from Assyria, Egypt and Persia. Some of the cloth blew against me, light as a Sudanese veil. Atthis had a length of it in her hands, a twisted flowered piece yards long.

"I'll make ribbons for your hair," she said.

Alone, I sank into patterns, colors and textures. Something brushed my cheek, a winged bull in gold on blue cotton... I saw an imperial snake in green on white silk, a mighty roc in black on grey wool... I heard friends asking prices, Anaktoria, Libus.

I heard mother say:

"This is the best, this one, darling, with temples and shields on it, this blue, soft blue! Don't you love it? Here, take it in your hands, press it to your face."

I saw ships and listened to their keels...sailors unloading bales...wasn't that a remnant on the water?

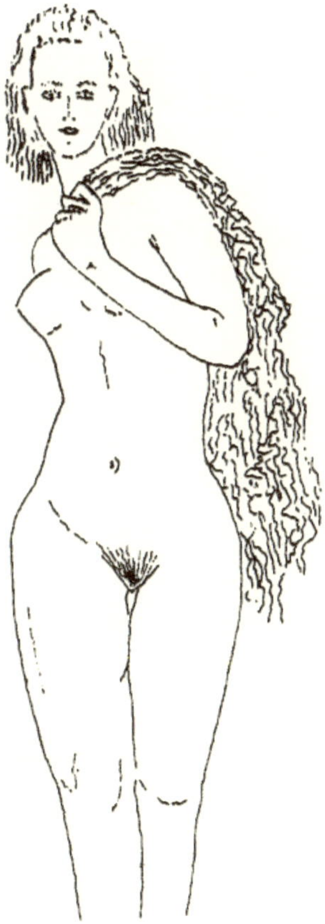

A suffusion of light envelopes the Venus de Milo,
revealing the contours and texture of her hair,
face, breasts, belly, and drapery.
Voices sing Homeric hymns.
A woman, as lovely as the Milo,
disappears in the golden light
beneath the Mediterranean.

Was it three years ago I met Atthis—five years ago Anaktoria? Was that another dream? I am not sure.

Awake, I thought about my girls and now much they love me and make my house a house of grace. I must have beauty: I must have peace: and they are peace and beauty. I recalled how and when I had met each and loved each one for her special qualities. Each had a place in my heart, gold on cotton, green on white...the sea was at each meeting and at each good-bye... I count my years but the sea has no calendar.

Sometimes I feel the sea thinks for us, its pensiveness communicates at dawn, its meditation at night, its probity sifting through the day. A stormy emotion—the sea. A period of tranquility—the sea. Fickleness—the sea. I could not be happy without its communication. For all its pervasiveness it seems on the verge of a secret: looking down through the waves I sense it, I sense it at night, when phosphorescence steals shoreward or when rain obliterates and there is no visible ocean, then, still, still it communes, insinuating mystery, legends from caves, legends stronger than any coral, barracuda and stingrays roiled under, sinking farther and farther.

As we eat, in the dining room, Atthis prattles about her new parrot, mimicking it.

Her glances, charming, rounded, sensual, inconclusive, ask for love.

Her mimicry, spoken somewhat under her breath, takes in the townspeople, theatre folk, the Athenian star, Alcaeus, Gogu, the girls. But, because it is kindly and feminine, the fun carries far.

Her eyebrows have grown to meet over her nose and the fuzzy little bridge gives her added years. Her breasts are larger, shoulders fuller. She could be a priestess: the face solemn, the lips pert; then laughter ruins everything and she is simply girl, joyous life, asking for love.

Dressed in thin summer best, she pokes her neighbor with her sharp sandal and before I can say a word a scrap follows.

As I went downstairs, I put my hand between the lion's jaws, stubby, mossy stone, oldest part of the house. Lingering, I watched leaves puff down the steps. By the fountain, I absorbed water shadows, warmth around me, an insect swimming toward a spot of sun.

A village girl brought me a bouquet of white roses, saying:

"You must let me join your *hetaerae.*"

She wore a twisted blue wool skirt, of darkest color, and no blouse. Standing erect, she offered her flowers and then spun around and fled: I could scarcely take in the clean-cut features, pointed chin, red mouth and new breasts.

I can't imagine who she is or where she lives but I must find her.

My working hours are longer and as I review my work I find it good: that is a sign of maturity: maturity is the seal I strive for and yet as I work I fear a loss of spirit: maturity is seldom daring and to be daring is to open doors: maturity, then, is balance: is it also the decorum people accuse me of? Parasol, tilted at just the proper angle? Mask, worn at the right moments? As I came home yesterday from the play, I remembered a winking mask, rather like one in my room: was that derision?

I saw a young man on the street who startled me. Though he didn't glance at me, I thought I had seen him in Samnos: ax beard and sullen mouth were the same; he had the same slouch, the same filthy clothes. Watching him, I recalled that Samnian fellow, his pleas and questions:

"...tell nobody I'm here...but I want to know about home...tell me the news! You see I've been here for three years...to escape the war...there are three of us...we came here on a raft...tell us..."

The frenzied talk was vivid as this derelict walked down our street.

In Samnos, I had sympathized with my countryman for his voluntary exile was no easier than an enforced exile: I drew him out and later met his friends, all hungry for news, all in rags, living from hand to mouth, scared. It was their fear that worried me and I urged them to make friends and forget the past, to marry and begin life in Samnos. I arranged contacts for them...

But, was this one of them sneaking along, hoping for luck? Pittakos, the wise, the clement, would have him lashed to death by nightfall, if someone discovered him. My pledge of secrecy is a pledge I'll keep. As I sailed home from Samnos, I thought of these men and was proud of their folly.

Roses are in bloom on the hills and violets are in flower around my house. Kleis will be married soon, so I am doing things wrong. I try to tell myself this is her happiest time and struggle to write a poem for her wedding. Her natural gaiety is infectious and yet, and yet...

We will have quite a ceremony, Libus, Alcaeus, Gogu, Nanno, Helen, my girls, sailors, half the town, Pittakos and rogues...Rhodopis and Charaxos...no, harshness is not in keeping with a wedding.

I can hear the male chorus.

I hear the surf...

Below us, the ocean eats at its rocks, above us lie the hills, around us stir the branches of the olives.

Peace: sacred grove, we dedicate these two: give them luck: a light will fall: the chorus will resume: a wreath will be hung.

Shall I play my harp?

Who is the god of illusion? Love? How is he to be kept alive through many years and many disappointments?

I shall try to help. Song has that gift, a gift nothing else has: to give the lost or hold it in suspension.

I feel utterly ridiculous, the greatest hypocrite: that is how it seems as I urge Alcaeus to curb his resentment for Pittakos.

I have tried reason but it isn't reason that moves Alcaeus. When he feels my sympathy, he listens: if he conceives of us as he used to be, his hatred subsides. Let him feel alone, he thunders, bends toward me, drags his fingers through his beard and sputters:

"To hear you talk, I'd think you were never mistreated by this man!"

"But you know better."

"You're a traitor to yourself!"

"That's not true. You want to have him killed and I say we lose through violence. I'm no traitor to myself—or you. You can be traitor to justice."

"Let's not say anything about justice, when we're fighting tyranny."

I recalled days with Aesop and said:

"I wish he was here, to advise us or hear our problems. I think I know what he'd say."

"What?"

"There's a way out of slavery... I didn't kill my master."

Slavery—there are all kinds.

It is a kind of slavery to long for Phaon and another kind to remember Aesop and another to hope. Perhaps Aesop would rebuke such thinking and say: Slavery is not in ourselves but in the misused power of others. Surely that is the commoner kind but I find slavery in myself and my girls and my island and my books.

Well, here is a story Phaon told me:

"Years ago, a slave broke into a temple on a deserted island and found lamps burning. On a rug lay a naked man, asleep. He'd been lying there for centuries, guarded by someone, the lamps filled and the wicks new.

"The King of Freedom, were the words on a shield beside him. His yellow hair streamed across the rug. Above him, a mask, fastened on the wall, spoke:

"'Shut the temple...let the lamps burn...make no noise...take a hair from his head...go.'

"The slave shut the temple, carefully.

"Years later, in prison, he bent over to examine the golden hair he had kept and it burst into flame and became a torch which he used to light his way to freedom."

His flames and heat are fuel
For seaman's muscles, his sea eyes,

Devil of laughter and devil moods,
His sinking-rising delicacy.

The initial union is relief
Of olives and cypress, breasts, birds,
Stinging and perspiration's siege,
Roots climbing out of centuries.

Beauty, the wedding is over and I am alone with my lighted lamps and moonlight across the sea, night's indifference.

Beauty, Kleis was happy...many of us were happy.

After the ceremony, Pittakos approached me, shuffling, dressed as I had never seen him dressed, in fine white clothes. His hate was gone, that was something I saw at once: I was seeing another man. Speaking guardedly, hands folding and unfolding his robe, he said:

"...They would have stoned me. What can I say...to make amends? You stopped them from killing me... You...you helped me..."

I grew confused. Remembering Alcaeus' threat, my hatred surged and I thought: Can he expect me to rub out the past because of an accident on my part? Can he ask such a thing?

Do you think that I have changed—that I went out of my way to save you?

My own harshness pained me. I had seen him at a distance, during the ceremony, and had resented his presence; as I played my harp and sang he remained near, boggling his head.

Our sacred grove, filled with people, trees streaked with fog, was still in my mind. I could see Kleis smiling and hear the wedding chorus, the flutists, the barking dogs, the cries of gulls.

Glancing overhead, I noticed them, passing, gliding, saying with their grace things I tried to say in my writing.

Pittakos turned away.

I could not say a word but stepped forward.

"...Pittakos."

He regarded me doubtfully.

"Yes."

Then I started to walk away.

"What can I say? I'm old... I can't erase errors. Sappho, I... Last night I stayed up all night...it was more than thinking: I looked at the past. I've been mistaken. Though we've lived here, in this town, we know only lies about each other..."

Shuffling, he made off.

All were there in the grove: Alcaeus, baffled; Libus, pale and aloof; Anaktoria, gay; Atthis, dreaming; Kleis, my herder... We ate together, drank, sang... The sun drank the fog and sunset ribboned the ocean.

I shall remember goats wandering through our grove, tinkling their bells...the mask-maker carrying my harp for me...trying to sing in toothless ecstasy...I shall remember the altar fire and wreaths of flowers, their incense and coloring... remember, too, the farewell of my pair, their backs and shoulders as they headed for their house on the headland, a small place among figs and tall white poppies, their world—not mine. I must remember it is their world. When Kleis flings her arms around me I will rejoice. At the same time, I must accept the fact that their marriage is their particular freedom.

May it be a satisfying freedom.

Mother's lamp, as I write, is nearly empty: she would have liked the wedding ceremony, the chorus singing my poem: terra-cotta lamp, do you remember her wedding? Did you burn for her ecstasy or were you snuffed out before the groom carried her to bed?

It wasn't long ago I was married: how I walked, my head high, the embodiment of innocence and grace: I thought life would be easy!

The wind puffs through my room.

The ocean whispers.

Charaxos and Rhodopis attended the wedding, staying apart with a group of their friends, no one dressed for the occasion. Since the man who had forcibly made love to her was there, I was disconcerted. I was ashamed. My face burned. What could I do? Would they interfere? But they seemed preoccupied, merely onlookers, most of them young men and women.

When they sauntered away, I enjoyed the wedding.

Someone among them, a stranger perhaps, gazed back at me, reminding me of Cercolas.

Cercolas, my mother, Aesop—each summons a series of images. When each one died, I thought: How can I go on? Now my thought is: What has replaced them? Husband, mother, friend... I am forever altered by their absence, emptier, lonelier. I seek them in others and yet never find them.

It matters to me how they died.

I am still troubled that Cercolas died on the battlefield. And it is tragic that Aesop died, beaten by a mob. At least, mother died beside me, comforted as much as human comfort is possible.

Death should not catch us unaware for then it cheats us doubly. Surely, it is hard enough to die without dying in some tragic way. Each of us deserves a last dignity.

Shall I tell Alcaeus that Pittakos came to me after the wedding?

I may never tell him because he will suffer more for knowing. It seems to me telling him could accomplish little. Hard as it is, unfair as it is, I must keep this to myself. Of course, some would disbelieve. And if Pittakos sees fit to remain silent, he and I will be better off. Lives will be less complicated.

Even unmolested, he has not much time ahead. We must be far-sighted and choose a leader...

Homosexual lovers in bed,
making love in the moonlight.
The light falls on their flesh,
faces, hands, legs, their passion:
laughter and soft moans and
the ocean below the villa.
Sappho rises and ponders her body,
stands by a window, facing the Aegean.

I took my lyre and said:
Here, now, my heavenly
Tortoise shell, become
A speaking instrument.

One by one, the poems have fitted into my book, so slowly time seems to have had nothing to do with its completion. Yet, my ninth book is done. When I had finished my sixth, I thought: this is all. When I finished my eighth, I felt I need go no farther. Will there be a tenth? What will make it distinctive?

Phaon lives in this book, insatiability floods everywhere: lyric by lyric, our smoldering hearts reveal our happiness.

When I shared lines with him, he laughed at their frankness, eyes dancing. He remembered some of them, and shot them back at me, to tease.

I have sent selections to Solon: what will he write me? Will their crudeness be too much for him? I think not. He has savored love.

My Egyptians are copying the book—conspirators, no doubt, mumbling lines to each other, shaking heads. I'd like to slip into their shop as they work, to overhear them: would I laugh or recoil? Probably I'd be annoyed. Well, tomorrow I must go to the shop and see how they are doing.

I have not thought of a title.

Villa Poseidon

I sought Anaktoria and together we spent the night.

In spite of her comfort, I could not get to sleep. Her arms around me, she lay motionless.

During the afternoon, we arranged flowers, taking them from the garden. A rainbow appeared over the bay and arm in arm we watched it, its arc faintly reflected on the water. Her myrrh was everywhere, her spirit too: the things she said were right: family traditions are a part of her and she adds just enough fantasy.

For a while, we practiced archery, her shooting more accurate than mine. A lost arrow sent us near the sea. Then games...games...what would life be without games and laughter!

Watch the dice in her fingers!

She's a magician of tricks and youth, my Anaktoria and, oddly enough, I can never bring it all together; it is too effervescent, too delightful: the moment swells over us: then, another moment, even while we are eating together, growing sleepy together: ours is a gift that has come from our island without men, years of femininity.

Someone sent me the doll Aesop had when he died, his Cretan doll. It came from Adelphi; badly wrapped, I opened it in my library, laid it on my desk, amazed to see it, startled, fingers fumbling. Someone had wanted to be kind, but it wasn't kindness to send it. What faded colors, what worn cloth, how had the doll gotten this old? It had suffered another kind of death.

With the doll in my arms, I smelled the incense of his house, dinner on the table, fresh fruit piled before us: the broad bracelet he wore bothered him and he shoved it higher on his arm: silent tonight, he listened to what we had been doing during the day: he had such heart for Alcaeus and me.

I could not keep the figure but packed it away. Its evocative intimacy, its forlorn quality...they would serve no purpose I could think of. I was glad Alcaeus could not see it. Yet, I felt I had rejected Aesop.

A sweltering day was made worse when Gogu had a seizure near Serfo's shop. Serfo and Libus carried him inside and I found them working over Gogu, kneeling beside him, Serfo's slave fanning the sick man, swaying his palm frond low, Libus' face tense and canvas-colored. Serfo turned his barbaric features, square-cut beard and blazing green eyes, on me, resentful when I placed a damp sponge on Gogu's head, when I suggested we pull him farther away from the wall. He growled and backed off, to care for some customers.

"Is it Gogu's old trouble?" I asked.

Libus nodded, his hands comforting the man. When Gogu's teeth chattered and his head and shoulders shook, Libus restrained him, hands on his shoulders. When he spoke to Gogu, I could detect an immediate response. The slave brought water and poured it for Gogu and Libus got him to drink: the frond dipping closer, rising and falling. "Libus—Libus," he said, and sighed, thin lashes over upturned eyes. The black hitched his broadcloth and sighed too.

The room was windowless and cool, lit from overhead. A pigeon cooed on the roof. For a while I sat near Libus but when Serfo offered drinks, we went into his shop where he displayed ivory figurines on his dusty counter, Amazons, ibis, Etruscan warriors and sacred cats, none bigger than my hand.

"The cats are from Luxor," Serfo said.

"Will Gogu be all right?" I asked, hearing his rapid breathing.

"He'll be all right by evening," Libus said.

So we examined the collection, Libus questioning their antiquity: I pointed out the yellowing and flaking: he held an Amazon in the doorway, dust cracks mottling her face and armor, the texture of his hands obvious as well.

He seems to be holding me in his fingers, as small. I felt the flakes of time—my life flaking, like Gogu's, less lasting than the ivory.

The hours I spend with Libus and his sister are hours of talk and wine, at his small house, in its garden of figs and olives, poppies in bloom along the paths. Their place, nearer the bay than mine, absorbs the bay's placidity. The furniture stresses comfort. His mosaics reflect his regard for ease...scenes of old days and old creatures.

I was glad when Libus gave up staying with Alcaeus; I had missed those visits to his home where Helen has taught me designs for my loom and reaffirmed what patience really is. She has read to me, acquainting me with books I would never have found...

Libus talks and toys with a loop of beads, in a thoughtful mood, his hands, as they move, remind me of their healing quality and his voice has that same beneficence, distinctly personal, meanings having extra meaning most of the time.

Helen's face has none of his ephemerality but has, instead, a country wholesomeness I love. She chats about flowers she has grown, seeds she keeps in jars, promising me a selection.

Their poppies, grey-leafed, sea-bitten, have large centers and bees loll on the petals and the sea lolls beyond them.

Why is it the hours loll here? I have seen whales from their garden, sporting near beds of kelp, their blue backs like so many watery hills. I think something lures them offshore...another something makes Libus' servants sing more than my servants.

A gigantic sea-rock assumes the face of a crying woman when the fog comes: some say she cries for our dead in the wars, some say it's for those lost at sea: I have often seen her, head bowed: she faces the town, staring: the sea sound is her weeping; perhaps it is the weeping of many women: if I walk by that deserted spot at night, with the fog about me, I cling to Atthis or Exekias. No woman goes alone there, when the fog is about.

The moon has set and
The Pleiades have gone;
The night is half gone
And life speeds by.
I lie in bed, alone.

Going to see Alcaeus, I met Kleis and she threw her arms around me and kissed me, saying:

"Mama, dear, it's good to see you! How I miss you!"

I tried to hide my pleasure but my heart sang and I held her close, my body remembering hers, fingers slipping around the back of her neck, staying in her hair.

Pushing me aside, she exclaimed:

"Mama, let's go to your house and be together, like old times. Shall we?"

How easy to consent—and we walked home, arms around each other, gulls over us, shadows skimming roofs, dusty cobbles asking for rain: I wanted to remember her chatter, each inflection...

I would see Alcaeus tomorrow. I needed time with my own...

Pittakos stoned...Aesop stoned...the mob's disgrace...

Year after year, is there greater calumny than our own communal perfidy? Is there greater stupidity? One man starts it, then five, then ten, manacled together.

For our island's sake, I'm glad I cheated death.

Like old times, we sat at our looms and Kleis showed me a periwinkle design, whispering confidences, saying he was good, saying the house was good, the sea...she put her faith on the loom, the thread of it going beyond life. Mother must have heard me say such things, reflecting the same hope. Finches gathered in the olive trees as we worked. I asked time to stop and let us have the day last, at least longer than evening and the shepherd's bells.

Charaxos brought him to my house, a castaway, I thought, dreg of the worst sea. Charaxos stood behind him in Cairo red, the sun blazing over the town, as the castaway bowed, holding together his rags, eyes wandering, skin and bones, nose snuffing at his hand, his mouth lower on one side, a canine look on his face.

Muttering, he fished in a sack tied about his waist and offered me something.

I hesitated to take it, feeling Charaxos' curiosity—or was it gloating? I grew afraid as the castaway insisted, wagging head and hand, Charaxos silent; forcing myself, I bent and peered at his hand...seeing a drachma.

I saw it had been pierced for a chain...taking it, I made out the letters my mother had gouged...in the metal...yes, it was her drachma.

I wanted to run, throw down the coin, send Charaxos away, turn aside the castaway. I wanted to crumble on the steps and bury my head in my arms and deny existence.

"Come in," I managed.

And the men entered.

Together, we sat down and I asked:

"Where did you get the coin?"

"At Cos..."

"You are from Cos?"

"Yes, I came from Cos."

"He came on one of my ships," Charaxos said.

I could not look at either man.

"He came from Cos," I said.

"Phaon died on the island...he and others...thrown on the beach...we have rocky shores...he was injured in the big storm...you see, we found him, my wife and son and I. He gave us the coin and sent me to you...he..."

So, he died after that storm, I told myself, and I got up, wondering where I could go: I saw the castaway's blazing eyes and torn clothing and the greedy face of my brother:

"Stay at my house...as long as you like," I said. "I will send servants to look after you. I will..."

What will I do? I asked myself.

Will I take the coin and sleep with it? Will it burn my bed? Will I place it on my desk or hurl it out my window? And I opened my fingers to see if the bronze was on fire.

Now, you have seen me grief-stricken, I thought, as I gazed at Charaxos. You may go and tell your friends. Tell them, Sappho is beaten. Tell them...

I excused myself and retreated to my room.

Far at sea, I saw a dot: Phaon's ship, and I opened my hand and laid his drachma on the windowsill.

Beauty, is he dead?

What has been gained by taking him from me?

Shall I go to Xerxes, and hold him to his promise? Couldn't there be a mistake? Better to find Xerxes and say to him, "Remember your promise," and take his powder. This is my inheritance, from parents, Cercolas, friends, this degree of misfortune, final degradation. Was love a mirage, or this?

Libus sat beside my bed, his hands alleviating the pain that dragged at every nerve: his hands warmed me, crossing my back and shoulders, assuaging with their mirage the storm that seemed everywhere inside me, bursting my throat, my brain, my chest, shattering my reason.

Yet, as he helped me, he reasoned:

"I hoped he would be back early enough for Kleis' wedding...he said something to me about getting back early... I hoped you two would go on...you know all of us watched you...our hearts were yours...it was like that.

"I've always thought your pride deserved love, Phaon's kind, free of politics. Yes, I know Alcaeus was sufficient, years ago; then our island women adopted you; then Phaon. It was his luck to give you what you needed..."

"My coin didn't bring luck to him," I said.

"A coin means what? Metal can't tell us about life...only we can tell...to one another..."

"What have I told you through the years?"

He paused a while, hands motionless.

"Beauty..."

"And now?"

"Another kind...in the making. I know your ancestral line...losses become gain...I recognize bravery."

His hands and thoughts continued their palliative, now the fingers, now the voice, as servants replaced lamps and closed windows, moving as slowly as if below the sea, finally to leave us alone again, the ocean's voice mixing with the crickets.

"Kleis will bring Phaon back to me," I said.

"Theirs is a curious resemblance...I agree."

"What will happen to his house?"

"It will be hers," he said.

"But she'll never live in town."

"No...she won't change her ways."

"Have you ever liked his house? I haven't."

"No," he said.

"Libus, why doesn't Alcaeus come to me?"

"He's not thinking of your problem."

"He doesn't know about Phaon?"

"He knows...but can't come."

"Shall I go to him?"

"Wait...for a while," he said.

My girls seldom leave me: Atthis, Gyrinno, Anaktoria, each brings flowers and gifts, bringing them surreptitiously or with a hint of jollity—sometimes compassion. Old Exekias pats my hands, kisses my skirt or turns away, tears unchecked.

Atthis, cheek against mine, murmurs her love. As we walk through our garden she says:

"I miss him too... I loved him too... We placed a wreath for him... We three have made a shrine in the woods..."

Gyrinno appears in the night, as I lie sleepless. Unable to mention the tragedy, she whispers hoarsely that she loves me and wants to help: Is there anything she can do for me?

Anaktoria has probed deeper:

"You must take care, Sappho. You must do nothing strange, that would harm us. We can't have you obsessed by melancholy. Let us look after you."

Eyes streaked with tears dim and I see him, imagine his body sprawled between the rocks of Cos and I hear his voice speak my name: I see our Leucadian cliff and know I could throw myself down, die as he died among the rocks, far below.

Then, I find Kleis as I work at my loom, and her voice, revealing her sorrow, eradicates the drama of self: the curse of death needs soft hands and blonde hair and blue eyes and tender mouth... "Mama, darling..."

Sometimes I try to brush aside feminine ties, but there they are, tightening about me: snatches of song come to me: I see women with babies at the fountain; vineyards creep over the hills, ascending through fog, under the wings of gulls, moving toward me, closer and closer: they are my father's vineyards, the vineyards of Alcaeus, Phaon's vineyards, Libus', Anaktoria's; the bone flute, the whole island is in them, in the spring leaves and autumn leaves, in the stark vines of winter: the weeping rock moves through them, the defeated fleet, the red rooftops of home, the bare hills, olive trees: I see a woman, called Sappho, leading a child, named Kleis: I hear shepherd's bells, and the silence of dawn spills up from the ocean's shore: a porpoise and a whale, beyond a belt of kelp, churn points of light and shadow: home, home is the red tiles and my mother's lamps and the view where the vineyards snuggle to sleep for the night: this is my inheritance, to keep as long as possible, that is what I tell myself, compel myself to feel.

Kleis has the grape leaf woven in her loom and as she weaves she faces me and smiles and I know how much love is in that smile.

Sappho stands by the seaward window in her library...
carved ivory racks hold books, ancient papyri,
Egyptian clay tablets, copies of hymns.
Blue from the bay inundates the library, her face,
obliterates the books.
Alcaeus, an old man,
holds a tattered manuscript.

Suddenly, he stood in front of me, in my library, dressed in black, beard soiled, deep wrinkles underneath his eyes.

"Alcaeus, I didn't hear you and Thasos."

"Exekias let us in. Are you working?"

"No...sit down."

"Are you alone?"

"Yes."

He leaned on Thasos: I felt that he hadn't been sober very long; he leaned forward, almost stumbling.

"Can I sit down?"

"Here, here," said Thasos, helping him, laying aside a package.

Silence troubled us.

I watched Thasos go and then Alcaeus said:

"I understand your loss. I understand what has happened to you. Phaon's death has overpowered you. I put it badly...but we have shared...be patient...I understand...Sappho; I have brought you my Homer. Remember, when I got it years ago? Remember? I want to share. I should have given you this before...What good is it to me?"

"Alcaeus."

"Where is the book?"

"The package Thasos left?"

"Yes...take it...open it..."

I opened it, remembering how we had thrilled long ago, and, after a while, reaching out to him, grateful, hoping I could make him sense my gratitude, I kissed his forehead and his hands, his hands motionless, the sightless eyes confusing me.

He went on slowly:

"I've come to share my strength...it's a poor strength, drunk, blind, but it does go on. You, my dear, are blinded by grief. Let me tell you your grief can't be as bad as mine. Or, if it is, let's share...share...we've shared before... I'll take your dark away...hide it in mine...lose some of your burden at least.

"Sappho, let me help.

"Accept the old book, find hope in it... I have kicked aside death on the field...look at my eyes and then look at yours...you need no mirror.

"He's dead...dead by the sea...you have your love of beauty to uphold you.

Let it live! Give it new life! Soon enough death will claim both of us, but, till then, let's find comradeship...come to my house tomorrow, read to me...

"Will you?"

I nodded, then remembered he could not see and remembered his gift and his grace and knelt by him and put my head in his hands and pressed between his knees, as he patted me, chuckling a little.

"I'll come tomorrow, Alcaeus," I promised.

"Good."

"I know your lot is worse than mine... I must find courage."

Beauty, I thought, beauty, what can I say to help this man?

"Yes, tomorrow; then I'll tell you, Sappho... I'll tell you what I've learned, living in my black sea. How my ship drags anchor. What I've heard. I've heard some strange things. I can sense someone moving, almost before he moves, a shift of air, let's say.

"Watch me play jacks with Libus, old soldiers at their fun. I could cheat you...if you gave me half a chance."

Again that chuckle.

The book lay open and his great arms lay across his lap, fingers up. My father had owned that book. With age it had come unsewed and hung in tatters: the smell of age was there: I rubbed my fingers over pages...

Quickly, he said:

"I like to feel those pages... I wanted to write a book as full of life...give back the thunder of the storm...look how the bugs have eaten the book...see that ripped page...well, where will you keep your Homer?"

And he smiled.

"Shall I read something?"

"Yes...now!"

Turning the pages so he could hear them I searched for a favorite passage.

I read as slowly and as distinctly as possible, allowing each word time.

Cercolas, mother, Aesop, Phaon...gone. When shall I go?

I have been unable to write for days. I have nothing to say...there is only emptiness.

Yesterday a nightingale sang, a song of tattered leaves, scraps of Nile, bits of Euphrates, papyrus against night, against impending doom, against depression. Tender notes whispered insanity. Other notes urged self-pity. Others shattered—with sheerest delicacy—any hope of contrition.

A feather drops...a pause. One could die during such a pause.

All of us wait—life waits!

A bubbling deceives the spirit, a trill alienates the heart. Something summons the past, other songs on other nights, other songs of other people, the bone flute, of course.

This was not a bird, not a beak, not a feather but sail and spar, rigged to go at dawn, course along many shores.

"Beauty, you're frail. Your bones are able to carry next to nothing and yet your song travels, spreading as if a pebble had dropped on water..."

I walked under olive trees along the coast, following grassy paths, the breeze with me until I met Gogu, carrying a piece of kelp and a shell. At first, he did not seem to recognize me. How thin, how sick he is! Shadows of the olives shadowed him. When he spoke, I hardly listened. Each of us is going the same way, I thought, and so we parted and stillness put its loneliness about me. The words he had said mixed me because I had not listened, mixed with my love-memories, adding incoherence.

Why was Gogu carrying kelp and a shell? Why was I walking where I had often walked?

In a hundred years, this path has changed little: the trees have become more gnarled, the shadows darker, the air quieter.

The marble shrine at the end of the path crumbles year by year and yet remains about the same: I can remember it when another brought me: Phaon remembered it: and now, memories are re-dedicated and burned, their ashes under my sandals, under my fingers and heart.

The best of life is illusion, I do not doubt. The best of Phaon may have been illusion.

Ah, the nettles of desire, the sleeplessness, the gnawing of regrets in my skull. These are emotions we can not share but must suffer alone till dawn, the dipper proving we are children.

I believe that we, as human beings, prove nothing: there is really nothing to prove except kindness and decency: all else is more illusion.

I take my harp but there are no words to accompany the notes. I urge Atthis to sing: play, darling, help me forget...let me see your face as I love to see it. Move your head with that fragile alacrity. Stretch your bare legs under your dress.

As I open the shutters in the morning, I miss him...the ocean has grown much, much wider.

My favorite olive tree says nothing to me.

Alcaeus wrote me:

"I know I can help you. Come over for the day. Courage, friend."

The note repulsed me. What could he know of Phaon, of man's cleanliness and beauty!

I did not answer. Instead, I climbed the hills with Atthis and Anaktoria, to lay a wreath at an altar that has been our shrine for a while.

The sea was rough and the wind was rough.

Tears overcame me at the altar and I made them leave me: I hoped to die there: I wanted my bitterness to kill me: Why couldn't it happen? Why couldn't there be this finality?

I pulled flowers from the wreath and wrote his name on the ground. A thrush hopped close by. The wind, gusting from the bay, scattered blossoms and I found Atthis beside me, kneeling to comfort me. We had shared so much, the three of us, days and weeks, grief and joy. She and Anaktoria got me to eat, under pines sheltered from the wind; she and Anaktoria fixed my hair.

Their sad faces made me long for happiness for their sake, and I tried to see beyond myself. There must be a trick that I can use to deceive others.

The placid sea carries a few boats,
small clouds on the horizon,
a series of silver cat's-paws;
and as though through a sheet
of green glass the faces of
Sappho, Atthis and Anaktoria:
a laurel wreath whirls above the Aegean:
herons fly, dolphins leap.

Kleis left her shepherd's hut and came here and we have talked far into the night:

"He liked a gold cup...he liked the mountains...he liked the cove...yes, he went farther out to sea than anyone...his sailors liked him...he..."

Kleis stayed several days and each day was a mirror of his personality. Her beauty brought out his quality, imaging it in various ways, her nature shaken from its customary silence to talk of him. I recognized the effort and appreciated the communication. I wanted to write her notes but she could not read. I wanted to thank her in some special way but it was she who thanked me, before slipping away.

Afterward I counted other friends: Alcaeus, Libus, Helen, Exekias, Atthis, Anaktoria, Gyrinno, Heptha, Gogu... I also counted those who have died. Dreaming, I counted our island, our town, our trees, mountains and sea. I added my home. However childish to enumerate like this, I went to sleep easily.

Perhaps, as I grow older, I may find an idea, a seed. Perhaps it can grow in someone's mind: compassion, courage, grace, love—it could become one of these.

I shall continue to put down my thoughts, the handprint of my days.

Could it be that the greatest thing in life is perseverance?

Somebody, I tell you,
Someone in future time
Will remember us.

We are oppressed by
oblivion, by the idea
Of nothing at all,

Yet are saved by the
Judgment of good men.

Christ's Journal

Peter's Home
Elul 10

The sun is setting. The evening is very warm. Across the fields I hear children's voices as they play.

This evening I have been reading the *Psalms* and their beauty fills my mind. I have decided to write my thoughts, not because I am a psalmist, but because I hope to get closer to the meaning of life. Of course I should have started writing long ago. When I was in the wilderness I had an opportunity. Now, it is hard for me to find the time, and writing is not a habit of mine and does not come easily.

However, like a shepherd, I shall gather together my thoughts, watching for strays. In spite of vigilance my thoughts may wander.

It is pleasant sitting here at this table, the night air blowing in; a star is caught in a tree. Peter is talking to a friend; Peter's voice has always pleased me, so deep.

Elul 20

Yesterday, when I was in Naim, someone pointed out a sick man huddled in rags at a street corner. It was one of those windy days and dust spun around us. The man reached up his arms and mumbled; I remembered seeing him before and maybe he remembered me. I felt his hope; I felt I could help, and I said:

"Pick up your mat, get up...walk... God will help you."

The fellow trembled. He seemed to shrink inside himself as if afraid of me. He closed his eyes and doubled his hands. I waited and then repeated my command slowly. Like someone in a dream he untangled his rags and knelt. As he rolled his mat I encouraged him. Glancing about furtively, he stood, tottered. I thought he would fall but he kept his eyes on mine and I urged him to walk.

"Master...master," he muttered, staring about uncertainly. "Master...where...

how can I?"

Limping, carrying his mat under one arm, he headed for the synagogue and as I watched he began to walk easily. He threw down his mat and began to run. Dust swirled around us and he disappeared from sight.

Later, someone told me he had been bedridden, crippled for almost forty years. Forty years—he had been crippled longer than I had lived! Now he was walking...running... I felt such joy, such joy, all day. I couldn't eat when I sat at the table at Peter's; his mother scolded me. To please her I nibbled a little fruit. I couldn't find anyone who could share my joy so I walked alone, roamed the countryside. As I walked I could see his tortured face, dirty beard, beggar's clothes. Forty years...

His name is Simeon.

Probably I will see Simeon soon. And what shall I say when he thanks me? What can he say? I will see a changed man and that will be enough.

Tishri 2

It seems only yesterday I was in Nazareth yet that yesterday was years ago. Regardless of the passage of time I feel the summer heat and hear flies buzzing. Father is at work in his shop. Whitey comes to me and meows; she's scared of the thunder rumbling in the distance; she's hungry too. Mama is cooking and the smell of beef is everywhere.

Father begins to saw and sawdust spills over his feet. I lean against a wall and sunshine spreads and I feel everything impregnate me, the stucco, earth floor, the bench, the broken handle of the saw, Father batting flies that try to settle on his beard. This will last forever. Caught in the web of time we will eat supper together, before lamp lighting, and Whitey will sit on my lap.

I recall another afternoon years ago—the same place. But Father is upset, talking volubly, denouncing Herod and his tyranny, an old, old story for all of us. I have tried to deny the truth of that story but there it is, Herod's soldiers slaughtering innocent children, hoping to kill me. Surely I hate the man and yet I have learned to pity his blundering.

As a boy I wandered, praying, asking understanding. The dry hills were uncommunicative. If it is impossible to forgive it is possible to look ahead. I felt too that my guilt might become a disease. I saw that the past can have too powerful an influence.

Peter's Home
Tishri 6

Tomorrow I am to preach on a hill... Peter says the weather will be fine. I hope so, after windy days. For weeks we have had wind and cold.

Here, in my room at Peter's, I am discontented. The windows try to send me outdoors. They face cornfields and the corn is waist high, brown and roughly swaying. I wish I could stretch out in the middle of a field, lie there and watch the clouds and listen to the wind. I am happiest when outdoors.

The sun is down but I won't light my candle; instead, I'll watch the coming night and perhaps I can summon thoughts for tomorrow; perhaps something will talk to me in the cornfields, something I can impart. Friends and strangers will arrive tomorrow...

Darkness has taken over and I can barely see to write...a cricket speaks...may profound thoughts come.

I spoke to them on a little hill, a rocky place. It wasn't windy or hot and we were not troubled by flies and as I stood before them, fishermen, villagers, friends and strangers, sitting on rocks and on the ground, on shawls and blankets, I was deeply moved. I was specially moved by an old woman near me who never took her eyes off me. Dressed in blue, her clothes in tatters, her face gleamed. Wrinkled cheeks were kind. There was kindness in her folded hands, but, most of all, it was the compassion in her eyes, soft, tearful, blue eyes, that had searched for so long and hoped for so long. Hers was the patience of the poor. Her spirit became my spirit as I talked.

"Blessed are the poor...for theirs is the kingdom of heaven. You are the salt of the earth—you are the light of the world. Let your light so shine before men that they may sec your good works and glorify your Father in heaven.

"Blessed are the meek," I said, "for they shall inherit the earth. Blessed are they that mourn for they shall be comforted...blessed are those who hunger after justice...blessed are the merciful for they shall obtain mercy."

The old woman had buried her face in her hands: she was my mother and every mother, sincerity and love, the symbol of integrity.

A breeze came and white clouds piled along the horizon. The crowd increased and the hill was covered with people. Shepherds approached and held their flocks in check, listening.

"...Rejoice and be exceedingly glad," I said to them, "...yours is the strength of thousands...yours is the strength of the chosen, the humble and the contrite, the pure and lowly...blessed are the lowly. Be ye perfect, even as your Father who is in heaven..."

I tried to express my sincerity, the sincerity that began in the desert, that has been accumulating, that is, for me, the essence of living. I tried to speak slowly, measuring each word. By the time I was finished I was very tired. I was glad to feel Peter's hand on my arm and hear him ask:

"Aren't you hungry?"

A lamb blundered against my legs and I stooped and picked it up and held it in my arms, thinking of my humble birth. There was such comfort, holding it; I felt my strength return. I thought of the stable in Bethlehem. When I went to see it years ago nothing remained but a watering trough and a fence. Time had also swept away the star and the Magi.

Men, women and children pressed around me, talking, praising, asking questions. When I put down the lamb it dashed away. Questions—there is no end to questions. I am glad and yet I am world-weary. World thoughts oppressed me. The moon was well up before I could get away and walk to Peter's; as we bowed our heads at the table someone knocked on the door.

Tishri 21

Sometimes people say I am an unhappy man.

That is not true.

For one thing, I like to remember happy experiences, and one of them was the wedding at Cana. What a pleasant stroll it was, the day temperate, the path climbing gradually above palm trees of the valley, up to the vineyards. Birds were gossiping in the vineyards. The blue of the Jordan flashed through oleanders. The snowy top of Hermon sent out a string of flamingos.

At Cana, Mother greeted me. There were old friends among the guests. Miriam was beautiful, more beautiful than I remembered. I thought of Solomon's song as I watched her, "Thou art in the clefts of the rock; let me see thy countenance, let me hear thy voice, for sweet is thy voice and thy countenance is comely..."

After we had eaten Mother came to me and said "there is no more wine... Miriam is distressed...a wedding without wine!" she exclaimed, gesturing toward the guests at their outdoor tables. Certainly it was Miriam's day. I thought of our friendship through the years and I decided to change water into wine, a token to their youth and their happiness.

I called two of the servants.

"Fill the water pots with water...now empty them into the wine pitchers. There will be wine for everyone."

"It's good wine," I heard someone remark.

Miriam thanked me and I hoped for acceptance on the part of everyone. A beginning has been made, perhaps a seal or symbol had been placed on my ministry. I tasted the wine on my lips as I walked to Peter's. Before I had gone any distance Andrew and Phillip criticized the miracle. They said I could change a man's soul as easily. They were afraid. Mother, walking with us, defended me and ridiculed them.

Alone, I struck out across a grain field where men were dismantling a tent; behind a stick fence donkeys brayed; day was closing behind its fence of clouds; I felt that the men dismantling their tent were also dismantling time.

Alone, the happiness of the wedding returned.

I tasted the wine.

Father is too old to work and I want him to sell one of the Magi gifts, help himself and Mother. This has been a poor carpentry season for him and for others. No use has been made of the gifts these years but he won't listen. He will not so much as hint where they are stored. Where else but the synagogue? He is afraid of the wealth, of robbers...

It is easy to get him started about the Magi. His eyebrow cocks, his head tilts, he pulls his beard and settles himself, legs crossed. He describes camels, accoutrements, attendants, a long, long story, growing longer with the years. The star and the angels are always there. He becomes eloquent like someone who had dabbled in divination.

"Casper...Melchior...Balthasar..."

Mother is pronouncing their names. She is fondest of the Babylonian king.

"He was tall and stately and wore a dark blue robe. His hair and beard were snowy white..."

It was a harsh journey into Egypt, some of the time without water, the heat so overpowering they walked at night. At an encampment, Egyptian soldiers provided food while Mother rested a few days. A sergeant repaired her sandals. They followed an ancient caravan route, asking for help. They lived with Gabra nomads—borrowing a white camel, a day or two. Father says "she was a real princess on that camel!" They hid in a hutment from Herod's men, his troops passing on maneuvers. A lone traveler gave them dates and bread. They begged eggs at a caravanserai...a little goat's milk...a little meat.

Mother praised her donkey. He never refused to carry her. For a while they stopped under sycamores where it was cool, a pond nearby. But they were very hungry. There, under the trees, the donkey died. They thought they would never get back to Israel. Father had the Magi gifts sewn to the donkey's pad but when the animal died he had to carry everything. Utterly disheartened, they trudged on. They got lost. There were sand storms.

Mother begged him to sell the gold cup. “It’s not mine to sell,” he objected. But he traded Melchior’s coins, “for the sake of our boy.” So they survived. Herod’s men continued to haunt them; then they learned that he was dead.

“Despicable men do despicable things,” Father said. “Rome is the great instigator of crimes. The *Kittim*! Political schemes are hatched in the Forum with the wild beasts. Rome appoints a governor for Jerusalem; the man is in exile so he devours us, his subjects.”

Last night I lay awake most of the night, haunted by these ghosts. The past can be a simoom. Maybe it is a good thing when today’s problems wipe out yesterday’s problems. When the oil in the lamp burned out I tried to find oil in the storage shed. There was no more. At dawn I read my favorite psalms.

A thousand hoplites marched through our town. Drums. Horns. Thud of spears.

Many people fled.

Last month the hoplites caused a riot in Naim.

I am unable to countenance such hirelings. I am unable to countenance military death.

Friends are still troubled by my miracle at Cana. As a group of us walked to Jerusalem their annoyance went on and on.

In Jerusalem I was annoyed by the bellowing of cattle, the bleating of sacrificial sheep. An ox screamed. Dust rose from underfoot as I jostled turbaned men... A woman in a striped veil blocked my way.

Passing Herod’s temple I searched for sky. Men had worked for years to build that temple—was it for dust and smoke?

At the temple I stood among money exchange tables and listened to men haggle. A strange, dark, bestial man lorded over everyone. At an ivory-topped table men quarreled and spat. A sacrificial trumpet shrilled. I grabbed my *taliss*, the one Father gave me. Knotting it into a whip I struck the money from a table.

Coins spun. An exchanger howled. I lashed another table, upset it, then another. A crowd jeered as I demanded that they honor the temple.

"This is man's place of worship. You offend God. Look, what you're doing... take your money away...you know our temple is sacred. God's temple is a temple of peace."

Later, when a judge demanded an explanation, I saw my own disrespect, my own violence. He was a lanky, stone-like figure, grey-haired, grey-faced, palsied. He understood my rebellion, the rankling perturbations of my life.

"I'm a Greek," he said. "I realize your alienation. I'm new here. I have much to learn. When a man revolts there is usually well-grounded reason. But be careful! The next time there may be fines or punishment; another man may not be lenient."

Heshvan 9

That night, after scourging the temple, I dreamed of home: I was working at the carpenter's bench, making a three-legged stool. I finished smoothing the legs and sat on the floor, Whitey beside me. She was playing with a heap of shavings.

Again I had that illusion that time was mine, that the sunshine and flies and smell of olive oil and earth would never leave me. And I thought, as I worked on the stool, how pleased Mother would be when I finished it for her birthday. I glanced at a mark on the wall and wondered if I had grown taller.

Galilee

A storm. The lake. Two fishermen drowned. Tents blown over. Next day as I bury the dead a little girl comes and throws herself at my feet, a flower clutched in her hand. What does death mean to her?

Heshvan 11

Wearing dirty work clothes I was readily admitted into the prison at

Machaerus, a citadel high above the countryside. Guards shrugged as I entered. A door clanged with a terrible crash: I was in John's cell. Kissing me, hugging me, we embraced: as always I felt he was part of me.

"How are you, cousin? I thought we would never get to see each other again...in all those rags they didn't know you. You chose a good time; there has been an ugly quarrel going on...we have new guards. Here, here, sit by me."

John has been imprisoned five months and is chained to the wall, a loop around one leg, letting him move a few feet. Rattling the chain, he nodded and grinned at me. I did not understand what he whispered. When he was certain we were alone he grasped his chain and forced it open, first one link and then another. Though he had been a wrestler and farmer I was amazed. Free, he clasped me in his arms.

"It's a great trick...nobody knows...I can get up at night and walk around... maybe there's a way to get out of here."

How often we have been taken for brothers because of our red hair; we trim our beards the same way; our faces are much alike except that mine is leaner. We were brothers as we talked, sitting on the stone floor, the chain between us.

John urged me to leave Capernaum.

"You can't go on preaching there. Antipas has men on the lookout for you. He's as cruel as Herod, you know that! Go in hiding for a while, Jesus. There's no good in it if both of us end up in chains. Our ministry will fail."

I had concealed bread and fruit in my clothes but John would not eat while I was there. I gave him a comb and he combed his beard and head, grimacing, laughing. I asked him to change clothes with me: "You can put me in chains," I said.

An empty cell, stone walls, chains, the Dead Sea glistening dozens of feet below, a cold floor, a little food...what could I do?

"Are there other prisoners on this floor, John?"

"I never see them... I'm not allowed outside."

"You know that we are trying to free you."

"Don't run any risks."

"We aren't afraid."

"I have enough to eat...time to pray."

"We need you."

He bowed in prayer.

To be born anew...that is our hope for mankind.

I went away embittered. Think of it, I left a comb and some bread and fruit for a great man, a man of God. As I walked through the night I heard and re-heard those words:

"May the Lord bless thee and keep thee, the Lord make His face to shine upon thee and be gracious unto thee; the Lord lift up His countenance and give thee peace."

Peace inside stone walls.

When shall John and I meet again?

Peter's
Heshvan 19

I have preached in the synagogues at Cana and Capernaum during the last few days. I do not like preaching indoors. The sky is best and weeds and grass make the best floor. Old laws become new laws outdoors. I stress repentance and faith—the time is now at hand. I try to speak with authority and yet avoid rigid precepts.

Usually I walk alone. Being alone, from time to time, is essential: there is a peace in the company of one's own shadow. After every meeting I am again surrounded by questioners, most of them respectful, some are quite idle and oblivious of anything but themselves.

At Capernaum, as I spoke, swallows flew in and out, swooping low. I wondered, as I watched them, are we the interlopers, have we usurped their place? For me birds epitomize the highest form of beauty.

Near Capernaum I met an officer as I rested under trees along the road. His horse was lathered with sweat and the man was tired; he leaned forward in the saddle and eyed me critically, in silence. I asked him to dismount and rest.

Joining me he said he had heard of my miracle at the wedding and my cure of the street beggar. He brushed dust off his immaculate uniform. Wiping his face he scrutinized me, then pled with me to come and heal his son who was, according to his doctor, dying of fever. I shared fruit and he introduced himself; he admitted he had sought me as a last resort. I pitied the young father, fond of his only child, yet so skeptical. Rising nervously, catching his horse's bridle, he urged me to go to his home.

"I can't wait any longer... You don't seem to understand that my son is dying. Ride to Capernaum. Take my horse. Ride...help my boy. Master, cure him...he has been ill with a terrible fever...for days... I must find help if you can't help..."

"Ride home," I said. "Your son will live; from this very hour he will improve. Ride home in peace...do not hurry... God has answered your plea, our prayers."

I felt my faith attend the boy as he lay in bed. For a little while he became my son—the son I would never have. I blessed him. My faith, God's grace, would renew the child. My power was adequate. I did not need to travel to Capernaum.

Never looking back, the officer rode off, dubious, angry. A breeze clattered dry leaves above me.

I knelt in prayer.

I am troubled because there are so many sick in the world.

Capernaum...Capernaum...the village might be all mankind.

Here I healed the mother of my host, a woman gravely ill of seizures. I had hardly helped her and finished my dinner when people clamored at the door, the demented as well as the sick.

Still riding his bay, the officer found me and assured me his son was recovering—his ardent gratitude was so bewildering, so nervous. As we talked in the courtyard of my host's home people jostled him. He tried to send them away, to establish a sense of intimacy with me.

Walking through the town at dusk I touched this one, spoke to another. A sense of anonymity troubled me: it was everywhere. The exultant friends, the overjoyed crowd, forced me to retreat. As I closed the door of the house I observed Roman soldiers. I asked to be left alone. I ate supper alone. Early in the morning, shortly after dawn, I slipped away to the hills.

Peter's

Simeon came. We sat on stools and he thanked me, tears in his eyes. Clean, wearing new clothes, a little shawl around him, he related how thrilling it was to be able to move about, to "really walk." He explained what it had been to be "a stone in the street, a stone to spit on." Eyes burning, he made me know what it was to be forsaken, abused, hungry.

He says he has told others of his cure. Only a few mockers doubt. Friends and strangers visit his house, to touch him. He imitated poking hands. Simeon is a pathetically handsome man, still frail, his frailty accenting his features. "My cousin Ephriam has promised me a job," he said.

"I'm fifty-three but you've made me young. My memory is coming back. Everything tastes good..."

I believe my faith will help people because it is a faith of hope, a faith that conquers obstacles; it is a faith based on patience and kindness. We have no right to kill, no right to inflict pain. Ours is the gift of understanding, contentment. Ours is the honoring of simplicity and honesty.

Sun on the hills is a kind of faith...the vineyard that endures is another...the wounded heron struggling on...childbirth pain...fishermen drying their nets on the beach...

Our Father Who art in heaven, hallowed be Thy name...

He is our guide, Father of us all, brother of us all, master of all. Seek and you will find. Our kingdom is at hand.

I have been reading a scroll, an ancient one.

I write outdoors, on a table, under olives.

As I speak in public I become more and more a master of words. I detect the difference in just a month or so. I am encouraged. I no longer have to think what I do with my hands and arms, how I stand. Thoughts flow.

Going from place to place I see the same heads. The sun streams over us at the benediction. The passion of living is obvious, touching each of us, offering kinship and peace.

Salt of the earth...

John is the salt of the earth and yet he writes me that he has been beaten by his guards. Several times I have returned to Capernaum to visit Joseph, the young officer. He has promised to use his influence to free John. How wary he is of becoming involved with the prison authorities. In Jerusalem my intercessions are ridiculed: John is branded treasonous.

Authorities are evasive or antagonistic. They ridicule our wish to uplift the world. I am told to take care.

Guards at the citadel refused to allow me to visit John.

Written requests go unanswered.

Peter, James and Matthew are no luckier than I.

A finch is watching me as I write under the olives.

Rain is threatening.

Conception. Birth. Death. Each is a mystery.

In my father's house I grew up among mysteries. I heard them talked, argued over, curtly dismissed. I have resented the unknowns, yet to plumb them is still beyond me. Each child is a mystery. The temple is a mystery. The shell that I pick up on the beach has its mystery. Some say I am a man of mysteries. Does the turtle have its mysteries?

Kislev 5

For days I have been too busy and preoccupied to write—preaching often, healing often. I am writing in a borrowed tent; James and Mark are asleep inside.

Yesterday, on the lake shore, I was circled by a crowd. I talked to them till late. I wish to record the promises I made them:

> *Verily, I say unto you, he that believeth in me hath everlasting life. I am that bread of life. Your fathers ate manna in the wilderness, and are dead. I am living bread. If any man eat of this bread he shall live forever.*

In keeping with my promise I passed out bread and fish in baskets. I blessed the food and there was an abundance for everyone, many of them hungry children.

Mark and James and Phillip passed the baskets till each was fed, the fish and bread always sufficient. At parting I reminded the people of the deeper meaning but some were overwhelmed by the miracle. A youngster ran about shouting: "He made the bread...he made the fish...with his own hands. Jesus made..."

A strange restlessness troubled almost everyone.

Phillip, Andrew and I strolled along a white path, as white, in the moonlight, as if made of crushed shells. Galilee was flat and silvery. Andrew continued to comment about the "bread and fish" at almost every turn of the path. His youthful, enthusiastic face warned me, warned me that youth is irresponsible. What is the proper age for wisdom? As for miracles is there a miracle surpassing the miracle of faith?

Peter has made me a tent. It is dark green, and big enough for two. The tent pole is an antique shepherd's staff. A charioteer and a number of untranslatable characters have been carved on the wood.

"Papa gave me that staff long ago. He said it is Assyrian."

I can carry the tent comfortably and the staff is never out of my hands.

Peter's
Kislev 6

Last night I dreamed I was a tree—a cedar tree.

"Don't cut me down," I begged. "I am shade...I am the home of birds."

I sat underneath the tree and fell asleep. I slept inside a dream.

Peter's Home
Kislev 10

John is dead. Murdered.

He has been beheaded.

The world has lost a voice of reason. I have lost my best friend. He was beheaded at a drunken orgy—his head was displayed like a trophy at the palace. What desecration, abuse, folly, horror. I can barely write...sorrow...resentment... my mind whirls to the days we passed together in the desert, our wilderness comradeship. His faith was my faith. Our bonds were those of true brotherhood.

I should have been able to free him. Instead I gave him dried fruit and a comb. The letters I wrote did nothing. My petitions were disregarded. I was too patient. I have sat in this room all day...nothing has come of my sorrow but more sorrow. Peter and James and Mark have had their say.

Late in the evening friends arrived, wanting to plan his burial. Permission has been granted: we are to be permitted to claim his body. It is best to have the sacred privilege of farewell. We tell each other that we must succeed for his sake, man of poverty, prison and death.

For his sake we can burn our lamps and candles and share late communion, get up early, walk many leagues and extol his faith. We will tell it on the hills and in the towns and in the villages. I feel his wrestler's hand tighten on my shoulder.

Kislev 12

We brought John to the ancient rocky crypts, a dozen of us. Some of us wound scarves around our faces. Mother suspected that we were followed. She insisted on two to act as guards.

Simon was there... Matthew, Peter, Luke, Mark...they helped us lay John outside his crypt, helped us cut stone. A torch burned Mark's arm; someone smashed our hammer. "Work fast," someone was constantly urging. Peter got defiant: "Let the Romans come," he shouted. "We have a right to bury our dead." Luke had to calm him. It was dawn before we had the crypt sealed; we were cut and bruised. No torches.

As I sat among the cliff rocks I tried to obliterate the tragedy, tried to refute his death. Hard to breathe. Hard to utter the final prayer. Think of it...we had buried a headless man, friend, friend...

As we stole into town we met the *Kittim* officer, riding for Capernaum; he did not recognize me of course. What a stark figure! I wanted to talk to him about his son but Mother begged me: we must not trust him.

She railed against wickedness and power.

Luke left us, to care for a sick man.

As we walked, Mother leaned on a stick. Her wrinkled face made me aware that the star of long ago was not around.

At Matthew's home we talked of John's betrayal.

Perhaps we should be somewhat mad to combat man's madness: we must chop up the two thousand crucifixes, chop them into pieces for firewood and with that firewood we shall bake our bread—our *pita.* Crucified bread is the bread of the poor, the waiting, waiting poor. God must help them; we must help them; we must help them as we must help God. Heal. Lift up our eyes.

Nazareth—home
Kislev 20

When I picked corn in a field with my disciples I was reproved because it was Sunday. When I healed the withered arm of a man I was rebuked because it was Sunday. I am threatened by various authorities for such "misdemeanors." Men spy on me and plot against me for acts of kindness. Kindness has reached the level of a crime. Officials remind me, rather discreetly, that John met a tragic death. The Sadducees hate me.

At the pool of Bethseda I helped a man who could not get into the water: I brought him health. He had been a paralytic for years. A cry went up because this was on a feast day. I explained that I intended to carry out my work regardless of the day.

"The son of man is lord even on the Sabbath," I said. "The world of kindness must be a part of our world."

At Nazareth, as I preached on a hill, the crowd turned on me. They insisted I perform miracles for them. Angered that I would not respond willy-nilly, men attempted to throw me off the cliffside of the hill. James, Mark and Phillip protected me; the four of us climbed down the cliff to a wadi.

Disgusted, Father feels I have gone out of my mind. He longs for the peace of my boyhood days. Mother understands: her feeling is intuitive. Though I disappoint and worry her she hides her concern, offering encouragement. She visits those I have healed and tells me how they have changed. Not all are like Simeon, grateful. Some do not want to have anything to do with me.

Peter's
Kislev 22

As I write Peter leans over my shoulder, reading this record that is such a poor record. In the midst of my writing I see John's face; I hear him. We talk about him.

"The Romans are going to take you, one of these days! What can I do to look after you? All of us...what can we do? Look at that madman the other day. He rushed at you... I thought he would kill you...he had a knife. And you cured his madness. There...there, he became one of us...or so it seems. Luke wants to help me look after you. You can't go on without any thought for yourself!"

Peter's voice expresses sincerity, warmth, education. Speech is man's finest quality. More than the eyes, the smile. Its powers are almost limitless. Its tenderness, the child, the babe. My mother consoles with a word perhaps. Out of the past it goes on and on with its revelations, its mirages.

Peter crumples leaves in his hands and reminisces as we sit around a table, the door open, his dog lying outside, flumping his tail agreeably.

"...No, Papa wasn't a clever fisherman. When Mama died he didn't look after our house; it didn't much matter to him what we had to eat. He seemed to be looking for her. I tried to light his lamp but it didn't work. He got very thin, weak; he coughed. I did all the fishing for us. I provided but I didn't do a very good job... I miss him...it was good to have him there, even when he was sick..."

Peter's
Tevet 4

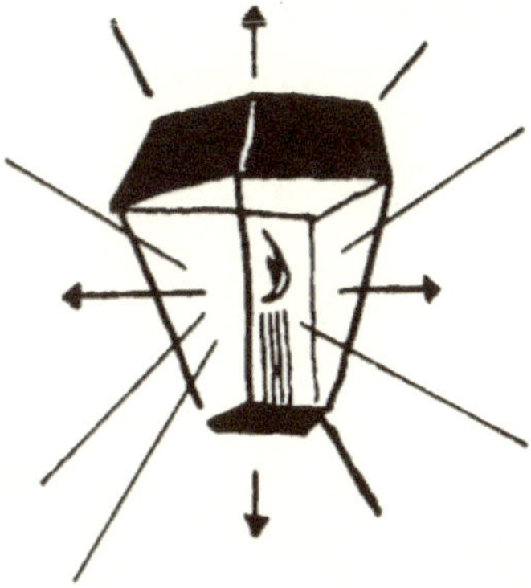

In this little, comfortable house I try to find time in the evenings to study Greek or write in my journal. I prefer my journal. Doors wide open, the lamp bright, I read or write. My legs get restless, my eyes blink and the next thing I know the lamp has burned out and my room is dark.

The other night, after tossing on my pallet, I dreamed that a woman came and brought an antique alabaster box and knelt beside me—to anoint my feet. I tried to say something to her but I couldn't speak. The woman was beautiful.

Suddenly I was standing on a hill. A man was near me; there was nobody else. The man began repeating a parable, imitating me, each word curiously vivid. He said:

"There was a creditor who had two debtors. One owed his master five hundred but the other owed fifty." The speaker stopped, adjusted his purple robe. "When their master forgave them their debts who was the most grateful? The one who owed the most or the one who owed less?"

Someone laughed uproariously.

Ah, the strictures of the mind: without discipline we are weak. As a boy I learned values. I learned how to accept and how to refute. I remember holding a scroll against the light in the doorway of the synagogue: I noted how carefully each word was written. Pen strokes. Such a frail thing, this wisdom.

I found other kinds of wisdom on a dune, at a desert pool, in an oasis.

Tevet 5

For days I have been trying to compose a meaningful prayer. I have trudged along the shore at Galilee; I have listened to the waves and gulls. I have tried to find words suitable for fisherfolk, villagers, countrymen. I walked the wadis, climbed the cliffs. I have lain in my tent and peered at the stars. I have repeated scriptures. Talked.

Last night, after supper, the words came to me:

Our Father Who art in heaven, hallowed be Thy name,
Thy will be done,
on earth as it is in heaven.
Give us this day our daily bread, forgive us our trespasses,
lead us not into temptation but deliver us from evil
for Thine is the kingdom,
the power and the glory, forever.

When I repeated the prayer to Luke and Peter they were pleased.

Galilee
Tevet 11

A storm woke me as I lay in my tent. The wind was churning leaves and I walked to the lake to watch the waves. I felt cold but pulled my cloak around me and continued walking. Clouds were traveling fast. When the rain started I retraced my steps. I heard voices and men at their oars. Waves were piling against rocks. The voices in the boat sounded familiar. Again the thud of oars. Yells. Wasn't that Phillip? It was Peter. Through rain and spray I made out the hull of the boat; then I recalled someone saying they had to land a catch before dawn. Someone shouted:

"We're sinking...we're sinking!"

I walked over the water toward the boat; it was difficult to see through the rain and spray. I recognized the boat. As I walked the waves calmed; the water was black underfoot. Two of our men had slumped over their oars. I shouted. Nobody responded: they were frightened at seeing me. Peter cowered. I called again.

"Peter," I cried. " Don't you know me?"

"Is it you, Jesus?"

"Yes."

"Let me come to you."

"Come," I said.

He sank as he walked toward me and I caught his arm and steadied him and helped him climb into his boat. Luke welcomed me. The boat swung toward me and I got in and sat at the stern with Phillip. Everyone began bailing. The rain was letting up and I pointed to the shore. We soon beached her and everyone began to talk, telling his panic, that they had been unable to see; they crowded around me; they thought I had saved their lives.

Luke built a fire of beachwood and as the sun came up we had breakfast together—some of them singing, everyone hungry, the fish tasting marvelous.

"Mark broke his oar," Luke said and laughed. He was drying by the fire, his clothes steaming. He explained that they had been blown first one way and then another.

Nain
Tevet 18

This has been a beautiful week because I raised a man from the dead and made a blind man see.

At Nain, a small village, my disciples and I met a burial procession headed for tombs cut in the side of a nearby hill. A young man lay on a flower-covered bier. I learned his name from a man in the procession: it was David. He and his mother had been my friends for years. I recognized Athalia walking behind the bier, weeping. Aaron, her husband, had died recently.

It was a warm, still afternoon. The warbling of a bulbul seemed out of place as the procession passed. As the bier scraped against a rock, as the bearers stopped, I approached one of them and asked them to wait.

"David...David...this is Jesus...arise..."

The disciples, astonished, bunched around the bier. I touched David, spoke loudly, shook him.

"David, you are all right. Your mother is here. Get up..." He sat up among his flowers and his mother rushed to his side. He recognized my voice and asked for me. I talked gently with him.

A happy procession. The bier was abandoned; someone threw flowers into the air as David walked...

I am overjoyed as I write. I see David and his mother kissing each other. Someone is singing.

From Nain I went on to see the daughter of Jairus as she lay in bed in her home. The curtains were drawn; the air was sick room air; flowers had wilted on her bed table; her dog cringed under her bed. I asked everyone to leave us alone.

"*Talitha cumi*," I said. "Daughter, I say arise...you are no longer ill. The fever has left you." As I prayed I also thought of John and his death. This little girl was not to fill a grave. I bent over her and took her hand. I could see her rolling a hoop, laughing.

"*Talitha cumi*," I repeated, and sat beside her, pressed my hand over her forehead, touched her eyelids. "Rise, my daughter...you must sleep no longer..."

Her eyes flashed; she was afraid because she had never seen me; smiling, I said:

"Your mother is outside your room...shall I call her?" She nodded.

When I came to the blind man in his home I pressed my fingers over his eyes and spoke to him. I wet clay and placed it over his eyes. I allowed the cool clay to comfort him as I spoke; his wife watched with an expression of doubt; as I removed the clay she stepped aside.

He made a curious noise, pushed me aside, stood.

Walking, he asked:

"Is this my home...is that my garden out there? Are you the man called Jesus of Nazareth? That must be a tree out there..." He was walking into the garden of his home. "Is that...is that a bird...who are the people watching me...and that, is that a flower?"

I write and the evening sun shines on my table and on my hands and it seems to me that I have lived many years in a short span; it seems to me I am very much alone; it seems to me I hear voices: Deuteronomy voices, Jeremiah voices. I hear and yet I am alone. Today is my birthday. I am thirty-three.

Shevat 8

As a boy I respected Greek—such a rich vocabulary, I found; I thought the language overly concise. Hebrew is the city man's tongue, best suited to argument. I prefer my Aramaic. It is more gracious and agreeable for public speaking.

Haran believed in learning three languages: he was the most intelligent rabbi I have met. To him I owe my background; his years of tutoring gave me freedom to think. Morning after morning we sat facing each other at his home.

"We have to think, not memorize...you memorize and then force memories to evolve into patterns of original thought. Yes, memory and thought are brothers. But, make no mistake, thousands repeat the law and the scriptures and only a handful think."

I see his sparsely bearded, wan face. He was a man who ate sparingly yet lived to be eighty. A great walker, he was as restless in body as in mind.

Haran was proud of two ancient scrolls—one of them on copper. The library at Qumran had greater rarities of course.

Haran said:

"Something lives in you...your mother has called my attention to it, an inner voice. When I heard you declaim in the synagogue I perceived it."

So, it is my privilege to help, merge dream and fulfillment: I believe it is a privilege no other man has had: I am the husbandman.

> *Come unto me ye who labor and are heavy laden and I will give you rest...suffer the little children to come...*

Tonight I see the world shining in their eyes; I hear hope in their prattle.

Tent
Shevat 12

Years ago I experienced the greatness of the Sinai desert, its crags and dunes, the heat and cold. I came to understand its desolation, its loneliness, its calm and fury. Now, during these troubled times, I long to return to the Sinai...have a lizard sit beside me, my straw-covered basket filled with golden dates.

In the Sinai I perfected my Greek to a greater extent and studied the classical

Hebrew until it came easily. The history of man became an important part of my meditations. Silence and the simoom became part of those devotions.

A tiny plant sprouted outside my tent and withstood the heat, cold and winds. It was my companion and incentive, a little calendar in leaves.

I found the same plant growing at Qumran, behind the monastery. While I studied there it survived several sand storms.

Locusts, dates, bread, honey—the wilderness taught me the true taste of food. During the months since the wilderness I have eaten well, too well, but the taste is lacking.

I have not thought as clearly as I thought when unencumbered by men. There, each morning was mine, each evening was mine. Worship was as natural as breathing.

My tent flaps billowed. They were pinned back every night by the stars. Heat and thirst were often there yet a sense of praise was foremost. Wonderment was on top of a dune. As I slept a mirage might come and bathe me in its cool water.

I slept on my boyhood blanket, one woven by my mother. She wove it when I was ten.

Nazareth
Shevat 15

I am leaving Nazareth—leaving home.

It is farewell to friends and places, all I have loved. Only in memory will I walk along the orchard creek and hunt for crayfish, think and stare as a boy thinks and stares. I had several pals... We had niches in cliffs where we often hid. We had an old fig we liked to climb; there was a cave where we lit fires. We found menhirs and dolmen—strange, strange things! In Galilee we had a stout little boat and we'd drift, drop anchor, fish for chromis and watch the pelicans.

There's a feeling to my Nazareth: the stars are brighter there, the sun seems a little bigger, the wind a little cooler. How good it was to turn a corner and think: Mama's home...supper is almost ready...Papa's working in his shop.

Nazareth
Shevat 20

Today was cool and windy.

I visited Simeon. I visited Mark. I visited Jude. I called on the captain, who has been transferred to Nazareth. His son sat in my lap a while. I did not say good-bye although I lingered at each place. I wanted to feel the peace of each place and keep it with me. I did not need to talk much. Being with friends was all I asked.

Oh, how the wind blew me along, flapping my cloak, flapping the olive branches, the weeds and the papyrus.

How hard it is to write.

Nazareth

Before I left home Father displayed the gifts of the Magi on his work bench, first removing his tools and shavings. He locked the door and lit two candles. Mother—so excited—seemed to be seeing the star as she handled the gifts.

"They haven't changed... Joseph, you've taken good care of them! Oh, they're so beautiful!"

And she knelt in the sawdust, the gold cup in her hands, its jewels redder than I had remembered. I had forgotten the gifts were so beautiful.

"Where have you kept them...in the synagogue? The geniza?" I asked.

Father nodded, frowning.

"We have decided to present them to the elders...tomorrow...at the meeting. They'll become the temple possessions. It's different with you going away... Mother and I have decided..."

But I wasn't listening; I was absorbed in Mother's appreciation as she handled the gifts, kneeling or half-kneeling, smiling; her shoulders lost some of their age. The myrrh box interested me, its aroma still evident, its chased lid yet untarnished. Mother lifted the clasp. The clasp was set with green stones. She called my attention to the ornamented hinges. She held out the gold cup to my father...

"I wish you hadn't worried about the gifts," she said with a sigh. "We ought to have enjoyed them...now we can see them at the temple... Look, Jesus, at this handle...ah, those were strange days in Bethlehem... God was with us..."

I loved her for her dreams and sacrifices.

I loved the hints of youth and beauty in her face.

Nazareth
Shevat 25

Tomorrow is my last day here.

As I lay on my pallet I heard rain lash our roof; I heard the wind in the trees. Then my mind dropped back and I remembered Mother singing, crooning to me, as I lay sick as a boy. I remembered songs in the evening. I heard her laughter as we played jacks. I smelled her barley bread... I smelled roasting lamb.... Father was in his workshop, his plane sliding; he was singing. As a child I loved his singing.

Now, silent, worried, he works in a preoccupied state, bothered by frequent visitors, concerned about my future. "It is wrong of you to go to Jerusalem, wrong to throw yourself into the hands of your enemies."

There will be no more Festivals of Light.

At Nazareth I used to have a pet goat.

Memories... I can not tolerate juvenile memories any longer. I am not an old man. Memories must not impede my ministry.

There must be beauty. Life must have beauty.

Jerusalem
Shevat 29

> *Thy rod and Thy staff will comfort me...yeah, though I walk through the valley of death yet will I be with Thee.*

As I walked into Jerusalem I heard those words. It was dusk. An immense caravan choked the air, camels, drivers, gapers. Again I thought of Herod and the innocents: city life brings Herod to mind. The *Kittim* are evident on the main streets: helmets, standards, shields.

A camel sank to the ground beside me, eying me, begging for kindness. Trumpets blared.

Crowds circled the temple, some chanting, some bearing fruit, some waving palm fronds. Flares burned. On two giant candelabra, perhaps eighty feet high, torches smoked, guttered.

Shall I be able to help the people of Jerusalem? Shall I remain? My loneliness here was so unlike the loneliness of the desert.

I was to meet Judas who was to take me to friends. When he did not come I bedded down in a booth of branches, with cattle nearby.

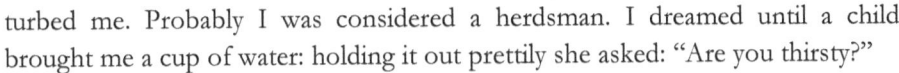

I slept and woke to their animal sounds, without dread. Someone roused the oxen, then the sheep; the beasts wanted to be fed and watered. Nobody disturbed me. Probably I was considered a herdsman. I dreamed until a child brought me a cup of water: holding it out prettily she asked: "Are you thirsty?"

"Yes," I said.

"My papa is taking care of the oxen."

Opening my pouch I offered sugared dates to the girl.

I found Judas at the home of a mutual friend. I had never seen him so well dressed. He drew me aside and gave me money from our treasury. He seemed forlorn. I am told he is having a love affair with the daughter of Pilate. Marcus, the son of a senator, has described Pilate's daughter as a beautiful, talented, ruthless woman. Marcus and I sat on a garden bench and he enthused about Jerusalem: "So unlike Rome, so much more oriental—can it be we are free of our penates here?"

That evening I stayed in the house of Leonidas Clibus. My windows were olive tree windows. Garden paths circled a tiny fountain where someone had tossed fresh oleander blossoms, red blossoms.

A copy of Horace lay on a circular table by my bed; lamps and rugs, hangings and x-shaped Roman chairs, cushions and inlaid boxes brightened the room. Propped on a cushion I read Horace for hours; when my candles dimmed a slave brought me fresh candles and volumes by Lucretius—recent translations.

> *...What's this wanton lust for life*
> *To make us tremble in dangers and in doubt?*
> *All men must die and no man can escape.*
> *We turn and turn in the same atmosphere...*

I went to sleep preferring the thoughts of Horace: his love of nature, his fondness for rustic surroundings, his boating on the river Aufidus, his fishing. He liked to play ball. I could visualize him, as a boy, when wood pigeons covered him with leaves as he slept on a hillside.

Clibus' Home
Adar 6

There are children here. What priceless looks they give. I love their delight in simple things, their warmth, their trust, so obvious, so quick. Truly, theirs is a special kingdom. I am happiest when they are around me, as they were yesterday in Clibus' garden. It was a birthday party for his daughter who is six. I told stories as they sat around me. What laughter, giggles. A little boy brought me a toad and put it in my hand, saying:

"It's for you, Atta."

Clibus

Of course I miss the great library at Qumran. The beautiful library in his home is a fraction of that monastic collection but bearded Clibus has invited me—with widespread arms.

A delicate bronze of Minerva stands on a plinth at the window end of the narrow room.

A book on my lap, I watched a golden Persian cat steal about, stiffly independent.

Though I can not read Latin I can understand titles and the names of authors and I appreciate handsome volumes, ancient volumes, family treasures.

Minerva—I used to think of visiting Rome and Athens.

Adar 15

I spoke to a group near the city gate. I was aware that officials were present, Sadducees.

I saw men dragging a woman, kicking her, letting her fall. She had been caught in adultery. When she was brought to me I suspected a trick. Why should I pass judgment when officials were in the crowd? Authorities wanted me to break the law by passing judgment.

I was shocked by the woman's fear, her beseeching face. As she stood by me a soldier hit her with a chain. Men yelled: "Stone her, stone her!" When a man shoved her to her knees she hid her face in her arms—pretty, a country girl, I thought.

To give myself time to think I wrote on the ground with a stick. I wrote and obliterated words, watching the crowd and the woman. I smelled death. It was in the smoke of sacrifices burning in the city. It was in the crowd around me. I had never smelled the death of a person.

Taking in the street ruffians and the officials I said, in a loud voice:

"Look at her, at her torn clothes. Do any of you know her? Think. Go deep inside. Think. Let the man who has not sinned throw the first stone. You accuse her...where is the man? Go home, all of you. Have you no pity? Remember the commandment: Thou shalt not kill. We are not animals! Let her go... I repeat, let her go. Go home—all of you!"

I helped the woman to stand. Someone had thrown ashes on her face and I bought water at a shop and washed her face and hands and bought oil for her cuts and bruises. Matthew found us and brought her food.

"Where can I hide?" she asked us. "What is to become of me? They will catch me...beat me... Master, master...what shall I do?" Her words mixed with sobs.

Matthew and I helped her out of town, beyond the gates. We sent her to the home of Talus where Luke cares for the sick.

I returned to Clibus' library but I was too disturbed to read. While I sat there, the *Sayings of Moses* spread before me, Affti, Clibus' Egyptian wife, brought a pillow and sat by me. She is as beautiful as Miriam; to have her there was a comfort but her words were not comforting:

"It isn't safe for you to preach in Jerusalem... Your faith is for the little towns and villages where the Romans have less influence or none at all...

"When James was here a month or so ago he mentioned going to Rome. Do you wish him to preach your gospel there?"

She went on to urge me to send apostles to Egypt.

"There are more than seventy of you now... I hope you can send two or more to my country...to preach in the villages...you are needed there."

That evening, after dinner, she rapped on my door: she is very tall, very elegant; dressed in an Egyptian gown, she made a little bow, and presented me with a bronze stylus.

"It will be better than your wooden one," she said.

While enjoying my stylus someone brought me a dish of lemon paste.

Sadly, more than twenty years have passed since our Nazareth synagogue acquired a scroll. Our scrolls are in tatters and all are asked to refrain from using them. Learning this, Clibus has offered several scrolls.

"I'll send two of my men...one to carry the scrolls, the other to see that the first man doesn't wander off."

Perhaps little Nazareth may have a worthwhile collection someday.

Jerusalem
Adar 20

My enemies come closer.

> *Verily, I say unto you, the man who climbs the sheepfold wall is a thief. He who enters by the gate is the shepherd. To him the porter opens and the sheep hear his voice and he calls his sheep by name and leads them...*

My parable is realistic but people do not listen. They push one another, talk.

When I encountered a blind man, a man who had never seen during his lifetime, I sent him to the Siloam pool. He bathed there and at my touch his sight became normal. He stumbled, fell, rushed about, shouted. Trembling he raced for home. He brought friends and there was great rejoicing. Then, stunning everyone, authorities questioned me rudely. Because he defended me and called me his healer he was put in jail.

I had to go before the local magistrate, affirm his honesty; then he was freed. I said to the magistrate:

"I came into this world to help men see..."

Last week I cured lepers on the Jericho road, men and women, all in rags. All were afraid of me, afraid of themselves. I thought I could change their minds but their minds were in tatters like their clothes. One man thanked me, a young man from Tyre; the others, quarrelling, pushing one another, tearing at their rags, left the road to crawl into a cave.

I asked the man from Tyre what he knew about the others but he could not concentrate on what I said: he was so moved, so pleased, so enraptured over his health he stood in front of me, smiling, laughing. He kept holding up his arms and hands—showing me. I asked him about people I knew in Tyre. He shook his head, laughed, kissed my hands, rushed off. A caravan was passing, camels, drivers, onlookers; he disappeared among the camels, the dust.

Jerusalem
Adar 25

Today I received a message: the *mebakker* at Qumran has invited me to return to the monastery for a second residency. He wants me to instruct others in the Messianic Rule.

I am no longer in accord with Qumran's rigid communal life: such sharing would be difficult for me; certainly none of my disciples would understand.

But I think of the Qumran desert; I think of the cliffs and caves near the monastery. Morning and evening shadows! What great fogs used to engulf us!

Urusalim
Adar 28

I spoke outside the temple and, as I spoke, men and boys picked up stones to throw at me.

Sadducees want me excluded from the temple; others want me excommunicated. They stamp me an untouchable. Such intrigue! How am I to help mankind? My disciples urge me to leave Jerusalem. The world is beautiful, they remind me: Go to Cana, go to Bethlehem, to Galilee, to Jericho. Date groves. Olive groves. Roses. As if I needed a reminder.

This afternoon I walked about Solomon's city to an impressive ruin, a series of roofless rooms, fallen columns, weeds growing through marble floors, lizards on walls. Birds dotted the sky. I tried to imagine the regal furnishings of Ptolemy's time. Underfoot were hieroglyphic slabs, a cartouche among them. I climbed old stone walls, were they Nehemiah's walls when he fortified the city? I found a broken scarab and remembered Egyptian words my mother taught me as a boy. In the street below the vast ruins a Roman soldier talked with another Roman soldier. Herod's workmen were capping stone pillars. Tall men in dark red robes, red turbans on their heads, prodded camels, heavily laden animals. Were they Syrians?

Somewhere along the way I met a blind man led by a boy. The sun sent sweat down the boy's face. Tired, they sat by a spring where women and girls were filling jars. People recognized me and soon a crowd formed, as I rested. The blind man, wearing a sash woven with gold, white-bearded, tall, erect and proud, asked about me. The boy whispered desperately to him.

"It's Bartimaeus and his son, from Jericho," a woman said.

"Son of David, have mercy on me," Bartimaeus pled, speaking softly. Then he cried:

"Lord, have mercy, that I may receive my sight. Are you Jesus of Nazareth? Will you help me? Will you touch my eyes? I must see again."

I sat close to him and talked to him, the aura of his faith evident. As we talked I realized he could see: his expressions were so startling. He embraced his son. Erect, silent, he stared about him. Everyone was silent. Fumbling a little, he walked away; then, he returned and knelt by me and kissed my hands.

"Master...let me follow you... I believe...let me be one of your chosen...let me tell others what you have done for me. I know about your ministry." He kissed my robe. "When I heard you speak yesterday I tried to reach you."

He urged me to stay at his home; perhaps he had heard me say that fox have holes and birds have nests but the man of God has no home. I warned Bartimaeus not to look back if he put his hand to the plough.

Lately I have not seen much of Judas. He refuses to visit me at Clibus' home. I hear that Judas has quarrelled with the daughter of Pilate. Faithful to our group, he collects and disperses funds. Our group is increasing in number—committed to everyone. Some of us provide food, clothing and shelter.

A nomad group is famine stricken. The babies need sugar and salt and we have provided packets by way of a caravan.

Clibus'

Through Clibus I have written a letter home. Mother will find someone to read it aloud. I don't want Mother and Father to come here. They dislike the city. Father has been unable to work and needs to husband his strength. He must avoid danger.

Getting up at dawn I have been able to memorize lines from Horace, lines that help. The tiny garden helps. The children help. But when John's cousin, Elihu, came, distortion returned as we talked of John's imprisonment, torture, death. Elihu is a frail soul, so unlike John. He is so in need of encouragement. He tells me that a storm flooded homes in Nazareth. They did the best they could with shovels and baskets.

Jerusalem
Nisan 8

I look forward to resurrection. The promise of resurrection sustains me although I am, at times, confused, confused because resurrection means a blurring of the future, perhaps a cessation of the future. I can not plan a sabbath. I can not say "We shall meet together at Samaria." Since the beyond is truly incomprehensible today is distorted as well.

I must warn myself of the onslaught of pain that will crush me during the crucifixion. How to bear it? Gird my loins, perhaps. It will not be easy to die for my fellowmen. Will my ascension help others rise from their tragic lives?

Dread eats away at me.

Hate undermines me.

Broken covenants...Golgotha, place of skulls...rocky Judea... Caesar Augustus, your crimes are everywhere...imperator...killer!

I need to be baptized with love.

With wisdom.

Yesterday, in this city of rocks, I noticed straw in a stable, yellow straw, fresh, clean, glistening in the sun. I took a few. Straw is simplicity. Simplicity points to a balanced way.

Bethany
Nisan 12

Yesterday I walked to Bethany. Martha and Mary said that Lazarus had died. Among graves and stunted trees, in a stinging wind, I became keenly aware of the days I spent at their home, with the three of them. How often Lazarus and I had done carpentering under his thatched shed.

Here, with his sisters, friends and relatives, here at the tombs, I knew death was not the answer. I walked to the crypt where Lazarus lay. Loose rocks tumbled underfoot. Wind whipped. A boulder blocked the crypt and I asked Martha to have her friends help me drag it aside. Men consulted and argued that it was useless; they glared at me savagely as they pushed and dragged the stone.

At the opening I bent over and cried:

"Lazarus...come... I am the resurrection and the life...come...this is Jesus!"

I needed him. His family needed him. Mary and Martha. Death did not need him, surely.

Men jeered and howled. But I knelt and shouted as the wind spat on all of us.

Ah, sorrowing women, yellow rocks, death, a man in his crypt, cold stone, a hawk screaming...

I called again and again.

"Lazarus, this is Jesus. Arise! Come with us! Remember us, remember I am the resurrection and the life. Come unto me...believe...God is here..."

It was late afternoon: the sun was behind the yellow cliff.

Martha clutched my arm and said:

"Lord, let us leave. Lazarus has been dead four days. He stinks."

A funeral procession passed by—men and women—the men carrying a child's coffin.

"God, our Father, help us. Give this man life again!" I beseeched with passion. I knew, as I prayed, that Lazarus would respond.

Swaying, wrapped in burial clothes, Lazarus appeared, a scarf across his face. He could not see or move his hands. I went to him and Martha uncovered his eyes. Mary ran to help. We unwrapped his legs and arms.

"Jesus has given you life," Martha said. "You are going home with us...you are one of us again."

Stumbling over rocks, Mary guiding him, Lazarus found a place to sit down. We unbound him and someone gave him a robe. Someone offered him a piece of bread. He shook his head, stared at us, turned from one to the other, his face birdlike, hawklike, white. He peered at his crypt. Martha hugged him, laughing. People gathered. Some knelt around us.

"Mary, what happened?" Lazarus began, speaking his first words.

"Why am I here in this place? Why am I wearing a robe? And these people... and Jesus! Was I sick? Where are my clothes?"

I longed to leave this place of death: it was closing in on me. The wind blew harder and a hawk leaped upward.

With Martha I walked away, listening to her happiness, her praise.

"We must have supper. What shall we eat? Will he be hungry, able to eat? Jesus, you have saved him. I love you. It's wonderful! He's back...think of it, after four days. Then, then there is no death for us who believe..."

At supper Lazarus was unable to talk; he drank a little and soon had bread wet with olive oil. No one had much to say. Lazarus sat next to me. Bending over his plate he gave me a few boyish grins—like old times. He had gotten into his work clothes. Putting his hand into a pocket he pulled out a small chisel and laid it on the table. But he said nothing. I urged him to eat Martha's fish or lamb, delicately prepared. Every face at the table expressed a wonderment and rapture. The candles burned down. The women ate. Suddenly there was chatter and then laughter—rejoicing.

It was difficult to return to Jerusalem, leave my friends. I lingered a day for the fields of barley, the paths that were peaceful paths. I had to have time to be with Lazarus, be with Mary and Martha, write my journal. Alongside the carpentry bench I have a table. I prefer writing outdoors. There is a vine on the thatched shed and it is in flower. As I write Lazarus is sleeping on the ground, in the sun.

Caretakers at the graveyard claim that one of the crypts has been robbed.

Jerusalem

I keep hearing the words of an old hymn as I go about; it was John's favorite, one we learned while at Qumran. Was it solace while he was imprisoned? I hope it was. It is a comfort to me—so gracious.

I give thanks unto Thee, O Lord,
For Thou has wrought a wonder with dust.
Thou hast made me know Thy deep, deep truth,
Thou hast given me a voice;
I continually bless Thy name.

I seem to hear John's commanding voice, his loving benediction as I left his prison:

The Lord bless thee and keep thee,
the Lord make His face to shine upon thee
and be gracious unto thee...

Ephraim
Nisan 14

I am staying at a beautiful old stone house in nearby Ephraim. I have allowed myself a respite, among pomegranate, olives, roses. Herons fly at dawn and evening. Children run in and out. A boy with shaggy head has a pet dove. A girl with almond eyes is learning to weave. My disciples are here, the new and the old. We have met in a low room, plain and bearded men, clothes new and disheveled; Ezra shows me his injured leg; Luke works over it; Lamech (a strong youth) is from Casarea, an expert swimmer, he said.

"I will walk to Jerusalem tomorrow. I'll remain there. The high priests will accost me. They may mock and scourge me, as they have many others...but I will return." I tried to speak calmly. I could not be forthright...

Calling me "Rabboni," a pretty girl knelt in the jammed room and anointed me with fragrant oil. It was a moment of calm, a moment of beauty.

Nisan 15

Holy Week has begun.

I walk accompanied by my disciples.

As we pass a tall wooden cross I remembered that the Romans have crucified as many as two thousand men at one time because of religious dedication. Almost every single one of us has witnessed a crucifixion.

Hail Caesar!

Ours was a solemn path on a clear morning, larks singing, the air brisk.

Carrying fronds, waving, hoping to speak to us, hundreds filled the paths and streets, wanting the miracle of love and life.

Our path crooked upward to the "House of the Figs," where I was given a donkey, a tall, white one. Children shouted joyously. For me, he was my donkey of peace. I waved as I rode along. Some women cut branches and tossed them in front of me. Others threw flowers and shouted "Hosanna."

Jerusalem spread around me, blocks of stone, yellow walls, piles of ancient masonry, new porticos, towers, shops... It was my city, my hated city; I esteemed the meaning it has for my forefathers, men who slept in the valley, with peaked cypresses above their graves.

Dust fanned over us as we followed a narrow way. Romans turned on me and turned on the crowd but I warned them to desist.

At the temple I found more money changers. The courtyard was cattleyard; waiting rooms were storerooms. Animals bellowed. I struck again at the vendors, toppling tables, hurling money trays. The crowd screamed, cheered. In the midst of this bedlam strangers, travelers, stopped Philip and Andrew. They insisted upon being presented to me. The four men offered me sanctuary in the kingdom of Edessa.

Priests, soldiers, young and old crammed around me as I explained the life eternal, the image of redemption, eternal salvation and the price we must pay.

God is our Father...the world of nature proclaims His goodness...men must share His divine harmony...you reach God from within...reborn, you recognize the light.

Children sang.

My love went to them.

Astride my donkey I preached to them in simple words.

As the sun slipped behind the city towers there were scores listening and we lingered on the terrace:

"There is light for you for a little while longer...walk while there is light... darkness will come...he who walks in darkness cannot tell where he is going... believe in the light..."

The evening air was becoming chilly; a wind was blowing in from the desert.

With my twelve I walked through the Golden Gate, passing great herds of sheep and goats, grey pastoral sheep and black mountain goats. I was proud of my men, proud of their courage and love, proud of their humility.

Jerusalem
Nisan 29

We met in an upper room—a white-walled room. Centering it was a long table and we sat around it, sharing bread and wine...below us roses were in flower.

God was with me as I told them, my legatees, that I must die.

"Tonight you are entrusted with the keys of the kingdom. Two at a time you are to go about the world, preaching the gospel. Faith is our church."

I loved each man. Such faces! Bartholomew, Matthew, Luke, James, Simon, Peter, Thaddeus, Judas, John, Phillip. I gazed at one and then the other, fisherman, cobbler, farmer, physician, lawyer...brothers.

"Your task is to save mankind!"

The lamps on our table shaped shadows on the walls, on the floor, far more than shadows. The white walls enshrined each of us. When the wind puffed our lamps blinked. Ours was an aura that may never recur.

"Soon my enemies will crucify me...one of you will betray me..."

What consternation! What hysterical exclamations! What accusations! Then the pleas began: you must escape! Let us help you! We can! Listen...flee...tonight.

"Faith is the miracle for everyone," I said. "Heal the sick. Remember Cana... Galilee...Lazarus...the lepers on the roadway..."

I reminded them that we are samaritans. Mercy is ours, ours to give. We are to help the heavy laden. Love our children. We are to teach by example.

Israel, I told myself, you are to nurture goodwill, tolerance, peace, hope.

So it was in that white room, at that hour.

Clibus'

By the light of candles I write, to shepherd words, to commune once more. There is little time for writing, little time for thinking. I feel that I must endure. By the flickering lights I commune with Father, Mother, earth.

I would like to go on healing the sick, alleviating pain, the body's pain, the soul's. To be a good shepherd, yes. Will my disciples persevere?

I can write no more tonight.

Peter's
Iyyar 2

Oh, Jerusalem, you killer of prophets, stoner of those sent to help you! How I have wanted to care for your children as a hen cares for her chicks under her wings. You would not have me!

Plotters have attempted to trap me. A group cornered me near the temple. Is it lawful to pay tribute to Caesar? they asked. I asked for a coin. I called their attention to the face on the coin, the face of Caesar Augustus.

"Render to Caesar the things that are Caesar's and unto God the things that are God's."

Not to be defeated, men queried me, as I sat in the court of the temple, old, old questions. It seemed to me they were stunned when I reminded them that God is not the god of the dead but of the living. Other interrogators appeared at noon. A huge grey-bearded priest demanded:

"Master, which is the greatest commandment of the law?"

I deliberated, wanting to impose on his arrogance.

"You shall love the Lord will all your heart and with your soul and with your mind...this is the first and greatest commandment," I said. "The second commandment is similar," I pointed out. "You shall love your neighbor as yourself."

By now I was angry and left these idlers and when I was alone with my disciples I shamed the trouble-makers who clean the outside of the cup and leave the inside dirty... I called them a generation of vipers...they are the ones who will persecute the faithful from town to town...crucify them...

Grief overcame me. I could talk no longer.

Disgusted with the day, Matthew asked if the world would come to an end soon. That question had to be left unanswered. Inventors of questions are everywhere. I wanted to add, watch, be on guard, pray ceaselessly, work... Don't be careless while your master is away. You can't tell when he may return.

Mother came to visit me, she arrived in the night, afraid. Rumors had reached her that I was ill. She was ill. It is a long, long walk, from Nazareth. Peter gave us melon and though it was long past midnight we sat at a little table under the stars and ate.

It is impossible to go on writing.

I see what is to take place. I am frightened. I must wait until I have risen from the dead to continue writing. I have spoken to Matthew. I will entrust my journal to him.

Judas, in a drunken rage, has gone to the authorities and has promised to deliver me to them for a sum. He ridiculed me when I refused to ask God's protection.

Here are my final thoughts:

I beg You, dear Lord, hear me. Be attentive to my last supplications.

I wait, my soul waits. My soul waits for You more than any who wait for the morning. I say, more than those who watch for the morning.

Peter's
Iyyar 10

I am alive.

A tremor roused me and I slowly unwound my grave clothes, noticing how beautiful they were. I looked at my left hand. I looked at my right hand. They had healed. The stone that blocked my crypt had been rolled aside. It was dawn when I went out. Outside I found a discarded robe.

The sky was grey but sun slanted across spring hills. I walked toward the sun on a path that led away from the tombs. Perhaps no one can grasp my bewilderment and my happiness. I tasted the air. My brain rushed about, rebounded from a bush, crashed against rocks. Light was splintering around me; inside that light was the realization that my suffering is over. I need not die. Life was living in me like a seed, but a perpetual seed.

Following a path across flowering fields I picked flowers; then, across the field, I saw Mary Magdalene. She was sobbing, crying. I called her and she ran to me, saying "Rabboni" over and over. "Dearest..."

Mary and Martha appeared. The women surrounded me, laughing, touching me, kissing my robe, my hands. Later in the day we set out for Nazareth, for my home, Mother and Father. Halfway Mother met us and threw her arms around me—no words were necessary.

That evening, as we ate together, Mother described Father's imprisonment. He had sold the gifts of the Magi to obtain bribe money: he planned to bribe the soldiers to free me. The merchant who bought the gifts summoned officials. By lying he got Father jailed for theft.

It required four days to free him, our Nazarene priests testifying...

Liberated from death I see life as a singular continuity, a continuity embodying my imperfections, many hopes. I find a new calm in all that I experience: as I project into tomorrow I sense this serenity. Simplicity itself wears an aura of riches.

Tonight, living in this composure, I write freely. Time, as a force, has dropped away. Pressures are comprehensible such as the stress at our last supper, the betrayal of Judas. Though I held my emotions in check I felt confused by many doubts: above all I felt that my ministry would fail. Ah, that white room, those shadows, our courage as we sipped salt water in memory of the Egyptian exodus. Those faces as we sang. Now those memories are glassed inside a mirror, unblemished. And I may open that mirror and experience a memory or I may close the surface.

I stand alone. It is a beautiful feeling. I stand here without past and without future. I am a naked man, a man of the wilderness. This is the miracle of self.

The mind owns itself. It does not ask. Acceptance blocks out intrusion. Each of us should experience the wilderness of mind.

Iyyar 18

This is how it was:

As I knelt in the garden I thought of John and his prison bars, for around me were bars of shrubbery, blacker than any I had seen. Immobile bars.

Death was in the bars and in the air around me, imagined but none the less real, as real as death had been in the street that day men wanted to stone the woman taken in adultery. This was my death—I listened for approaching soldiers, for the voice of Judas.

"If it is possible," I prayed, "let this cup pass from me quickly."

I heard the brook below: it had a place to go. I had this, this waiting, this expectancy, my disciples asleep on the ground.

Death...death is the ransom for man's sin, I reminded myself.

Cries of sentinels rang out.

Judas knew that I was here, that I had come here to pray; presently I heard the unmistakable clank of side arms and men's voices, foreign speech. I could wait no longer. I stood up and waited for Judas to identify me.

Stumbling over shrubbery, Judas called.

I answered.

"Who are you looking for?" I asked a soldier carrying a torch.

"Jesus of Nazareth," he said.

"I am Jesus."

Lanterns and torches appeared. Peter saw and heard the soldiers and snatching a sword from one of the guards he slashed a man's ear. I rebuked him and cared for the guard, an Arabian named Malchus, who was singularly afraid of me, afraid of the garden, his task.

"We shouldn't have come...you were praying...this is the garden where you come to pray," Malchus said.

"Is Judas with you?" I asked.

"He has gone... I'm captain here...you must come with us. We have been commanded to take you to the high priest, Ananias."

"You take me with swords and shields—like a thief. I taught in the temple... I prayed daily for you..."

Malchus, his face in torchlight, mumbled in Arabian and turned away.

"Leave him alone...get out of here," Peter shouted; I saw the guards struggle with him.

Malchus led me along the narrow streets, dark. People lay asleep in corners and doorways. Donkeys were hobbled together. We walked over piles of garbage. As we filed toward the house of Ananias wind smoked our torches. At the door of the house we were kept waiting. Two of my guards fell asleep.

Amid bickering I was led into a small room and left there; then, late in the morning, I was brought before Caiaphas, before scribes and elders, in an open courtyard. There I heard someone say that it is expedient for us that he die for his people.

Caiaphas asked me about my teachings and I responded:

"I have spoken openly. I have taught in the synagogues of Nazareth and Cana and Capernaum and in this city... I have said nothing in secret. Ask those who have heard me what I have said." I spoke tersely because I realized this was a false trial.

One of the scribes struck me across my face and hurled me to the floor.

Witnesses were brought—citizens. One testified that I had vowed to destroy the temple within three days and rebuild it without hands. Other witnesses disagreed. A woman said I faked miracles. A man testified I had threatened to depose the governor. Others disagreed.

"Are you Christ...are you the man the people call Christ?" Caiaphas asked.

"I am."

A priest gestured; he seemed to tear his robe. Caiaphas smiled.

"You have heard this blasphemy," he said. "We need no more witnesses. I condemn this man to death." I knew nothing more could be said in my defense.

As I sit at my table, underneath the trees, at Peter's home, I write as if I were writing about someone else, a friend perhaps. I write without prejudice. I am shaken by man's corruption and yet my lack of faith in man does not influence my writing.

I was left in the hands of guards and palace servants and then I was led into a room where my hands were roped behind me. I was thrown on the floor and beaten and kicked and spat on. Men placed me in a chair and covered my eyes and asked me to guess who struck me, everyone laughing.

I fell asleep on the floor and was wakened for a trial before priests, elders, scribes, in a marble-floored room, Roman insignia on the wall, the room icy, airless, officers and soldiers at one end, one of them in battle gear—to impress me, I thought. But I was scarcely able to stand, scarcely able to think. My hands on the back of a chair, I put my mind to work: I singled out my home, its doors, its windows, the grass growing in the street. I forced myself to visualize my mother and father. Though I was in pain I remembered my little friend, Amos: we were kneeling in the dust before my house, playing marbles: dust flipped as we shot.

I was asked if I was the son of God.

The trial was not a trial. There were no witnesses.

Temple officials conferred.

Roman authority was not involved.

A judge or priest condemned me to death.

Such authority had been denied forty years ago by the Romans. Being aware of this added to my resentment; I tried to speak out but was silenced. From the courtyard I was marched to the paved square called Babbatha; troops lined the square, spectators gathered. The sun's warmth lessened my pain. One of the guards, secretly, gave me bread. I saw Judas with Pontius Pilate; Pilate was accompanied by councilors, guards. I felt I had been hurled into a wholly alien world—enemy world.

Pilate, stepping forward in his robe, asked Caiaphas the nature of my crime. I will remember that scarlet robe.

Caiaphas, annoyed, said:

"If he were not a malefactor we would not bring him before you." Pilate understood the evasion. He responded:

"Take him, judge him according to your law."

A priest declared:

"We found this man saying he was Christ the King."

Perhaps Pilate was remembering his troubled past, the servitude of his ancestors, some problem, for he hesitated, suspecting a ruse, that the priests were deceiving him. He must have known that I had not preached revolt.

"Are you king of the Jews?" he asked, motioning me to come closer. "Your people have brought you here. What have you done?"

"My kingdom is not of this world."

"Are you a king?"

"I was born to bear witness to the truth."

Pilate shrugged.

"What is truth?" He resumed his seat.

I did not respond.

"What is truth?" he repeated. He waited a little while and then said, looking at me closely: "I find no fault in this man."

Spectators and priests protested. Someone shouted:

"He stirs up the people from here to Galilee. He's a troublemaker. He drove us out of our temple market."

At that moment Pilate may have become aware of my accent or remembered I was born in Nazareth for he ordered me brought to trial before Herod, the local governor. Herod, I thought, the name stunning me as I recalled his crime.

We crossed a bridge, a hostile crowd following; young Herod welcomed me because he had heard of my miracles and wanted me to perform for his benefit. Was I wizard, necromancer, fakir?

I could not speak to this murderer: I envisioned John in prison, waiting, waiting for the liberty that never came. I saw his decapitated head on a tray, displayed for a dancing girl.

Because I could not speak Herod had his men throw a purple robe over my shoulders and place me on a chair. They mocked me, spat on me, and demanded I save myself.

Herod refused to try me and ordered guards to return me to Pontius Pilate. It was then, as we recrossed the bridge where the populace jeered, it was then I attempted to think of home. Something like an actual wall blocked me. All the emptiness of life, the savageness of the wilderness, the enmity of mankind, came into being. I prayed but prayer was useless. A man held my arm or I would have fallen: his sword hit my side.

Peter's
Iyyar 25

Pilate resented a jeering mob and tried to establish order.

He commanded men to assume positions in the Babbatha yard. Calling several priests, he said, shouting at them:

"You have brought this man before me. You say he perverts the people. I find no fault in him. I will punish him and release him."

He sat on his tribunal chair, his wife beside him. Raising his hand he resumed:

"I will free a man. Who will it be? Barabbas? Do you want Barabbas free or Christ? Choose your man."

"Barabbas...Barabbas," the priests shouted, and the crowd repeated his name, a man known for his crimes.

"What shall I do with Jesus?"

"Crucify him...crucify him."

"What has he done?"

The crowd answered: "Crucify him."

Shall I continue this journal? Will others accept my account? Shall I simply destroy these words? As days pass I am able to re-live the sadness. There is a chance to diminish man's cruelty. I take that chance. We are here in this world to make life worthy. We are here to teach others. Teaching is no easier than learning. No one has ever had my vantage point: this permits me to continue.

I searched for a friendly face among the mob...Peter...Mother...Matthew... Clibus...

Barabbas was brought before the judges and liberated with jeers and laughter. He passed by me, a great, tall man. As he walked away I was led to a whipping post, bound, and lashed with thongs; I was lashed until unconscious. Courage, where was my courage to bear the crucifixion.

I tried to think...

In a barren hall soldiers stripped me and put a filthy robe around me and forced a crown of thorns on my head. Six or eight men confronted me. They mocked me.

"Hail, king of the Jews," they hollered.

Priests appeared and cried: "Crucify him...he calls himself the Son of God. Kill him." Pilate appeared and asked: "Who are you?" I could not speak because of pain.

"Speak to me...don't you realize I have the power to set you free."

I was thinking of Judas.

A Roman officer spoke out: "He's an enemy of Rome...he defies Caesar."
"Our emperor is Caesar," a priest shouted.

"Take him away," Pilate said. "He is yours." He took water and washed his hands before the crowd. "I am innocent of the blood of this man," he said.

Again I looked for my disciples but now a centurion in cuirass and armed soldiers, carrying shields, grabbed me and forced me outside. "To the cross," someone said. "To the cross," another repeated.

I was amazed to find myself walking. It isn't far, it isn't far, I told myself.

We descended a stepped path. The bridge lay ahead. People jammed the bridge. We climbed a steep bank, passed houses, trees, rocks. The centurion ordered me to carry the crossbeam. As he compelled me to take the beam he gave me water.

It was nearly noon.

I shouldered the beam, fell, tried again. The officer ordered an onlooker to carry the beam. I heard a priest shout: "If any man wishes to prove the innocence of Jesus, let him speak." His voice, his robe, the beam, the crowd... I can't remember. Yet I remember men selling dates, hawking fruit. I wanted the food of earth, life itself.

My mother broke through the crowd and embraced me. A little farther on I heard Lazarus call. I saw Martha. She was kneeling, reaching toward me. Peter, Luke, Clibus, Mark. I saw. I loved them, their faces like old graven coins.

I saw them all the way to the spot where they laid the cross on the ground. I prayed for courage, strength to endure, as they stripped off my clothes.

Then men pounded a nail through my hand and I was blinded, torn with pain. Then I felt greater pain as they pounded a nail through my legs and then I felt no more pain until I hung on the cross.

I looked and looked but could make out nothing; then I saw two men hanging on crosses beside me. I looked at them and they looked at me. I saw people below me; I heard women and children crying. I tried to speak to them. But as I hung there everything began to move away from me: a great distance swam around me. I thought of a mirage. Someone put a sponge to my mouth. Then I saw my mother, I saw Martha, Lazarus, people I had cured. A soldier shoved his spear into me. I tried to say something... That is all that I remember.

Joseph of Arimathea obtained permission to remove my body from the cross. He and my disciples placed it in his family crypt. He provided a robe and cloth to cover my face. I lay in his tomb, myrrh and aloe about me; there I lay for three days.

Peter's Home
Sivan 2

Peter is a descendant of a nomadic tribe. Euodia, his mother, is a gnarled woman, dark, serious. She and Peter built this house after her husband died. She had had enough of desert privation. Last night she spread a special table for my homecoming: pomegranate juice, melon, cheese, bread, nuts, chromis and another fish, clarias, my favorite. Euodia is an expert with olive oil—perhaps some are nomad recipes. At supper time she accepted me easily; Matthew and Peter were wary, afraid, shy.

While we were eating, Peter said:

"Master, how can it be you were crucified eight days ago... Can you say that you are well?" He brushed his hand over his yellow beard. "I couldn't forget the terror...will you help us understand? When all of us meet will you explain? Is it faith?..."

We were eating at a makeshift table under Peter's olives; it was well after sunset and we felt the quiet of the extensive fields that make Peter's home a retreat.

Matthew, picking at his supper, nervous, kept watching my hands—I knew he was studying the scars.

"I hope you never return to Jerusalem," he exclaimed.

I agreed: I agreed for several reasons: one reason was my desire to send my disciples to remote places, villages, towns.

"Our work is to be carried out among our countrymen while governments interfere."

"We love you...we had nothing to do with the crucifixion," Euodia blurted out.

Love, love after crucifixion is a brilliant but black enigma: it proffers and denies. We know that love helps us forget pain; however I ask myself whether it is evil to forget evil. But I can think of resurrection as a form of love, a love beyond supplication. I take that step and realize that immortality is another form of love.

Desert air pushed in as we finished our meal and we soon felt chilled. I wanted to shed my fatigue by reading but we discussed visiting the spring at Neby. I suggested we leave early if it did not rain during the night and bog the paths. At Neby I wanted to work out a plan for James, Peter and Matthew, if

James joined us. When government cruelty diminishes I want Peter to preach in Rome.

In my bedroom I read *Ecclesiastes*—drowsing at times, aware of my familiar pallet, the good pillow, the candles. I was able to dismiss the imminence of departure. I put it away like a shell under sea grass.

Ecclesiastes meant more to me than weeks ago as I read and re-read passages.

Rain woke me during the night—a pleasant shower smelling like spring. So, we would walk to Neby another day. Here I would be able to go on reading *Ecclesiastes* and Peter's copy of the *Psalms*. When I told Peter that Clibus had found the *Ecclesiastes* scroll on a trip to the upper Nile they were astonished. They had never seen so ancient a scroll.

Peter's
Sivan 5

Judas is dead. He took his own life. His body was found by the daughter of Pontius Pilate. Since he was one of us we have buried him; at his grave a downpour struck us and drove us to a shelter. In a few moments the earth was flooded. I can't recall such rain and thunder.

Judas, born in Gamala, vineyard proprietor, dead at twenty-eight years. As *Ecclesiastes* says: "Woe unto him who is alone when he falls."

Startling, on a hillside, on a hilltop, a contingent of Roman soldiers, a new encampment, white tents in rows, banners, standards, smoke. Shields flash as men drill. Camels are hobbled behind the tent town. We can make out men in half armor, men wearing helmets, men at work shoveling, men erecting a large striped tent.

Is this always glory, power and death?

Peter's—early morning
Sivan 8

Shall we be like trees planted by rivers of water? Shall we mature slowly like the olive? Shall we endure two hundred years? Shall these men replant? They are humble men. Are humble men more or less successful with their lives? These men know ambition and is ambition the safe route? Verily, verily "all is vanity and vexation of spirit," if we listen to *Ecclesiastes*. What will evolve when the silver chord is broken? I have answered these questions in the past but I wish to answer them once more.

Peter's
Sivan 10

Sivan is a beautiful month, a month of subtle changes.

I lay in deep grass yesterday. While I lay in the grass I remembered the fields around Nazareth and I remembered climbing olive trees at harvest time—how we sang and shook down the ripe fruit onto nets.

Mama made the finest olive oil in Papa's oil press, the finest in Nazareth some Nazarenes said. I hurried to fill our baskets... I wanted to gather more than anyone. I never did.

Tomorrow I go to villages and will heal the sick...it is a joy, a joy rather kindred to lying in deep grass in the warm sun.

I have read my journal. I will return it to Matthew's care. Among our disci ples he is the most reliable.

Sivan 12

So, as I write with my bronze stylus, I listen to the evening, familiar sounds; through my window I see the Milky Way and the great constellations and I am aware God is affirming his handiwork.

I write very slowly, lingering over each letter, the square letters superior to the old script. I go on listening. The lamp burns steadily. There is no wind. There is gratitude.

Nazareth
Sivan 17

Father has suffered from his imprisonment. His hands tremble. After seeing me on the cross he is unable to believe that I am alive.

I held out my arms to him as we stood in front of our home. He backed away.

"...Father, remember how we visited together at Qumran? Remember that old long-bladed saw, how I repaired its handle three times?

"Mama gave you that shirt at the Feast of Lights..."

He turned and walked away, trembling.

When I was staying at the home of Gehazi, after preaching in the synagogue, after healing, Barabbas appeared. Jamnia is his village and he entered the house of Gehazi without knocking. A great tall hulk, he loomed over me; then he knelt and begged me to accept him.

Dressed in goat's skin, his face and beard wild, he seemed ill, perhaps deranged. I tried to calm him, to reason with him.

"I should have been crucified," he repeated in a hoarse voice.

For a long while we remained together, talking, praying, hoping.

Peter's
Sivan 24

Patience—we need patience.

Going from village to village, town to town, means walking five days, four days, two. It is a five day walk to Nazareth. It is a two day walk to the village of Gehazi. Most walks are pleasant. It can be cold, windy, hot; and when it rains there is seldom any shelter.

Sometimes we travel together; sometimes we walk alone; these days I prefer my solitary walks. I am aware of close communion when alone. Patience, patience...but the calendar moves on: Shevat, Adar, Nisan, Iyyar, Sivan...

Peter's
Tammuz 3

I will miss Peter's little house, its rough walls, its crooked windows, its clumsy thatched roof. The floors have interested me. He found pieces in some Babylonian structure; he hauled them here in an ox cart. I have come to love this isolation, its olive trees.

Today is a summer's day.

Great clouds, great sky.

Peter sought me out as I sat in the bedroom reading. Again he asked for forgiveness. Kneeling by me he promised he would carry the word... "to Rome, if you wish. Teach me courage, teach me strength, teach me to be wise..."

He and I have worked at the carpenter's bench lately, in Lazarus' shed. It took the three of us to line up a door. Of course it was very old. Laughing, we had to admit our clumsy workmanship.

We are proud that there are more than seventy of us now. I send them out in pairs.

The home of Lazarus
Tammuz 8

It seems to me I view mankind with a sense of compassion—a constant perception. Mine is a brief, swift looking back: I heal the sick, I renew lives... I remember the hart and the brook...man's insatiable thirst.

Children come and animals come...the ox and the donkey have been friends. A shepherd, I still follow hills, hills of resurrection they may be. Perhaps history may call me a man of righteousness. Perhaps history may not stop. I speak to history. I say, once again:

"Go and teach all nations, baptizing them in the name of the Father, the Son and the Holy Ghost..."

Teach as I have taught...remind them of grace.

Tammuz 11

I leave no tomb, no crypt, no marker.

Finality may not be a friend...

When I leave shall I carry a handful of earth with me?

James, Peter, Matthew, Mark...Mother and Father...Lazarus...Miriam... each one is mine but for how long?

Peter will pick up my sandals and say:

"These were his."

Father will say:

"He helped me make this box."

The Godhead is before me and I struggle with delight and with astonishment.

Tammuz 12

I am entrusting my journal to Matthew. Since we have friends at the synagogue in Capernaum he will leave my journal there.

Verily, verily I say: Fear God and keep His commandments. This is the duty of man.

Farewell Thoughts

I hope these thoughts may be helpful. It is very late and lamplight flickers...

Inside a man of light there is light and with this light he lights the world.

The angels and the prophets will come to you and give you strength.

Blessed are the ones who have heard the Father's word and kept it in truth.

Have you then discovered the beginning so that you ask the end? Where the beginning is, there the end will be.

The kingdom is inside you. When you really understand you will know that you are the son of the living Father. If you do not understand yourself you will be in poverty.

Split wood and I am there. Pick up a stone; there you will find me.

Come to me because my yoke is easy, my lordship gentle. You will find rest.

The kingdom of the Father is spread over the earth and men do not see it.

Blessed are the solitary and the elect; you shall find the kingdom because you have come from it and you shall go there again.

I say, whenever one is one he will be filled with light, but whenever he is divided he will be filled with darkness.

Love your brother as your own soul. Guard him as the apple of your eye.

There will be days when you seek and you will not find me.

NOTE:

These logia appear for the first time in a journal.
They are from the 4th century Coptic book,
The Gospel According to Thomas,
discovered in Hammadi, Egypt,
quoted through the courtesy
of the translator, Dr. Ray Rummers,
Chairman, Department of English, Baylor University.

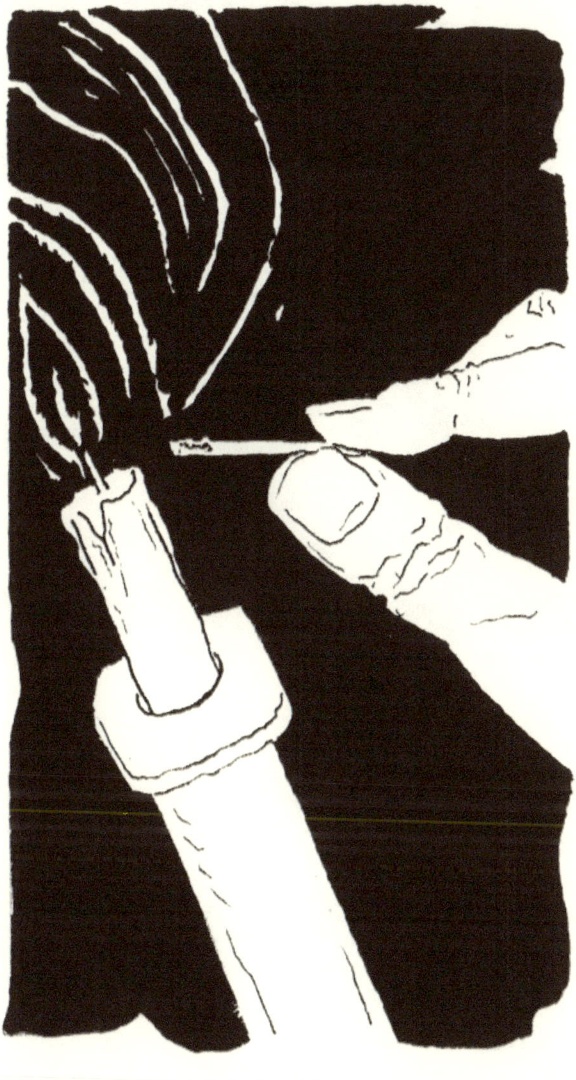

Leonardo da Vinci's Journal

"Both those who recently attempted to fly came to grief.
Leonardo da Vinci also tried to fly,
but, he, too, failed."
– Girolamo Cardano, 1555

For Elizabeth

Leonardo da Vinci

APRIL 15, 1452 – MAY 2, 1519

Illustrations

The illustrations are originals by the author—interpretations of work by da Vinci.

This journal was kept by Leonardo da Vinci during the years 1516 to 1519 while he lived in France as the guest of King Francis I; there, he lived in the small residence of Cloux, near the King's summer palace at Amboise on the Loire River. Leonardo writes of his boyhood, his mother, his friends, his easel and mural paintings, his dissections, his colossal bronze horse.

He tells of his attempts at flying, his inventions... This is a codex of his mind as he divulges his art and the scope of his interests.

To the end of his life he was painting, map-making, carrying out architectural commissions, arranging his treatises on perspective, anatomy, horses, flight, and the arts. His patron, King Francis, called him "Mon Père." Da Vinci's last years, at Cloux, near Paris, were friendly years.

1516

Cloux
December 10, 1516

MEMORY . . .
MEMORY. . .

I remember that hot, dusty afternoon in Florence. I ordered everybody out of my studio. I got up from my workbench and demanded that they leave: the tattlers, the oafs, the bores, the faithful. I packed them off. Yelled at them. Stormed. I had work to do, work that would keep me until dawn. I had to have serenity, no ribaldry, no disgruntled silence, no questions, no interruptions of any sort.

I slammed the doors, bolted them.

A mouse scuttled across the room.

Until I resolved the perfect angles, sheet after sheet went into the making of that pelvic drawing.

Queer how memory is: I can see that messy workshop, easels, clay figures on stands, rags, canvases, frames, chisels, pigments, brushes... I can see the mouse watching me from beneath a basket. Again I sense that long afternoon, that long night... I had dried bread, cheese, and port. I remember the church bells. At dawn I slid my work into a special portfolio, then concealed it. I was often hiding things in those days, hiding sketches, hiding determination, hiding frustrations, goals.

Memory...it gives you what you want and supplies absurdities as well, like the dream that I had in Florence, recurrent: I was lying on my cot... I was dead... I was carried to a morgue and dumped there, among cadavers...blood and mould saturated my drawings and my writings...my canvases were being eaten by termites... how well I remember that dream.

I remember a fat Milanese who used to haunt me while I was decorating the walls and ceiling of the Sala delle Asse: he was a pompous member of the Sforza household, a great nose-picker, who had done nothing at all through his long life. While I worked, he sat, hunched in a princely brocade chair, in elegant clothes, sometimes asleep in spite of my assistants, ladders, and scaffolding.

That Sala delle Asse work was boring. Like many a commission it was compulsory. To arrange masses of foliage on walls and ceiling seemed absurd.

Designs were refused, at the outset. The employment of immense tree trunks satisfied. As I painted, I mingled knotted cords with the foliage, intermingled branches, established a rhythm. I kept my greens from becoming monotonous. I achieved a kind of helmeted bark on the tree trunks. Before I finished, the Sala's canopy, the forest umbrella, became more meaningful.

My fat friend slept on and on.

How much did I earn? I have forgotten. Was I ever paid?

I would like to return to the castle and walk through that Sala; I would like to be alone; I would like to try to think as I thought in those days; I would like to sense my aspirations; I would sit on a bench under that deluge of foliage: I would list geology, hydraulics, painting, sculpture, geometry, anatomy, medicine...

⚜

Cloux

When Michelangelo showed me his cartoon for his mural in the Consejo, I complained that a scene of idling nude bathers was not the best way to depict war. He was critical of my cartoon, saying "you are more concerned with horses than men."

My objective was to show war's anguish: pain was to be sixty feet long by twenty feet wide. Twelve hundred square feet of pain. All of my draughtsmanship went into this *Anghiari* conflict: I painted rage, rage against war, the rage of dying men, the rage of the wounded, my hate, my affirmation.

All of 1503 and 1504 went into my preliminary sketches. I often rode about the countryside to sketch horses, sketch riders; I sketched in the Sforza stables; the stablemen posed for me; my apprentices posed. Friends had their chance to exhibit their horses in action. Gamin posed. The militia.

So, I did not paint a wall: I painted the smash of steel against steel, the plunge of steel into flesh, the grunting of frightened horse against frightened horse, men stumbling, men falling, dying, their helmets of fear, helmets of pain...yellows, blues, greys, reds.

On Friday, June 6, 1505, I began to paint the Anghiari battle. It was my greatest challenge. Here I could render something more meaningful than the madonnas. Not Christ on the cross, but man on the cross. Pigment and light were to come together in harmony. The day that I began to paint was beautiful but the weather changed quickly for the worst. Some of my assistants were called away—they were ordered to attend a trial.

The wind caught me unprepared and ripped the cartoon. In a few minutes the storm took over in earnest. I laid aside my brushes and pigments and dismissed the remaining apprentices. Half of Florence was inundated that night.

PAZZIA BESTIALISSIMA!

That is man's disease: he can not refrain from political madness. Again and again he is willing to be duped.

The central group in my *Anghiari* mural is the struggle for a military flag: I painted life-size horses, life-size men, life-size hatred: the central struggle fans out across the mural, expressing this futility.

I seldom eat at the King's table although I am always welcome. Sometimes it seems like a long walk to the château, sometimes it is raining. In the evening fifteen courses are certainly gourmet adventures, but a little late at night.

The King often sends me three or four trays—a retinue of pages brings them to my studio, laughter and ribaldry, and then decorum as they file into the studio. Soufflés, artichokes in cream and butter sauce, crêpes, pastries, glacés, Vouvray. I am partial to grapes and someone on the royal staff hunts them up for me.

Sometimes I find five or six silver dishes with as many kinds of nuts. Francis claims that he could not survive for a month on my vegetarian diet.

Maturina fusses over almost everything the King sends:

"Now, let me see, let me see," she mutters. "You should eat this first...it's better for you that way...and these pastries, why they're much too rich for you!"

She arranges the dishes on the dining table (you must not eat in the studio); she places my chair, lights the candles, unfolds my napkin and spreads it across my lap. What a splendid old ragamuffin she is! Too bad she has lost most of her teeth; her features are leaden, her hair is twisted under a net in lumps, her arms dangle crookedly. She is bones hooked together with shrunken gut. She has been working as a servant for thirty-five years, she tells me. I've had her for fifteen years.

⚜

Cloux

The French call this place Le Clos-Luce, and it is a bright enclosure. I think of the royalty who have lived here through the years, the many mistresses who came and went. As I look across the lawn of the manor house I can see the little chapel of St. Hubert and the rooftops of the château; it often seems to me that I have been here before! With Francesco, Salai and Giovanni busy in the adjoining studio, I try to believe I am a young man...time is of no importance!

Salai rushed in as I worked at my easel.

"Look, look at this..."

He had found a sketch among my sketches, a sketch he made in Florence long ago, when he was about ten. It shows a bicycle. There it is on a scrap of paper, among pornographic scribbles and graffiti.

"You did pretty well, riding that thing...at first," I reminded.

"There weren't any brakes, remember?"

"Well, when I connected the chain drive to the pedals and adjusted the handlebars you rode it into the Arno."

"Some splash!" said Francesco, coming in with Giovanni. "You could have gotten the bicycle out of the river...it floated," reminded Giovanni.

"I couldn't get hold of it...the current was too fast!"

"It should have been made of steel, to last." I said.

"Let's make a bicycle for the King," suggested Salai. "I'll show him my drawing...no, you make one for him. I can see the courtiers riding about...we can improve on the one we made in Florence."

⚜

Cloux

Certainly a bird is an instrument performing according to mathematical laws which are within the capacity of man to understand. How does it climb, dive, spiral, hover? I asked these questions yesterday as I watched a flock of ducks along the Loire; I asked the same questions in Florence, in Milan, in Rome. If we ask questions we can eventually achieve some kind of answer. Persistence then!

Why does the heart pump a certain beat? What starts it pumping? Just when? Why, at that given moment? Does a nerve trigger it? Heart beats in the womb must be automatic.

If we understand the mechanism of the heart we may be able to help when it is damaged.

What are the essential differences between the heart of a squirrel and the heart of a man? Between the heart of a cat and a man? Between the heart of a cow and the heart of a man? Knowing the differences should help.

I must check through my anatomical drawings and compare notes and analyze the results. There is so much to be learned. And it is all there, ready to be apprehended.

⚜

Amore sol la mi fa remirare... love only makes me remember; love gives me pleasure...

So it was, long ago, when I loved, when I composed a rebus every day. There was so much to sing about. I played my lira da braccio. Made notations. As a boy, I thought seriously of becoming a musician. Perhaps a troubadour. At Andrea's shop I created a silver harp, in the shape of a horse's skull. The fame of that harp took me to Milan—changed my life.

"The song of men is the remedy to pain..."

I almost believed that.

I designed drums, multiple beaters; I could change the pitch of my drums through holes in the sides...I built three portable organs... I designed glissando recorders...I made a lute for Nicolaio del Turco...I made a wind-chest *con gomito* for the prioress...

Perhaps I should compose some rebuses for the King.

No.

The music I hear now is not that music.

I might have spent my life in the world of music; yet, often, even as I played, I puzzled over the enigmas of ocean and mountain, the enigmas of the body, of sound: why was one sound more resonant than another; why were there echoes; why was a woman's voice unlike a man's; why were there changes in the songs of birds?

Ah, those apprentice years!

⚜

Those apprentice years!

Getting up at dawn, working before breakfast, working till late, forgetting to eat, going for a swim in the Arno, rushing back to work, forgetting to sleep; work, work, it was a beautiful thing.

I was forever gathering plants, drying them, mounting them, identifying them. I roamed alone. Good to get away from the studio. I was forever dissecting animals and birds. With every bird I asked: how does it propel itself? How can man go aloft? Those birds, those caged birds...it was right to hoard money, to buy them, to liberate them. I followed them, I sat with them, I ran with them, studying every possible angle.

I filled sketchbooks with sketches of the hawk in flight, the raven, another with the sparrow.

My glider, based on the studies of the hawk, flew around our workshop. Again and again we tested it, wondering why it flew.

Andrea had me working bronze...there was so much, so much. He was always encouraging. What a fine master. What a fine artist. Now with gold leaf, now with new pigments, now something in the way of a discovery with silverpoint.

He had so little money. Sometimes he went hungry. Sometimes we had to find money for him and his family. Little Lila, little Lila had to have a toy. Tony had to have crayons. Bread, milk.

⚜

Writing this journal I am attempting to indicate the important things in my life. However, I am perplexed: I can't decide what has been significant, I am trapped by small things...little things crowd the important. If life is a mural then every detail is important. As I write I am learning who I was. And the omissions, are they carelessness or are they deliberate? As for important lapses I must make an effort to fill them in, if there is time. If weariness does not overcome.

Looking back at Milan, at my first year there, I remember: no, *remember* is not the word: I have never forgotten that meeting at the Duke's *festa*: I was playing a lute; she was introduced to me; she wanted me to repeat the song; we talked. Love? That is not the right word. But is there better?

Caterina had my mother's name; that meant something to me.

I wish I could describe her as I saw her at the *festa* but she has become unreal through the years. I see her in the sunlight, I see her as I sketched her, I see her as she lay dead. There is no easy way to describe our love. I am unable to separate beauty from tragedy. I wish I could.

Caterina was nineteen. She was my blonde, my Leda. Was our love unique? Maybe it was rather ordinary. That does not matter. It matters that there were long brush strokes in the mind. There is no need to retouch our emotions. Certainly her death and our daughter's death need no retouching.

I hear her singing one of my songs, a song I composed for her... I hear her laughing and I hear our daughter laughing, as they play together. Laughter—in memory—does not blur as words and faces blur.

Nineteen, twenty, twenty-one...we had three years together: there was money enough: there was time enough: then Milan was besieged. Both were killed by the bombardment. But before they died, Mother visited us and for a while I had two Caterinas, two loving women, two gentlewomen. Our child was learning to walk. Not many people know of those three years.

Cloux

Today, Maturina has served me her special pasta, several kinds of bread, dried figs, camembert, her three-layered pastry, and Moselle wine. She appreciates my fondness for sweets.

I asked her to sit down with me. As usual, she declined.

"I want your company...everyone's away."

Boltraffio, Francesco, Salai and others had gone for the day. Another holiday!

"Are you homesick?"

Her sad face became a little sadder. She sat down and clasped her hands in her lap and stared at them.

"I think you should visit your people."

She nodded.

"...But I couldn't leave you."

"For a month or two?"

"It's a long, long way to Vinci...and alone!"

"Salai is returning to Florence soon..."

"But I can't..."

"You should see your family. People in Vinci would like to hear about us, how we're getting along. We have money enough."

Abruptly, hands to her face, she got up, and shuffled away. "I'm too old," she said.

Cloux

As we rode along the Loire, following the river road, Francesco and I talked:

"So you received a letter from your mother yesterday? How are things at Vaprio?"

"Quiet...everyone is well. Papa has fully recovered. Mama says that conditions are very bad in Milan...fighting in the streets...hungry mobs...looting."

"Vaprio continues to escape...I hope nothing changes that!"

"You asked me about the pigments I bought in Paris. We have a good assortment. I've been grinding them. We'll have a beautiful green, that laurel green you're fond of."

"I'm still partial to green. I suppose you bought the Dutch pigments..."

Our horses, side by side, kept an even pace: both from the same stable, they liked walking together: the road was familiar to them: the afternoon was sunny; shafts of light rebounded from the Loire; a pair of squirrels chittered at us; hunters and their dogs passed—someone saluted us with a playful toot of his horn.

"Mama insists that we stay away from Milan...she warns us...she said that I'm to tell you."

"I understand. We're lucky to be here; Cloux is like Vaprio; beautiful countryside; a sketch here, a sketch there."

"We should ride to Chambord."

"I prefer the river trip..."

"Shall we go on the river?"

"All right, Cecchino. You arrange the trip. Certainly, there's no finer château than Chambord. Let's spend a few days there. We can find new paintings, new marbles and bronzes...from Milan...Athens...Rome...the greatness of stolen art..."

As we left our horses at the stable, Francesco asked:

"Did I mention that the Princess de Lamballe has a son? He's my age. He wants to study painting. Do you want a Prince for a pupil?"

Cloux

The King and I talked far into the night.

Youth can be so sincere: youth can evaluate and assess: last night, on the part of others, he apologized: the Gascon archers were much on his mind...

"I have thought of them many, many times...those Gascon fools...nothing else to do...made a target of your *cavello*...our archers..."

Bronze for cannons...he knew about that...he searched about for a solution, as if it might be possible to cast the horse. As he saw it, he felt he had rescued me. Had he? I turned over that thought. Recompense? Was Cloux recompense? He did not say so. I think we both wished to believe it was respect, admiration. His talk made us feel awkward at times.

I had not complained: I had not mentioned the monument. Divulging his sincerity got Francis beyond his scope.

He referred to Amboise and Cloux as my home. Haven, of course. Retreat?

Voluntary exile. Those thoughts could be brought in. I tried my best to avoid any embarrassing approach. Presently, he was excusing the battle of man against man. Again we were faltering. His innate shrewdness came to our rescue, and we discussed architectural changes at Amboise...

"We must do everything we can to improve it...it can never be like Chambord ...help me give it a manorial feeling...walk about with me tomorrow...let's write down some of your ideas...that stairway...the entry...we have to make it less grim...harmony..."

IL CAVELLO...the words haunted us as we said good night.

I lay down under my canopy. The bed seemed to grow immense. On one side I saw a child, a bend in a river, a hill...the bed drifted...the room changed... I saw men pouring bronze into a mould... I saw a great horse in a city square...

⚜

SALAI—He is either in studio rags or elegant, foppish; he bursts with energy (has a brisk, haughty walk); he is quick with his pigments; he is as lean-featured as a fox; he is yellow-headed, tall. He has a wonderful laugh, a tooth-spread grin. His brown eyes are spoked with yellow. A girl-chaser. My Salai will never become an accomplished artist. I still have to remind him to wash himself. Ai, Salaino! And will he ever quit that foreign habit, the habit of smoking?

⚜

Almost everywhere I travel I am troubled by poverty: I talk with the workers and some of them say they are hungry all of the time: I talk with them about their tools, and try to improve them. Shovels. Spades. Rakes. Forks. I have suggested a more efficient roasting spit—I have made detailed drawings. I have improved a wood-planer and a file-maker. I have designed a textile machine, a better barrow, a good water-lamp.

For most field laborers, theirs is an ox-life.

Horse, mule, donkey, ox, man...they are inextricable.

Landlord and tenant, the struggle goes on and on: they are as much at loggerheads as pope and duke. Serfs, beggars, greed, knights, fools—pathos.

At Vaprio, I sometimes ate with a farmer and his wife, in their tiny stone farmhouse. They did not complain, yet they slept on mats, ate meat now and then, worked from dawn to sundown, shivered through the winters, saved florins in a clay pot. Their hands at mealtime were the hands of old people and yet they were not old.

In the Vaprio region the people have to pay exorbitant milling fees, pay to use a common oven or wine press. Fishing rights have been stolen. For a few gentlemen there may be no wood for winter; for many others there may be no wood at all. Some want a civil war to put them on their feet.

At Vaprio, I recall a child of nine or ten: I saw her often on my visits there: she reminded me of that *festa*, in May, in Florence, when I fell in love with my own Beatrice, when I was eleven or twelve years old. My Beatrice was beautiful, her features delicately formed, her behavior gentle and agreeable, full of candid loveliness... I thought of her as my angel.

In those days, in Firenze, I often passed Dante's home: his wooden door had a bronze knocker, a simple braided ring. I used to imagine knocking and saying:

"Is Dante Alighieri at home?"

I expected a housekeeper to reply:

"He's been dead a hundred and fifty years, you fool!"

I would have dashed off, laughing.

Cloux

I suppose I must admit it: I am a parasite of royalty.

During forty years I have had nine royal patrons.

Each one has hindered me; each one has helped.

I could not have survived in my vineyard at San Vittore: I need artists, sculptors, apprentices, courtiers, women, princes, jousting, masques, jewelry, perfume... I need great art. I need antique art. Libraries.

Last night, at Amboise, in the garden, at the pergola, I explained some of my observations of the moon. Courtiers crowded around. A duke was there. A princess. There was an earnest exchange as I passed around lunar drawings, in the lamplight and torchlight.

"The details are as accurate as I could draw them...notice the craters, pits, the rills...you see, if you keep the moon under careful observation over a period of time, you'll become aware of fixed landmarks. I made those drawings from the Coliseum...in Rome..."

Francesco has copied this. It was written in Florence, in 1508. I thought it rather interesting, so I have included it here:

For several days I have forgotten to hang my notebooks on my belt. I must see to it that I remember. Tomorrow I must write down exactly what I observed when I dissected the pigeon I found dead in front of the church.

Se sarai solo, sarai tutto tuo...

NOTE: when you sever the man's legs tomorrow afternoon, lay them on the floor beside him: measure length, diameter, muscle curvatures. Dissect each foot, and record differences. Since the man was very fat, try to discover ways of overcoming this problem.

Remember to borrow the lancet from Tomas.

I warned my new assistant: Cosimo, squeal on me and I will see to it that you never become a member of the guild.

He has threatened to write the Pope (or one of the Cardinals), and expose me. He could. He knows how to write. Now I pay him more *soldi* than any of the others. Blackmailer!

Ah, you Florentines, look, look! I render a skull—yours! You tremble. You are afraid of learning! For centuries you have been afraid. Afraid of yourselves, of others, of God. You are trapped in stupidity and lassitude.

Blood—how it scares you: You whimper at the sight of blood. I remove a man's guts. You are horrified. But you will batter a man to shreds on the battlefield, and show your gory sword. You will dump boiling oil on him...you will blast him with gunpowder...but you won't dissect him...you won't learn how we are made!

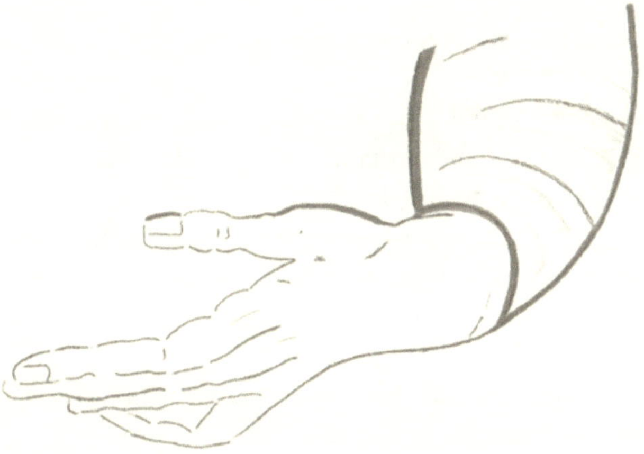

Sometimes kids overran my studio; maybe because I never could yell at them. They would sneak in from the street; they had to poke, to see, to talk, to giggle. One afternoon (I remember it was such a fine day, a day to chuck everything and walk out of town), five or six boys and girls came in and before I could figure out what they were up to, they rushed out with two of my models. Two or three ran toward the Arno; others ran off into the countryside. I couldn't follow both. Whooping and hollering, the kids flew their model over the river. I watched it soar away, dip, glide, plunge into the water.

When I found the other kids, in the country, they had my Red Hawk: they had it launched on a cord, and kite-like, it was climbing, spiraling, staying aloft.

Kids—I miss their laughter, their enthusiasm!

There was a time when I had dirty waifs sleeping on the studio floor. We took in two or three; then others came. Their parents had died in the plague at Santa Maria; I guess it was at Santa Maria. Those were hungry weeks for all of us; yet we somehow managed, managed to feed them, get clothes for them, find homes for them—and kept on working.

Cloux

Copied from my 1504 Florentine notebook:

As soon as we met in the Town Hall there was a big wrangle. Ten or twelve of us, bearded patriarchs and upstarts, were at odds. We must decide where Michelangelo's *David* was to be placed. We must situate it where it had shade part of the day, where it was protected from the weather; we must have it mounted on travertine; we must move it carefully; we must see to it...

It was lucky for us that Michelangelo was not around. He would have exploded—and told us off.

We walked around Florence for several hours, fighting the heat (and each other); then, we reached our one and only mutual agreement—to go somewhere and eat.

Later, I went with Francesco to Michelangelo's studio, and we sat there, the two of us, and talked about his *David*, sitting on a bench facing his work. We agreed that it equaled any classical masterpiece. It was a little difficult to accept such beauty coming from such a troublemaker.

It required four days for men to move it, by windlass and rollers, to a site alongside the Town Hall: how carefully we worked, the statue suspended in a sling. Sometimes there were thirty of us at the job. A downpour drenched us. As we moved forward over slippery cobbles I thought the figure would topple. *Cargadores* bellowed. Michelangelo was on hand and beat one of the *cargadores* with his fists, screaming at the top of his voice.

When we had *David* in place we arranged a party. All the Florentine artists. Michelangelo was absent.

⚜

A while ago Niccolò Machiavelli wrote me from his Tuscan farm, where he is still exiled from Florence. His disturbing thoughts linger:

"Mornings, weather permitting, I hunt or snare thrushes, reading Dante or Ovid to make the hunts more agreeable. After lunch, I visit an inn and throw dice with the yokels, to taste my malign destiny in their brutish company.

"When evening arrives I go to my library, after I have shed my muddy, everyday clothes. Now I am dressed as if about to appear at court, as an envoy from

Florence. Elegantly attired I enjoy the presence of great men of the past. They receive me cordially. I talk with them, speaking confidently; they are at ease. For a few hours I lose myself: I am not afraid of poverty and death."

Familiar...the thoughts of the exile.

Yesterday, I wrote Niccolò and invited him to Cloux.

"We will be a pair of exiles. Stay with me a month or two. Amboise won't bore you. There's a superb library. The King has welcomed you. There will be no expense on your part. I will see to that."

How he helped in Florence: I remember that I owe my *Anghiari* commission to him. And that night Cesare strangled my friend...it was Niccolò who provided the horse.

⚜

A library.

A library can erase problems.

A library is a kind of stained glass.

Francesco and I enjoy the Cloux library. Handsome room. A fine Mantegna—in an old style frame—hangs on the far wall. Its mythological scene is pleasantly antique. The shelves hold parchments, vellums, velvet-bound books, illuminated manuscripts, scores. Francesco has turned up a score I wrote for the Medici, one I used to play.

There is a white marble table with alabaster legs where I spread out the manuscripts and books.

The librarian, keys at his waspish gut, is a defrocked Jesuit, ashen-headed, ashen-faced; he admits that he has never lifted down half of the books.

A lovely *prie dieu* holds a Latin volume, its pages ornamented with pastel watercolor and gold leaf. The carpet is a mouse-chewed Turkish weave, red on red on red, with colorless, limp fringes.

The unchained books are in Spanish, Latin, French, Greek, Dutch, and Hungarian—collected by King Francis' father. He loved this room. He died there.

⚜

Sitting under the green pergola at Amboise, King Francis and I sipped *apéritifs*, the afternoon warm, a lazy hunting dog at his feet.

"I don't understand how your army crossed the Alps in six or seven days."

"Five days," he corrected me.

"By the Col d'Argentière?

"Yes...do you know that Pass?"

"I have camped there. I have seen some of it when I was collecting fossils. But for an army to get through, it seems impossible. You had cannons, horses, mules..."

"We were determined to surprise the Milanese."

We watched dragonflies circle above lily pads in a small rock-rimmed fountain, their orange wings on fire in the afternoon light. Near the fountain men were planting young columnar cypress. Other gardeners were spading paths because the King was re-landscaping. Someone, pushing a barrow, with an enormous red wheel, asked the King if he could plant the roses in the circular beds already prepared.

"We had good weather," Francis said.

"Think of it...it took me almost a month to reach here."

"But you were in no hurry, Mon Père."

"Snow...mud...ice..."

"I realize."

"Did you think of Hannibal?"

"I did."

"What Pass did he use to invade Italy?"

"Some say the Mount Genevre."

"He was a great tactical genius."

"Our army was well led...but there were times when I wished we had some of Hannibal's elephants...but fog was our worst problem...morning fog, thick as an elephant's hide...maybe that fog helped us...our scouts encountered shepherds in the fog...stopped them from informing others..."

⚜

Most men fail to come to grips with nature's intricacies. When they find a fossil they are satisfied with a cursory look. As for flowers, insects, animals, birds, they turn away from them if they serve no practical purpose. And because men do not care to probe, they resent or fear my studies. I have been made to feel this through the years.

They accuse me of wizardry...alchemy...vile practices.

My studio door is banged open.

"Help me, Maestro...oh, God, help me!"

And I try... I draw out pus... I patch a hole in a rogue's leg... I sew up flesh...but the same man, when he is well, whispers lies about me :

"He steals bodies from the morgue! He steals dead men's legs...he slices men's skulls in half!"

The body's secrets, the mind's secrets...we must unlock them!

⚜

In his Amboise armory, facing the Loire, Francis showed me his trophies and gear: his new armor from Cadiz, engraved with floral patterns; his father's armor inlaid with gold and silver (from Milan); a plumed helmet with the regal salamander in brass and copper inlay; a circular shield inscribed AFTER DEFEAT VICTORY.

We spent a morning among spears, pikes, swords, scabbards, helmets, bows and arrows, arquebuses...standards...saddlery. The King admired a Toledo sword and a pair of antique Hungarian spurs. I was taken by an engraved dagger from Greece—Homeric lines along its shaft.

Leaning on a pike staff, Francis spoke excitedly about his conquest of Milan:

"...How we fought! Was it for twenty-eight hours or longer? I thought our cavalry would mow down the Swiss...the Swiss kept rushing toward us...it was our artillery that destroyed them...I fought on my great Conde, the chestnut you admired...he was wounded, badly wounded...I had to leave him...I had my visor smashed...my shoulder was sliced open...it was like your *Anghiari*... horses...men...smoke and dust...at times I couldn't see...everybody yelling...drums beating...the Venetian troops saved us...

"By God, it was terrible...sometimes I felt alone...sometimes I thought my own men would kill me."

"Is it true that 15,000 men died?"

"Yes...yes...15,000...12,000...who can count the dead? Some wounded crawl away to die...peasants began pilfering, killing...maiming...our wounded filled the

Maggiore Hospital...you must have heard...the halls and loggias were filled...

"Milan was poorly defended," I said.

"The walled area of the city? Few tried to stop our entry. News of defeat had spread throughout Milan...little resistance...futile..."

I returned to my studio thoroughly disheartened: it is this repetition: city against city: pope against duke: the stupidity seems endless: what shields protect us against the fools of the world!

Yesterday, I enjoyed the King's dinner—another hundred or more guests: Cardinal Mercier, De Brosse, Ambassador to Holland, military, priests, courtiers, beautiful women. I sat opposite Francis and enjoyed his scarlet-gold suit, sewn with diamond chips. I believe he was wearing five or six rings; one of them is rather like the stone I gave Mona long ago. Francis personifies youth, hedonism, and royalty. Watching him, listening to him, I forget the tedious round of courses.

Princesse de Lamballe, sitting beside me, a lovely woman in her forties, dressed in blue and nakedness, praised the banquet:

"Francis has such wonderful chefs...the food is fresher here than in Paris...I'm so glad to get away."

"Tomorrow," the King said, leaning toward me, "all of us are leaving Amboise...we're going to Chambord." He waved his hand, and smiled. "All of us!"

All of us meant about a thousand people, as the King headed for Chambord. I watched his retinue (I declined the invitation): I estimate that there were four hundred horsemen, two hundred mules, mounted archers, stablemen, the Chamberlain, musicians, clergy, wizards, cooks, doctors...the archers wore black and red, the musicians wore yellow and green; the King wore a hat with a yellow plume and a yellow cloak flecked with white fleur-de-lys. The musicians played oboes, trumpets, tambourines, and drums. Such discord. Away they went, pennants, banners, oriflammes.

Suddenly, it was quiet at Amboise.

In my studio I sat at my desk and looked down on the peacocks and some pheasants: Francesco came: we began to work: I dictated pages from my treatise regarding horses.

⚜

FRANCESCO MELZI is a proper, thoughtful villa-man, handsome, slight, middle-tall, grey-eyed, blond. He is my patient friend, my gracious friend (gracious to everyone): he has his father's agreeable manners. He is horseman and archer. Flutist. A painter for fifteen years, he handles chiaroscuro like a master: he is best as portraitist. No woman-chaser, he is dedicated to Latin, Greek, Hebrew, French...and all of the arts. When he trims my hair and beard he likes to flatter me.

I am searching for a glass that reflects a Florentine face—not a wrinkled, bearded patriarch.

GIOVANNI BOLTRAFFIO—Tony—has always had wealth behind him (like Francesco); here, at Amboise, he wears satins and silks, claims that the King's tailor is "the best in the world." Tony is so enormous, so muscular, his satins often split. Blue-eyed, genial, bowing, a little too obsequious, he sometimes dabs perfume on his paint-messed hands. He has big hands, big feet, big skull—topped by curly brown hair. With him decorum comes first. He is always aware of his sedate heritage. He sings beautifully, and is an accomplished lutenist. At home he is devoted to his cathedral choir. In Amboise, he is considered a notable fencer. He'd rather fence than paint. He'd rather eat than paint. He will have nothing to do with dissection. Right now, he is involved with a red-headed hussy who champions sex.

ANDREA DEL VERROCHIO—tall, with not an ounce of extra meat on him...it seems to me he is still a young man, that we are at work together in his studio. But no, no, the Arno roared throughout that night, as we mourned his death. Many of us. Corpses lodged against supports of the Puente Vecchio. Plagues. Madness. Work. We cherished him, his frailty. Guild-member at twenty. Such kindness, such classic renderings in stone and bronze. We revered his *Saint John*, his serenity in stone.

We exhibited his sculpture in every corner of his workshop and yard. People. His *Dolphin Boy*. His *Christ*. Ghosts from his metal and chisel.

We learned how to use the abacus together; we learned about mixing oils; he taught me silverpoint and charcoal; we worked with pastels, with gold leaf.

Ai, Andrea—what a scalding rain on the night you died. We sat about, we drank wine; then, next week, we returned to our casting, our horses, busts, angels.

Most of the years in his studio were tranquil. There were wonderful days, when, like John in the Desert, we detected our own worth—in the mastery of his work. His home was mine. His garden was mine. His florins.

I see him painting a madonna's drapery...weeks of work, painting delicate, gilded folds...he gave me books...

He said: genius is dedication.

He also said: art and friendship.

1517

Cloux
January 6, 1517

After walking along the Loire, the water grey, swallows passing underneath the grey arches of the château bridge, I sat where I could study the supports, estimating their bulk and weight. No notebook. Too many unfinished sketches and treatises. An ancient bridge and my face—ravaged by time.

At the little chapel of Saint Hubert, which I admire so much, so complete in itself, pigeons were flying about. Wings again. What are the correct angles for flying? Which wing structure can lift the most weight? How to estimate the camber?

Rain splattered me as I walked about. A drum roll reminded me of the thunder at Vinci. I climbed the Tour Hurtault and was a boy again, as I watched the rain, as I had watched it at my mother's house. Then I used to try to estimate the number of drops, measure them, weigh them.

What a superb château—this Amboise! I admire its bulk, its age. It is no wonder that kings have lived here! Amplitude. Privacy. Gardens. The gardens tempt me to walk on and on. Yesterday, I sketched the Tour des Minimes—emphasizing its massive base line, the skillful masonry; as I sketched a playful squirrel climbed a birch, flipped from branch to branch, nibbled. I must remember to sketch the bronze doors of the chapel. The sculptor stresses texture in his composition. Somehow Florentine!

Wander...

I wander...

I wander alone or with Francesco.

Inside the château, if it is raining or cold or misty, we prowl through the halls and public rooms. Halls, rooms, people. A door opens and there is someone. A door shuts, and you are alone with a dozen doors. Cold windows merge into cold mirrors, a door opens. Here are tapestries from Bruges. Someone coughs. Feminine laughter sounds.

As I walked toward Cloux, lights blinked in window after window; a light appeared in my studio; someone passed carrying a torch. Maturina has a fire in my fireplace. She has the table set for Francesco and me. Glaring at me she scolds me for my damp clothes. "Your cough...you know! You never think of yourself. Your supper has been ready a long time. I've asked Francesco to look after you but he forgets. Only yesterday I said to him..."

Whenever the Egyptian sultan presented the Florentines with a new animal, I made sketches. At one time, there were several lions in the town's menagerie. An old lion had a stubby grey mane and a black splotch across his face. Since one of his paws was crippled, he limped badly. As he walked or stretched out in the summer sun, a friendly ibis often pecked about in his fur. Old and wise, he ate only two or three times a week...and outlived younger lions. Bruno, a keeper, let me measure him. Skull. Neck. Spine. Shoulders. Rump. Paws.

I suggested large cages for the menagerie animals but no one listened. When I designed a cage for a lion on two levels, with a tree in a corner, nothing came of it.

One night, in winter, a friar opened a cage and let a sick lion go; for days the young man had tried to cure the female. Running amok through town, she created quite a scare until she was trapped in a cul-de-sac by some of my apprentices. Muzzled, growling, she was returned to her cage where she died.

It was only a few blocks from my studio to the menagerie and I often heard the animals roar while I worked.

Cloux.

Cage.

Our incessant feuds, wars, brutalities, our pettiness, have rotted our minds.

For years I have heard men describe roads frozen with sleet and dead, bloody ambuscades, military gear trapped in mud, mules and horses floundering, desolated villages. I have seen victory and defeat...Milan... Pisa...Bologna... Perugia...

Surrounded by death, I have known many men who want more and more of it. I have remembered that as I painted my mural, my *Anghiari*. Some of my war sketches have been aberrations. It would have been wiser had I confined myself to my atelier. Among my drawings, sketches, cartoons, models, among my plants and fossils, I should have gone on and on painting. Who, better than I, through my anatomical studies, know the marvels of life! Now, I shun crossbows, guns, chariots. I have asked Francesco to destroy those sketches.

Once again, as in Florence, as in my youth, I am putting art foremost. I am painting.

Tomorrow, Francesco and I will go along the Loire, sketching. If tomorrow is a rainy day we will try the next day. I think he is overly concerned with the problems of perspective. We will talk about the elimination of detail.

Painter and friend, I am lucky to have Francesco, my Cecchino!

These days, I sleep longer, but, through the years, in Florence, in Milan, I never slept more than three or four hours a night. There were too many plans, sketches, paintings, bronzes, portraits, models, commissions...three or four hours...that was enough...

Lie down, sleep...catch the dawn, the window shutters open. Mist on the Arno. Plunge face in icy water in that old white wash basin. Tie sketch pad onto belt. The town is sleeping; the birds are waking up. Careful, open the door quietly. Don't disturb Andrea. Is that the moon, still hanging in the sky?

I made my way to the Boboli Gardens...passed the *David*...rows of crooked cypress...marble satyr...pool of frogs...a beggar whined...

A town sleeps a thousand years every night.

⚜

Cloux

Occasionally, while playing chess, I imagine there are no pawns; I imagine there are no knights; the good bishop has vanished; the castle has gone; there is no stalemate; instead, we are walking across checkered fields, Caterina and I. Soon, we'll sit down to supper; then, when candles have burned low and lamps are dying down, we'll lie in each other's arms.

I have never been a clever chess player: I have spoiled games by envisioning a spiral staircase, by designing a parachute or estimating the cost of draining a marsh instead of planning my next move. I can cast bronze better than tackle chess strategy.

When King Francis and I play, I know the rules—those unwritten rules—and abide by them: the king must win.

Checkmate...what are the rules in life...checkmate...how to play the final move?

Someday our earth may be burdened with people (but I will not be there).

Numbers cheapen us.

Collective folly weakens us.

Man and art drift apart.

However, who can create man? For that matter, who can create a common pigeon? Or the mangiest dog? Or a horse?

And there is such mystery in this arm, this wrist, these fingers as I write. I would like to be able to trace these impulses: the thought, as it takes place in the brain, the thought as it becomes the letter L, as it becomes da Vinci, as that word connects with another word.

A dot becomes a sketch. A sketch becomes a tree (a tree becomes a sketch). Must there be limitations to the mind's probings? Experience can shackle us. I resent shackles. I still believe in flying.

I love the horse more than all the animals because he gives me a sense of flying. Racing across a field, half-naked, bareback, I was free as a boy. I was above the earth. Galloping along a road, my cape fluttering, I was outside myself. Trotting underneath the stars I sensed another kind of freedom. The clopping of the horse was a drumbeat for liberty. I was often carried away.

Nuzzling my hand, I stroked his head, thanking him for this ecstasy.

March 2, 1517

Yesterday, a traveler, a Spaniard, a navy officer, a guest of the King, claimed at dinner that a Spanish explorer, Juan Ponce de León, had discovered a land, and named it Florida. He said that Ponce de Leon discovered it four or five years ago.

"Where is Florida? Is it an island?"

I had a page bring my maps but the Spaniard could not locate Florida. He was ill at ease as if he had divulged a state secret. The arrogant officer's face still bothers me, like the face of a diseased rat. Florida? A Spanish name: does it have a special meaning?

"Mon Capitan was hunting for Bimini...the fountain, the great fountain, that cures all diseases," the officer said, pushing aside my maps, less like a traveler than a spoiled child.

Travel...

Francesco has never read the *Travels of Marco Polo*, but he is reading the book to me; he reads in the afternoons, maybe when the warm sun is in our western windows, maybe at the pergola, if it is pleasant. Sometimes, when I am tired, he reads to me by candlelight, beside my ducal bed.

I respect Marco Polo. I believe what he wrote. He was no *millioni.* He was fortunate to find a Rustichello to record his story. Perhaps Francesco is mine. When I visited Polo's prison cell in Genoa someone showed me the painstaking calendar he had chiseled into the wall beside his cot...Chinese characters along the top section of the calendar—a dragon underneath.

In Florence, in Andrea's home, I read Polo's book and dreamed of crossing the Lop Desert on camelback; I imagined visiting the Khan's great cities; I dreamed of sketching palaces, temples, courtiers. I wanted to climb lofty mountains; I thought of mapping rivers.

I told this to Francesco; he smiled and nodded. India? China? Tibet? For him they are words. He thinks only of his Italy, his Vaprio. I am afraid he considers that I have stolen years from his homeland by keeping him here. He writes his mother and father faithfully; when there are lapses in their correspondence he is troubled.

Alas—Salai and Tony have left me!

At Cloux they have spent less and less time at their painting on their own or under my tutelage. They have become infatuated by the King's women—the prostitutes. Finally, in desperation, I urged them to return to Florence. Tony has serious family problems and is needed. Salai plans to build a house for himself, on my vineyard property. I will miss them... I will miss them! They have been an important part of my life! Francesco is pleased there will be no more rivalry and friction. Yet, apart from that, ours was a sad farewell, lingering, the wind blowing about us harshly. It was our last good-bye, I know. I know. They promise to write to me. When are letters alive!

NOTE—Baron Sabran visited me last week. We strolled about the château, and he related another of his wild boar stories as he glanced over some of my paintings. I enjoyed his visit, his chattiness, his effort to be friendly.

Today, I hear that he has passed away: Time...today's friend, tomorrow's enemy.

Cloux

How well I remember:

I was riding with other horsemen, perhaps a dozen of us, Duke Lorenzo on his favorite mare, both of us a little to the front of the Medici pennants, flags, and jousting gear. As we approached the Duke's stables at a canter, he leaned toward me, and said:

"He's yours, Leonardo... I know you like him! Tell the stable boys where you want to have him kept."

A smile, no more.

Cheppo was a three-year-old, four-gaited, almost as distinguished in bone and muscle as Cermonino, yet wider across the withers. I sketched him, studied him, studied him as I had studied Cermonino. Cheppo had a way of shaking his mane, flopping out his upper lip—nuzzling. He was a competent beggar: if I failed to remember a treat he would squeeze me against the stable wall and regard me sadly. Once I was in the saddle he was obedient, alert.

Cheppo had been Lorenzo's favorite. Certainly no one else could have given him more competent training than the Duke. I was so pleased to have him and spoiled him, until I left for Milan—never to find another his equal.

My mirror writing came naturally; it began as a boy; I have always been ambidextrous; yet my left hand's skill surpasses that of the right. There were reasons for my mirror writing: for abbreviations and symbols, the prying of idle apprentices, the intrusion of rivals, the circumvention of blabbers. It also satisfied me personally—esthetically.

Tonight, I am alone, writing: the manor house is still.

It is raining hard, and has been raining hard throughout the day. The fire in the fireplace is comfortable. The lamps are well trimmed.

As I sat at my desk, continuing the journal, someone tried to pry open the door lock. Metal on metal. I waited. Again I heard the intruder. The rain beat on the door; the door shook. I heard the lock give. Picking up a broken easel leg I waited, in case the lock gave way. The man outside coughed. He shuffled about, then left.

Perhaps I should get a dog.

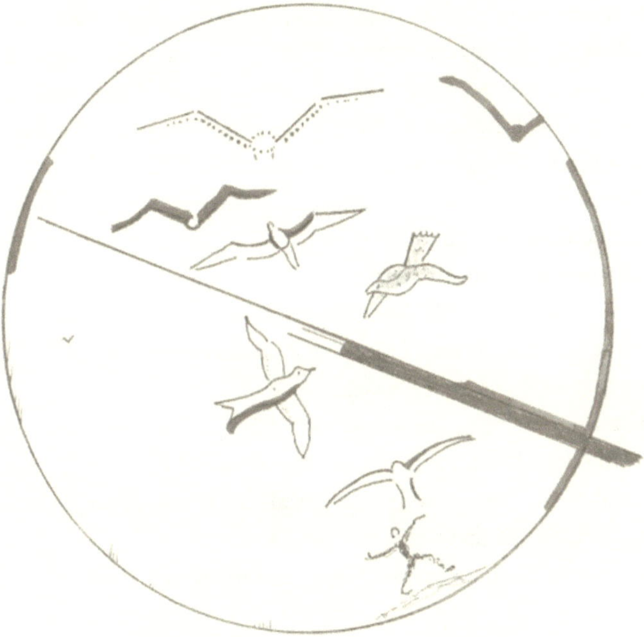

Devotion is the best quality, human devotion and devotion to one's art. Certainly my devotion to Francesco—trust and affection—has been reciprocated.

And, when I am dead, he will remember me. That is what artists need—men who care. If there are those who care, it is as if one's atelier continues on and on. And, if the apprentices think along the guidelines already laid down, that is another continuation, another defiance.

One of these days, Francesco will return to his Vaprio, to paint. He may set up a studio in Milan. Perhaps there will come a time when he places a canvas and sits on his stool and paints my beard, thinning hair, protruding eyebrows, strange nose and strange eyes.

He will say to himself:

"That's how the old man looked, at Cloux.

"Shall I paint on open window behind him...shall I paint some rock formations in the distance?"

⚜

Although the King and his court go out of their way to befriend me I could not tolerate this voluntary exile, this foreignness, this remoteness, were it not for Francesco. When he is away, at the château, in the village, in Paris, traveling somewhere, I am at a loss. I glance about: where is he? When will he return?

Often, when Cecchino comes back from one of his rambles, he has a gift or two, a plant, a seed, a leaf, a rock...he tells me what happened, details. He's good at verbal paintings. Excited sometimes. No matter. He may have sketches to show me, charcoal, pencil, chalk.

"This is something you must take a look at, Maestro...here, this face? Isn't it Greek, the nose, the forehead? And this gypsy woman, what about her? And this fellow...ever see anyone dressed like that? And this fountain..."

He sits on a bench beside my easel.

"We must ride to Paris...we must visit Cluny...the churches...there's a great Van Eyck...and Chambord...now is the time to visit Chambord, when the court's away...we ought to see how your canal and irrigation jobs are coming along...remember, Sr. Migliarotti is pretty lazy..."

Francesco hopes to make me feel like I am thirty years old.

⚜

It is May and I am in the Amboise garden, soaking up the noon sun, courtiers milling about on the many paths; yet I am alone, with my sketchbook, to write, to think. And I am thinking about Francesco, how he arrived at my studio in the pouring rain. Drenched. He had ridden from Vaprio. I don't forget that rain, that stormy Florentine afternoon, that eager, wet face of his, his mud-spattered horse, his servants' horses, how they looked in the street, as Francesco spoke to me. Cold, very cold, even for April. Tiled roofs were choked with rain. Drowned cobbles. Leaves and mud.

But there he was at my door, bowing, smiling.

"Maestro da Vinci...I want to be your pupil."

That was seventeen years ago. Was he only fifteen? It doesn't seem possible he was so young. He was my favorite from the start. I love Salai as a son, but this young man, this gracious young man, is friend and ardent disciple. Painter! When I have been his guest at Vaprio, I am honored. Francesco's father and mother make their villa a place of rest. I know. I have fled there, from the *condottieri*. I am always protected by the Melzis.

His illness upset the studio.

"Melzi's sick! Francesco's sick!"

Fever day after day, hands like ice, coma. Shivering though his apartment was sunny. I thought he might have malaria. The plague. I called in the best doctors; I sent for Francesco's father. His uncle came instead. Other doctors came. And in his delirium, Francesco painted a large canvas, with a flock of white birds in the sky, carrying a blue tree. October, November—bad months for sickness. But by December he was up, skinny, hungry, forever hungry.

And there was his father's gratitude to me, his uncle's gratitude, as if I had been the physician. That summer, as Francesco convalesced at Vaprio, I vacationed there. The family purchased my portrait of *A Boy*. That rolling land, the swift Adda, those canals, the villa gardens with their Roman statues and roses...roses...the women in the gardens, picking roses. But I have written about this before? ...I am getting forgetful.

We sketched and painted.

I remember a puppy lying in my lap as I dozed in one of the gardens, the one with the apple trees. Good food, good wine, summer, that was Villa Vaprio. I learned about summer there—what summer really means.

Cloux

The King wants me to move to a spacious studio in the château. I prefer a smaller room. Small rooms sometimes discipline the mind. I have explained that my studio, in the manor house, has everything essential to my work: cupboards, cabinets, tables, shelves.

"Do you need pigment...oils...turpentine...brushes?" He is impatient... you must want something!

We have space for our paintings. We have the right amount of light. We have quiet. And on our mantelpiece we have a place for my Greek and Roman antiquities—things I collected in Campania (along with malaria): iridescent vases, bronze and alabaster lamps, household figurines, a few coins. I have one with a porpoise leaping. The Greeks were master minters-designers. Francesco says he knows a place in Paris that sells Greek antiquities. If I can ever get there I want to purchase an ivory Venus for my desk. We have not surpassed those ancient artisans.

Such things make a bright enclosure.

I am fortunate...I have had many friends.

I had many friends in Florence, Milan, Rome, Genoa, and Venice. I shall name a few: Marco d'Oggiono, Vitelli, Tomaso Masini, Amalia, Father Pacioli, Ferrera, Machiavelli, Francesco, Mona, Cristofer, Andrea...and now King Francis.

I see them in my sketches as I leaf through them now and then: Benci, in pen and ink, beside a juniper tree; Andrea, at work on a bronze figurine; here is a pastel of Ambrogia, puttering over his careful palette; here is red-headed Filippo Lippi finishing the background for a madonna; here is Cecelia, sipping wine, asking for sweets...Madonna Lisa and her graceful beauty, her soft voice, patience...

She and I had many hours for the *gamboa*...we ate together...played cards, talked about my *Anghiari*...when she posed I had singers for her... I loaned her little sums; she lent me money; she sent me baskets of fruit; I gave her sketches and drawings.

If all these friends could be with me, at Cloux, to walk with me, visit the château and its gardens, prowl the mirror hallways, enjoy my studio, my latest paintings...talk...talk...

⚜

As an apprentice I longed to fix in my mind every detail: I must look and look, a second and a third time and a fourth. I must fill a notebook. Quickly. I must follow that bearded Corsican and draw his face.

All of us apprentices respected Andrea del Verrochio, as artisan, as teacher. We were at home in his workshop. We were proud of his accomplishments, proud of our own accomplishments; at the same time we were eager, pushy, ready to challenge other artists. Ready to consider a commission, evaluate it, carry it through to perfection.

And what were my best years, the best of my mature years, I ask myself? Those dedicated to my mural, my outcry against war, years that included many paintings? Or was it the time dedicated to the creation of the Sforza horse—IL COLOSSO? If I could have had the metal and cast the statue it would have been that success above others. And the years that went into *The Last Supper*. Three years. There were also the years of dissection and anatomical studies. Best years? There were the easel paintings. I suppose there have never been any best years. There were discoveries and discovery made another discovery possible...and so the years went along.

Last night, Francesco burst into my bedroom.

"I can't find them," he exclaimed.

"What?"

"I have looked everywhere...your letters are missing."

"What letters, Francesco?"

"I have your list...letters from King Francis...from Duke Lorenzo...from Christopher Columbus...Machiavelli...Father Pacioli...Beatrice d'Este...Cesare Borgia...Salai..."

"Did you open the trunk in the storeroom? They may be in there. Look carefully. I want to destroy some of them...let's go over everything together."

"We had them in Milan..."

"Look again... I'm sure you'll find them."

(Yesterday, in the château's hall of mirrors I saw Caterina: she was talking with a young man, a man her age: she had on a summer gown, with one breast almost bare: she smiled at her companion who was dressed in grey.)

⚜

Cloux
June 1, 1517

After I completed my silverpoint of Francis, he ordered his tailor to cut an elegant velvet smock for me. In carnelian. Two pockets. Belt of silver lozenges hooked together on braided silver wires.

Francesco is framing the portrait and it will hang in the château library, along with a Rafael, a de Predis, a Bosch, a Dürer. Francis has his eyes on Francesco's new canvas, his *Columbine*, but I tell the King it is not finished.

"Not finished? Of course it is finished, Mon Père." But Francesco listens to me.

I continue with my drawings of the deluge: I go on with the terror, the falling of buildings, the erosion of life, the force of wind, the weight of torrents... I go on with this feeling... I must express it.

The gloomy air must be beaten by the wind and perpetual hail...there must be ancient trees, uprooted trees, torn to pieces by the fury...the fragments of mountains must spill into valleys...immensity must burst the barrier of rivers.

It is my last judgment...certainly there is nothing that does not have an ending ...twisted forms...fear...puny man...

I hear the resounding air, the lamentations.

Mountains are to be torn open for their minerals...all animals will languish...all will be pursued or destroyed...trees will be laid level...due to man's malice there will be great losses...how much better for man to go back to hell.

⚜

Cloux

It is late.

A fire burned all evening in my studio, and King Francis has sat by the fire with me, talking. He was depressed because bankers have been demanding exorbitant sums: he plans to sell royal titles to recoup funds.

"All this will take months...there are many hazards..."

Abruptly:

"Do you see something in my face, something ominous?"

"I don't understand..."

"It seems to me...I feel that the future has something tragic... I'm worried... Do you believe in foretelling?"

He had been jousting: I blamed fatigue. But he would not be put aside by a few casual words.

"Mon Père...tell me...some say that you can foretell? Is that true?"

"I can not."

"Who can?"

"Nobody."

"Nobody?"

"Divinations...those occult doings...forget them. You must think clearly, your Majesty. Don't let men hoodwink you. Nobody knows tomorrow."

"Tonight, as I walked through the tunnel from the château...tonight I had three guards... I was afraid...like a Borgia...assassinations...pretty bad..."

He laughed at himself.

It has been sunny and cool for several days: I have gone on pleasant walks, along the river, through the château gardens, through the grove that leads into the King's forest: paths are becoming familiar: I shake hands with old trees. At the château I have watched the King play tennis: they are having a tournament. Francis plays with ugly ferocity. His partners play warily. I see that diplomacy begins on the tennis courts.

Studio
September 3, 1517

My lamp is guttering. Candle stubs are smoking.

Was it thirty years ago, in Milan, that I understood? Windows were open and heat-lightning was flickering beyond my studio. My anatomy drawings were spread on the corner table. Then I saw. Saw clearly. Knew. Saw that man's blood resembles the tides of the sea; from the seat of the heart it circulated throughout the body. Let an artery or vein burst or suffer injury and blood raced to the injured spot. Incessant currents of the blood, passing through the arteries and veins, caused them to thicken and become callous. So, I had additional proof of circulation. Each dissection revealed further confirmation of the system. Why was I slow in grasping the obvious?

I have explained my theory to some but was often rebuffed and yet when I told her—using my drawings—she grasped the significance. She understood many things. And when she lay dying there seemed little left for me... I held her hand. Her eyes were closed. Grey eyes. She never spoke. God, how I stumbled down those rat infested stairs, stairs with a cross gouged in each step. Ah, those flooded streets!

Some men of science and art have copies of my first treatise. Some. They hesitate. Resent. Last year I explained circulation to King Francis. He was not interested; he fondled his diamond-studded belt and stared stupidly at me. I must tell Francesco that the treatise is packed in the third trunk—the one with the smashed lock.

I must sequence my drawings:

1 - Skin
2 - Muscles
3 - Tendons
4 - Bones

Indicate effect of emotions, labor, illness, age.

⚜

Cloux
October 15, 1517

Francesco is copying this:

I have been unable to write or work for several days. These days she is in my mind all of the time. Maturina begs me to eat...my appetite has gone. The weather is perfect but I can not go outside. Here, in my studio, I have her portrait to console me; sometimes I have to turn away from it. I thought that she would live for many years. I thought that she was contented. Her family loved her.

The letter, written by her brother, says nothing about how Mona died. Was she ill a long while? I can't remember when she wrote me last time...was it as much as a year ago? Why am I confused? Did the plague kill her? Was she with her family? How they will miss her! The letter took four months to reach me—a hundred and twenty days! She died in Genoa, on the 2nd or 3rd of July. I can't make out the date.

The King knows of her death. Francesco told him, because I can not ride with the hunters... I can not ride... Francis has presented me with a small jeweled hourglass. A note accompanied it.

Life and death...old friends, old enemies.

My face is a cemetery.

Gossips said that Mona was my mistress.

We were friends.

In those days, when I was beginning her portrait, I had Gorgio play for her: she liked his viola da gamba skill. He would usually appear a little late, but always with a smile, a bow. Sometimes a choir boy sang motets; it seems to me he recited poetry too. Did he always wear a brown cloak?

Our sittings were often far apart: there was illness in her family: she was away from Florence for months at a time: on her return it was hard to recapture our mood. She was patient with me but I have often stood before her picture quite perplexed...especially if the light had changed...my colors had changed.

I was late for one of our sittings and she put on an apron and scrubbed brushes and mortars, made my apprentices scurry; then laughed at my objections.

"Next time you're late, I'll clean your leggio," she said, and smiled teasingly.

Her smile...I used to think of it as hiding family secrets, feminine secrets, her own loneliness ("Yes, Leonardo...yes...there are times...")

I could not always arrange for a musician; when she posed during those silences I felt the bonds of our friendship...when we ate together, when she described her travels, it was another aspect of our friendship.

I was welcome at her home. Her distinguished husband bought fine pieces of art. They were happy to share.

At her home and in my studio we often talked about my *Anghiari* and she was eager to follow its progression.

⚜

October 29th

Masculine skies...feminine skies...at this season of the year they are mostly masculine, with snow falling, wind blowing. My feet are cold because of the weather, or is it because my fireplace chimney needs cleaning? Cold, I have moved to the library.

As I mull over my papers I observe the great books around me. I must concentrate. I must push on. There is so much to be done with the organization of my treatises. So much.

Maturina rouses me.

"You are cold, Maestro...it is chilly in this room."

So, I am cold!

Perhaps I have cathedral sickness!

It is good to be writing again. My journal suffers when my hand is unsteady.

Francesco is away; that troubles me.

I wish I were young and could bend horseshoes instead of two sheets of paper.

Maturina has found a bird stricken by the cold; we hover over it. A dove. A flyer. Where are my sketches for the glider? The one Francesco and I tested. He must find it for me when he returns.

Interruptions...interruptions...

Francesco has adopted a stray cat, from among the dozens that haunt the château. The cat beds under his easel, among cleaning rags. He always stinks of turpentine and oil.

I have never seen a cat so eager to sleep; perhaps half of his life has gone into carousing. He is bone white, has one orange ear, a twisted nose, one orange foot, and a black-tipped tail. His greenish eyes glare out of skinniness.

Crabby.

Maturina hates him.

Francesco calls him "Michelangelo."

My four-poster must have been made for a cardinal or bishop, or someone's mistress. I am tempted to remove the garnet canopy and drapes. But it's a snug bed when it's cold. I often lie there and watch the fire playing about. It's a chance to weigh the past—and plan ahead.

Sometimes, when I am very tired and have turned in early, Francesco rolls his easel into the room, and sits on the side of the bed and we talk brush strokes or ways of grinding the new pigments, how much overpainting is feasible, the dangers of black as an under pigment. Shop talk.

Cloux

ANDREA SALAINO—Why did I adopt him in the first place?

That's an easy answer: because I loved him!

What a waif Salai was! I took him into my household, my studio, twenty-some years ago. It can't be possible that so much time has lapsed.

He stole...stole shirts, shoes, brushes, gold leaf. He stole gold leaf and sold it. He took money. I was right to christen him "Salai." It took months to straighten him out...if I really did. Yellow-headed, curly-headed, tall, foolish, loveable... when he puts his arm around me...

He is a capable artist, incapable of continuous effort; perhaps time can change him but I doubt it.

Now that he is gone...I often think I hear his voice... I think, ah, he has come back for a while...

The King and Queen have asked me how I had hoped to cast *Il Cavallo*, so I placed my drawings on tables in the salon, and we walked from one to another and I explained them.

"Mon Père," Francis mumbled, as he examines drawings and sketches, "Mon Père...these are workable."

I am silent.

"When did you begin actual casting?" the Queen asks. I try to disregard her obvious skepticism.

She is dressed in white and gold; he has on one of his dark cloaks lined with down; he has rings set with emeralds; she reeks of cologne and sweat. Her pinched face is regally ugly—somehow provincial.

"I began casting the horse in December...'93...casting it on its side. I placed the mould in a shallow cavity. I opened it on the left side. I could have completed the casting if there had been sufficient bronze. I am sure you know that cannons had priority at that time."

They knew, too, about the Gascon bowmen.

I understand they had watched the archers, as they used my clay model for target. Watched my *Cavallo* disintegrate.

I watched, hating, hating those bowmen. How they cheered as arrows pierced the model.

Now I watched the King and Queen.

"In Milan, in those days, the Sforza stables were at my disposal. I chose a magnificent horse—Cermonino—as my model. Alone, or with a groom, I would ride into the country, where it was pleasant and we were free of gapers. I would dismount and sketch my horse. Or the groom would lead him back and forth, while I sketched, to record a sense of motion.

"Other times I would ride Cermonino, race him, sweat him; then I'd draw his distended mouth, his swollen nostrils, his wild mane...

"Leaning forward in the saddle, baton in hand, the Duke was to symbolize leadership and power...he was pleased...his baton would have been more than thirty feet above the ground."

Visitors and courtiers annoy me, though I do not show my annoyance. I have learned how to patronize. I pretend I have nothing to do...my life is one of leisure. Then, at night, through most of the night, lamps and candles burning, Francesco and I work with my drawings and texts.

Francesco realizes that I am homesick but he does not quite realize that I am homesick for a Florence that does not exist. I don't admit it but I am also remembering Vinci, the only home I ever had. I would like to walk into the rambling stone house and sit by a front window. I would like...but why go on?

Botteghe or ateliers have their points but they are never home. Guilds, with their rivalries, their rascalities, are continually broiling. Greedy apprentices. Raw apprentices. Rowdiness. So many crowns for this piece of work, so many *soldi* for this job. Dissension over models. Spats about religion. Muddy sex.

Perhaps I should have lived out my life in my vineyard. Much sun. Quietude. Animals. Olive trees in the sunset. The mistral. Peasants. Fidelity.

What delusions.

Tomorrow I look forward to working again on my *Saint John*. I have decided to darken the background.

I knew Sandro Botticelli well. Now that he is dead and I am far away, leaving this personal journal to a mere boy, I can write about him. We called Sandro "Our Little Barrel." He was fat enough, to be sure. Success favored his belly. Drink gave him a pleasant stupor.

I thought his *Primavera* a piece of ostentation: the picture flaunts showmanship in many ways. The background is especially weak. I have shied away from gigantic canvases. A painting should not pretend to be a mural or a fresco.

However, Sandro's illustrations for Dante have a lightness: his lines are right.

Maybe I am not respectful of Sandro. Michelangelo dislikes my work. Who is right?

When my fellow Florentines legally murdered Savonarola I was repelled. Savonarola was reformer, dictator, fanatic. His bigotry alarmed me; all bigotry alarms me. I prefer the Alpine heights and passes to heavenly promises; I prefer rivers and lakes to the Dantesque. Savonarola's ashes were thrown into the Arno... I anticipate further degradations...ashes... whose ashes were thrown into the river? Ours? No matter what we say in defense of religion there seems to be another road. Some things surpass religion. My mother's gentleness, for one thing. I say, let us worship beauty. Now, in my old age, I say let us worship beauty.

Thinking of beauty, I hoped for many years to do a bronze of Hercules, Hercules firing his arrow at the Stymphalian birds, head back, eyes upward, his right arm tensing the cord, fingers ready to let the arrow go: Hercules in the nude, among rocks, one knee cocked at the same angle as his bow arm.

1518

Cloux
February 1, 1518

It is snowing again.

The ground is white. Trees are white. About two years ago, on our long ride from Milan, we stayed at the Pericord Monastery; snow was falling. Outside my one-eyed cell lay a deep drift. A path led nowhere through the snow.

While at Pericord, most of us ate in the refectory or the kitchen. Were there thirty monks at the monastery? All of them were dirty and resentful. This hermitage wanted no outsiders. Although we paid, we were gross intruders. This order had the Biblical fish engraved on its coat-of-arms but these men no longer remembered what that symbol meant.

Bread, cheese, dried fruit, sunflower seeds, eggs, wine, herbal tea—they offered us these and we tried to express our thanks.

Each enormous deal table had IHS chiseled in its center. IHS...smoke from cheap table candles mixed with kitchen smoke as we ate with shutters closed against the snow and cold.

Painted black, a large wooden cross leaned against a corner of the refectory.

Fealty far from any hamlet—what is this monastic fealty?

As I stayed there, recovering, troubled, I compared those thirty faces with the faces of the disciples in my *Last Supper*. I understand more about human nature now than I did twenty years ago. So did the artist who had painted a primitive fresco of demons in the Pericord Library. His demons are Borgian nightmares.

We have more snow this winter than in many winters, I am told. The Loire has frail ice edges and some of that ice traps leaves and twigs and resembles tortured stained glass. I like to walk alone, along the river—snow tracking: fox, rabbit, deer, raccoon, and boar.

Snow crystals in my hand, on my glove, I analyze their geometry.

In the comfort of my studio I sketch from memory: I am able to reproduce plants, birds, people, machines. Years ago I lost an important sketchbook and was able to reproduce more than fifty drawings. Any capable artist should be able to do this.

As the snowfall continues, I shall go on tonight, red chalk and charcoal.

Rome proved to be a harsh experience.

Living in the Vatican was an impoverishment: the roof of my apartment leaked with every rain; the light was bad; sewage odors were frequent. Gamins—so many gamins! Threatened. While others hunted rabbits in the Coliseum, I sought libraries and worked in my own laboratory. But work was difficult because my old kidney complaint afflicted me. For a time I was at the Hospital Spirito. I became as desolate as Hadrian's Tomb. I ate only fruit and nuts, but fruit is often scarce in Rome at certain seasons.

Rafael was friendly; Paciola was faithful; Bramante was friendly. I blame the city, its somber tufa buildings. Cities, like mistresses, betray. Fleeing Rome, I

visited my vineyard; then, again lured by the wrong magnet, I returned for more Roman punishment.

Tibullus and Ovid were there. I opened their pages and read. But my optical experiments were thwarted: a violent quarrel with my optical expert undid the work of months. He smashed all the equipment in my laboratory. As soon as possible, half-recovered, I joined Salai and Francesco in Milan. They had located an apartment for me, Salai lauding its grand style, its perfect studio. But the studio was not for me. Milan was not for me. At Vaprio, I began to recover in the bracing air. My friends helped deceive me: I was not growing old; so, I began a little fresco for the Melzis.

Throughout my life I have been willing to attempt various disciplines. I am alien to most men because they limit their interests. Almost all of my friends thought in terms of a single field of endeavor. Ambrogio cared nothing for geology. De Predis shunned mathematics. Boltraffio scorns cartography. Fra Luca shrugs off all but church music. Luini favors frescos. Who is interested in oceanography? Or flying?

I think men should reach out. A rut can lead to a dead end. The portrait artist need not paint portraits all his life. Andrea was one of those rarities (an inspiration!): his world was brush, pastel, oil...marble, bronze, porphyry...cenotaph, altar, sarcophagus...portrait.

⚜

Cloux
March 12, 1518

Sleep comes hard: there is frequent pain in my back and legs: insomnia exhausts me: I think of stairways, dikes, weaving machines, cylindrical sails, cadavers, faces...

Many times I have seen Christ's face—as I painted him in my fresco. I remember him, lying in his ghetto... I remember him so ill he could scarcely walk... I remember taking food to him...there, over there, on the wall, is his face in the candlelight.

Sleepless, I have gotten up and sketched those who have been dead for years. Friends, neighbors, filthy seamen on the coast, mountaineers, shepherds, brigands at the Borgia castle.

Here, at Cloux, I have found a girl whose profile is perfect: I have asked her to pose for a silverpoint.

Here, in the heart of France, when I am listening to Francesco talk French I am listening to a clever Frenchman. He could speak the language fairly well before coming—he has perfected his pronunciation, his pauses. He says he learned from a boyhood tutor. I ask him to correct me but he never does. Most of our château friends speak several languages. When I am explaining technical drawings to the King or members of his court I have to have help when it comes to the vocabulary relating to hydraulics, gears, fossils, and such.

March 18, 1518

My journal is in danger.

Time is leaving me.

I go weeks without adding a thought.

If I see a horse riddled with arrows, a mural that is scaling off—where is the joy? Where the beauty?

Let's go to that valley along the Adda River, in May. We were laughing then: being alive pleased us. Let's go to Piombino where I sketched the little ships in the harbor, ships and pounding waves. Let's walk in the castle garden, among the senatorial statues; I played the lute and both of us sang. And Rustici's! What about Rustici's and that pet porcupine of his?

In Pavia, I lost my way among narrow lanes; it was dusk; it was summer; it became dark; a lantern appeared, another; I found myself at a house of prostitution: the loveliness of that meeting, those unexpected caresses, that girl... O, sleeper, what is sleep? Sleep resembles death. Yet, there are happy dreams. And actual dreams, such as rolling the *Colossus* into the square and seeing the Milan populace mill around it. And another...my mother, Caterina, embracing me when last we met.

There have been other dreams: working with wood and silk, to perfect a wing...there was that brief moment of flight...my wing...being aloft...lifted above trees and town... I feel that lift as I write. Joy. Beauty.

There were rows of candles and water-lamps shining in front of my *Last Supper*; I stepped back to contemplate my work; I looked around; I realized that the fresco was finished. I felt tears of joy, tears that never fell, yet existed. I felt another overwhelming satisfaction in my *Anghiari*: the horses were alive and came to me as I looked at them... I remembered their names.

Andrea Verrochio came through the refectory door and shook my hand. When I write to him I will remind him...but he is dead.

I have always thought the penis handsome during copulation, otherwise pitiful. I have never worshipped it as have some men—and women! As a boy it was tantalizing, always there, always a reminder of sex, most often a mystery. I saw copulation enjoyed before I enjoyed it with a girl. It seemed to me that it wasn't much fun. I had to mature. It seems to me that the penis often has a life of its own, as during the night when it rouses a man, a sentiency of its own perhaps. I note that women like the size of the penis as large as possible, but a man wants the opposite in a woman's organ.

The Greeks and Romans were penis worshippers. As a fertility symbol it amuses me. I wonder how the Egyptians regarded the penis? They have had centuries to think about it. Young women enjoy displaying their breasts; some men want to show their masculinity. There is something quite amusing about these sex thoughts. Juvenile! Life has so many serious problems: hunger, plague, crime. The ecclesiastics laud the cross and crucifixion; I suspect that some of their fervor is part of the penis contemplation. With the penis there can be a kind of holy ecstasy, for certain. I had an ivory penis in my studio in Florence: was it African? Some thought it Babylonian. It does not matter.

Men will always fight among themselves, sexually, politically, socially. I have realized this for years. Can it be that this realization urged me to fly, to escape perversion and mediocrity? Flying can be a celebration of the mind.

Well, sex means little to me now. Silence means more. Friendship. Calm. Hope. Ai, those workshops of my youth were so noisy. On crowded streets. Near alleys. Vendors howling their wares. Mule teams. Horsemen. One of my workshops was close to a smithy. Steel on steel mixed with palavering.

Amboise is my silent *bottega*, walkways, garden, flowers. Here I have so many of my favorites: nasturtiums, ranunculas, roses, poppies, violets, iris, pansies.

Maturina keeps flowers in my studio and my bedroom.

Writing in the sun along the Loire, remembering, *remembering*:

I recall details of my dissections of pigeons... Sketching, measuring, I concentrated on bone structure of the wings, then the tail, the balancing properties of the entire bird. Using those dimensions I calculated wing lengths and wing widths for my glider. I laid out a narrow area for a man to lie on, exactly between the wings.

I constructed the glider with the aid of my apprentices. I launched it at Mount Ceceri. Ceceri seemed the likeliest hill since wind currents had to be strong, and constant. Men lifted, pushed, yelled.

"Now...now!"

I dipped into the wind, slid with the wind, lifted. It seemed to me that I hovered for a while above a big willow. Rooftops. Then, in spite of my attempts at balancing, the wing swung down, dropped, spun... I crashed.

That wing measured 15' x 3' x 9'.

⚜

I can visualize Milan's pink and red buildings, its fortress Castello between moats, its drawbridges, the fumbling city walls, the filthy streets. Though not as old as Rome, I often felt Milan's shabby antiquity. It was a lesson in futility. So many sieges: 1497, 1500, 1512...military engagements that disrupted every fiber of living. (There is nothing like the filth of a city under siege.)

During the last siege, in 1515, the cannonades drove me out of the city. In my absence my apartment—with its view of the Alps—was looted by riffraff.

The city gates...I remember them: Porta Comasina, Porta Romana, Porta Orientale. Near the Orientale I found a bronze figurine, on one of my walks. Its small head had been uncovered by a recent rain. A priest, carrying a rice bowl.

How I worked during those Milanese years: apses, loggias, transepts, windows, frescos! Survival jobs. "This door needs immediate repair...place that medallion lower...no red marble here..." I could not equal Donato Bramante's architectural skill. Friend, I wished him well.

Did I spend almost three years in the Castello, in those maddening salas, those perfumed rooms? The only place to avoid the stench of sewage. I urged the Duke to plan a city with upper and lower thoroughfares, a city where there was air space to lessen the danger of plague. Fifty thousand dead in '09.

Sieges...death...

Milan...all focused on my *cenasolo*...my *Maria delle Grazie*...that refectory...that was my world...those faces, those outspread hands, that table...there is more than one way to break bread...more than one cup.

⚜

Cloux

It is satisfying to return to my study of curvilateral stars: evenings, after I have had supper, I begin—if there are no royal interruptions. The cat now curls at my feet, as I sit at my desk among my lamps.

Perhaps Michelangelo and I can become friends.

To amuse him I roll balls of paper and snap them across the floor. He responds—with an obvious effort.

I work to reduce a segment of a circle proportionally so I can make any number of identical segments which in sum are equal to a segment subtended by a side of a hexagon inscribed in the circle. I can make any number of curvilateral stars of which the sum of the triangles is equal to the sum of the segments subtended by the side of a hexagon inscribed in a given circle.

I much prefer doing this to working on the plans for the château at Romorantin.

The point of the center, where there is no movement, suggests peace.

Cloux
April 9th

Today, I had a brief letter from Salai.

I remember the Arno at sunset, the yellow and the gold, the yellow underneath the gold, the gold identical to gold leaf, a metallic sunset overlaid with misty hues, the bridges silhouetted, the darkest spans cut out of charred steel. The force of sunlight lay between each bridge and turned the river banks violet, the violet merging into cobalt.

Ai, to walk there, to think there, again!

As a boy I used to fish there, but never had much luck. Papa insisted that the tastiest fish came from the Arno. He was a good fisherman and should have known. Maybe fishing was better in his day. I wonder if there are any fish in the Arno now?

Fishing or wading or splashing in the river—that was a half century ago.

April 11th

IL CAVALLO

I solved all the construction problems in 1493. Bronze horse. Bronze rider. Weight of horse: 185,000 pounds. Horse to measure 23 feet from hoof to mane. Total height: 34 feet from hoof to helmet of rider. Total weight of horse and rider: 205,000 pounds.

THE HORSE:

We began to pour the metal at night, a team of sixteen men. We had metal from salvage. Our caldrons blazed as the metals combined. We had our supply of wood stacked under a thatch, another supply in a shed. As we worked the shed ignited and burned. Shouts. Orders. Warnings.

Shortly before dawn some militiamen arrived—drums, not sunrise. The *commandante* of the city fortresses—on the Duke's orders—requisitioned all bronze for armament. I read the Duke's order... I read, and stepped aside.

And the Duke lost his city, and his life. His horse.

Cloux
April 12th

ALBIERA AMADORI—My friend Albiera was as beautiful as her name, beautiful to me, beautiful to her family, her friends—all who knew her. In my sketches she appears as an angelic one, an ideal woman. She was delicate. Always. Busy with her large family, her housework, yet stealing time for her lute. There in her garden, among her irises. There in her garden, by her fountain. Singing as she played. Dark hair, dark tint under her eyes. Her voice a little frail. Perhaps she was too good for us, although we loved her dearly.

After she died I used to visit her grave and bring or arrange flowers. Her little bronze bust had a special place in my studio.

"Albiera," I hear Florentine voices calling.

Somewhere perhaps in the château garden—a bird sings and seems to say: "Al - bi - era."

Cloux
April 14, '18

Tomorrow evening, Pietro Papini will play his lira da braccio for us, music I composed in Milan, when friend Atalante and I played and sang. Papini is Court maestro and master of the lira. He'll be playing his amusing instrument—moustached *mascherone* on the sound box.

Good Francesco has searched through my manuscripts for rebuses and notations, and he and Papini have put together a song that begins:

Amore sol la mi fa remirare, la sol mi fa sollecita.

Tomorrow is my birthday.

Princess d'Arezzo will wear a gold mask I designed for her. Pity to hide beauty behind a mask. The King is wearing my skeleton cloak. Three dwarfs will appear as miniature elephants. I will wear a replica of a camel's head. Francesco is to impersonate a Hindu seer. Countess Benci—sixteen years old—will be naked except for silver slippers and an Etruscan helmet of silver foil.

It will be gala!

Cloux

I did not know it was raining until one of the King's pages brought me a rain-spattered note, ink and coat-of-arms smudged.

"What is it?" Francesco asked, standing by me protectively, holding the door.

The page grinned and wiped rain off his face. Probably he was perplexed since he could not understand Italian.

"The King is sick," I said, reading the note. "He wants me to come to the château and talk to him."

"In this awful rain!"

Water was sluicing off the page's cap.

"I won't let you go out...in this cold rain," protested Maturina. "You have no umbrella...it's being fixed."

Francesco tugged my sleeve.

"The tunnel," he said. "We'll walk through the tunnel, to the château. It's been worked on...we'll keep dry... Shall we?"

So, with torches, the page, and a couple of my servants, we entered the old shaft. Almost at once our torches died out; there was a brisk draft; some of our torches were wet. Somebody went back to the manor house for candles. The passage was difficult for a tall man. I had forgotten there were several curves. Bats annoyed us. We had to wade across rain pools where water was oozing in. I stumbled over bricks and stumbled over a rusty cuirass someone had leaned against the wall.

Holding up my torch I made out crude foreign names and initials and dates... VITELLI...was it really VITELLI? I thought I saw 1502 on the wall. Latin names. Gascon. 1601. 1502 again. Cesare Borgia, that Papal bastard had had Vitelli strangled on December 1, 1502. His name went on and on, as we tramped through the tunnel.

My hatred was everywhere.

The page opened the château door, and we ascended several flights of stairs, walked along halls, were stopped by guards at the King's suite.

"His Majesty is asleep now," a guard said.

Borrowing umbrellas and raincoats, we returned to the manor, preferring the paths and the road to the tunnel route.

How fitfully I slept while in Cesare Borgia's camp...like Alexander the Great I slept with the *Iliad* and a dagger under my pillow.

It was Niccolò Machiavelli who stole horses for us—made our escape possible...horses...rain...all night the two of us rode through the rain.

⚜

Fibonacci's dog-eared book, *Liber Abaci*, still interests me: what tattered covers, foxed pages, and scribbled margins! Too many fingers have flipped through this book. No matter... I have tried his famous rabbit problem once more and then once more. I see that each number is the sum of the two preceding numbers, continuing *ad infinitum*. And it is true I can divide Fibonacci's number (after the fourteenth in his sequence) by the next highest in number: it is precisely .618034 to 1.

.618034 is nature's proportion—her golden mean: it exists in sunflower seeds, shell spirals, spider webs, ferns, the perfect rectangle, in playing cards, the Parthenon's façade.

Another night of memories, a night for murder. Incessant wind, rain...

Vitelli...

But there was more than this young man's death. There was Giamina Andres da Ferrara. GAF.

The officials of Milan murdered GAF...the officials!: They had him hung, drawn, and quartered, in the Public Square.

GAF.

I fled to Mantua, as if I could forget in Mantua!

So much of life is fleeing.

So much is trying to forget.

Rain...

Those youthful faces...Vitelli, 24 years old...Ferrara, 33 years old...artists... good men...friends.

Perhaps there is something to be said about this remote château, this little manor house, these woodlands, paths, fields, this Loire; I should be able to put these things together and say something; when I am alone here, or alone with Francesco and Maturina, when I sit in my studio or in the library or walk in the fields or along the Loire, I hear something like wisdom: it seems to suggest greater dedication, calm, calmness, like a stag in a clearing, alert, watching.

⚜

August 15, 1518

Another summer at Cloux.

(I have not written my journal for months).

Birds—orioles and finches—are singing along the river. Willows and birds for miles. Old trees, some of them half-drowned by a heavy rain, seem determined to flourish. Where the Loire widens, meadows of water form islands.

Yesterday or the day before, Francesco and I spent most of a morning searching for a species of frog that interests me. We crossed and recrossed the river at shallow points.

Close to the château, by the tenth century bridge, I waded over slippery rock. There I fell. Old shanks!

I'll just lie here...the pain won't last...

"Maestro, your sketchbook is ruined...let me help you!"

I was overcome by my own weakness, by the ugliness of my bony legs. It's true I'm an old man!

⚜

August 20, '18

Sometimes France becomes alive—not in the geographic sense: it comes alive as a fresco of bogged willows, a row of pencil-pointed cypress, a field of yellow rye, a woodland village, a pagan altar, a tired bridge, a flock of charcoal ravens ...these are the enchantment, along with August cicadas and August storms.

Swans and cygnets are also there, and a knight in armor!

I stand at my studio window: there, below me, stretches the garden and the garden leads to the woodland and just inside the first fringe of trees is a stag.

From the château I watch the blue water of the Loire flowing by; the blue water changes to grey: the Seine.

I taste the antique taste of time and illusion: my telescope focuses on wayfarers: I see them in mirrors: years of princes, priests, soldiers, artists.

Maturina is Italy: toothless, sickly, yet eager to carry-on! Smiling, smelling of grease and herbs, she offers me her famous soup, her haricot beans, her red jam, her Vinci cheese.

Behind her, as she sets my table for supper, gawks a young Midi apprentice (a possum-faced individual). The Midian is talking about Brussels sprouts, how her mother used to prepare them. When she takes Maturina's place and her teeth fall out, she will be ready to impart her culinary skills to someone else.

⚜

Cloux
September 14

Suddenly, Francis appeared in my studio.

He was dressed entirely in black, his suit sewn with pin stripes of diamonds and pearls. We embraced warmly. We had not seen each other for several weeks...

"What has happened to you?" I asked, shocked by his appearance, for his hair had been scorched and trimmed; his forehead was livid; his cheek was scarred by burns; his chin had been gashed.

"It happened at Romorantin," he said, laughing loudly at me. "Didn't you hear about the accident?"

"I heard something about an accident but I didn't know it was serious. I've been in Paris, with Francesco. What happened to you at the château?"

"Come, don't take it so seriously, Mon Père. I'm all right. The scars will disappear. My hair will grow back. I came to talk with you, to get away from the roisterers at the château... I need a little peace and quiet."

"But what happened to you at Romorantin?"

"Games...we were playing games in the field alongside the château. It was dark. I shoved a wicker basket over my head and one of my cronies set fire to it with his torch... I couldn't yank off the basket." Francis showed me his burned fingers. "This is what I get for playing the fool.

"Come...let's go into the studio, where you keep your fossils from the Alps. I want you to explain again how you have estimated the age of the earth from your shells and ferns. I can't seem to grasp that the earth is as old as you say it is.

"Look at this rock, Maestro, with the snail imbedded in it. Where did you find it? Did you find it in the Argentière Pass?"

"No, I found it when I climbed Monte Rosa, when I was making notes on the quality of light among the glaciers and snowfields. You see that snail came from the ocean...it's an ocean snail..."

⚜

Today the new barber trimmed my hair and beard.

He is chief barber for the King, a Corsican, red-faced, rotund, about forty; he seems in the prime of life. As he trimmed my beard he ranted about autonomies, puny city against puny city.

"War is a sewer," he kept repeating. "Man is crap...he is great. But he must stop fighting." All very private, in his red-carpeted shop, mirrored, hung with dirks. One of many small rooms along a château corridor.

As I was about to leave, he said:

"I sing...you like music, I know... I sing for you... I am an exile too, but I sing."

His tenor voice was at its prime. He poured out song after song, as others gathered in the corridor and room to hear him.

(Tomorrow, he will extract a molar for Francesco.)

As I write in my studio, rain splashes across leaded glass and sputters on my autumn fire. I dictate. Francesco nods at his desk; it is late, well after midnight.

> Fame, in the figure of a bird, should be depicted as covered with little tongues instead of feathers.

> Pleasure and pain are best shown as twins, back to back, since they are inseparable.

"No, no," Francesco objects. "I think we should write down important things."

I agree.

I pick up a paper and read about heat...fire...vapors...water sucked from the ocean.

Yes, I must discriminate. I have over a hundred treatises to work on...the days are passing quickly.

"Let's stop for now... I know it's late. Tomorrow I will arrange fifteen figures, fifteen nudes, in sequence. On the basis of those drawings I will make various comparisons, the horse with man, the legs of frogs with the legs of men."

Cloux
October 6, 1518

This is my second autumn at the château—cold, cold! Windy. Bundled up, I walk. Maple, oak, chestnut, pine...lightning-scarred oak, crippled pine, friends... I walk alone or with Francesco or the King, paths for every direction. Alone, or with Francesco, I am aware of the past.

Tonight, at supper, by our studio fire, talking with Francesco, I talked about my maestro, Andrea.

"I was twenty, like you, Francesco. And I was always hungry—like you. Andrea was thirty-five then, maybe thirty-six...twenty...thirty-six. I was lucky to have him for maestro."

His skill with jewelry was something to remember. I remember his setting a fire opal in a gold brooch... I'd been his apprentice for several months, maybe a year. Not a word was said while he worked, an entire afternoon. A smile, a nod...

The opal was rectangular and its blob of fire was at its base—resembling a setting sun—the gem surrounded by finely woven wires.

And there was a day when Andrea's famous sphere was polished and ready. How it glistened! How proud he was, how proud all of us artists were! We crowded around; we left the workshop to sing a *te deum* and drink wine as it was hoisted aloft, to embellish the dome of the cathedral.

"Verrochio...Andrea Verrochio," we yelped.

And the copper sphere is still there, above the red tiles, unharmed by lightning.

He was a flawless craftsman with the porphyry and marble walls of the Medici sarcophagus. And his beautiful *putto*, boy and dolphin, are loved by everyone.

F's drawings of Andrea's *David*, and his silverpoint study of Andrea's great bronze horse are treasures of mine.

Well, his *bottega* was a place of magic...subtleties in metal and wood.

Again it's late. Francesco is playing cards at the château—Parisian girls. The cat has disappeared. Lamps need fixing on my table. Will I every finish revising these treatises, re-arranging them?

Di me se mai fu fatta alcuna cosa.

Andrea dead at fifty-three!

Di me se mai...four words...scattered among my mathematical papers, among my drawings: *Is anything ever done!*

I was twenty...he was thirty-six...genial.

He believed art was the zenith. He asked: What do men respect most? Laws? Writings? They respect the bronze horse, the jeweled necklace...the alabaster vase...the cameo...the bas-relief...great murals...antiquities!

Old thoughts now, but new then, important then.

Andrea often praised such accomplishments. How often we talked in his small garden, trellised with wisteria and grape, his sister, Margharita, looking after us. He had a scar across his right cheek, a special smile because of it. What an aura there was at his home—like nowhere else. Simple, family accord, everyone doing his part.

I remember something Andrea said:

"When I shivered as a child, I knew an angel had passed by."

Cloux
Manor House

Early morning. Good light. Francesco and I worked at our easels until lunch. Cold.

At lunch, F said:

"I lost again at cards last night... I can't speak French well enough to win. It's lucky for me that everyone's leaving here this weekend...off for Paris."

We talked about Paris and the King's departure (how desolate he would leave the château!): we talked about the Alps. I mentioned my climbs and the fossils I found...the caves...with shells on the floor... I showed F my memory-sketch of huge male bison painted on the granite walls of a cave, painted there before any Florentine painted. I tried to find a primitive carving on a piece of bone but couldn't locate it: I wanted him to realize how clever those ancient artists were.

F was interested in the avalanches, and asked me the best season for a climb. He will ask his father to accompany him on an Alpine trip...he's eager to return to his beautiful Vaprio. I certainly understand. Last month the Melzis renewed their invitation but I lack the strength to make another move; perhaps, in a year or two, I might leave here without offending the King—perhaps I can obtain a commission in Milan; then I could use the Villa Vaprio for my base.

In the afternoon, because it was sunny and inviting, we had our horses saddled and rode through the *bois*...a fox plumed his tail in front of us... I tried to sketch on horseback but my sorrel was very restless. What fascinating shadows in the woodland—when the sun is low! How to blend them.

I am confused, cold.

I wrote in my journal a day or two ago, it seems; yet, tonight, I can't recall the date; I seem to be in an unknown country, not France, not Switzerland. This place is not my place. I am somewhere by a warm fireplace fire. What confusion. The fire stares at me.

Through the open doorway I see my canvas of *St. John*...the painting assures me. Ah, the King has gone. F has gone. It is as if I had been asleep.

An assistant and I are making and repairing brushes; we are also grinding pigments (how hard it is to find someone who cares to do quality work); having discovered that my scale is inaccurate I am checking the grinding. It is no wonder my *Saint John* colors blend poorly. A faulty scale is a great hindrance.

I am troubled by the shading in John's face: underneath his eyes—so important.

"Patience," I say to myself.

I have heard that admonition through the years, hollow, utterly sadistic.

The pleasure in painting is perfection!

I have heard that.

Pleasure and perfection are illusions, friend!

An artist frames his illusions and gilds the frames and people gape at the illusions and then foster more illusions.

Years ago, as a youngster, I liked to sit in front of the marble façade of Santa Maria Novella.

In the wintertime it could be a balmy spot.

Girls...but I would sit there and imagine that the twin obelisks in front of the church were being lugged off on the backs of their immense bronze turtles, four turtles for each obelisk. (What mad sculptor designed turtles to hold up obelisks!) Ai, the marble columns tottered across the piazza; the monks and priests, with penises dangling, dashed out of church and monastery, shrieking to heaven for help.

Maybe it was helpful to think such ridiculous thoughts; maybe it erased problems; there were always problems...on Sunday no hawkers were permitted in the piazza...pigeons took over, kids, wings, laughter.

⚜

Francis, so young, so arrogant, showers me with praise at every opportunity. He introduces me to his friends: "My Leonard!" He introduces me as "Mon Père." He calls me "Maestro...architect...engineer...he's designing the main staircase at Chambord...this is Count de Senlis, a connoisseur of art." The Count, an old man, is one of Francis' "oldest friends." Monsignor Marais admires my paintings. Lingers. Cardinal Chambiges compliments my work with sincerity, makes an offer on behalf of his church in Rheims. There are artisans from Suresnes. There is an Italian group, enroute to Paris. However, it is not so much the visitors, the guests, as the King himself—his fondness for me.

Surely Cloux is everything I need.

Old paths, old benches, newly pollarded trees, beds of flowers, autumn leaves, moonlight...at night I hear the owls talking.

⚜

Cloux
Studio

Winter evenings, cold evenings, before a roaring fire in my walk-in fireplace, my lamps lit, I sometimes read aloud two or three of my fables. Guests applaud. We enjoy *hors d'oeuvres*, sip claret. What lavish trays arrive from the King's kitchens!

The King has a poet in residence who likes to recite female poetry—for the pomades and perfumes! He is a hunchback, with a sharp tongue and tragic grey eyes in his young blond face. Courtiers tell me he has completed an epic poem about my *Battle of the Anghieri...*

A couple of weeks ago, Galeazzo, a local hunter, dragged a bear cub into my studio. He was quite docile for a while and then became too frisky, and had to be led away. Galeazzo promises to bring him again, and I will sketch him.

⚜

Francesco found this fable of mine in an old notebook, one of those I used to keep in Italy:

A stone lay on a mound where an attractive woodland shaded it. Herbs and flowers of many colors grew around. As the stone looked about, at the stones in the road winding below, it wanted to drop down onto the road.

The stone said to itself: "What am I doing, sitting here, among these plants all day long? I want to be with the other stones, my sisters and brothers."

So, during a heavy rain, it managed to roll down and stop among the rocks of the road. In a short while it began to feel the weight of the cart wheels, the crack of horse and mule hooves, the tramp of cattle, the kick of travelers' shoes. A man knocked the stone to one side, another spilled trash on it. A cart wheel chipped it. The dung of a cow splattered it. The roadway became very hot.

The stone gazed back at the place it had left—its place of solitude.

This is what happens to those who think they can live tranquilly in cities.

Francesco feels this is my best fable, although he does not think much of any of them:

"Remember, Maestro, you are not Aesop."

A nut, carried by a raven to the top of a tall campanile, fell into a chink. As it lay there, it asked the wall, by the grace of God and the fine bells in the tower, to help it survive since it had fallen into a chink without any soil. The wall was sympathetic and was glad to help the nut roll into a place where there was soil. After a time, the nut began to split and send out roots. Soon the roots worked their way between the stones of the tower. As it grew stronger it began to destroy the campanile.

The old tower bewailed its destruction, but it was too late!

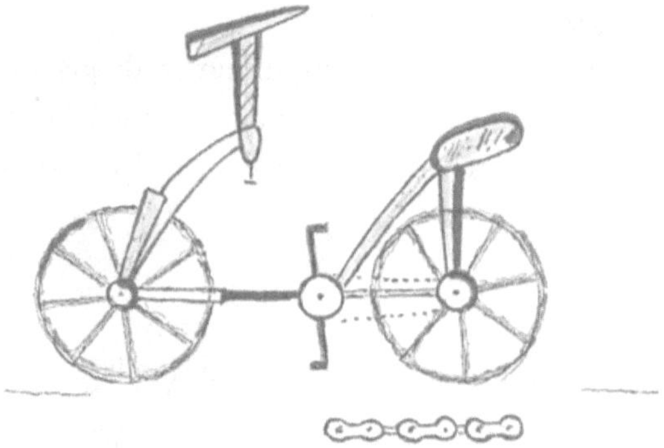

Tonight, Francesco and I have been working for hours: he sits at his big desk with two water-lamps close to his bearded face, his silhouette on the wall. He is only twenty-two, but appears to be older in the lamplight.

He will be a great painter, when he is free of my influence. He should set up an atelier of his own in Florence or Milan. He comes alive in Milan. He endures this exile out of respect for me: for him I am both maestro and father (in his own father's eyes the world of art is unimportant). In his patient, almost ecclesiastical voice, Francesco repeated the outline we have prepared; here are items we have sorted out for further evaluation:

1 - The inequality in the concavity of a ship.
2 - Inequalities in the curves of the sides of ships.
3 - Investigations as to the best positions of the tiller.
4 - The meetings and unions of water coming from different directions.

5 - A study of shoals formed under river sluices.
6 - The configuration of the shores of rivers and their permanency.

These studies should be of value to mariners.
Francesco finds that much of the information I had recorded is spotty.
Tomorrow we will begin with item 1.

October 28, '18

A lavish autumn!

Gold leaves float on the river, and, as I walk along, admiring them, a handsome riderless horse crosses, shakes his mane vigorously, plunges wherever the water is deep, then stands on the shore for a few moments, regarding me.

Again and again the fog becomes total master here: blanketed by this Loire curtain, we are obliterated almost nightly: a visitor would have a hard time locating the château. King Francis, and his retinue and parasites, have fled to Paris for the winter.

I have hours to contemplate his Italian plunder: in his salons, his superb collection of Mazzoni marbles—twenty-one major pieces.

I study and admire the King's Bataille tapestries. My private gallery. My autumn sun, as well. Sometimes Francesco makes the gallery a gallery for two. With autumn rain or wind. He sketches a Mazzoni bust; I sketch a Mazzoni figure. I am learning to appreciate the man's skill: it helps my exile.

Yesterday, as I left the château, the handsome horse re-appeared, trotting along a path that leads into the forest. Bobbing his head as if in recognition, he walked toward the manor house with me. He's a grey, with mixed mane. It was growing dark and his color blurred into the dusk.

I came to Amboise three, or was it four years ago?

The easel of time totters against invisible walls.

I grow thinner.

Maturina urges me to eat more.

"Give up your vegetarian food. Let me fix you a strong beef soup...let me casserole a chicken!"

A letter from Salai.

He is completing his house on the vineyard property. As usual, his letter is brief—painfully brief. Where is the love we once shared? I know that friendships are like old clothes, they wear out. But we were more than friends.

If we live long enough we may achieve maturity: we will have the past to guide us: we will confront the future more wisely: I write this, wondering about myself: is this something, this saying, that applies to someone else? I know that blind courage sustains me. I know that somehow we must circumvent the Cesares and Savonarolas.

⚜

December 2nd

At Vinci, winter, spring, summer, we used to attend early Mass: Mother had her favorite seat, near the altar, close to her Jesus: I remember her somber clothes, her yellow hair in a spiral. Her face was the face of a madonna, and the way she looked at me lit up my face; so, we walked, hand in hand, or with her hand on my shoulder. Through the years I have seen us walking there, at Vinci, a hundred times: were we always alone together? It seems that way. Was the church beautiful? It seems so.

She disapproved of the sermons:

"Latin rote...I can teach you...listen to me."

I listened.

"There are three things for you to remember. One is gentleness. The other: honesty. The third: beauty. Look...look at this sky, the clouds, the birds, our cypress trees, our church."

I looked.

⚜

December 4th

Alone, walking in the fog along the Loire, in the early morning, I saw him. Magnifico. Crossing. Splashing. Approaching.

That night he appeared in a dream: the Christ of my mural was walking along beside him, His hand buried in Magnifico's thick mane. Christ was saying something about feeding him: plenty of grain in your stall, we must see to that.

A week or so ago, Judas visited me. In the dream he seemed to be standing at the foot of my bed: he complained about the cold, the falling snow: his face had become scarred; he appeared much older. Feeble.

Alone...I have learned there is something sacred about being alone. I was...

For next Saturday and Sunday

Write to Machiavelli—invite him again
Draw steering armature for bicycle
Collect leaf specimens along Loire
Re-sketch stairway at Romorantin
Invite the King—arrange sketches for him—show him Francesco's copy of my *Salvator*

Cloux

Visiting here, the Parisian architect, Pierre Arconati, admires my canvas of Saint John and my Mona. What a genial man, a student of the masters, devoted to all of the arts, dapper, young, fluent in Italian, he brought a portfolio of exquisite architectural renderings of Parisian commissions.

I showed him my drawings for the Chambord and Romorantin châteaux. We went over them in detail and he was especially interested in my spiral staircase. He, too, is a vegetarian. We had lunch together and swapped dietary ideas. Of course he can find unique foods in Paris—things we can't obtain at Amboise.

As I showed him around the château and manor house, he was enthusiastic about living in the country...when the gardeners' pet fawn ate out of his hand, he turned to me:

"I find the city difficult... I hope Amboise is right for you," he said. "How did you like Rome?"

Here is my list of drawings and sketches at Cloux, work I wish retained:

Façade of a residence.
Dome of a church, with cupolas.

Lock on a canal.
Motor, with falling weight and ratchet arrangement.
Proportions of man (Vitruvius).
Star of Bethlehem plant and spurge.
Machine for grinding telescopic mirrors.
Life preserver.
Parabolic compass.

Sforza horse (Cermonino).
20 silverpoint drawings of horses.
Sketch of sailboat. Weaving machine.
Pincers for hoisting heavy objects.
Sketch of windmill.
Planetary clock.
Parachute.

Birds in flight—30.
Man in flight.
Gliders.
Helicopter.
Insects.
Drawing of Ginevra Benci.
Crayon of Cecilia Gallerani.
Silverpoints of Boltraffio, Salai, Marco d'Oggiono, Francesco Melzi.
Head of Christ.
Disciples.
Series of *Last Supper* drawings.

Astronomy: distance of sun and earth.
Anatomy: 60 drawings—
Muscles of upper limbs,
muscles of legs,
muscles of back.
Bone structures,
veins.
Complete skeleton, skull, hands.

Studies of horses for *Adoration of the Magi.*
Preliminaries for *Leda.*
Studies for *Anne.*
Saint John.
Geologic studies.
Deluge drawings.
Châteaux drawings.

FIFTY YEARS OF WORK:

	Hours of work
12,000 Sketches	20,000
400 Major Drawings	10,000
20 Easel Paintings	20,000
125 Treatises (still incomplete)	16,000
Murals (and their cartoons)	15,000
Bronzes	15,000
Dissections and Anatomy Studies	10,000
Engineering Projects (canals, locks, swamps)	20,000
Architecture, Music, Horology	10,000
Maps, Geometry	5,000
Geometry, Hydraulics	5,000
	146,000

N.B. I have destroyed 188 drawings. I have retained several maps, and I may retain several drawings of people here at Amboise. Francesco is to destroy most of the military sketches and drawings because many are lifted from old books and manuscripts. It was my intention to compile an encyclopedia of machines of all kinds.

1519

Cloux
January 3, 1519

I am very tired after a long horseback ride. Francesco and I rode miles along the river—exploring. Where the ground became swampy we road through forest (the King's Forest), following vague roads and paths. Somewhere, in the thick of the woods, we roused an elk. The animal crashed into a ravine, and disappeared. We saw fox and squirrel, ravens, an owl. The bird was dumbwitted on a stump, too sleepy, too careless to fly. At a clearing we alarmed poachers who raced off, leaving their slaughtered buck, their bows and quivers beside it.

Tired of the thick shade and the monotony of old trees, we headed for Amboise, but soon found out that we were lost. It was a tedious ride before Francesco detected the sound of water; it was good to dismount and drink at the Loire.

Back in our saddles, we trotted along a sandy road, wide enough for a carriage. Cecchino began to sing and whistle. There was sunlight. Evening clouds built up a sunset. Presently we saw the hulk of Amboise in the distance.

So we began the new year!

"*Bonne Année*!" Francesco yelled at the château walls.

January 7, 1519

BEATRICE D'ESTE—Painting Beatrice d'Este was troublesome because she seldom kept her sittings. She was moody, flighty. Her sallow features defied changes in light and shade. I wanted to impart a special quality to her portrait, a sense of youth, interest beyond the face itself. I tried animals in her arms, birds, flowers.

"You're too fussy, Leonard...all this bother...let's get the ugly thing finished! You don't remember that I'm busy. When I'm late, you fuss at me. Scowl. Tomorrow is the Spring Ball, yes, yes, it's tomorrow!" And she would babble on, in French, in Italian, stamp her foot, gesture, swear. Child-wife, she was child-model.

She felt I should concentrate on her favorite jewels, her rubies, her pearl snood, her diamond shoulder-pin!

"I insist," she would storm.

It was Boltraffio who painted her jewelry—when she was away from the studio.

"I hope the paint cracks on her jewels," he snorted, disliking her.

When she died, in '96, I tried to visit the Duke, to present the finished portrait. He refused to see me. Inconsolable, I was told.

Beatrice was twenty-two or twenty-three when she died; she had been married to Ludovico for seven years. Everyone said the Duke loved her profoundly. He also adored his mistress, Lucrezia. He also adored Cecilia. Love, for Duke Ludovico, was living.

Inconsolable? How long was he inconsolable?

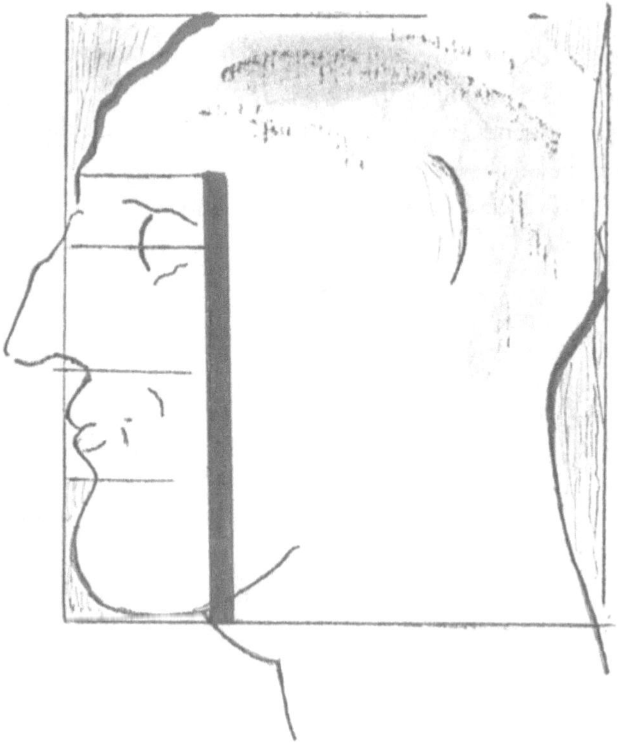

GINEVRA DE BENCI—I painted her in the autumn and painted autumn into her hair, painted it into the juniper trees in the background, in the dress she wore, in her eyes.

I was twenty-two!

She was a sickly person, cold; yet I admired her: she posed with patience, understanding my tedious brush strokes, praising my skill. A woman of scientific inclination, she had learned much from my friend Amerigo, her geographer father.

When I studied geography with Amerigo, at his home, she would appear from time to time, and I would try to memorize the contours of her face, the coloring of her skin in different lights, her bearing. I wanted to appreciate her personality.

Sometimes, in the studio, Ginevra would preach her father's ideas; I think she was trying to see how much I respected his concepts as cartographer. She could be rude, blunt. She tried to sail to the New World. She wanted to be the first woman to circumnavigate the world. She thought I had no right to discourage her.

"You are no sailor... I have sailed more than you!"

In her boldness, she dictated changes in her father's maps. This was forty-five years ago, when some of us believed *Virtutem Forma Decorat.*

Cloux
January 10, 1519

CECILIA GALLERANI—It was totally different with Cecilia's portrait: the painting and the sittings went well.

As Ludovico's fourth or fifth mistress, she had learned artfulness: she was smiles, warm hands, long, slender fingers, warm embraces, kisses. Always in agreement. Soft-voiced. Fond of poetry. Music. Enjoyed eating, sipping wine, walking, flowers. When we were in bed together, she knew how, when. Her breasts were small. Ivory. Her body was compact, delightful. The shape of her skull was more to my liking than any woman's.

I like to think that all of my models are still alive...

Here is Cecilia's ermine, eating from his dish...he's very much alive...here he comes, trotting across the floor, jumping into her lap, cuddling, ready for another pose.

Cloux
February 2, 1519

Tomorrow there is to be a sumptuous banquet in the château, again royalty. Three hundred guests, I hear: Germans, Dutch, Austrian, Swiss, two or three British, a Greek potentate; the majority will be Parisians and the château people. I will have one of my puppets, dressed as a hunter, in fur cap, etc., relate my fable about the great elk of Scandinavia.

I have constructed a papier-mâché lion—in yellow, black, and pink. He will walk a few steps down the center aisle of the banquet room, growl at the guests, then open his mouth to reveal a bouquet of white lilies.

Last week I was ill (my whole body ached), and I could not attend the masque ball.

At the ball, boxers fought in an arena, sawdust-floored; there were Swiss dancers and yodelers; sword swallowers performed: they are the rage now.

Michelangelo sleeps on my lap.

Cloux
February 11

Outside, as I write, a girl is singing, in the chilly, windy afternoon:

Châtaignes piquantes!
Châtaignes chatouillantes!
Que chatouillent la cuisse,
Mais qui piquent la poche!

Now I hear another child—an Italian, a boy of six or seven, way back in time, singing, as he runs an errand.

When I was a boy...it's true...I was happy: Mother made me happy: hand in hand we walked, at sunset time...she liked to sing as she worked in her kitchen...we sometimes sang together, "bread songs," she called them.

I made drawings for her, little gifts, on scraps of paper, a flowering geranium, a lizard, the figure of a clay dog...

Vinci...its hills, its sun, the trees, the caves, the rocks...they made me happy...grapes made me happy, the *clairette*, pinkish and very sweet; the yellow-green muscats, so fat...grapes, laughter...kindness...

I still taste those grapes on Maturina's table.

⚜

Cloux

In the afternoon heat, it was a long drive to Pliny's Villa, outside Rome. Enroute, I witnessed some of the wretchedness of Rome's slums; we were detained by waifs and by a number of mentally retarded. My driver's glib humor, levelled at the poor, gnawed at me until we reached the villa among its cypress and olive. There I walked through derelict rooms, some with views of the Tyrrhenian Sea...summer rooms...winter rooms...dining rooms...library. I saw swimming pools, fountain, turrets, Numidian columns, Luna marble. The sea boomed and Pliny, the upright Roman, governor, senator, consul, killer of Christians, stood before me in his white toga:

P - I respect your portico mural but it must be finished by the New Year. Our banquet hall will be ready at that time...we are preparing festivities—you understand. Your unicorn motif is overdone in color...several sea creatures are neglected, it seems to me.

LdV - Then you are dissatisfied?

P - I wouldn't say that, but changes, changes might be made.

LdV - A matter of details, perhaps?

P - Correct. A matter of details. You are to consult with Valerius. He will...

LdV - And your payments? I must remind you...they're in arrears.

P - You will speak to Antonius, my secretary. This is a bad season...the harvests are poor... I have obligations...charities. It was exceedingly hot in Rome today...good evening.

And those walls, mosaics, turrets, frescoes, pillars, arches; what sort of luck had their artisans, fifteen hundred years ago? The opulence of Pliny...the opulent sea...millions of sesterces...banquets...Nero...Otho...Titus... Can Rome become an art center?

After exploring the villa, I ate my bread and cheese by the shore, sitting on the sand. Sketchbook on my lap, I sketched seabirds and a torn shoreline tree.

Kicking aside leaves from a mosaic floor, I visioned a mosaic: in my mosaic of green, brown and white were squared circles, spirals, nudes, sea horses.

A pretty girl passed by, selling figs from a shoulder basket. I bought six, three for me, and three for the driver.

⚜

Cloux

Was it ten years ago, at Piombino, that green shadows sprawled across the walls of bayside houses, with sun, hot sun, on the bay? Sun on the moat of the town's doddering fortress, on the plumed helmets of its entry guards.

I made sketches at the harborside inn, made them on a long balcony table; I made harbor maps and drawings for a windmill; I added sketches of a spool-winding machine; I remember I evolved my machine for polishing crystals. My sketchbook filled...my ellipsograph, my new perspectograph, a pair of improved compasses.

Yesterday, as I sorted these sketches, memories came back.

And here at the château, I must see to it that the pale, long-legged, crooked-nosed Frog finishes my brass compass. He has kept me waiting for more than a month—these dilatory French! Can the artist live forever—like a Pope!

At Piombino, a fisherman helped me locate fossils on the beach. A small lizard, a multi-veined leaf. What was the fisherman's name? Giorgio? Paolo? Doesn't matter. We became friends. Bearded rogue. Fat. In his rowboat, we sailed the harbor, weathering calms and wild gusts, in and out of bays, eating cheese and bread, sipping port, catching fish, his oars a pair of misshapen flippers. With his tools, at his home, above the bay, I designed oars, shaped them, edged them with thin copper. When he tested them he found that he rowed with ease.

"Fine...Maestro, fine!"

Blue rowboat, blue bay.

We rigged a sail, a drab hunk but it worked. His name? Not Paolo, but Rimini. Obese fishmonger Rimini. Excellent bread was baked by his young, mute wife. Bread, cheese, wine. Rimini often sang, with his Piombino slurring, sang as we drifted, sang and rowed. We sailed far away from the odious wars, from weaponry, forts, and death.

Rimini's gulls, black-tipped gulls, followed his boat, ate out of his hands—perched on my shoulders. Ah, those wings! Those flights!

Occasionally, I slept at Rimini's thatch, where ducks always woke me. It was pleasant to wake to the quackings of Rimini's pets. His drake had been his pet for years, I won't guess how many. But I remember his glossy plumage and proud head, and how gluttonous he was.

When Rimini's pretty wife (woman) became bedridden I prescribed omitting meat. She agreed, through our sign language. Within a week she was out of bed. Rimini had a *festa*, to honor her recovery. Poor man, he thought me something of a wizard, an ogre, because I could explain to him what the interior of the stomach was like.

⚜

February 13

Francesco and I have spent hours at the Château Romorantin, where remodeling of the old rambling building goes badly. The weather is mean. Cough weather. Stormy. Romorantin is no place to live in February. My drawing papers go limp there.

The King is seldom around; his disreputable workers look as if they had come out of a tenth century nightmare. Some have quit because of the weather; I am told that the head architect is sick.

My supervision nets me nothing, does not help the King.

Francesco groans as we make the rounds of inspection.

Enroute to Cloux the carriage breaks an axle as we near the château and manor house. Rain. A few days later we backtrack to Romorantin on horses. Carriages would not get through. The sun comes out... Francesco and I work in the main salon.

As I work on my rendering of the new staircase, an old pine tree crashes against a window, shattering it. Workers snigger as I jump and drop my pad. The present stair may collapse at any moment.

We eat lunch before a handsome Gothic fireplace. A woodcutter tosses on chunks... I continue working...the King appears...he is gone before I can speak to him.

⚜

Romorantin again: the Queen occupies a wing that has been recently renovated—she and her court. I have learned that when the King is too preoccupied with his current mistress, the Queen moves in. Up go her tapestries. Up go her pictures. In go her dogs, cats, guards, maids, pages—and favorite chef.

As Francesco and I strolled through corridors, hunting for the illusive architect (now recovered), we find doors open into the Queen's suites; there is sun; the weather has improved; at one of the open doorways, Francesco grabbed my arm, and exclaimed:

"Maestro...look...look in there!"

"Where?"

"To the right...through the door...on that easel...that's your painting, your *Leda* and her swan!"

I can't believe what I see!

"Yes...yes..." I mumble.

"It's your painting, your missing canvas. How did the Queen get it?"

"Come...we'll find out about it...come away...don't go inside."

"But it's yours."

It was seven or eight years ago that my *Leda* painting disappeared. We blamed this one and that one. We offered a reward. The Duke promised to help...

Back at Cloux we have talked and talked about *Leda*. What can I say to the King?

Why has he never mentioned the picture? Had he purchased it from someone? Had his father purchased it? Was it a gift? Or is it a copy? We could ascertain that if we could inspect the painting. There were too many questions for the moment. We needed to think. We needed to concentrate on our work for a few days.

We will talk to people at Romorantin...some of the Queen's girls will talk...perhaps what Francesco saw is an excellent copy.

The weather improves...but I am depressed: I will not return to Romorantin.

In the sun (cold sun), Francesco and I ride slowly along the Loire. I hope to see Magnifico.

⚜

HORSES...

Francis has some of the finest horses in France. His stables are comparable to those of the Medici's.

Though I seldom ride now, except to walk the horse or shake my depression, I still visit the stables: I can spend hours there among their warm bodies: I note ears, nostrils, teeth, manes, tails, rumps, shoulders, hides, colors.

Colts.

Mares.

Stallions.

Favorites!

Sickly animals become mine: I feed them, pamper them, talk to them, comb and brush them...hostlers are sometimes irritated... I do not care...in that stabled world I become one with animal life.

I gather grain and fill a trough.

An old girl needs water: how grateful she is! This beautiful pinto needs liniment.

Horses...

My drawings show their illustrious qualities, their courage, their stamina.

⚜

Cloux

A young Parisian portrait artist visited me; he was wearing a new grey velvet suit (in the King's honor, he pointed out). With arms crossed on his boyish chest he defended his dedication to portraiture.

He examined my paintings with friendly admiration but bristled when I said that it is not enough to paint one thing well. I said that anyone studying a single aspect of art for a lifetime can attain a measure of perfection! An accomplished artist must paint nudes, seascapes, animals, birds, plants.

Spitting into my fireplace, coughing, the fellow said:

"Do you call your *Mona Lisa* and your *Saint John* landscapes?"

I could sense that he was annoyed by my French.

So, his handsome, goateed, disappointed face went out in the rain—rain on his velvet suit.

And I began rethinking: why have I painted few landscapes, seascapes (in the Dutch tradition); why have I painted so many madonnas? I should paint deluge scenes, glaciers, Vinci.

Rain on his velvet suit.

⚜

How can I continue my journal when it grows increasingly difficult to write? Left hand or right hand, I am troubled. I am troubled in other ways: I walk into another room and can't remember why I left my desk. Where is that sable brush Francesco brought me from Paris? I am unable to recall names. And F—sits there, perturbed, as I attempt to remember. I also forget facts, and I am at a serious loss. What is to be the outcome? As I review my treatises, I am aware that they are worthy; it seems to me I have an adequate grasp of language; yet. Writing is not my *métier*. I prefer a silverpoint or a chalk drawing or the infinite pleasure of oil colors. Sitting in the cold window sun, I sip Chablis...

Francesco, wearing his newly tailored suit, continues his portrait of a young woman—progressing nicely. He hates to lay down his brushes. If I have a suggestion it is a minor one; he absorbs whatever I say with pleasure.

As I stand in his room, before his easel, watching his brush, appreciating the light, I think:

"We are moderns...we are scientific artists. The face, a. b. c. d., responds to light on opaque pigment, as we have determined. We realize that a shadow can distort; we must estimate the value of each overlay..."

Then, sitting down, aware of the pleasant viridian background in Francesco's painting, my eyes blur: I feel like I am falling asleep: then, the river horse, my Magnifico, appears inside the pigment.

Yesterday, or the day before, Francesco learned that my *Leda* is a copy, purchased by the King's father, five or six years ago.

I do not miss the dirt and stink of the *botteghe* or the sink holes of Florence, Milan, and Rome. Too often they smelled alike. *Botteghe* was spilled glue, dust,

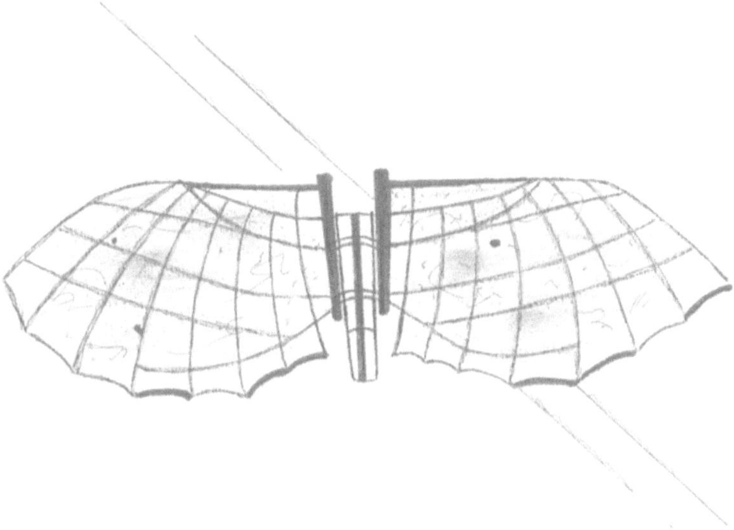

roaches, flies, antique casts (how quickly they got broken), rusted pots, rags, gold leaf (always being stolen), sketches, frames, saws, chalk, nails, rats. Someone was always leaving food around, wine bottles; there were broken bottles, cracked pestles, chunks of clay, mineral samples, stools, grease, brooms (that nobody wanted to use), mauled papers, waste paper...brushes...brushes...brushes.

To paint, to write, to think.

Life's chiaroscuro!

⚜

Under chestnut trees, in the grove near the château, I sat alone on a bench, aware of the evening's beauty; as I sat there, the sun became a red ball behind a string of pines. I felt that Caterina was beside me, she and Magnifico. I think I stood and shoved my fingers into Magnifico's tangled mane as Caterina whispered to both of us. It was almost dark but I could outline the oval of her face—her mouth and eyes smiling. Around us, in the grove, the wind was dropping leaves. The night promised to be cold...

Cold.

I looked at the Milky Way, as Caterina and I had in Italy, from our bench in our small garden, while the city slept. She said something to me about our daughter.

"Who will..."

For some reason, a reason I can not understand very well (a fumbling reason), I have gone through some of my luggage. I have come across some drawn work Mother made: flowers and angels, in perfection: *punto en aria.* How white the threads—after all these years! I see no lace like hers. She was first or second at every annual *festa.*

And my father left me a legacy also: his is a literary legacy of four curt letters, notary letters: our home life, under his coercion, slowly disintegrated. Coercion and promiscuity. Fatal combinations. But why glance at ruins? I glance at them because they are a part of me.

Francesco has repaired my portable bathtub. Soon I will be able to luxuriate again.

I hope there are sunny days ahead... I am reading Aesop... Confused, I feel I am repeating myself in my journal; I must check through my pages. Weariness says I must stop writing and yet as I write I think of the sun in the garden below and the peacocks below and I think of the sun that has burned for me for many years and I think of the shadows I have observed, the shadows of weeping willows, the shadow of a lifted marble arm and hand, the shadows of birds... I think of spring foliage coming...the first spring flowers and there is a wonderful haze in these thoughts tied in with the sun...the haze makes me feel I am young; I am able to climb hills, ride Magnifico; tomorrow I start a painting of Hercules firing his arrows at the Stymphalian birds. As I put away my journal some of that light blurs in perspective, and I think how light bends at night when lamps are lit.

I seem...

Cloux

The date, does it matter?

My right arm has become paralyzed. Gradually. It has happened gradually. Now I can not manipulate my fingers. For a while I could manipulate one or two. I hoped they would recover. I think this affliction began on the strenuous ride from Milan to Amboise. I think it began in the monastery where I was stricken for a while.

The King's physicians have tried to help...they are trying to bring back muscular control. They have prescribed herbs, poultices, hot concoctions. Strange, very strange, to have a hand that hangs by my side, a hand that does nothing, that is already dead.

Cloux
March 2, 1519

The greater one is, the greater one's capacity for suffering. It should be that the greater one is, the greater is one's capacity for courage and understanding. Why do we suffer?

Nec spe nec metu.

Cloux
March 5

Fifty years ago...fifty!

Whether it was *chiaroscuro*, *sfumoto*, encaustic, or other technique, I was sincere. Few days were long enough.

Florence, fifty years ago...it was my town. I fitted in. The place is no longer the same. The guilds are different. The workshops are different. Most of my friends are dead or gone. There is another kind of politics.

A half century ago life was adventure: life was new: friends were new, work was new: there was love. When I was accused of homosexuality some of that libel pervaded my thinking for years. A personal plague. How easy it was to brand a man in those days: the "telltale" box hung on the church door. You wrote your accusation and dropped it in the slot and scurried off.

So much of life is focused on sex, is wasted on sex. I have been a masturbation man. For long my body has nothing to share with any woman or man. I am immersed in thought. In my bed I have loneliness as mate. I patronize no one.

⚜

One of the château gardeners, a Venetian, who has been very friendly with me, has presented me with a caged oriole. In a woven reed cage, painted black.

Black!

I carried the cage outdoors, into the morning mist; I set it down. The bird fluttered, trembled. How long had it been captive? I knelt. I could see where he had chipped off black paint with his beak.

Black!

I opened the door.

A male, he battered the reeds with all his strength, found the opening, and hurtled into the sky.

⚜

I have forgotten more than I can recall: perhaps this is true of most of us who have lived a long life. Many of the things I have forgotten I have wished to forget. I find it hard to live and harbor grudges, but it is also lack of wisdom to erase the mind; then it may be necessary to experience our mistakes again: that's being trapped twice; a fox avoids that.

As for survival, I have survived because I found something to discover: discovery is the key: new sinew, new mineral, new color, new face, new canal, new lamp.

In Andrea's studio I discovered perspective. There is so much about perspective that eludes one—a continual challenge.

Perspective may be the most important of all the art disciplines. In this branch of science, the beam of light is best explained by mathematics and physics. Since the axioms are long I will abridge them now:

There are three branches of perspective: 1 - The first deals with the reasons for the diminution of objects as they recede, and is known as diminishing perspective. 2 - The second deals with the way colors vary as they recede. 3 - The third is concerned with the way objects in a picture must be finished in relation to their proximity. I amplify these three in my treatise on perspective.

I have admired hands, respected them for their capabilities. As I dissected, I marveled at their intricacy and perfection... I admire all classes: the feminine, the masculine, children's hands. I made drawings of my own hands, in the days I could squeeze the crabprongs of a horseshoe with ease. I remember Mother's loving hands, Caterina's sensual hands, Andrea's clever, slender fingers. There have been clay and bronze and marble hands. The hands of beautiful women have appeared in my dreams. I can perceive, as I write, the hands of Christ and those of His disciples.

Perhaps there will be a few, reading this journal, who may care to know some of my thoughts about painting:

a - All colors, when placed in the shade, seem of equal degree of darkness. b - All colors, when placed in full light, seldom vary from their essential hue. c - The eyes, out-of-doors, in a illuminated atmosphere, perceive darkness behind the windows of houses which nevertheless are light. d - The eyes perceive and recognize objects with greater intensity in proportion as the pupil is dilated.

⚜

Sleep is a curious thing—resembling death.

Sometimes it is totally blank, as death must be; sometimes we see destruction.

Flames rise. Buildings collapse. Sometimes we hear animals talk. Without moving, they run away from us. Sometimes we fall from great heights—without harm. Sometimes we talk to those who are unseen. Sometimes we meet those who can't speak. If we do not sense death in our sleep we may sense confusion. Confusion in black and white. Or grey. We dream of bucolic scenes in grey, a grey stream, a grey tree, grey boulders. We stroll through grey air, grey birds in the sky.

Now, in color, a great hawk threatens us. Angels appear. There is a cave with a ragged mouth. It wants to swallow us. Now cadavers threaten. Enemies besiege us.

Now, a friend appears—a childhood friend, unchanged by time.

Christ descends from the refectory wall—leaving a terrible hole.

Cloux
March 4, 1519

I am writing very slowly now.

While painting *The Last Supper* I lived at the Santa Maria delle Grazie some of the time, working day after day, often sleeping on the floor, on a bench. I painted by day and at night, with the help of lamps and candles, placing lights on benches, on tables, on my scaffolding. I was altering forms, changing colors, imparting greater age to a face, lessening the impact of a gesture.

I might stay an hour, or remain for days: Ai, Matthew's eyes might move; Luke might raise his arm; John might turn his head—or so it seemed. I was always there when the light was good; during inclement weather I might shove my key into the lock, and shut the door. A few grapes, some nuts, bread and wine... I didn't need much food. With a basket or a bowl beside me on the scaffolding I would go on painting.

I was forty-three.

When Christ's model became ill and finally died, I retouched His face, imparting what I had learned while observing the dying man. I remember: to soften the shading I retouched with a lamp in my hand, holding it close to His face.

As I painted there were two dead men watching me.

I discovered Judas when he was drunk. I found him in a *borghetto*, slumped at a table, a big table sticky with spilled food and wine. Flies. Sipping wine at another table, I sketched him. So it was: I would not have to hunt any longer. That night, although he was drunk and unsteady, I got him to my studio and put a robe over his rags. We talked, we ate. His name: Carlo Macchini.

Carlo came and went. He never accepted a *soldi.*

Came and went, usually a little drunk. Kindly.

He was an assistant baker. Hated his boss, hated his job. Hated.

When I had completed his face in the fresco, he contemplated it for a while, shrugged, patted me on the shoulder, walked away...not a word... I never saw him again.

Before I finished the fresco, Luke had died. The last I heard about Peter was the news that he had added another child to his big family. Ninth. As for Mark...he was living with a prostitute. Sick. No job.

I made many sketches of each man: filled sketchbooks. I worked them into my cartoon...slowly, slowly. I wanted the faces to express the gravity of life; the clothes that they wore must not distract; the food on the table must not distract. I made the tableware similar to that used by the monks as they ate in the room. It took me almost a month to arrange the food and dishes. Twenty-six hands must tell their story but not overdramatize.

I strove for simplicity: that resolution haunted me. So many times, when rain drummed on the roof of the refectory, as I sat alone, I heard that word: simplicity, simplicity of color, design, shadowed by the past.

And while I painted, the beautiful refectory was flooded by a storm: I saw water two feet deep: pigments were washed away, brushes were lost.

Ai, I see it now: at least one of the disciples should have had a scarred face, should have been crippled perhaps. Life, in those Galilean days, did not let one escape unscathed. Out of the twelve, one would have suffered.

But there, there they are, with their Lord.

I had a brief letter from Salai today. If he had remained, we would have made our bicycle.

Tomorrow, I...

On my birthday, my friends, Father Luco Pacioli, Phillip, Donato Bramante, Abbaco Alberti, Peter, Francesco, John, Toscanelli, Andrea, Luini, Credi, friars, priests and many artists, gathered at the Grazie, and we burned lamps and candles for the first showing of *The Last Supper.* Standing on a bench, Father Luco said:

"Milan is indebted to our Leo...to him and Il Moro and the prior and his people. We have watched the fresco come to life. For three years we've seen it move along. It has meant something special to each one of us. It is Leonardo da Vinci's miracle. A symbol of man's desire for a better life."

How well I remember those words!

⚜

In Milan, my *Salvator Mundi* attracted crowds when it was exhibited in my studio. King Louis had expressed his public approval of the painting and the curious had to be satisfied. Since General de Galen had come to Milan to deliver the painting to the King, I asked his protection. Onlookers came out of the alleys as well as the palace. Alley folk jeered. They shouted "Christ the Juggler;" they called Him "El Puto"..."the glassy-eyed Gascon."

Riffraff threw mud and garbage.

I had to cover the painting...but that was yesterday...the jeers and criticism should remain in the past.

Here, at Amboise, at Cloux, all is respect, a respect that originates with King Francis. Courtiers and guests and workers often approach me in the gardens; we pass the time of day. I get along best with the gardeners because there are new plants and flowers to examine and sketch. Sit me on a bench and I am lost by a bed of flowers. An old maestro, toothless, stooped, a man from Padua, knows how to please me with a leaf, a flower, a seed.

"These roses I grew in my own garden...what colors!"

Thinking of Jesus, here in repose, I realize the Savior lacks an aura of gentle mysticism, the aura of my Jesus at the supper table. The globe He holds in His hand lacks the obvious meaning of brotherhood—the great concern of the disciples. My Savior's eyes are not the eyes of a shepherd from the hills. He has a city man's face. He is younger than the Christ at the table. His benediction is for all men and yet carries a sense of restraint, perhaps a sense of doubt. Perhaps it is my own doubt, a doubt that I feel keenly at Amboise, a doubt that seems based on my inability to bring together the meaning inherent in my studies, my optics, my hydraulics, my engineering work.

⚜

Dreams...dreams...

It is evening, and the kite comes. He grips me in his talons and helps me fly, over the Arno, over the town; he becomes my black-brown-grey kite with wings 18 feet long, wings of wood, cloth, wire. I hear the wind.

Francesco has been amused when I describe my experience with the kite; however, it is too old a dream, or experience, for me to dismiss. How many times it has encouraged me.

As I write, I hear someone calling my name.

⚜

April 2, 1519

Again, my health is failing rapidly. I can not continue my work with my treatises. I can not write my journal. Sometimes I can not speak. My vision is going. Francesco and I had begun to bring ends together; I had hoped for days ahead because there is so much to accomplish.

At night, in my room, the walls become a mural of Amboise, the manor house, the Loire, old bridges, royalty, paintings, rearing horses, Francesco, wings, rocks, caves, Galilean faces...like maddened bees.

⚜

Cloux
April 3

Yes, most of my years were years without sexual intimacy. I experienced ecstasy but it was often bitter later on. So, I comforted myself with sham comfort. I gained time through my solitary living and lost time that could have made me more human.

Yes, I had a woman for three years.

My own illegitimacy was often slammed at me...bastard da Vinci...that stigma harms the mind.

Dedicate?

Of course, dedication...but I have explained...art, music, sculpture, geology, mechanics...not one is bastard.

DEDICATE:

A priest outlaws distractions. What is an artist but a priest! Joyous children, sick children, they are part of most married lives...that little girl on your lap, sucking her thumb, kissing you, stroking your beard...she...she is dead.

Here, at the château, there are hall mirrors, mirrors in ornate frames: the artist observes himself in those mirrors: he also sees a rusty spatula and shredded brushes: sometimes, late afternoons, I see in those mirrors, someone in Milan, I see her smiling, I see the spiral of her yellow hair.

I hear her laughter.

I hear...but that is our staircase creaking. Or is it Francesco working in his studio?

Food has become tasteless.

What is wrong with my château wine?

Maturina scolds.

I think of those hungry days as apprentice, when eating was such a pleasure! I think of our kitchen, at Vinci. Mother's. Fresh bread. Milk from that blue pitcher.

Paix, paix, Satan, allez, paix!

⚜

Machiavelli is here. Unexpected.

He is enroute to Paris to collect a bad debt. A man owes him 600 livres. I have offered money. Niccolò is proud, too proud.

He has malaria and shuffles about in a great coat though it is warm. Last night by a studio fire he huddled in his coat. Perhaps Dr. Pedretti can help him. We'll see tomorrow. As we sat by the fire, sipping wine, he railed about politics at home—-wretched deceptions. Scoundrels!

Most of his three days have been spent in bed. In his elegant clothes he bowed before the King. The two got along well. Lying and vying. Francis has offered one of his carriages for the trip to Paris.

Niccolò has lost weight. He was always skinny but now he is a shadow of himself. He resents my paralyzed arm...says it is God who is to blame. Then laughed—or was it a sneer?

He thinks Amboise is a true haven.

He is wonderfully clever with his tongue, Latin, French or Italian.

⚜

Sometimes loneliness has embittered me.

Last night I asked Francesco to come to my bedroom, though it was late. He came and sat by my bed. He understands my sickness; and he also knows he is going back to his Vaprio.

It was a cold night. A fire burned in my fireplace.

Francesco wore his grey wool gown, stared at me sleepily, flames on his thin cheek bones, on his hands, bringing out their veins.

Cloux was forgotten as I talked of home and my mother and my first days in Florence, at the Verrochio, first days so different from Francesco's first days when Florence had more patina. I rambled on about Milan and my paintings and the siege and Milan's bombardment and deaths—pell-mell thoughts. Francesco brought cups of wine. For us this was a father/son relationship. We two had been father and son since we left Italy, since Francesco cared for me during the big snow at the monastery. It pleases him that King Francis often addresses me as "Mon Père."

Ivory-faced madonnas...regal pomp...commissions that failed, commissions that succeeded...my flying wing...I was reliving my life! Francesco asked about the men who had posed for *The Last Supper.* Faces, thoughts, words...flooded. We talked about Peter and James and Matthew; we found drawings of Jesus and He seemed real in the firelight.

Francesco added two or three logs to the fire.

He brought in a wine bottle and refilled our glasses.

Wind gusted smoke into the room.

We talked about Paris and our trip there. I told him that Rome was far more interesting than Paris. I related the story of the mirror-man, at the Vatican apartment: that story involved me in anguish. I stopped talking, to listen to the wind.

We talked of fishing in the Loire...when?

"Tomorrow," I suggested.

"It's tomorrow now," he said, laughing.

"How time gets away from us."

"Maturina will be rattling the breakfast dishes soon."

"Then you had better get some sleep."

"Good night, Mon Père," Francesco said, and laughed that good laugh of his.

⚜

So, you won't paint again! Where you are going you won't hear the pestle grinding pigment. How insignificant my sketches, my trees, faces, water...as a boy I thought every sketch would open up the world a little more.

It was only a month ago I made the four small bronze horses, moulded the graceful contours of Andrea's face...it was only a year ago that...

I hate the body's frailty, that dead arm! Work was life, but no, there were hours to prowl the hills, to climb the Alps, to sit by the sea. Maturity came during those hours as well as during the hours of work. I remember, while painting *The Supper...*

I remember a little plant in the evening light, that frail light that shadowed the corolla. I remember a sorrel leaf, I remember a small fern. Small? What is small versus big? I should know.

A madonna in the evening light—her smile.

And the world shrugs.

Pigments reveal how I have erred...tell me green, tell me saffron, tell me royalty, tell me death.

And you, red chalk, speak!

⚜

Cloux

We think we are learning how to live but we are only learning how to die.

I, Francesco Melzi, write:
Maestro Leonardo da Vinci is dead.
He died at Cloux, in the manor house,
on May 2, 1619.
He was sixty-seven years old.

Cloux
April 4, 1519

DURING THE LAST WEEKS OF
LEONARDO DA VINCI'S LIFE,
I, FRANCESCO MELZI,
RECORDED THE MAESTRO'S THOUGHTS,
AS HE DICTATED THEM:

"You ask me what my apartment was like in Milan? It was an apartment of tapestries and antique furniture, paintings, mine and others. Sculptured pieces. I bought many things at the Thieves' Market. My Camjac tapestries covered three walls. Made the room warmer. My paintings covered the fourth. This was my *sala*. A large stained glass window faced the street. You remember that street, of course. Lodi Street. Western exposure. Hot in summer. Dusty. But my apartment was on the fourth floor, had a wide, shaded balcony. There was a small courtyard of plants and a pair of little tiled fountains with squirting fish. Sometimes the courtyard was a refuge. Cypress. Old ones.

"With my big iron key, I stepped into my rooms. Five. My studio had good light. Of course I painted the walls black. You would have admired my Roman pieces, heads, busts. You, my friend, were living in Vaprio then."

We moved his bed into the sun, and pulled open the drapes. He enjoyed lying there. "Spring is beautiful," he said.

Cloux
April 5, 1519

Da Vinci talks to me with difficulty. However, I go on:

"Perhaps those years in Milan were the busiest years of my life. Irrigation projects, *The Last Supper* mural, easel paintings, the horse...yes, the horse...

cartoons. I tried to interest the authorities in an ideal city. I made models for them. Planned double-decked streets. Vehicles would use the lower level, pedestrians the upper. There would be proper sewage. I wanted to show men that the plague might be avoided through sanitation."

He has eaten a little fruit, and sipped some wine.

"In Milan, I went on with my anatomical studies, this time working in a clean hospital, with proper light. I had adequate leisure. I dissected male and female ...eight or ten cadavers...over the years. Made my drawings in various media.

"Illness laid me low...

"I never trusted physicians. They know nothing of anatomy and less about illnesses. I suffered alone—with my servants. They fed me, administered my concoctions...my kidneys. Nature cured me. After about six or seven months I was able to get about, to walk, stride along. There was kindness then...but kindness is your specialty...your kindness has never failed me."

⚜

Cloux
April 6, 1519

"Remember this—I was forced to work for Cesare Borgia. Remember, Vitelli and I tried to refuse him. Refusal was impossible. We were like hostages in Borgia's camps. Of course we wanted to escape...planned...we were afraid. Pay was high. So...we continued ours jobs as cartographers. Close friends, fellow artists, we looked to each other for support.

"As I sketched Borgia I realized his animosity. Vitelli and I were aware that his soldiers disliked us. They made it pretty obvious most of the time. I talked to Niccolò Machiavelli about this antagonism. He scoffed. Laughed at me.

"Yet Borgia, always demanding, arrogant, worried us. He went out of his way to annoy Vitelli. I tried to play down his swaggering. I tried to play down our apprehensions. Then...then, he had Vitelli strangled. Strangled in Borgia's tent. Enraged, afraid, I left that night. Niccolò provided my horse. He rode with me. We escaped through the rain. Our horses fast. Solitary roads...hoof beats... I remember. Vitelli murdered. In the tent.

"We said little as we rode.

"At an inn we dismounted, drank, warmed ourselves. Niccolò could not justify his Prince.

"Ai, that murderous rain! His name, his face, that Borgia face, assassination rain!"

It is late as I finish writing down his words. He is in pain. Last night he slept very little.

April 7, 1519

"No, not purgatory and not hell...

"I esteem the horse and the dog because they are free of perversions...no *misa*, no confessional...

"Animals exact little...make no covenants.

"I can't forget the Papal wars, the crusades, the Savonarola fanaticisms.

"When did robe and aspergillum exorcise evil?

"I'm still searching...but, in this world of ambiguity, I think there is no answer."

Today...only these words, as I sat by his bed. Visitors annoyed him. Several times he asked for his mother.

Cloux
April 9, 1519

It is afternoon. The sun is low. Da Vinci speaks:

"When the old French King saw my *Last Supper* he was determined to remove the entire wall of the refectory, and have it transported to Paris. He discussed it with engineers and architects who said it was impossible.

"What a study...the King is scarlet, pompous, in a very bad humor, his syphilitic face grey. Flailing his arms, as he stood before my mural, he roared at the men around him, kicked a dog that had wandered in.

" 'Your fresco can't remain in this wretched refectory!' Everyone was amused.

"Later, when I painted his portrait, he was affable. I painted him in profile, a good study, in good light. He insisted on having a book on his lap. Ovid. I remember he said:

" 'In Amboise, I have a collection of fine books...Ovids.'

"He was willing to pay any price for my *Madonna of the Yarn Winder.* So, he paid...and carried it off to Paris."

Stroking his beard, da Vinci watched rain streak his windows. Lifting one arm, he said: "No more today, Francesco, no more talk."

Cloux
April 10, 1519

"Come, let's get on with it...I have something to say:

"My deluge drawings express weight, gravity, power, fury, terror. The overturned, whirling chunks of masonry, the enormous waves, defy. This is the end of man. I believe such a cataclysm is going to overcome the earth.

"The drawings were inspired by my visits to the sea, by my trips to the mountains where I saw avalanches. Sound...the crash of falling boulders, the crash of a raging ocean...they warn. Finality—in one form or another—surrounds. We can't escape.

"Rage, rage...much of life is rage...desperate rage.

"Here, far inland, I can hear the tumultuous sea!"

Sometimes I can barely make out his words. I served his supper. He ate very little. He remarked about the pigeons cooing on the roof.

Cloux
April 12, 1519

Royalty have visited us. Alone with me, da Vinci said:

"Yesterday, I dreamed that the sun was coming through my window at Vinci...there were bunches of grapes on our table...bare table, in the sun.

Caterina was sitting opposite me, her hands in the sun. I seemed to be about thirty years old. She seemed to be about the same age. Our dog lay on the floor, waiting for me to take him out.

"I felt imprisoned by the sunlight, happily imprisoned... I was imprisoned by the beauty in Caterina's face. My eyes followed the grain of the table, mixed with the bunches of grapes, went out into the street, returned to her face, her smile.

"...You have asked me about happiness. Does anyone know what happiness is? It is so often illusory. For you, Francesco, it's a woman...or a swim in the lake. For me it was always work. If a great discipline haunts a man throughout his life...well, he's lucky. You have seen me happy. You didn't throw in your lot with a bitter man.

"We see King Francis...we watch him...he is eaten up with regrets...he is scheming, plotting...worrying...battlefields gnaw his guts...if we want sanity there are Vaprios, little rivers, little hills."

He asked me for another cover.

Cloux

This was our last conversation—on April 23rd.

Melzi - I heard that you created a mirror machine while you were in Rome.

Da Vinci - I tried to amplify the stars—study them.

Melzi - Please explain.

Da Vinci - A series of mirrors and lens.

Melzi - To catch the light?

Da Vinci - I could position the mirrors and the lens. You have to visualize them, in a shallow cradle, some pieces one and two inches square, some pieces two and three inches square, most of them concave, all specially ground, to fit together like an eye, to focus like the eye. They could be raised or lowered, tilted, under a lens which I could also focus.

Melzi - They brought the sky closer?

Da Vinci - All of the mirrors and lens were destroyed by the man who had cut and polished them. He smashed them. Malice...fear...envy...

Melzi - A bitter experience, Maestro!

Da Vinci - That's how it was...in Rome. The Pope learned of these experiments and ousted me from the Vatican.

He fell asleep.

⚜

Cloux
May 20, 1519

As requested in Maestro Leonardo da Vinci's will, sixty men, each carrying a lighted taper, accompanied his coffin to St. Hubert's chapel, on the evening of May the 4th. Royalty, château-pages, soldiers, visitors, servants made up the procession from the manor house to the Amboise chapel. It was a cloudy, threatening evening. The chapel bell tolled.

A bearded priest, in black vestments, performed the requiem. Royalty crammed the chapel. The royal green flag, sewn with hundreds of white salamanders, blanketed the casket. Wreathes of roses and carnations leaned against wall cabinets where there were lighted candles. Men chanted a Gregorian chant.

The Maestro was buried close to the chapel, under chestnut and cypress, buried by torch and taper light. The chapel doors were wide open as someone played the organ. Six men lowered the coffin.

Leonardo's death was the saddest moment of my life.

When King Francis returned to Amboise, later in May, I walked with him to the burial place and he laid flowers on "Mon Père's" grave. Fog filtered the grove and dripped on us. A hard day for the monarch.

King Francis has retained all of da Vinci's paintings.

I was willed his drawings, sketches, journal, treatises, music, and correspondence.

Soldiers accompanied me on my return to Vaprio.

⚜

Villa Vaprio
July 13, 1519

My father and mother welcomed me home.

Father gave me a northlight room, on the third floor. I will place my easel near the windows that face the Adda, face the little bridge where the Maestro used to fish for temolo.

I have hung my copy of his *Mona Lisa* on the entry wall and have laid his red velvet cloak over the back of a chair.

I am arranging some of his drawings on a center table.

There is ample space for his *Anghiari* cartoon on the inside wall. I have ordered broad shelves for his books and his small bronzes, his drawings and treatises, his brushes and pigments. I will purchase a leather box for his correspondence.

I will do what I can to bring order to his writings.

Under this stone are the
remains collected during
excavations outside the
royal chapel of Amboise.

It is surmised these are
the bones of
Leonard da Vincy

1452 – 1519

Author's note:
This epitaph was placed on da Vinci's grave in later years.

SHAKESPEARE'S JOURNAL

To my Elizabeth,

for her loyalty, love and genius

Henley Street
January 28, 1615

To invent can become an aberration, a mystery, at times a querulous searching to remedy an irremediable loss. Shall we say there is a larger purpose? Must there always be a purpose and justification? I can not believe that. Then, there can be stumbling, burial, burial violets around a grave, an absence. These thoughts must be weighed, reassessed, subtracted from physical ailment and sickness of mind. Surely the stage was not intended for a single player.

. . .

Stratford
February 2nd, Candlemas – 1615

On Christmas last I sang carols with Ellen and her friends, in her London apartment, candlelight on her frosted windows where trees, like menhirs, listened. Some of her friends were drunk and raucous parasites; some were manikins; some were overly friendly; some, Countess Bardolph, Lord Fenton, Lady Page, were perfumed bores; the Irishmen were troublemakers...

The Captain of the Guard requested a dance, and musicians appeared on a small wreathed stage, a candlelit tree at one side. Sprigs of ribboned mistletoe decorated the window drapes and the frames of all Ellen's paintings; she wore a sprig and her Scot mouth met mine under the portrait of a highlander. Caroling and wine went on and on:

Joseph and Mary walked
Through an orchard green,
Where were cherries and berries
As thick as might be seen...

Mummers paid Ellen a call, accompanied by a dancing jester wearing furs. By now it was snowing and the storm sprinkled the jester and the costumes of the torchlit merrymakers with him, as they trailed about, singing. A glass of wine with Ellen... Egypt, it seemed an easy dive to the bottom of the deep, to pluck drowned honor, but there was Ann, pinch-faced, wanting to scourge, and sting with pismires.

Joseph and Mary walked through their orchard bewitched, and Ellen's thick tree burned with its candles; the Yule log burned and cat-spat; thick-eyed musing came with scalding wassail; then more dancing and then sleep at their side... Later, I'll tell her about my play, my plans, secrets of the stage, boyhood delights... I'll reveal the wildness of the world, and beyond this, the tranquility of poetry itself.

She'll share her Edinburgh, her theatre, her books, her home by the lake, her work for the priory library.

She told me:

"Life is to hold warmly in our hands. It is to be made better for our passing."

Her intense face considered mine: the fine lines of her mouth, those eyes, lochs, and then there were her dark, dark hair, her perfume, the pressing of her fingers into my sex...necessities and no better...

Carols continued while snow stuck to her window panes and the pine boughs put resin on the air...a day and then another, her hair on her pillow like a fern...and nothing else was needed.

On the blue frozen Thames
skaters zip past people, booths, flags.
A giant ox roasts on a giant spit.
Arm in arm, Shakespeare and Ellen skate:
Over a glassy spot in the ice they peer down
where a blue cloak floats:
fish below.
Singing carolers pass on skates.

Henley Street
February 8, 1615

One year the Thames froze and above London Bridge it became a market, hobbled with ragged booths, stalls, flags and streamers, peopled with courtiers, beggars, soldiers, priests, merchantmen and their families. An ox was roasted—and as it steamed and smoked—walkers clustered around the carcass as if it were Holland. Skaters spun close, stopping to chat or buy and eat, then spun away over the ice.

For days the surface was free of snow and one afternoon I brought Ellen, and we skated arm in arm, the sky unblemished; we swished between ice-bound frigates, toqued sailors leaning over, waving and jeering. It was almost Christmas and carolers sang around bonfires. Royalty had set up tents and we were welcomed there, the tents and flags reflected in the ice, purple, red, yellow—pennants squares gay—men and wenches tippling—musicians trying to keep their feet warm, strumming bravely.

Ellen, in plaid scarf, yellow cloak and jeweled tam, stands alongside a striped purple and gold tent, laughs alongside the scabby hulk of a frigate, warms her hands before a fire. Ellen...your face is real... I can reach out and take your hands...you smile and sway in the wind.

Singing with the carolers, your breath puffs its toadstool alongside my mushroom, and we laugh and hug each other. Inside a carpeted tent, we toast "Wassail!" and glance at velvet cushions heaped in a corner.

Henley Street
Stratford

Mine was the wish to bind society together, expose the floor of heaven, make immortal real, show man's folly and labor, extol faith and uphold beauty. Beauty, as I felt it at the outset of my career, is no longer here: it is a long way from *Venus and Adonis* to *Henry VIII:* there were grim diversions, rude and costly failures: my goal it seems is beggared: if I had the capacity I would reach back to beauty and carry it forward with greater maturity: I am thinking of poetic beauty.

Farewell! You were too dear for my possessing,
for such riches where is my deserving...?

I lost sensibility and communion in pursuit of plot and character for the ricochet of horror and death, for the mockery of crime and subterfuge.

At times, I was in sleep a king—but on waking, no such man.

I have been awake to my losses a long while: there was no recouping them in France and Italy, alone with hegemony of rocks, promontories, beaches, hierarchy of seas assailing nakedness...here in Stratford, here I have illness as exchange.

Sallow yellow:
Men, women and children dying in the streets:
Church bells tolling.
Three men drag a dead youth to the Avon River,
pitch him in.
Church steeple, reflected in the water, sways:
The church registry lists column after column of dead:
Not a sound.

In Stratford, the plague moved down Mill Lane, Butt Lane, Rother Street, jumped to Henley and then Church Street. Father and I worked on Mill Lane: finding Charles collapsed by the whipping post, we lugged him out of the sun...shivering...sweating...vomiting...and we could not find anything to cover him, and he begged us for a cover.

"Something to cover me, Will...just something?"

"But there's nothing left for you."

"Everything used up?"

"All used, Charles."

"So many of us sick?"

"Lie still. I'll bring you hot sack. That'll help you feel better...there's a rug..."

"I'll see if I can find something to cover him."

"No, you're tired. I'll bring hot sack and a cover."

Pigeons swooped low, then rose: were they afraid?

Six people had died that day.

During the week twenty-six died, men, women, and children. Our town heard the bell toll morning and afternoon and evening. At times the tolling seemed to be right in my ears; at times I forgot it, bringing water or food, medicine or cover, anything to help. Father and I worked together as much as possible...his word or nod kept me going.

The Avon seemed blotched and diseased for there, there was the plague's mucous caulking the water and the water was grey and beaten and unmoving, locked in its own foetidness, dead by the weir, dead by the church and underneath the bridge.

Stratford
February 14, 1615

I remember the plague, how, with our theatre closed, I worked to aid the sick and cart away the London dead. Appleton...I remember his red beard, his cough, his scared grin. Meerie, talking Irish, blamed us, saying "there's narra a plague in Ireland—it's your filthy London—you damn filthy foreigners!" Miller cursed the altar and the saints behind his head, as he struggled to breathe. And that gargoyle-like fellow, Fackler, crawled off to die or recover, we never learned: he said the open field was the proper place to get well, or die.

The Cheney twins died right outside the Globe: they had been working as stage hands: clever lads from Sussex, faithful, hard-working: they got sick on Tuesday; as the bells tolled on Thursday evening they were dead, dying a few minutes apart, their hands clasped, eighteen years old, flax-headed, tall.

Why did that young woman, with hair to her waist, run about laughing, eating handfuls of earth? Why did that Dorsetshire man stab himself with a dirk? How did the graves of the Boothby children get left open, deserted for days? Was God in the heavenly lectern those days...to save us of our sins!

For days the sun chewed us in Blackwell. It gave us a chance to kill some of the rats. Caesar, don't let one bite you! Worms crawled out of the earth. Caesar, beware! Whenever I passed our cemetery I smelled new, raw earth—as terrifying as the death smell. 'Sblood, how many deaths does it take to satisfy the earth?

YOUTH—

What is this vomit, this black gunk pouring out of your mouth? Are you only fourteen...with death on your face?

This is our boy, Slade, who walked to school last week and fished where I fished.

"Papa, let's carry him into the shade. We'll cool his hot face and give him water. Our medicine has to make him well. We need him, to grow up and catch perch and pike, and marry Jenny."

Papa is washing his face. There's fruit. There's sleep. There's tomorrow. There's kindness. There's forgetfulness.

Best to cover him.

I'll cover him. There, that blanket may keep him from shivering. His mother's sick too. I'll rub his hands and arms. Water, Papa, give him some. There!

"Papa, you get some rest, while I stay with Slade. You'd better go home and turn in. You didn't sleep much last night. Things are better now. No. I'm not hungry. I'll eat later."

I'll sit with you, boy, and we'll deny harsh fortune. Did you ever see a play, boy? The play's the thing: it takes you out of yourself. Listen...I'll recite some lines for you...

Farewell! a long farewell, to all this...

This is the state of man: today he puts forth
The tender leaves of hope; tomorrow blossoms,
And bears his blushing honors thick upon him;
The third day comes a frost, a killing frost;
And, when he thinks, good easy man, fully surely
His greatness is a ripening, nips his root,
And then he falls, as I do. I have ventured,
Like little wanton boys that swim on bladders
This many summers in a sea...

Farewell, he's dead.

Papa, you and I have lost him. He'll never race across the fields or pack his creel or kiss a girl on the bridge. The plague has killed him.

Was it you who wanted a new cap?

Now you'll have a cap of dirt.

I throw my heart against the flint of time. O sun, burn your great spheres... I importune death a while. The passing of so small a thing should make a crack at least. Stained with his own blood...

Grey yelping dogs chase a coach through London fog:
Fog drips from coach lamps, from trees, iron railings.
Someone in the fog screams and
a cloaked figure stabs Ellen
as she gets into her coach.
Ellen's cloak, blood, fog,
Shakespeare's anguished face.

Henley Street
February 20, 1615

Fog, that old-year-treachery, steals round my house, thief at every window: renegade, despot, carrion-maker.

That night the fog mauled us after we left the theatre, Ellen and I. I thought of throwing my cloak around both of us, as we walked along: dark blue cloak in white fog. Instead of covering both of us I covered her...

The play had been well played, Alleyn up to form, Marlowe's lines appreciated by a better than usual audience, some of them royalty. *Tambourlaine* usually appeals to royalty. This was Crown night, Christ's crown, hell's crown, fog on every thorn, thorns sticking through our laughter, to be remembered, in that cloak, bastard thorns.

Like dogs they followed us as we left the theatre, late, our arms around each other, the cloak flapping, fog leaving us inconspicuous. I saw her carriage approaching, inching the fog, fog through the spokes of her wheels. And then outcries, and Ellen beside me, falling, and as she fell I turned and saw my cloak slide with her, lantern and dagger on the road, *misericord.*

Here it is now: yes, here it is: I have it, pricking thing for future pricking, if need be: long, needle-pointed: Toledo steel: the right length to kill her—or me.

Laughter and fog, spines and theatre, the royalty of crime in a London gutter; time doesn't remove them, can not remove them.

When we could we located guards—trustworthy men—and with a constable informed her servants and posted guards. Later, Jonson and I sat with her doctors and learned a little more about pain. I went for Ellen's brother and he came, a cold young man who resembled Ellen, a slight fellow in handsome black. Hand on sword, he drew himself up, face ashen, mouth trembling...

"I'll comb London for them...get them..."

Jonson often visited her, his words and thoughts the stuff for those days, my brain run dry, bats coasting out, Enobarbus memories:

Why, sir, give the gods a thankful sacrifice. When it pleases their deities to take a man's woman from him, it shows the tailors of the earth; comforting therein, that when old robes are worn out, there are members to make new...so grief is crowned with consolation.

Did I write that?

Henley Street
February 26, 1615

I am not able to write poetry and yet I must write, must tell the teller, crush the shards of illness. What is life, the undone and the done, the foolish and the great? I hate drowning in real and invented apprehensions but mine is the stumbling, after the play, after the compliments and the celebration, a mixture more brew than sanity admits.

My pen jerks and my hand wavers and my head aches, and I watch faint light creep into the sky, exacting a promise from me to defy pain.

I hate sleeplessness on a foggy night like this, for there is something in the fog that makes death come alive, that sears the sordid into the mind...what was the cause: contorted memories? Am I afraid to die, be laid in straw or committed to a sulfurous pit?

Give me my rope, put on my crown...

Memory is for me acting in a dissolve, cloud of rain, concatenation of nothings, performing yet recalcitrant, ambiguous and poor. Here, in this town, this room smelling of spilled wine, the candles ugly, I see a woman, the filaments of yesterday's straw tangled in her hair—selling love for a price. Why is love obtuse, ruthless, rain-buried, eerie and demanding, slinking one to the other?

Stratford
March 2, 1615

I write with rain across my oriel, and the fire almost out in my fireplace, and my loneness sniveling in its pot. I am sick of self-pity. I taste with wretched appetite, so be it! To be generous, hungry, guiltless, and free...what would I give!

Pincers, pinch harder at the rushes, keep the light burning as long as possible, for each of us.

At my age, I am guilty of longings that I can never realize: dreams hawsered to nowhere. I have been guilty of this all my life. I copulated with commas. I hunted dreams on paper—cheap privateer! I was priest, pharaoh, general, slave, glutton. Paper is a sickness, a sweltering fever, clammy forehead, thudding pulse, ague within ague: so I am a man of paper, elongated, soggy, contorted, multiple of calligraphic speculation: paper bones, paper heart, paper skull, paper blood, paper penis.

Listen, isn't that time rustling a sheath of paper?

Snow buffets Shakespeare's cottage:
Snow enters a window.
There are varnished ceiling beams,
varnished furniture,
books and manuscripts.
A stunning woman appears, smiles, fades,
beckons seductively, disappears.

Henley Street
March 5, 1615

Yesterday it snowed, and during the afternoon I fell asleep and dreamed I saw King Henry and Shallow crossing the fields beyond my windows.

"O God, that one might read the book of fate," I heard King Henry say, as I followed, hidden from view. "I wish to see the revolution of the times make mountains level, and the continents, weary of solid firmness, melt itself into the sea and, other times, to see the beach girdle the ocean..."

"There is a history in all men's lives, figuring the nature of the times deceased..."

Was it Shallow who said that?

Though I am confused, I recall the gaunt face of Alleyn as he spoke those lines, that stormy night, when our theatre rattled. He was infirm with fever and yet played on; he seldom let us down.

Winter is here again, to make our beds uneasy. Oh, for a muse of fire that would ascend the brightest heaven of invention, and return me to my youth!

This is a document in madness because pain seldom leaves me...

Oh, to be young and tumble a naked woman on a bed, quarrel desperately and make up, burn the night learning and unlearning lines, defy the elements, dally along the Thames, out-shout the gulls, see a mermaid behind a rock.

Youth has such powers! Youth's rule rules his own court by championing a hundred causes, ordaining and cancelling, defying and acknowledging, digging canals, raising temples.

Slave of every beautiful woman he meets, he presents her with lasting riches and eternal potency. He conquers every country for her: his grail, his fleet battering an endless Armada to bring her into port, no gale too wild.

Henley Street
Monday, '15

When I taught school at Snitterfield, Jonson came now and then to prime my Greek and Latin. He used to say, "You should have done a lot less fishing in the Avon, boy! Why, these fellows will never learn, not the way you teach. See, they grin at you. They love you. Call them churls, cane them; make them scat when you appear!"

Away from school, Jonson would slip into theatre talk and urge me to rejoin him: "Your poems are remembered. You have to come back, Will! I'll find you a patron. Now's the time to write plays... I'll help you put them on the stage."

I told him I was afraid of the London plague. He scorched me with a "haw-haw." "Teaching's your plague, man!"

Henley Street
April 20, 1615

Teaching was forgotten at Fair time, good food, acrobats, cockfights, gambling—there was something to keep us spellbound spelling laughter! Games and dances went on at all hours. Cinquepace was the fast, new step. How I liked it! There were plenty of pickpockets but I had nothing to pick but my loneliness. When I danced with a red-cheeked girl there was sperm in every movement—those giddy curls and hot hands, the smoke of sizzling fish, howls of the stinking bear baiters.

Stratford

Trumpets blared... I heard them days after the Fair.

I stayed on as long as possible in Snitterfield, to contribute what I could to my family's upkeep in Stratford. Then came the day when the school board asked me to find another job; so it was back to London again, to Jonson and his half-ass promises, back to city trumpets, strumpets, rattle of carriages, pismire poverty, paunched patrons and perfumed snowballs for the Queen's masque...

Stratford

While I was at Snitterfield, I had the companionship of a girl whose fourteen years should have been double fourteen to equal her double sight for fox, hawk, raven and snail: she was unreal because she could bring me to the brink of fantasy by gesture or word: "Hush, there, over there, in the grass by the stile." Her flip-smile had the best of both pook and pagan. What she wore seemed a part of her blondeness, a blondeness often eerie with an eeriness that worried me, to be quickly saved by her smile or laughter. Her low voice set the stage for confidences—thread between goldenrod, rabbit lying in the entry of its burrow, lark rising.

Faith and I had lingering afternoons and saw the first of fog before dark, heard the last of bird sounds before sleep: her house next door to mine taught me, by window and door, the wretchedness of her life: her father's drunken beatings, kickings, savagery: so, to escape the village clod we escaped together, to sit by a woodland stream and hear words by leaves as they sifted down. Faith had her legs in the water, up to her knees, or lay on the embankment, the color of her flesh gleaming. Her beauty was not a pair of breasts but a pair of hazel eyes and a dimple in her chin. She was tall, a cathedral figure in caenstone, the stone so alive yet ecclesiastical, erect, her posture one of graceful expectation: repose flowed from her: her thin hands lifted to her thin face: her hair straggled to her shoulders and down her back or was combed into a flaxen haycock. I thought my teaching infinitely poorer than hers and went with her whenever possible, helping her withstand the disgrace at home.

I thought many times of going back to see Faith Stanton but even the changeless changes and woodland jewels, claiming socketless eyes, reflect only images of the mind. Drunkenness outlives beauty—the clod burying haycock, bog and girl.

Henley Street

Goddamn my hair!

My hair, with its copper and red, used to say: This is your world, boy!

Damn my wrinkles! My gallows neck!
My face was once all right.
Now one cheek has begun to cave in under my eye, the wince of lechery, no doubt, and meteors, no less. Lines around my mouth give the impression that I have never had a good time—never laughed. My eyes, when I swivel them in a mirror, warn me that grave changes are taking place inside and that denials will get me nowhere: grey hairs, wrinkles, poor vision...they are the roistering gift of time, markings on the stone, to remind myself that I am here, that escape is never, that courage is all that counts, humor with its leg lifted on the monument, peeing on vanity.

The sullen bell called me to school and I went reluctantly, leaving my fishing pole behind the door, pike and trout lost to me. Early morning was almost beyond endurance; I rubbed my eyes and stumbled downstairs, to eat amid yappings, survive, survive.

I did not resent school when Hunt read aloud in Latin, reading masterfully, giving us Caesar, Antony, and Cleopatra. When he read, I wandered beside the pyramids, the Nile dotted with boats, ibis, and heron; I tramped battlefields, fought with black spears piercing the hot, dusty air. It was along the Avon that I sensed man's struggle. I saw. Heard. As the water grew greener and greener and deeper and deeper, the air motionless, the past was there, Hunt's past, Cleopatra's...her barge, like a burnished throne, burnt on the water; the poop beaten gold, purple the sails, so perfumed that the winds were love-sick with them; the oars were silver, which to the time of flutes kept stroke...

When I dared I got away early and went to fish or loafed at the mill pool where I hung my feet in the Avon and counted dragonflies, my line thrown as far as I could throw it. Sitting on a mossy mound, I heard the warblers and lark spell morning into warm sun.

Thirty-five years ago!

Summer:
Naked swimmers, five boys, penis fun, laughter:
Naked girls in bushes along the same river bank:
Church bells in distance:
Behind a copse boy and girl kiss and squirm.

Henley Street
May 4, 1615

Growing up, our greatest fun was swimming, our greatest anguish church. From church, as quickly possible, we got into nakedness, rival of summer lightning. We swam the Avon in laughter and rowdiness, three, four or five of us, and if others were at our favorite pool we chased them off, our penises flying, rocks and yells going everywhere. We scared them half to death, or, if we were in proper mood, we adopted them, kids like us; we swam and climbed on them and trampled the ooze of plants, and the ooze slicked our bodies over their bodies: I can feel it almost like a lover getting ready to make love: and that's about what we did: we made love to the day and we made love to the water: we yelled and slapped it and cuffed it into obedience, and orgasmed it, and tore our legs till blood pricked, and then we swam and I was pretty good and I out-swam some though some out-swam me, and we swam until we felt cool and easy, and then lay on the grass by the mill, to watch the swallows and gape and groan, like lovers after their bout in bed: our spirits ebbing for the nonce, then rising to dress and yell and pull and sing and chase each other home.

How I reveled in summer haying.

Usually, I loaded a small wagon pulled by Burt, Burt eying me, snuffling at me as I pitched the hay: he was getting old and the grey of his wooly hide was shedding outrageously; he lifted each black hoof slowly, often fetching a fart. He liked working the field alone but I preferred working with others. Stripped to the waist, hatless, I forked and grunted and Burt pulled and farted. Some of the time I had to sing, the smell of hay and sun inspiring my songs: sometimes, when I worked with others, all of us sang, horses perkier for our merriment.

Mildred was as good at the fork as I: working side by side, we often bumped and her blue eyes would widen and light up: pretty, blonde, barefooted, she wore a blouse, skirt and Dutch apron: our field ended at the river, an apple grove along the other sides. Two or three of us, in teams, harvested Papa's hay each season: I still smell the timothy and the girl.

Wonderful, wonderful and most wonderful...and yet another.

Henley Street
May 10, 1615

Choir singing was boring—just sucking melancholy out of song—and whenever I could, I skipped it and went off with Becky. No matter how icy, there was fun, hands linked, our runny noses beatific: Becky, whose giggle alerted every boy, was my girl whenever we could steal away and turtle hunt—that was our joy: tirelessly, we combed the creeks and river, staying long past staying time, scolded but not caring.

I see her giddy black eyes, brown mop, skinny legs, tiny hands and tiny feet—barefooted beside me, wetting herself to the legpits, screeching or silent, often too silent, wading lustily. She loved to steal apples, raspberries, strawberries, turnips, hungry from morning till night. I peeled turnips for her and we munched them on a stile, then raced one another, slithered downstream:

"There's one, see, on that log. Be quiet!"

"I'll get 'im."

"No, let me. It's my turn. He's tiny. He's for me."

"Go slowly."

A few times Becky and I rang the church bells for the sexton; together, we stole buns and cookies at home, but best of all we stole happiness, books in running brooks.

She married a seaman and lives in London: I warrant you there are eight children, a happy family—God bless t'em! I would not change the story.

Henley Street

Mother—memories of you are mostly memories of songs you used to sing when sleep was near, lovingly, patiently, sung in my room, close to the varnished beams, curtains drawn, as you sat or lay beside me or rested in a nearby chair.

Our favorite song was "Happy be thou, heavenly queen...man's comfort and angel's bliss...of all women thou hast the prize..."

And I remember each word of Sanctus—and hear each word as you sang it lingeringly; sometimes your hand kept time; sometimes your fingers covered mine.

Stabat Mater Dolorosa...

So many years have lapsed that I have forgotten how you looked, only your eyes and thin figure and voice remain: I hear you when you called us in from play: "Too-lee-looly-loo," you called, shepherding your six for supper and bed.

I roam about, room to room, stooping for a bedroom doorway, floors creaking, the varnished beams always the same, three floors of thinking about me, windows you used to look out of, beds you used to make—or was that another house, another time, another illusion? My house, your house, our house—who owns, who makes traitorous gifts, decisions, contracts, to pile millions of acres of dirt on top of us later?

At the Globe, when I was young, I received quite a visitor! Ben Jonson brought Sir Francis Drake. Ben was a sharer of friends. I was dumbfounded but "El Draque," contemptuously at ease, sat on my backstage table, his plumed hat and red gloves flung on top of a litter of plays. He and Ben discussed a masque Jonson was to produce.

Young as I was, it took courage to speak to "El Draque" because even his purple hat shocked me. But I managed to ask about his attack on Cadiz. Lines warped his mouth, and he said, stroking his corn husk chin:

"It was a matter of guns...we singed the King's whiskers through our superior armament. Ah, good winds too. We had great luck! Don't you believe in luck? When you write a play, isn't it luck, lucky weather, luck with your players, luck with your attendance, the right kind of royalty attending at the right time?"

I saw him again after the defeat of the Armada, at a crowded Thames anchorage. Wounded, he looked older, livid scar on his cheek, the fire dead in his eyes, his expression one of cynicism and fatigue. He wore a squat, official hat. No rings. Leaning against a spattered capstan, he seemed smaller than I had remembered him; he did not recognize me.

"Our fire ships forced the Armada out of anchorage, broke up their plan!" he said, talking to a group of officers.

"Put yourself on a fire ship," he boomed. "You're at the rudder. She's aflame—flames are roaring aft! Your whole ship's blazing but somehow you bugger her against a Spanish hull. You're beaten off. They're afraid you have a powder mine in your hold. There's cannon shot! You dive overboard. It's a long, icy swim. Most men never make it out of that water...

"What we needed was more gun shot, more ammunition, kegs and kegs of powder; then, by God, we'd have run them clean to Spain, run them, not waited, our guns useless. We had to sit it out, wait—no powder. We didn't dare take a chance. Think of it, everything to our advantage but we dared not move. We had to bluff."

I wrote down his words—but I still hear them, it might be five or six years ago, not thirty!

Deceptions of mind bother me: unrehearsed, the brain bedevils and stacks lie on lie...in the lays of time. I turn my glass and am alone, the cuckold of myself reflected in three hundred sixty-five mirrors. My spirits, as in a dream, are bound up, and like the Armada, strewn on shores and still more rocky shores...

Henley Street
May 18, 1615

Memory's snowfall rattles every door and window in my house. Was it the once lost winter thirty years ago in London? From door to door, I begged for work: my hands blue, legs quaking, face frost-galled. Belly empty, pocket empty, I harried taverns, bakeries, homes. People mistrusted me, that wild-haired kid, goat-bearded—doors slammed in my face. Blinded by snow, I headed for the Thames, for the bridge—shelter there. On the way, I passed a tavern and opened a door: a crowd of young men faced me: I asked for work and was given a scullery job, supper and a mat by the stove: I'll never forget the warmth of that mat by that stove: I wanted nothing more: cherry voices and warmth: it all comes back!

A piece of bread in one hand, I fell contentedly asleep. An elephantine man, with florid face and scraggly beard, wakened me roughly.

"Next time you go to sleep don't let the rats share your bread," Falstaff guffawed.

Stratford
May 23

Falstaff helped me find an old cloak and helped me borrow boots and gloves. He got me a stagehand job. Later, he showed me where I could purchase stolen things, sharing his room with him: ribaldry, punning, gargantuan laughter, thievery, friends, foolishness, foppery, wit and wine. Little did I think of using him in a play during the weeks I lived with him. In those days, I had never written a line.

Like an umbrella, his character sheltered me from depression: he introduced me to Marlowe, Kyd, Jonson. Years later, I introduced him to Alleyn and Burbage; Burbage wanted him on stage but Falstaff had his own stage where he could dupe and bedevil, unmolested by paid gapers. By then, he was getting old and liked puttering and sleeping best.

Those were mad times, those days with Falstaff, and yet, behind every laugh lay the threat of poverty, the knife blade of quarrels, reason gone unreasonable. Night after night we went to sleep hungry. With glue and nail we pieced our shoes together, for one more day. With needle and thread we patched our clothes. Falstaff pulled my wisdom tooth to save the barber's fee: "Open wide, yell! There, I've got it, Will, spit now. Spit, boy."

In a few ways Falstaff resembled my father: both were unassuming, generous, dilatory: their fat portraits hang side by side in my mind: the last I heard from my friend was a brief word from Dover where he was working for a shipbuilder and lived in a shanty by the sea.

He would have roared at his role in my plays: he would have objected to his cowardice, upheld his zeal, begged me for a thousand pounds, and tried to bribe me for the address of a pretty woman.

Friend...you were eel-fish, bull's pizzle, dried neat's tongue and stockfish! When you were born the front of heaven was full of fiery shapes and the goats ran from the mountains.

Henley Street
May 25, 1615

A cockroach creeps about my room, an X on its back, the only roach branded in my roost. I see it in the morning, when I sit down to write. It favors a corner, where there is a deep crack, in case of an intruder or wrath on my part. It has a stiff carriage—much more so than any of the others. Ruler, no doubt, with excessive responsibilities! So I have decided to call it Bill. Certainly all other roaches seem afraid of this Conqueror. When I find it on my table, I make a pass at it and it leaps with a scut. It eats paper—old and new. It munches leftovers, liking cheese best, though I think the cheese is pretty well divided between the roaches and the mice.

Henley Street
May 26, 1615

Why am I disliked in Stratford? Is it because I drive a hard bargain? Is it because I have assumed, at least at times, an actor's air? They say I stand aloof but is it possible to cross the Avon to their side? My side is Ptolemy's, Priam's, Cleopatra's, Coriolanus'. We four are difficult to appraise as we walk along Henley Street. The local folk have never heard the creak of chariot wheels.

Lonely...I have been lonely and am lonelier now, but which is lonelier, the pod with one pea or the pod with aliens? True, I have sued for money; true, I have acquired property. And the city man and country man mistrust one another: the writer fits in nowhere: yet, since this is home, I try to accommodate myself, say "yes" to Mr. Combe, and help if I can. "Yes, M."

I never could introduce Ann to Londoners and she has been unable to introduce me to Stratford people. If I were well, if I could write, I would spit on Avon.

Combe is the only person in S. who has seen any of my plays; however, when I talk with him, he confuses scenes and characters; his appreciation is based on pride that says "I can speak of Shakespeare." A Puritan, he patronizes incoming Puritans more than most, helping them infest this town, making it a sawtooth of moral crud, chair and whip in line, summoning whispered inquisitions.

Monday

What fools we mortals are, for I who wrote of shrews married a shrew who is more shrewful than any Kate from Padua. I laugh at my own defeat, a shrew beside a shrew, players nodding at my marital bewilderment, I, the drunkard drunk on illusions. Shall we list her infidelities—country-man at Fair, con-man, neighbor? Shall we name names?

Shakespeare and Ann, at ruins of Kenilworth castle,
copulating in the grass, happy in their bucolic lust.
The two trudge, hand in hand:
Ann ups her skirt and they flop again, giggling:
"Twins," she says.

Henley Street

I married a shrew and yet thirty years ago, Ann and I knew hot jollity at Kenilworth, the grass a hide under us, pigeons reconnoitering castle walls, a falcon lawing the sun. Since Ann and I had a few days for ourselves, we had ridden to K. She was Sweet Villain, and when we pastured the horses and unstuffed our knapsacks, we stuffed ourselves, and sacked ourselves, gorging in sun, the horses stomping and snuffling beyond us. Sweet Villain pulled up her skirts after we had drunk more than we should and I was glad I had not married another. She said "Your hair's redder," and I said "Your hair's yellower," meaning where, and our laughter went bounding.

We sacked that old busky castle from wall to wall, writing on scalded plaster, pushing over abutments, throwing rocks at a fox. From some crater corner, we looked up, our heads dusty, holding each other sexround, our fierceness there while falcons fought, clipping each other, beaking one another, feathers falling. Kenilworth and kings: we smelled unsavory dungeons but pushed our falconry over them, our naked seel better than intercourse of power and time: among the marl, we viewed puffs of smoke from country homes, saw water gleaming, a windmill turning, sheep among sheep, their woolly backs humping toward a rainy sunset.

Soon, soon, time was to tear away our love, but we did not suspect: we were the confidents, our jollity amusing because fastened to laughter, no wrack or confusion: it was slap of hands on bare buttocks, "ah" over breast, mouth sucking, suckling, surprising, surfeiting, back again for more: the taste of love's bite the waist around, the hand up, down, and the grass its hide browner, browner than our flesh, her flesh ignited from within, so burned for me.

Stratford-on-Avon
June 1, 1615

We ate off wooden plates, tulips blooming in the garden, blue and white Chinese plates hanging on the wall, and lilacs blooming in the garden...in a dream I confronted him and he was monarch and he said to me: I am Hamnet, come, we'll go to the guild chapel and hear the sermon...it was a cold sermon but honeysuckle was blooming in the garden...orioles were singing above the oriel. Columbine, ferns, and lilies were on the cabinet: she said to me: Come, Will, eat! I said to her: listen, I hear the pegs moving inside the beams: that is for integrity. Ivy grew on the east wall of my house in those days.

Henley Street
June 3, 1615

Alone, following the Roman wall, as it girdled London, I used to speculate where the Roman gods had gone; thinking, as well, of those of Egypt and Greece...time with a scroll on his back, asking alms. Smashed bricks, *memento mori,* along that vast, yellow, unweeded garden, were questions in their own right, broken, to be kicked aside, as are our own questions concerning mortality.

Gazing at the Thames, I hoped for hope from the wide wall, wider river and broader mystery. I went over my plays...Ulysses...Cleopatra...Prospero... The wall, with its imperialism and legion of whispers, said "no, master, no," speaking in the voice of Lear's fool.

Ellen and I climbed the castle where Caesar lived, the tallest site in London, the Thames below, flowers and vines crawling over ruins, the walls of yesterday saying "Et tu Brutus."

Danger knows full well that hate is doubly dangerous: we are two lions littered in a day, and the litter of stones crumbles underfoot, but Ellen cries out to me, and I catch her by the arm.

There is a white sail on the river...

Ay, me, how fine a thing the heart of woman! I thought it then and think it still, the very best of her is gentle subtlety: it is this that takes a man in.

A flock of blackbirds lit below us, covering the fallen stones like black hail.

We went many times to that castle and walked along its ancient yellow walls; she asked me for poetry and I repeated lines: what were they, I wonder?

Now...most noble one...the gods stand friendly today, that we may, lovers in peace, lead on our days to age:

I am constant as the northern star, of whose true-fixed and resting Quality there is no fellow in the firmament...the skies are painted with unnumbered sparks...they are all afire, and every one doth shine; but there's but one in all doth hold his place: so in the world...

The stars came out, a summer's night on Caesar's place, and we heard frogs and the tittering of lovers, ourselves loving that place, our flesh, that empirical wisdom. We went so often we called it "our castle."

Henley Street
June 5, 1615

At Christmas skirling bagpipers, piping a *waulking* song, greeted us at Dunira. Ellen's room, in a squat tower, faced a narrow lake with ragged shore pines and a small island, wild geese and ducks resting on the water, cold, cold, moss blue water.

Sun crossed the bear rugs and tiles of her floor.

Her bed was canopied with green velvet embroidered with golden shields and

crossed spears, seen on her coat-of-arms.

She called my attention to the pulls on the heavy drapes, each pull a carved ivory ball enclosing a ball inside another.

Hand in mine, she showed me her collection of silver, gold, and ivory fans, fans from Egypt, Greece and India, arranged on her walls, some open, some in cases, flabellum with bone handles, Venetian lace fans, tomb fans with gold-encrusted ribs, a Greek fan like an acanthus leaf. I can see the movement of her lips as she described them; I can see her hand, pointing.

We often walked around the lake and through the pollarded garden, its cypresses like stone columns: we walked the moors until Christmas cold sent us shivering to the big fireplaces where we talked and ate and sang and drank.

Someone kept the fire blazing in her fireplace and we would sink down on her bed or lie on the bear rug and make love, the firelight skirling her ivory, her fans and the canopy's yellow silk lining.

Hugh opened our door one morning very early, while we were busy making love, and with a boisterous laugh he said:

"I just finished with my woman; when you're done, we'll go hunting. The horses are saddled. Better lock your door next time!"

Hugh—his huge body on a huge hunter—led us hunting along a loch, where the ocean, squeezed as in a glass case, shuddered, as though resentful of its trap, as though it considered everyone as intruder. I was awed by the water's dark and the chasms menacing it. Deer eluded us and while we followed the loch, I lost interest in the hunt for the quarry of sea and earth, spirit and well-being.

Hunting, walking, eating, drinking, love-making, this was the happiest time of my life. Her brother's acceptance amounted to adoption; he often came to my room and talked at length, sharing intimacies; the only misadventure during my stay was an attack of hungry peasants who swarmed the castle court, shrilly demanding food, some in kilts with silent bagpipes.

Ellen and I visited the ruins of a sprawling Cistercian abbey on her Dunira property; there, under the vaulted archway, where roses climbed, I felt inspired, and, staying on I wrote *Cymbeline,* scenes and words coming easily, happiness a constant companion: the sweetness of her personality seemed altogether mine. Words and flesh—they were mine, in that sun and cloud world of Dunira.

The weather settled into a steady spell, my room overlooking garden, lake and bluecap forest. London might have been at the bottom of the sea: I could not have cared less. Its dirt and beauty—I never missed them.

Visiting the abbey frequently, we met several of the monks who resided in a section of the refectory; their geniality contented us and we lingered with them, in their herb garden, by a fountain—pigeons about. A marvelously tiny man, spry though old, gave us a parchment book, one he had rubricated, pleased to see us in love.

Hugh accompanied us occasionally to bring food for the brothers, making the short trip with donkeys carrying loaded panniers. He, too, would linger, sharing our mood.

Abbey garden, fountains, vegetables and herbs in rows:
a collection of rare fans on a wall:
Hugh and Shakespeare drink at a refectory table:
a peasant enters and Hugh beats the man
who is asking for alms:
skirl of bagpipes.

On the Scottish coast the sunset prowled the lowtide combers, rolling cloud into cloud, wave into wave. The clouds absorbed orange with yellow and the yellow took on red, the red brooming low, sweeping shoreward, reaching the sand at our feet.

Is it true that we saw the sunset together, her arms around me, the rocks beyond us red, the sunset extending for miles? The moon rose out of a rust-colored sky?

Stratford-on-Avon
June 11, 1615

"Darling, ours is a supreme happiness and we must cherish it," she wrote me long ago.

For years I kept her letters in my desk at Blackfriar's house, to lose them when the place burned: waxed, ribboned and perfumed letters, from France, Italy, and Scotland. I could rewrite some of them from memory—some.

At the time I received her letters I thought that a number of them had been detained much too long and I thought several of them had been tampered with. I put this aside as fancy for I was willing to be blind. As I think back it's odd I never suspected censorship. And why was it I never knew till later that she and her family opposed the Queen?

The knife of one's own stupidity cuts deepest!

A year or two after the attack on her, when she was back in Scotland, she wrote that Hugh was assassinated in Glasgow—an Elizabethan courtesy, someone said. The shock was more of a shock coming from her: Hugh dead, big Hugh, with his cleft beard, bushy eyebrows, and mop of greying hair: the bigness of his Dunira castle comes to me, along with his hospitality.

For years I was driven half insane by a dream of an enveloping cloak: the cloak swallowed my house, trees, sun, and stars: I heard a woman scream inside this luminous thing. Behind the folds was a bearded face, coming closer and closer.

Henley Street

I was headed for home when I met Ellen and the autumn sun favored us, potentates meeting by a river, our kingdom the leaves along the shore, the ash red, our introduction friends, our hopes instantaneous. I saw beneath her gloves to her veined hands; I saw her veined breasts beneath her dress; I saw beneath her smiles the invitation, rebuffs, wiles...

Yet who dares to know royalty outside the theatre!

Home, I reminded myself, is Stratford; but, who among us remembers home and fidelity?

I loved home once, my Ann, my children, and the sharing of the things a man wants to share. I loved these in my groin and the raves of sweetness summoned me, over and over, till I was worn out and imperious insomnia stalked and kept me at my desk or sent me.

How can it be, in the midst of aged foolishness, Ellen appears, to convince, to distract—those devil eyes of hers and that black hair and her white, white skin begging love. When she speaks, I listen: I turn and listen: I turn and listen again for she is theatre, its hush, its compassion, its folly.

Jonson was right to introduce us; he thought to kill my pen and wit. It was his plot to make me plotless—great jest! He was right, for sleepless nights swept around and the pulsing indirection of sex carried me to her for yet another rendezvous.

Did I ever come to my senses: was it a week, month, or year? Was it she who nailed the fog over my soul? Ah, crucifix between her breasts, so soft, so impaled! What graciousness!

London was too small for us for everyone perceived the unperceivable, impaired our pairing and yet...but all this is past and the last seat empty.

We thought to escape to Rome, that eternal place for eternal mouths. She offered me money and I refused. At the theatre she begged me to accept, for us, for time, for love...and I accepted. On stage I swore to testify but I hugged my testament and my lines faltered.

We have played our parts too often, our thighs packed with wax, our mouths with honey; we bring it to the hive; and, like the bees, are murdered for our pains.

Henley Street
June 18, 1615

For months I kept at the writing of *Antony and Cleopatra*—Ellen seldom out of my mind. Yet the writing was an abatement of anguish, scenes lifting me out of maelstroms, Antony's turbulence alleviating mine. Apartment and theatre were all I allowed myself, sharing time with Jonson, dividing mutual crusts.

Rain—rain—when has it rained more! It was well I had the Egyptian sun to keep my bones warm.

Some scenes evolved easily; others fought me, full of sound and fury. I could not visualize certain scenes on the stage and sometimes strange actors walked the boards and stole my lines, fixing them with their own personalities. Alleyn stalked as Caesar, and I had to re-write again and again.

Baxter affronted me with his buffoonery and I had to cross out his lines. Phips—our cheerful homosexual—had Cleopatra in his perfumed arms, jeering at me. Kempe jigged.

On top of all this, insomnia set in and never left me for weeks. March – April – May, it was the warmth of May that unlocked its crossbow and shot me outdoors, to sit and sit for hours.

There, in the sun, my shirt open, shoes off, grass alive, lilacs alive, birds twirping, I knew I could make *Antony and Cleopatra* successful. There in the sun people and river came alive. The sun's gnomon wrote. I bowed my head and waited. At my desk, I hurled my sentiency... alive, it must come alive, to hurl aside life's muddle: alive: these people from the past must speak: nothing is more remote than yesterday: speak to them: make them chroniclers: break their sleep.

The Thames with anchored and sailing ships:
Ellen and Shakespeare on board a coaster,
leaning on the taffrail:
She settles her tam and quotes from Two Gentlemen of Verona.
They talk of Naples as sailors leer at them
from on top a stack of boxes.

Henley Street
June 20, 1615

Ellen and I sailed the Thames, the water stippled with gulls; our hands locked, we stood at the stern and hoped for a smooth voyage, with love, our rudderbar credulous to us, the wind mild and lasting. In Venetian wine there would be happiness, we promised each other...

But why are you lost to me and I alive?

Ellen—what is this, that reaches round us and never arrives; what is this that promises return?

Ours was a proper departure, landing us on the Italian shore, love in a town of disinterested people.

Perhaps I want the impossible: yes, yes, I want that time when we were there in Naples, when we strolled the seaside; when we sailed the waterlanes and walked Roman streets and her fountains watched us with sleepy eyes, spray beaded on some bronze arm.

I dislike borrowing things and yet I'm borrowing memories, borrowing time, those bronzes, our return, our boat bucking seas, sending us north, ice off the larboard, back to reality, debts, conniving. We said good-bye but our good-bye was postponement. Our wheel became St. Catherine's. At a gypsy teller's tent there was a kind of double silence.

I lived for my work, starved for it.

With my pen I quartered the earth and green pastures and made them live for her and the witchcraft of hope, to shake off sadness and burst the anarchies of soul.

Incorrect to heaven, some say.

June 22, 1615

What a cocked up play, my *Coriolanus*. To fill my pocket! To fob off bad for good, that was it. I leaned on one crutch and fought with another—and fell. Too many of my plays were crutched. I borrowed too much from Plutarch and others. I worshipped royalty. I was too conventional, too romantic, borrowing plots, borrowing, borrowing, double sure, never sure, cocksure.

Henley
Midsummer-day

And I must guess the identity of her attackers—or why they wanted her life. Christ, we had our list of suspects. And what came of our grim suppositions? Nothing. We said: was it robbery, I prithee? Jealousy? Hatred? Politics? We said. We have said and I go on saying. Thrift, Horatio, thrift...and I have not saved.

Henley Street
June 26, 1615

Hamnet...

Today is your death day.

After you died I went to the shore and the sea's clods of wood and detritus infused in me a loneliness that nothing has every wiped out: a wrangle of foam goes on and on inside me; the grey that topped the abyss of ocean finds a darker grey in me; the gulls are sleep-flying for you.

Hamnet, my son...

Prince of my house, I loved you. We had such fun. Good day, sweet boy, how dost thou, good boy? May flights of angels sing you on your way. When you died, Stratford teemed with monsters. Your hand in mine, such a cold hand, you said adieu. What God was this to snuff you out at eleven. Grief stiffened me: I feel it today, when there should have been a birthday party not a remembrance. The sea rolls back on me as I sit here, my legs unable to move, pain working in me.

The Queen and her killings...time and its murders...they are alike! The unfairness of life, O what angels sing the truth? What angels! Go, fetch me a quart of sack; put a toast in't.

God took him from me...damn the God that steals your son.

King of grief they might have called me. Now, all is mended by many years:

ours be your patience, your gentle hand lead us, and take our hearts.

I had thought to leave him something beside my father's coat-of-arms. I had thought to introduce him to the theatre, have him think about my plays, have him know the better part of London. He would have been a friend of Drake's; perhaps he might have sailed on Raleigh's Virginia voyages. Perhaps Jonson might have taught him Latin. Perhaps is my treadmill, and I wear it thin.

He went to a few plays with me and thrilled to them. He respected me. Loved me. What were his thoughts, as he died? To be such a short, short time on stage! Was he resentful, bewildered? I think he was confused because of the great fever. Good God, what was the use of his flowering? It was an error of the moon...it makes men mad.

To thine own self be true, they say, and I, still harping, I ask your credent ear to listen: we shall not look upon his like again?

Speak... I go no further.

Stratford-on-Avon

Flowers in my hand, I thought to visit his grave, but as I limped across the yard, thinking of the bone house and how each of us ends there, remembering those underneath my shoes, under the tree, under the threatening sky, I laid the flowers on another's grave, and the dove carved on that granite nodded, as it were, pecked me across the grass, among the weeds, reminding me of other men's grief.

That woman, over there on her knees, isn't that Nancy Richards? I recognize her shoulders and the back of her head. Her father died last month.

What stupidity, this crawling, mewing, kneeling, this unresurrectable world, with weeds that smell of dust.

I remember a king's grave in Denmark, with falcons carved on it, falcons of black marble, perched on top a branch, carved black centuries ago.

I walked through the rain, moving as fast as my legs would let me, my soul full of discord and dismay, wishing I had not gone, resolved to confine myself to myself, incarcerate my grief in my writing, or, if I could not write, be ennobled, not afflicted as other men are with contagion.

The fault, dear Brutus...

After his death, the dissentious Judith and Ann used to side against me: "He's no good, Judith," Ann preached vehemently. "What does he care for any of us! He's always away in London. You've heard him say that life's but a walkin' shadow. We're just so many shadows to him!"

I would stare at Judith after one of Ann's outbursts; I would look at her and through some sort of necromancy I would see Hamnet's face—I would remember our fun, our fishing, our swimming in the Avon.

It was not the constant conspiracy of Ann and Judith that drove the final nail; it was Judith's resemblance, same color and texture of hair, same blue eyes, same half smile, same propensity to giggles, same way of rubbing her hands on her clothes. I had always favored Hamnet because he and I had shared more. Now, now that Judith lived, I could not accept his death. Of course I never wanted her to die. As long as the twins lived there was accord. If death must steal one of them...but I couldn't, wouldn't choose. Yet, in ugliest anger, I had shouted my preference. And she knew I often saw Hamnet when I looked at her: I've seen her run when I stared at her: I've heard her cry: "Mama, he's looking at me that way!"

"These are my twins," I used to say, showing them to people. *Twins*—for how long!

I bought her a goonhilly pony, an excellent pacer, and taught her to ride. I got her a lamb and a puppy, I brought her gifts from London. I brought her things from France and Italy. There was little chance to get through to her because of Ann. If I won Judith for a while, I lost her when at work in London. She never wrote to me...or Ann destroyed those letters. During my years in the theatre, in London and touring the provinces, all those years, I received no note. She never expressed a desire to see one of my plays, seemed disinterested in my life in the city—unless it was to suggest I bring something when I came home.

Home?

July 1, 1615

I am that wanderer of night, full many a morning have I seen flatter the mountain tops with sovereign eye...

There's memory, that's for remembrance; pray, you, love, remember...and there is pansies; that's for thought...there's fennel for you, and columbine; there's rue...you must wear your rue with a difference.

Through the years they mangled those lines! How cold to hear them back-stage! How cold to hear them now, here, in my room, echoing from varnished beams, off-stage in my oriel of yesterday.

But I should not have gotten sick: I should have stayed in London to the end, fought the Puritans, fought the King, the tax collectors, the players of the shrew's men!

Pain shut me out: the body must have its moments of solace—the mind its soothsayer!

I would give you violets...but they are planted around a gravestone.

I was a young man when I wrote those lines; like Ophelia I ride on bawdy repetitions, error on error.

The table of my memory is dusted with crumbs.

Off-stage, the wind gushes; on-stage, there's a frenzied pitch of "no!"

Chorus, players!

This love, this royalty by jackanapes brought to earth, the stage to my back: what can a man affirm in such a position: flight? I speak to her and she puts her fingers on my lips and holds her beauty like a whip over me. The curtain came down quickly: fie, the curtain often comes down swiftly, manipulated by fury, a last sound snapped out, muffling resolution, covering courage...

There is a curtain for love and one for hate: there is a curtain for youth and another for age. And when we finally realize these things we are dotards, and our realization laughs.

The executioner's curtain is no doubt the swiftest. The jig maker's safest. The priest's dullest. The mariner's loneliest. The lover's saddest.

Henley Street
July 8, '15

These pages are so unlike my plays and sonnets and yet I have to struggle to get anything down! Here is my mock dukedom; since I can not write any longer I look back across time from the shelf of my memory, longing to improve my existence: I am certain that the old word-chattels gladly deserted me, looking for a young man, no doubt, an upstart from Snitterfield, enroute to London, riding a brood mare, humming...hey, non nonny...

...Heaven mend all!

Henley Street
July 9, 1615

Elsinore has a tongue of land that licks at time, a place that ends with defeat, its castle and its people falling into apparitions.

Usurping night, Elsinore made me face the northern ocean, irresolution. There was no illusion to being there: rain cusped out of sky: the snow fell: it was a bitter time to see the place, a blastment. I had shaken off that incessant pain that stabbed the roof of my skull each time I leaned over, that writhed through my eyes: I would rub my eyes and feel something click in my brain as if it had fallen into place again. But I was still weak from this ailment and tired from long journeys and longer thoughts. I was filled with new dreads, especially here, under the rain. Irresolution: it is wrong to deny it for there is no denying its power.

There is something like death, being alone in a foreign land. With determination grappling, the loneliness and death-sense grip harder. So I felt that I was borrowing from everything around me.

It is a custom for some of us to think and yet I turn against that custom. It is better to live, simply as simple people live. I wanted to live without the paper-world, to shun its distortions, escape its death head, the charnel house of yesterday.

As I stood on that tongue of land, I heard the slobber of the sea: I heard old men whisper: I heard old passions. My blood was young and yet I could not get away. The porches of my ears wanted friendship, I, the kind hand, the kinder mouth.

"If you were here there would be reason enough. Without you, there is no more than walls and sky and food. To be sure, I eat. To be sure, I move about. You understand what I mean. I find that there is so much in life that never gets said. When I am with you I am unable to say it...old plaint. I try to convey with my presence—that is help. You, too, have this desire, and have expressed it. When we were in bed, mating, there was a beauty in that union that sufficed...until tomorrow. Then, caught up in time, I sensed the old longing, to share the unshareable, to reach the unreachable. Here, in this cold room, I am trying to make life a little more livable, for you, for me."

So I wrote her.

Stratford

YEARS AGO

At Oxford, it is pleasant to recall, I stopped at Duvenant's inn frequently, the rooms and meals much to my taste. Madame Duvenant, dressing like someone from an Inigo Jones' masque, her rosy sex refreshing, greeted me with a favorable eye. Veal, shoulder of mutton, rabbit, green fish...gingerbread...strawberries...claret: she knew my favorites, sharing my meals and bed. When I arrived, tired by travel, she had someone look after me, prepare my meal; then, we enjoyed each other's company in the dining room she kept for private use. A Londoner and play-goer, she fixed her lusty eyes on me, hand on my arm, and made me feel I had never been away. She asked no promises, required no letter-writing, no payment. "It's late. Will, shall we go up to bed?" Why are there so few generous women?

Henley Street
July 13, 1615

I'd like one more ferry trip across the Thames, in the morning, the water dark, Sly at the oars, telling me about the latest girl, of the girls he has ferried, girls he wanted to love but could never love, old, old Sly.

"There's one, Will, you just can't beat. She's about this tall, tiny around the waist, and she makes you know, before you know it, that she can be had for very little, very sweetly done too, that's the game of it...that's the game of her, that little one, Portia, they call her. Portia, the one with grey eyes and small mouth. When she stands up beside me in the boat to pay her fare, I groan. It's terrible being old, Will, when you can't do it any more. And I want to do it to her, to be young again. That Portia, she comes mostly in the evenings, I guess you know why. But she's not always alone, but when she's alone, we talk. That she, she is little around the waist but has melon breasts, the kind, you know how they are. I will give you her address, if you want. Shillings, now Will! But she's not one you'll forget, I warn ye. That mouth of hers and them eyes of hers. Faggots for her, that's it, Will, faggots for men who see her..."

The boat shifts, Sly's oars are cracked, his old face crisped from the sunny crossings, the winds and fogs. He's been boatman for forty-odd years, he says. He has worn out a dozen boats, which he builds himself, to make them stout enough. Sun on his boat, the water dark...

I'd like to cross once more with him, though he's been dead a long time, cross with other boats around, small boats and schooners, some with sails unfurled, seaward bound.

St. Swithin's Day

If I knew where I was going to die I wouldn't go near the place.

Stratford
July 20, 1615

Today, warm sun and silence were mine and pain alleviated: I hoped for recovery, hoped to write again, hoped that my memory might outlive death half a year; so shall I progress, ant-wise, day by day: ants, as you creep over the woodwork, stumble against the grain, think of me and the words I summon: conviction me to another Rosalind: the Touchstone will unblacken and reveal pure, pure gold: alchemy of ruffians and angels:

Tongues I'll hang on every tree
For the souls of friend and friend...

The sword in my chimney corner has not been unsheathed for years: when I bought it I thought I had the keenest blade in London, sharper than my rapier: when I carried it I liked to give it a flick now and then, to catch the eye of a woman: I kept it polished: it saved my life in a street fracas: Hamnet liked it: he used to shoulder it and parade about: I thought it would keep me young forever: I thought it would cut across time, loosen parchment and paper, let flood a bevy of immortal words above a sea of faces...

...for Thomas Combe.

The Roebuck *on the Atlantic, bucking water,*
sailors topmast, Raleigh in his cabin,
one eye on the compass, another on a manuscript:
Books line the walls; a monkey chitters:
the Roebuck *pitches:*
Raleigh's jewels flash on his hands:
"Mermaid," yells a bow sailor.

Henley Street
July 24, 1615

I had thirty-five days at sea with Raleigh:

How he commands, respected by his seamen, each crewman called by name. There is adequate leisure aboard his frigate. I never saw anything done "on the double" as aboard an Essex ship where the captaincy seemed insecure.

On board the *Roebuck* I kept at my writing, lolling and writing on deck or passing hours in his cabin where I gave up to his booked walls: volumes in French, English, Italian, Greek, manuscripts in Latin and Hebrew, his literary world broader than mine.

In his cabin, under his table lantern during bad weather, during squalls, I wrote an act and then, at Raleigh's urging, read it aloud. Feet propped on a mother-of-pearl chest, he listened gravely, smoking his clay pipe, brandy in reach, his comments as mellow as his drink, Oxford accent to my liking.

Ere we were ten days old at sea I had written several scenes—writing in the sun and spray, sitting on coils of rope, a gun lashed in front of me, gulls mewing.

"Mermaid...mermaid," a sailor yelled aloft, and we scuttled to the starboard rail, to see something break water and then submerge, its pearly back toward us.

She swam and dove, flipping in and out of swells, the bubbles foaming around her, making off at a 40 degree angle from our stern, pearl or green grey, though I never saw her distinctly.

The excited sailor who had spotted her claimed that he had seen her face...

"such a beautiful face!"

Raleigh appeared.

"They're deep swimmers," he said, as we leaned far over, hoping she might reappear. "She'll likely stay down a long time. Must have powerful lungs, those mermaids."

He told of other mermaids: he had heard one call through fog and mist on the Orinoco river; he had seen one off the Cape, near a small island; he said that seeing a mermaid spells luck.

He went on talking of a trip upriver, jungle river, heat, crocodiles, green birds, monkeys with beards, butterflies, solid white butterflies, bigger than your hands: his descriptions sent my brain going: I too was the Queen's favorite, Shepherd of the Ocean, sailing a *Golden Hind:* I would find El Dorado in Manoa.

His accent sometimes thickened to a brogue and it was difficult to follow. Talking of his travels, his eyes grew nervous, searching, searching, seeing inside, greying: his arms gestured.

We leaned against the taffrail, as the ship heeled under a wind, white caps racing after.

His *Roebuck* is splendid, new, well-equipped, faster than others of design. He and his navy draughtsmen spent months on her, and she cost him a fortune.

On this run we fired new cannon, firing them to test their recoil, trying a device designed by his chief gunner: for Mr. Ames the firing took place after dawn, when the ocean was smooth; I was wakened five or six mornings; the great ship rolled in protest and rigging and beams creaked. One morning I was on deck to witness the testing.

Legs spread, soap on him, he rode the swells, while a sailor threw water over him, a sexful man, proud, and that same pride was at dinner in his cabin while being served among his officers and it was there while he read to me at the same table, eatables cleared, read me from the Greek poets, Pindar's ode on boxing, Simonides and his Perseus imprisoned in a chest at sea, Anakreon: reading the Greek and then translating as if it were his tongues.

It seemed to me he might be fit to govern the new world...a great, wise colonist...

On our trip we visited Madeira Island, disembarking at noon, the cambers keeling us into warm, shallow water, the weather perfect. I had a carcanet that I was determined to give a girl, in exchange. The priest, in the town, was very determined to detain me: to please him, I had to see the hairs of the Virgin, treasured in a box: the coil of hair kept the convent free of famine, he insisted: with his gigantic paunch I felt he might cause a famine of his own: he had a tree-filled, bird-filled cage he wanted me to see, strung with brass wires, where hundreds of birds lived. Negro girls, naked except for the cloth pad underneath the calabash shells they carried on their heads, wandered past the cage to see the birds, and found me most amusing. Their smooth, dark features, slick jet hair, round waists and small breasts were delightful. The priest had to leave—called by the convent bell. I gave the youngest my carcanet: the bushes slid about us, our hands together, the leaves cool, the cool stream cool beside us, giving us water in our hands: birds in the aviary whistled and sang, while she fondled the carcanet and lay with me: I had never had anyone so young, accomplished, kindly, wooing, mouth tasting of fruit: she peeled fruit taken from a bush and we ate together: she filled her calabash at the stream and left me, lying, dreaming of her smiles and stroking hands...

Stay illusion.

I liked sprawling in my bunk, the ocean light illuminating the ceiling, a book or two beside me.

From above came the pad-pad of barefoot sailors, shift of rigging and cordage, yaw of boom, sough of wind and flap of canvas; from below came the gurgle of seas and jab of crested rollers that sometimes held the ship suspended for a moment and then permitted her to careen as she drove down inclines steep enough to shake the reaches of the sails.

When I dozed I felt the vastness, ringed vastness, and I was monarch through nearly closed lids: I was ruler of my inconsistencies: I dreamed an island, chained by surf and reef, where life was incredibly carefree, a warmth of flowers, fruit—women.

At night, in the bunk, oil lamp swinging, I imagined the uncharted waters beneath us, porpoise and whale, creatures that pursued us as we floated across a valley, across a hill where coral studded the top: I saw monsters pass and re-pass, dark blue, grey, orange, fins fluted like fans close to our keel. Streamers of kelp and seaweed tangled crab and shark and I fell asleep, my play forgotten, the lamp burning, burning, burning...

Screaming, a seaman plunged from our topgallant, to die on deck while we were outrunning a storm.

Raleigh had his body wrapped in canvas and tossed overboard. No ceremony. Giant, wind-wracked combers.

"Do you know his name? Is there any record?" I asked.

"Timothy Parkes."

"Where was he from?"

"Dover. He was wanted there for murdering two women."

"Was he a good seaman?"

"No. And he was eaten up with scurvy."

And Raleigh's face said: "What kind of ship can an officer command sailored by rogues?" But he was all man: I saw him, in his canvas sack, as all men, falling...falling.

There was never another voyage for me after Raleigh's...nor was there ever another Sir Walter. I should have been his champion. He needed me to fight for him. I have often shut my eyes and seen his books and sensed the cradling lull of his ship and felt the grace and power of him standing beside me: books, beams, a pointed beard, a swinging lamp, smell of oakum and ocean.

To think that I witnessed his trial and made no attempt to defend him...to think that I saw him in prison...to think...cold venison! Cry your mercy!

Henley Street
July 28, 1615

At the Mermaid Tavern, Raleigh laughed over his ale, his lanky body screwed on a rickety chair, the wind and rain howling, people coming and going, their clothes soggy, the wind gusting inside with each arrival. Most newcomers made for the fireplace, stamping and shaking out their coats; boots and leggings steamed.

Grinning, Raleigh lit his pipe, a dozen men around our table, elbowing Ben Jonson and me.

"Come on, Ben, smoke another, and you, too, Will."

Raleigh's coat was ripped, where a sword or cutlass had slashed; he pushed a tobacco pouch and pipe toward me.

"I'll drink with you—but not smoke," I said.

"Try again. You'll learn to like it."

"You experiment," I said. "Once was enough."

"But I'm not experimenting. I've smoked on the long watches. It settles the blood and calms the mind. The Indians..."

"We know about the Indians," Jonson said. "Just remember, we're not Indians!"

"You might better be! Here, lad, bring us more ale! Let's drink!"

"Here's to your return! London's London with you around."

"Have you seen my new play?"

"What play is it?"

"*The Winter's Tale*," I said.

"What—a chilly play on top of this miserable weather! Why a month ago I was basking in the sun...you and your plays! Is this Denmark and another Hamlet? Tell me, Will, was Hamlet named for your son—are those lines in his honor?"

Jonson interrupted and answered for me:

"When my boy died I wrote something for him. I was in prison then and the jailer grabbed my manuscript and spat on it. Bah, that's the kind of crassness that shakes you. I've forfeited goods in payment of my stupidities but I haven't forfeited my hatred of injustice! It's another kind of injustice when a boy, a stripling, dies. Will made Hamnet into *Hamlet,* an outcry against this world."

He drank his ale and I saw him examine his thumb, where they had branded it when he was in prison; he nodded to himself; I suppose his thoughts were of his boy, a victim of the plague...

Jonson eats poorly. Prison treatment has hurt him. His hair is greying, particularly on one side, sweeping down, showing when he talks with gusto. Teeth are missing. Today he wears a suit of black wool, his cuffs clean, his collar clean. He hardly seems one of us.

Raleigh's sword scrapes against the table as he leans forward, talking of his voyages. His is a perpetual struggle with storms and mutinies and his flashing eyes convey a courage one has to take into account. He has sent the idlers packing and smokes with his pipe in the bowl of his palm, its brown the color of his hands, the five or six rings on his fingers blazing: opals and rubies, I am told.

I am also told that if he sold the jewels he wears he could pay for the construction of a ship-of-the-line.

Henley Street
July 30, 1615

I came across several old letters this morning. Raleigh's is hard to decipher:

Portsmouth
March 9, 1608

Will Shakespear—

We have taken an old carrack, the *Madre de Dios*, and spoils clutter her deck as we lie at anchor in Portsmouth Bay, spoils, things the Queen would grow sullen over, wanting them. Some of them bloody and soaked with spray, they have a cheapness about them, a liar's eye. You and Ben would know how to laugh and knock them about. Here's a green gem in a brooch a negro queen must have worn, its horse's eye staring through a slash of sail canvas. Here's a rope of skulls carved in brownish ivory;

here's a tiara ornamented with pale yellow gems I can't identify...a pile of brass bracelets alongside a smashed cutlass. As for me, I'll take the wind in the rigging and a clear landfall.

How are your plays going this season? Sometimes, when a sea rages, Macbeth howls in my ear, Othello lifts his hand as stars dive below the washed horizon.

Shun the Queen's condemnations. It is usually her freedom—seldom ours. Stay clean!

But if I could write like you I would try to destroy political chicanery, though meddling with the Crown may spell my doom.

Well, I will make London late next month, and see you at the Tavern.

Raleigh's pen dug into the paper, and the signature has almost disappeared for lack of ink.

The Tower

Will Shakespear—

When I scribbled verses on a window, our Queen was pleased. I did not know—my crystal would not divulge that I would become a chemist in the Tower, alchemist of solitude. I thought the compass mine, shrewdly boxed...

London
April 9, 1593

Will—

For years I have been planning an expedition up the Orinoco, to locate a gold mine. The fabled mine is near Spanish

> settlements and these may present hazards to any English force. A Spaniard, a Captain Berrio, is entrenched there, along the River. The expedition will tax my resources but I am determined for the sake of the Crown: to carry out my plans I will require several shallow draft frigates and several small boats; there are no accurate maps and the mine is in fever jungle. Certes a month or two will go into exploration, hacking this way and that. The roguish crew of prison perverts will contribute their share of complications, no doubt of that, my friend. Console yourself that you will never know such an experience as dealing with deckloads of cutthroats. To be a voyageur you must condone scapegoats, assassins, rapists, thieves...but you know our maritime history. I have been accused of bad voyages...who has not made bad voyages who dared voyages? If this expedition can be materialed the victualing will be a matter of months. Wish me well...wish me God's speed.
>
> I am contributing £3,000, and it seemeth to me this Empire is reserved for Her Majesty and the Nation. I can find the gold King of Cundinamarca: *el hombre dorado*. Who knows, as in Sergas de Esplandián, we may reach the Island of California, inhabited by Amazon women with passionate hearts and great strength, where there is abundant gold.

There were other letters in this vein, about his future. As explorer he was to the manner born. Thou canst not be false to any man—his letters seemed to say.

The Tower

> Like our ship *Revenge* I am surrounded by an armada of enemies, all my pikes splintered. In the beginning of the fight I had a hundred for me; volleys, boardings, and enterings have done their damage...this composition and exile are the dullest and longest in the history of our Tower; the book I am writing is for Prince Frederick, a slow, slow tacking about; yet you, who respect writing, realize the salvation. Tell me, friend, that I will fare well with my *History of the World*...

It is still my error that I never assisted him: it was my error to have shut my mind: there are many I could have helped as I went along. But to pass by some-one great—that is great misfortune.

I hear him telling about how he burned the town of San José; I hear him telling about the treachery of the Tarawa Indians; his terrible thirst when his ship ran out of water at sea; he is boarding a Spanish frigate, raiding for guns...

'Sblood, the Spanish are a cruel lot, chaining the caciques, scorching their naked bodies with hot bacon, beating them, starving them, decapitating them...

The Tower

> Write to me, lad, before thought's relicts utterly obsess me and the ghouls remove me in their stinking chains. I have seen and heard them, ghouls and ghosts of this town and tower, seen and heard them cringe and bully, nightlong. Stones multiply their menace. There's an old seadog from Dublin crumpled in a cell here, a grumbling bag: he claims he used to sail with me; by his own confession he is the murderer of his crippled father. He is to be freed in the Spring. Freed? Free—are we ever free, my lad? When I sniff the brined air I am hard put not to cast myself off the Tower—I still hope to see the sails double-reefed and porpoises rising off the bow...

Later he wrote bread—bread—bread. "Time drives the flocks," he said: "I am reading the *Amoretti*... have you read Spenser recently?

"*None can call again the passed time*," he wrote. I repeated those seven words. I repeat his bread...bread...bread...it is not bread we want. I did not care. Who cares now?

Henley Street
August 1, '15

What times we had, Raleigh, Marlowe, Jonson, and I, Marlowe and his wit, Raleigh and his tales of the sea, Jonson and his satirical pomposities in Latin or Greek. Then, then...Marlowe's murder crept through our veins and left us dumb or feverish, our very gatherings viewed with disapproval.

Hail drubbed our windows, the chill of complicity and duplicity spread over cobbles, the clatter of horses' hooves meant torture on the spit of tomorrow: these were hitched to our beads of sweat.

We had seen our share of slings and arrows. Was it important who killed Marlowe? We weren't sure. All threads of evidence were thin threads! We praised Marlowe, shuffled through our worn pockets to bury him—Raleigh at sea now. We excused, blamed, made our exodus.

Ann said, with scorn:

"It's the company you keep! London! Always London!"

As if our plays could be produced in Stratford!

"It's men who blaspheme God who find the gutter! Listen to what people say about Raleigh! He'll have a bad end!" So they prophesied over sour beer.

Chris Marlowe was squat, dark, tousle-headed, many-freckled, with wretched teeth and poor eyes. He weighed far too much for a small man—his clothes were sacks at times—his body lost inside for all its bulk. He had character and a voice that conveyed character—his speech superior to many actors. He could memorize lines quickly, and speak them sincerely, interpreting with sound thinking behind them. When nervous he picked his teeth and jogged his foot, when writing or talking, not on the stage. He slumped in his chair habitually, as if he had been on his feet for days. When he spoke, there was Marlowe, bringing you to attention, his eyes serious, the warmth of him coming to you, a piece of currency.

Stratford

Marlowe and I worked throughout the night, troubled by reeky candles, rain and chill. He kept us grinding by saying we'd soon see the sun cross the roof tops.

The sun...where was it?

Our playwriting went badly as we worked at rephrasing, changing, cutting, adding. I would write a scene and he would recompose it, or he would start out and then I would revise. We had to have our three acts finished by noon, for our players.

Red-eyed, Marlowe sipped ale, his quill chronicling, squeaking, or head on his arms, he snatched a fragment of sleep.

Rain over the house, over the mansard, clicking against the glass, sounding colder and colder, dampening our spirits and our paper, making my knees and ankles ache...rain.

I wanted to toss myself on the cot and smother myself with blankets and call it a day. Marlowe said we'd soon see the dawn. God's bodkins!

In that four-square room, cluttered with Greek and Roman masks, posters, books, and dirt, we wrote *Titus* over and over. When the manuscripts were ready for the theatre even the rain sounded tired.

In those days, for economy's sake, we often cut each other's hair, sitting in the doorway or on the steps, when the weather was good. Draped in sheet or towel, I sat on a chair while Marlowe snipped. Scissors and comb usually put him in a whistling mood. Gently puffing a tune, he scissored away—the slowest barber in London. He liked to complain about the color of my hair, saying he wished it was as black as Othello's so he could see it easily.

"I've cut so many bad lines from your plays this job should be easy."

Chris was better at barbering than I. He said I didn't keep my mind on my work.

"If I had the money, I'd certainly excuse you. Come on, no more time out for jotting down lines. Let's get through this mess. Presently, it will be dark. I never trust you by candlelight."

In separate crimson frames:

Sir Francis Drake, Sir Walter Raleigh, Ben Jonson, Shakespeare:
A mirage of Armada, sails rattling, guns roaring...

At sea, Sir Francis tells yarn of brave seamanship:
a man stabs another in the eye with a dagger.

Silence.

Stratford
August 5, 1615

Spelling God backward gets dull after a while: at the clandestine meetings where Raleigh, Greene, Marlowe, Drake, Jonson and others crucified everyone's beliefs, they gradually dulled their arrows, for me: I thought: Lucifer can smell too strongly of sulfur too often. "Am I not a mighty man who bears a hundred souls on his back!"—talk like this was to little purpose, to my way of thinking. How much saner to keep convictions to one's self: Yet some, surly as a butcher's dog, paraded their beliefs. Gulled, I never went too often: the suite, in the Duke's Thames house, had about it an air of trouble brewing, trickery, and the abrupt appearance of men-at-arms. The talkers walked or sat about, under brilliant chandeliers, shadowing their shadows on the polished floors, starched cuffs thrown back over satin sofas. Whiffs of cologne and perfume over-topped the whiff of garret. Rapiers shimmered. The Queen, if she chose, could do away with each of us: a nod of her wig. I seriously suspected all their pattery, branding it half-hearted conspiracy, mistrust and defamation. The passage of time has confirmed, not denied my feelings: perspective has brought out the folly of guffawings at creeds.

St. Grouse's Day
1615

For weeks, after Marlowe's murder, I avoided the Mermaid Tavern. When a courtier from the Queen's court came to me at my apartment and suggested, with coughs behind his perfumed handkerchief, that I leave London for a while, I agreed... I was rather unaccustomed to such visits!

Meeting Jonson, as I left the city, sensing evasion on his part, I felt ill at ease, suspicion stepping in. Later, he visited me at Stratford, brief visits, but he was aware of my doubts; my reserve must have told him.

Jonson said:

"The Queen has been spying...last week your London apartment was searched...if you're smart, stay away...she's making up her mind..."

I turned that over.

What could I pin on the Queen? What could she pin on me? Which play? A broadside? A pamphlet? With Jonson back in London I sent out feelers. When I was convinced that he was loyal I would remember that he had killed two men. Queen? Pawn? Right? Wrong?

September first
1615

Months after Marlowe's murder, I learned that the Queen had had hirelings kill him. I confided in Raleigh as we stood on a pier, near one of his frigates...the Thames wind whipping our clothes.

How well I recall his expression when I told him. Mouth tense, eyes afire, he grabbed at the hilt of his sword and exclaimed:

"I command nine ships. How many cutthroats do you think I have at my beck and call? In a fortnight, Marlowe's murderers will be dead. Our Queen will know that she has been out-maneuvered, that there are plotters keener than she. She killed Marlowe because he was too rabid an atheist..."

Those were vain words on Raleigh's part: he did nothing: I did nothing. How gutter-cheap we are in times of stress, how obliterative, given to expediency, wedded to her and safety!

Next Day

Come live with me and be my love,
And we will all the pleasures prove
That hills and valleys, dales and fields
Woods or steepy mountain yields...

And I will make thee a bed of roses
And a thousand fragrant posies...

Chris never knew what it was to have a bed of roses, not even for a fortnight.

He might have gone on to splendid heights. His verses mean much to me. I liked him for his clowning, his patience, his kind words, his persuasive pen. Glover's son and shoemaker's boy—we had many a boisterous time. Of his plays I think best of *Tambourlaine* and *Faustus.*

From jigging veins of riming mother wits
And such conceits as clownage keeps in pay
We'll lead you to the stately tent of war...

As we collaborated on our plays, he was constantly fighting debts, his mistress riding him hard. Our tankards full we worked in my place or his. I shied away from his association with the School of Atheists, leaving that to him and Raleigh.

No writer could have had a better guide for *Titus, Henry* and *Richard.* M__ had learned to smoke and like R__ had to putter with tobacco, pipe and flint.

One afternoon he used a scrap of poetry to light his pipe. Letting the paper burn and then char on the floor, he said:

"That was a poem well used."

Was it another "Shepherd's Song"?

I should have collected his works and seen them published. Now I could not track down his pieces. Ah, the shoulds of life...

This is the anniversary of his death, another churlish scruff of day with wretched rain...the rain it raineth every day...true, boy, come bring us to this hovel...the tyranny of the world is too rough at times...give me your hand.

Jonson received a letter from Ellen, Ellen in Edinburgh, writing at home, expressing her friendly concern for me:

"Will has written me but I am worried. Can you look after him?" She was afraid after Marlowe's death. "Will you write and reassure me?" she asked. "Edinburgh is far... I'm sick with a cold...so much rain."

And it was raining as Jonson read me her letter, in his apartment. I opened a book of his and leafed through it, standing by his window, the rain leaded on the pages, long, grey, thin lines, tracing problems that threatened us, a bond tying in with her concern, lessening that distance between us.

The wall felt damp to my shoulder and I smelled stale bread and stale cheese on Jonson's desk.

"What came between us?" I asked.

"Are you talking to me...or to her?"

"To you."

"Bad luck...the thing that comes between most lovers."
"And what do I do to change it?"
"You know London's soothsayers...they're ready to help you. Pay them."
"How much?"
"Pay...oh, with your life, your work. Pay and she's yours."
"It's stupid to talk like that."
"It's stupid to fall in love. Just fuck and go."

Stratford
September 9, 1615

When Raleigh was brought to trial by the Crown and condemned to life imprisonment, I began a play, thinking to defend him, troubled by the royal hatred leveled at him, for his loyalty to England was unquestionable.

His trial was pure sham.

SHEPHERD OF THE OCEAN

Scene I: Courtroom, in winter

> Raleigh: You claim me guilty, but I am innocent. In no way, at no time, have I conspired against the throne. At sea, I defended our country against all enemies. I supplied ships for the Queen. In Virginia, my colony is dedicated to all that England stands for. Sirs, I protest!
>
> Judge: Damned you are, damning our people with your stinking guilt. You have conspired! We have every proof...there's not the slightest doubt of your perfidy! You defended Queen Elizabeth against the Earl of Essex but he was the King's friend, never his adversary. You have every guilt upon you. You are grossly guilty of plotting against our nation and our King. King James sees fit to sentence you...

Maybe the King had secret reasons for Raleigh's banishment but I doubt it. Some call Sir Walter the "King of Liars." His letters from prison no longer come and Tower over me, filling me with guilt.

Should I burn his letters: could there be family involvement at some unforeseen time? I should burn many things—many memories!

Ocean Skimmer, you pilloried yourself. We were friends: those were good days but not good enough to last. What lasts?

The oriel outlasts us! Its quarrels outlast ours!

September 11, 1615

In my mind's eye we meet at the taproom of the Mermaid's Tavern...

Raleigh: ...At sea, weeks away from port, alone on the deck, rigging and sails creaking, I've felt it... I've felt it in the smash of waves and moan of beams...felt it in the expanse of sky...that there must be a god.

Marlowe: Should be a god! Put it that way.

Raleigh: No...let it go as I've said it. As you ride at the bow, as spray hurls on board, there are certain certainties, rebuffs of personal fancy, declarations of a godhead.

Jonson: The Greek helmsman felt those same declarations, and his god was Zeus.

Marlowe: I don't go for such thinking on my part, Sir Walter. It shuts me inside a cage and the cage has a door with four heavy bars: f-e-a-r.

Raleigh: You know that each country has had a godhead.

Marlowe: Each country has its diseases, debts...despots.

Shakespeare: Are you denying your "School of Night"?

Raleigh: I'm not on trial here. I was speaking confidentially, no, intimately...that's a better word. I was trying to share an emotion and I ask you to respect it as an emotion.

Jonson: You ask for respect. God be at your table. Everyone's highly respected here—even the waiters. (Laughter)

Marlowe: Ah, shut up!

Shakespeare: We didn't come here to quarrel.

Raleigh: Maybe we can do better with politics...or is it too hydra-headed tonight? Let's talk about Essex. Cautiously.

Marlowe: But why cautiously?

Shakespeare: We'll do better trying something else, not so risky. Supper's ready. Here it comes.

Jonson: Pour the ale, boy.

Marlowe: Hugger-mugger, my cage lost its bars. The bird of fear has flown ...hunger picked the lock.

That's how I remember an evening at the Tavern, Raleigh in his finest, wearing green velvet cloak, red trousers, black boots, black hat, sword; Jonson, Marlowe and me in our snuffbox suits, wearing our swords because of recent street fracases.

The Tower of London...
A cracked stone stairway leads to an open door:
Inside, windowless, Raleigh sits at his prison desk,
with maps, letters, books around him.
He is writing; he coughs:
Frail, he seems to be listening:
An armed guard trudges by and looks in.

Stratford
September 15, 1615

In '10, sometime during the autumn I think it was, I stopped outside Raleigh's prison, thinking to visit him: there he was, at his deal table, books, globe, maps and papers piled about him. His door was flung wide: his pen moved: perhaps he was writing his *History.* Sun lay on the floor of his room. A wren sang. His hand stopped. I stepped forward, then faltered. His hands moved over the table: he leaned on his elbows now, coughing. He had on a grubby red woolen cape, sleeves smudged with wax. He coughed again—his shoulders shaking.

He was the one who had dared the wild and secret lands, who had sweated men and ships to reach a goal. Winds luned, storms crashed; yet he had kept on. He had wanted to explore the world for himself, for mankind! Books on board his ships, books in his brain: wind stirred parchment on his table as I stood there and he read. What if he should turn and see me? What if he should get up? Would he recognize me?

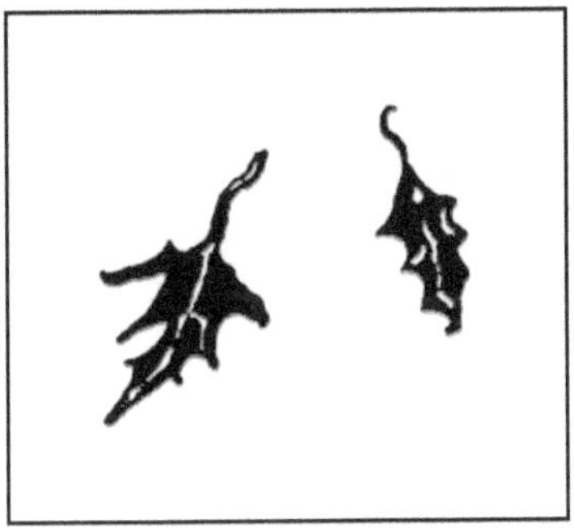

I thought: who are his friends? The thought cut me: the Great Lucifer is forgotten. Look around you. The liar is captive, will die behind these walls. They say he concocts an elixir, and gives it to his friends. No, I was not included. He needed his elixir more than I.

His white head was dirty...where was his youth? No, he had concocted hope. People said his rooms would be unguarded...so they were. But I made no sound. The ugly Tower was still. What has happened to his Elizabeth: is she memory?

I wanted to talk to him about Spenser's *Faerie Queen*, and say...Spenser...you know...no, Raleigh sailed to the Canaries, to Florida, Manoa...Hispaniola...cloak-thrower...knight...names...and his map, a large parchment, came out of the wall and stared at me, rebuking me: cloak-thrower...patron...names...John White said that he admired him...John White said...where was White now, now that he's back from Roanoke?

Pushes hand through hair, coughs... I back away, wanting to put the wall between us. I shuffled down a few steps, disgraced, down to the street, cockroaches and rats scuttling, ivy blowing in the wind.

Let him finish his *History of the World.*
I had no right to disturb.

The blue cloak slips from Ellen's shoulders and through the stabbed hole I see moon, stars, and fog, each flecked with red. Fog soaks the hole and then, then, there's the face of an attacker, scarred, piratical. Something behind him fades into her face, so white. I see her smile her dazzling lover's smile and I hear her laughter and the sound of her bracelets.

In the funeral procession
a small black casket is accompanied by Ann, Shakespeare,
his daughter in black, and others.
A flower falls from the casket and Shakespeare
picks it up and puts it in his pocket:
A church bell tolls:
Blue cloak over a tombstone.

I buried Hamnet, buried father, buried myself... What is this death that eats our lives as if we were pieces of bread on a dirt plate, sacrificed to whim and time? Our crosses top a hill, row on row, a row for each generation, across fog hills, across sunny hills, Italian, French, English, Scot.

Escape with me:

Now at the prow, now in the waist,
the deck, in every cabin, I flamed amazement:
sometimes I'd divide and burn in many places,
on the topmast, the yards, the bowsprit...

Henley Street
September 23, 1615

Now, now thought is closer to death than love: I live in it, longing for her, for intercourse, the ice of this winter-house aging me and the wind, poor wind, scuttling nowhere, nowhere to go.

Go to the oriel, then.

Henley Street
September 24

God, the rain, the rain at its cobble-sop, common rain on cobbles, rising out of them, climbing the ivy, moulding thatch, hurting places of the mind, shivering our secrets, insinuating with lashes, coming again and again, thieving.

The dropping of one drop can absorb a soul: its alchemy traps a man: so, we, reduced, debased, encompassed, are carried to sea, to finality, ourselves made useless, noiseless, like a million others.

I heard rain throughout the night, from lying down to getting up, no sleep, only this endrenchment, intent on obliteration, transforming life into a comedy of errors.

I was twenty-eight or so!

All morning I sawed wood for props; all afternoon I practiced lines; all evening I rehearsed. My costume didn't fit: the crown was badly torn. At four in the morning, there was no food for us. That was life at the Globe, when I first tried London.

I estimate that I have earned less than a hundred pounds from my thirty-seven plays. When I divide that by thirty years of work, I see what it represents. At least I see that much.

Henley Street
1615

"Small coals! Small coals!"

"Hot peas!"

I wish I could hear those raucous London street hawkers! I'd like to see the Thames crowded with little boats. I'd like to see the people packed in front of St. Paul's. I'd like to be back at the Exchange, for the armorers and booksellers and glovers. I'd like to stare off-stage at a thousand rapt faces.

I miss Burbage more than anyone. He and I worked hand-in-glove for more than ten years, seeing each other almost every day. He played Hamlet, Othello, King Lear, and his was the finest Lear voice-transcending. Lear was Burbage and Burbage was Lear. There were no weaknesses. Weaknesses?

I have mine—so many weaknesses.

Today I have been up and round but last week I was in bed throughout the week. When I am up and about, I freeze. My sight fades. My heart bangs. I must get to the composition of my will, the final act in my play...no applause...no whistles...silence.

Burbage could take my lines and recite them for me, adding, subtracting, modulating. If there must be rewriting I knew, through his skill, what I must do to improve a scene.

What amusing letters he used to write home, when he was traveling with the Company. He and Alleyn were as domesticated as tea.

"Dear Jug," he would address his wife. "Dear Mouse," Alleyn wrote his.

"Dear Jug, let my orange-tawny stockings be dyed a good black, against my coming home in the winter," Alleyn wrote.

He wanted his wife to sow spinach in his parsley bed at the proper season.

"...Sweet Jug, farewell, till All Hallow's tide, and brook our long journey with patience."

We brooked many a tedious journey with patience.

October 1, 1615

Gargoyles and ghosts: they are always a part of pain. Here is a prescription: pulverize a gargoyle in a deep mortar, shred one carefully, mix with ample wheat and milk, add salt, bake two hours, serve piping hot. Add surfeit of prunes, against the inevitable her.

Globe Theatre:
Elegant and seedy theatregoers.
Hand bills read Hamlet*:*
Actor Burbage mounts the stage
behind candles, rushes, torches.
Backstage, actors hustling, yacking.
A soldier outside pisses:
Curtain rises.

Henley Street
October 3, '15
Evening – late

We players, playing in the provinces, walked all day to reach our destination, our horse cart lumbering behind us, stacked with costumes and gear. Sun blazed. Rains soaked. Chewets followed us. We walked from inn to inn, town to town. At two o'clock we played *Tambourlaine,* and the soft verse of Marlowe. Then, packed again, we walked until another two o'clock, somewhere along the way. Our comradeship on the road, sleeping in the same rooms, sleeping on the floor as often as not, eating at the same table—those were our bonds! Burbage, Alleyn, Kempe... I could name a dozen. Week by week, we played our plays, our *Lord Chamberlain's Men,* banished by edict and plague, protected from jail by contract, cheered by the Puritans! We worried over money, badgered, confronted, schemed. We placated the constabulary and loved the *annuncios*—the children!

Sometimes we sickened of one another and quarreled, our masculinity distressing us: *men and boys, men and boys*—that was our disease! What women would have meant to us, in London especially, where the theatre was spoiled. What it would have meant to have a girl strut across the boards and smile a smutty smile. Chafing would have disappeared.

I longed to see Desdemona as a girl would play her; I wanted to see Cleopatra acted by a woman, Lady Macbeth by a skilled player—not castrated boys, our sexless wire-sounding temperamentalists.

Who wants boys primping, boys in women's hats, giggling over skirts and bows? Scratching fleas in baboon areas? Crying for their mamas?

Our groundlings wanted women to go to bed with.

Lords, ladies, and soldiery wanted women.

Everyone is sick of boys!

Soldiers, in their half-armor, jeer at us!

It is afternoon—warm and sunny!

Women, wearing eye masks, are chatting and taking seats at the Globe. Hawkers, bright yellow bands around their waists, are selling books and cakes and ale, passing among the theatre crowd. Dandies are getting settled in an area close to the stage. Swords clatter as soldiers find seats; a captain bows to a Jesuit priest. Someone strums a zither and croaks a bawdy ballad. Workers shove their way past the gate, afraid to miss a word of the beginning.

Popping open the little door of the hut atop the theatre, a trumpeter blows shrill blasts; the play is about to start: *Hamlet, Prince of Denmark*.

Henley Street
Sunday afternoon

Theatrical voices—commanding, secretive, beseeching, vituperative—are not voices I want to recall. I prefer the normal and kindly, an intimate Scot voice, a man's educated speech, someone mouthing thoughtfully, an older person whose words show profound mellowing.

Ann's voice was once full of witchery, stealing my guts and senses, leaving me hot. Marlowe's was low and persuasive. Queen Elizabeth's crisp. Raleigh's burly. Hamnet's birdlike. Ellen's warm.

Not the regal! Not dotards and thieves, but a voice combining generosity, ease, and hope: is the voice I invent when insomnia takes me: for a moment it speaks out of the past.

I never enjoyed the children's theatre—always wondering how they produced even one creditable play a season since they whipped their boys to force them to learn their parts. Clifton, I recall, was kidnapped and compelled to act. They whaled him, fed him badly, did sexual malice to make him perform—hardly the way to create a star. Clifton's father had to appeal to the authorities for his boy's release. I went to see him, at his home, and the tales he told me matched his tear-streaked face. His little hands trembled and his mother had to reassure him he wouldn't be kidnapped again.

Whippings, threats, nagging—they were the stuff that kept the children's theatre alive in London, while the council shrugged and patrons furnished subsidies for these odious and grossly amateurish entertainments. I talked and fought. Marlowe talked and fought. Alleyn and Jonson used their influence. The cruelty continued.

London was a place of whippings: the public whipping of offenders through the city streets and post whippings repelled... Jim was one of those I saw...and Hardy's body hanging naked in chains...

Stratford-on-Avon
Wednesday

Damn them in Luddington and Walton, the groundlings who pelted us with fruit and eggs, those smelly coxcombs! That day in Luddington was blazing: the sweat ran down me as I stood on stage: then, the first egg struck, then a rotten orange: I waited, hoping. The play went on, drowned by laughter, and then, as if by prearrangement, a barrage of fruit and eggs hit us: our tragedy was hounded off the boards.

Walton had a couple of hecklers who were supported by the audience and broke up our play: we got eggs from many Waltonites: putrid, smelling a dozen feet away, saved, undoubtedly for our arrival: it was two days before we could play again since we had to wash and press our clothes. What a jangling of nerves that bred.

Why not give up the acting and the writing? Why not go back to Stratford and work with father? Why let these slovenly cruds, these barnyard bastards ruin my life? Days later, humor came slanting through. When we were well-received and the money tinkled we forgot; we called ourselves ninnies and threatened to arm ourselves with eggs for the next affront. We found goodness and warmth in lines well-delivered. We saw our comradeship, our triumph over slogging days: there was magic flowing through our blood: that fulsomeness, that nothing could tarnish or remove.

Globe Theatre is on fire...bucket brigades,
smoke around men with pails,
smoke around boys with pails,
smoke in trees, smoke in the rain:
Jonson talking and gesturing to Shakespeare:
Burbage screaming orders...
A wall topples...
Inside the conflagration
books and manuscripts burning.

Jonson and I watched the Globe burn—the afternoon cold, with rain falling. People crowded around; there was mud and water underfoot.

"Someone must have set our theatre on fire, Will! Jesus, how it burns!" Jonson cried.

"No. I was inside. I saw the thatch start burning."

"Wasn't there anything you could do to stop the blaze?"

"We tried! We got ladders and buckets!"

"Lord, look, now! A wall's toppling. The hut's gone. Why it has fallen off. Will, our props are afire. Our scripts! The flames are roaring..."

"Stand back!"

"Stand back or get burned!"

"How long has it been burning?"

"Maybe an hour..."

The flames seemed to meet in a giant peak, a peak that had at the top a great tree of smoke. It was raining harder now; the crowd had moved back.

God, wasn't it enough to have to fight the plague? One month our doors were closed, next month we were open, next month we were shut again. That was bad enough, but no theatre meant no chance.

"Kemp is sick...the Globe is gone," I said.

"Let's go and get drunk!" Jonson said.

Later, Burbage told me it was a cannon, fired during my own play, that set fire to the Globe. We met in the street. Yanking his beard, swearing, he spat on the cobbles, and turned away.

Henley Street
1615 All Souls' Day

Pain is gross companion, inducing lecherous thoughts, destroying temperance, stability, mercy, courage, fortitude. Craving release, I fought all day to remember better times. At night, with candles lit, blankets around me, I find ease... I remember...

I am in a lemon grove, naked stone pillars stabbing out of the tops of the trees, Greek pilasters by the sea. We are eating on a terrace overlooking the water, a lazy meal, with old wine. The moon rises, drunkenly, fat, water-distorted, closing in on us, in rhythm to the waves below. We hold hands. The moon spells urgency, urging us to the grove, where we lie side by side.

"Ellen...Ellen..."

The lemons are yellowish in the moonlight: there is something stage-like about their motionlessness: it is rather as though we were in a velvet box, facing the sea. Stars have something to do with the fragrance drifting about us, the only movement apart from the waves and rising moon. I suggest we go down to the beach, so inviting. Ellen says no and I forget everything but her fragrance and the fragrance of the lemons, her whispers, her kisses.

That Scot profile, so chiseled, that bluecap voice, so warm, that hair of hers, softer than Juliet's... A great rock, a sea boulder, surrounded by waves, glows in the moonlight...her skin is whitened: a ringlet glows on her neck.

Marlowe, Jonson, Raleigh, Spenser have had their days in jail; I have had mine—those county sties where pigs and dust ate my manuscripts and foetid odors ate my skull, jailed by the local thief who deemed each man a thief who thought:

If all the world and love were young...

But Raleigh it never was except in fancy and during the dead reckoning on paper: that is why the five of us stumbled backward in time, learning and escaping simultaneously.

We used to play chess, many of us, pawns, varlets, kings, knights, evenings, one play bastinadoed on another, Caesar against Titus, Hamlet against Lear, Portia against Cleopatra—always a gamble, along the stinking alleys, along the nocturnal slugtide Thames, along the turtle sea: stonehenge of concupiscence, murder vs. philandering, octogenarian vs. boy, sex vs. cuirass, check vs. cul-de-sac.

Everyman knows the exquisite desire for a woman; he also knows the ravening need...when there is no woman.

With Ann opposite me at supper table, I peered outside at the leaves, beyond the oriel, and denounced myself as I ate, enumerated my festering faults. I tasted little, wishing for sensible words and tranquil mind. But there was no shutting the door.

"Eat, Will," she said, and I nodded, but dared not glance at her, to find the stranger and myself. I resented her as if her infidelities were yesterday's, as if my side of life could be ruled out, as if we were young...

Patience has not helped. Only forgiveness can.

Leaves drop from the trees and the kettle bubbles and we feed ourselves, grieving. Our shields are in place but the lances were broken years ago. Our visors are down, our plumes awry. Our horses have been killed in the field. Without pennons, we move our gauntleted hands in rusty bewilderment, slow-gaited with many, many abysmal hungers.

Henley Street – '15

I kept a stray in my London apartment: after feeding him while on one of my strolls along the Thames I could not shake him: Pericles had a soothsayer's mug dripping with ignominious grey whiskers, a privateer's baleful eye, a silver-grey hide, a black tail, three white feet, a black-booted foot, and a bark like a tin pot clipping the pavement. When it came to food, Pericles was greedier than Shylock for a pound; piercing me with piratical eyes, he sat up, wagged for pity, then slumped in grief, moaning better than any stage madonna. Pericles and Jonson became the best of friends: pieces of bread or cheese from Ben's pocket ordained him lord and master. Along the Thames, Pericles flew after every bird, yapping incessantly; it seemed to me he could run all day and never tire. When left to guard the apartment, he kept to a mat inside the door, gradually sheathing it with a coat of silver-grey hair.

Shakespeare and Ashley meshed in fog:
They duel in a fog meadow.
Fog blows away before Julius Caesar's ruined castle
among rocks and weeds.
Shakespeare's dog tangles with Ashley,
caroms against Shakespeare:
Shakespeare falls.

November 7, 1615

Fog sopped the grass and weeds when I fought my duel, by Caesar's castle. I could barely make out Jonson, Pericles, and friends, among the pines and bush below the castle ruins. Phantasma? I asked myself.

Ashley and I had quarreled over money: as one of the King's Men he had cheated me roundly; now he faced me, privateer, poet, rich man's bastard who would defy immortal Caesar: on twelve-foot legs, bearded, cloak over shoulder, rapier in hand, fog creaking against him, he closed in. On stage I had dueled many times; today I must put fakery to test.

As Ashley and I fought I heard Pericles barking and heard voices, saw Ashley's men and my own, now in the fog, now out of it, shifting distorts.

My rapier hilt felt icy; the whip of steel on steel had a ring to it I had never heard. I hated the fog, telling myself I must make it serve me: it was to my advantage as well as his. Our blades spat fire. I drew back. The ruins caught the inserting sun and stood distinctly above us: in my inner sight Caesar's legions were amused at us. Other watchers appeared—grinning. Death is always grinning.

Ashley drove me back, steadily, steadily, forcing me toward the base of the castle where blocks of stone menaced, strewn amidst thick weeds. I fought to keep my footing and tried to beat him off. He was fighting savagely: his blade had a whiteness about it I couldn't understand. I felt that whiteness slice my white belly: so, stumbling over Caesar's masonry I was to die.

But I am 'gainst self-slaughter and somehow drove him in front of me and got yards away from the wall, deflecting blow after blow. Ashley was fighting like a privateer with a cutlass, each blow shoulder-down. My wrist felt beaten. I parried a series of terrific blows and then staggered.

At that moment, Pericles hurled himself on Ashley, playing, growling, jumping joyously; with a bound he leaped at me and before I could call off the dog or beat him off, I fell. As I came to my knees, Ashley was waiting and shoved his blade into my groin.

The fog and woods...they were there in that pain, and Jonson's voice was there...my rapier, I kept thinking, where is it? Will they pick it up? I felt that months had passed, that I had aged a multitude of years, like the stone, like the battlement: age, that alchemy, filtered through the fog and sun...

I remember them carrying me.

Henley Street
November 8, '15

Jonson took me to his apartment in his carriage and bragged about his Holland duels and the men he had pinked. As I lay in bed, feverish, during the days to come, father appeared, expressing pity—the pity he had shared with the plague-stricken. "You there, you, boy, I've something for you. This will help you." I understood. I cared. I wanted to talk to him. I wanted to sit with him underneath our apple tree and feel the summer's sun.

"The fault, father, is not in our stars, but in ourselves," I said to someone. "Yours is a fair name, fairer than mine...

"I am singularly moved when the sway of earth shakes like a thing infirm... this is not a dream, father."

On Jonson's bed, I went through hellish days—thirst, hunger, the bungling doctor bungling me, cold, cold remembering, sweatful forgetting, spouting delirious lines from plays... I accused the world of every crime, and managed to include my own.

I was afraid alone, yet distressed to have others overhear my ranting. The bed boards gaped and between each board I sweated another chill.

"Will, here's your supper," Jonson said. "Will, here's breakfast. Will, I've brought you a book."

Pericles licked my hands. Lying under my bed, he thumped his tail, saying: "Get up, master, there are birds to chase along the Thames."

–S–

Without asking me, Jonson wrote to Ellen, and she came from Edinburgh. Was it her coming that pulled me through? Her care, beauty, her hands, her smiles of reassurance? Love put on its Oberon and scrubbed the grey out of the windows.

Quintessence.

She found a better doctor, brought me better food, got Bill McFarland to look after me, an old friend of hers, agreeable yawning fatness, eating half our food behind my back, gossiping with Jonson's neighbors, bobbling and drooling his words, coddling me.

When I improved she took me to the park; later, we sailed the Thames...on shore larks sang... I was grateful and tried to repay too soon...on top of rolls of canvas at the stern.

At court there was a wedding celebration and a mock battle and fireworks spilled across the river: how the fireworks turned water into sky...the guns thundered.

"For us," she said. "For your recovery," she said. How like a paragon...

The diamond on her velvet blouse winked at me; I put my head on her lap: pain melted: seagulls mewed as our boat rocked gently.

–S–

So, Ashley and I settled our accounts. I saw him years later and we turned our backs on one another. I suppose he was embittered at my recovery.

The best of us is both participant and confusion, but I, I am stranger because estrangements have put a lie to my living, making it stranger still.

Stratford
Monday morning

While recovering from my wound, my brothers, Jim and Dick, paid me a call.

They seemed quite uninclined to sit, skeptical of Ben, afraid of Pericles, contemptuous of the apartment with its manuscripts and shelves of books. Wearing their farm clothes, they smelled of dung, dirt, and rain-soaked cloth.

Jonson, wanting to be friendly, told how Pericles acted during the duel, winking at me, falsifying his ferocity. Brothers—were those men my brothers? Long ago, they had washed their hands of my life, Pilatewise. Mother praised them when I visited our home, ah me.

"I had heard that ya killed that-tar man, in yer duel," said Dick, pawing his kneecaps.

Jonson clapped him on the shoulder.

"Wish him better luck next time," he guffawed.

Jim and Dick had brown, flat faces, flattened by hunger, by defeat, lust, work, illness and sorrow. They had lost their children during the plague. Their teeth were blackened, or missing. Their clothes...what is a bundle of dirty clothes topped by a voice and a dead mind?

The afternoon sun poured through the open door. "Your hair ain't red like it was," said Jim.

"You're getting bald," said Dick. "The hair's slipping down your neck."

Bells of London startled them and helped send them on their way, and I went to sleep, amused by Jonson's mimicry and laughter, as he sprawled in his chair, head thrown back, one hand on Pericles' mane.

Stratford

My brothers' visit reminded me of our hometown Ned.

Ned used to lie on the ground with pads underneath his shoulders: an anvil, weighing two hundred weight, was lowered on his chest by huskies, and three men with sledges bent a bar on it as he lay there. Ned performed at every Fair, girls ogling. The picture of him and his admirers delights me: hero with anvil and hammer. How I used to envy him. Ann thought he was a wonder. He was. And now I wonder what became of him?

Henley Street
November 13, 1615

One night, Pericles and I got into a talk: he squatted by my bed and we went over the business of writing for a living... He said the market was poor. He said my plays were very wordy. He said he had it tough before I took him on and suggested I see if I couldn't buy stock in a Company, one that was really *enduring,* he said. "No use getting in with one that is here today and gone tomorrow. Wisdom," he snuffed, "is a thing you get when they crowd you off the dock into deep water, or when you grab for a mutton bone and it isn't there."

Our talks were not long as a rule. Pericles could drop asleep when I was in the midst of telling him something interesting or trying out a few lines on him. If I offered him a chunk of bread his interest quickened, and there was tail action too. He could listen attentively to a stanza, let's say, if I held the bread (or piece of cheese, preferably cheddar) above his head, just out of his reach. I sometimes did this to improve his mind. However, a week or so later there seemed no sign of improvement. Perhaps dogs, like some people, are impervious to poetry.

Shakespeare, Stratford sleepwalker, walks about his bedroom,
stumbles, tries door handle, raises window:
Ann, in clumsy breasty gown, wakes him angrily:
"What on earth were you trying to do?"
"I was listening to Burbage and Alleyn
recite lines from my plays."

November 15, 1615

Again I sleepwalk, from room to room, standing in doorways, waiting before windows: I wake and there I am, unseeing, window, door or wall in front of me, the crime of myself, the assassination of my past confronting me. All the perfumes...all the words...all the concern defeat their purpose and I ask myself when will I get up next time and walk the floor, to disturb and be disturbed—for what reasons? Reasons for the unreasonable, reasons for the sickness of a mind—how can they be called reasons?

I wake to remember a dream, or wake to find the moment as bare as slate, or I feel that I am somewhere in the past, with my father, bending over people stricken by the plague, the plague bell tolling, the rain streaming over my face, someone weeping.

"Where is my new cap...where's my new cap?" The dying boy pleads, huddled against the church wall.

Alleyn—on the stage at the Globe—informs me of the plague and warns me in his stentorian voice to leave off helping people, let them die; then, he carries away Puck.

Alleyn stalks across the stage, his voice cutting the dark, my sleep, my sleepwalker's darkness. Dressed for *Tambourlaine*, forked beard over red cloak, he swings through lines, a torch gleaming, smoking behind his shoulder.

Henley Street
November 18, 1615

When to the session of sweet silent thought
I summon up remembrance of things past...

It is not love-making I call to mind but an August afternoon, the paths that led us on and on, underneath giant oaks and elms, the ground wet with sun, our happiness as sure as the trees. We walked through groves and across fields, the pathway winding past cattle and horses at pasture, men at work scything grain. Sitting on a rock fence, we listened to the swish of their scythes, their friendly calls to one another. Wandering, we ate at a farm, the people happy to have us. Butterflies and children were part of that farm: it was as simple as that, and since it was so simple I would like to have that afternoon back again, a small favor to ask of time, just an afternoon and a lunch at someone's farm, dogs lolling on the ground, a cat on Ellen's lap.

Like as the waves make toward the pebbled shore,
So do our minutes hasten to their end...

I have not found a way to cheat the end: my glass is broken and the sand has sifted through. I am too much i' the shadow, it seems.

Confidence diminished as my memory failed: this began in a certain way: during one of my plays I could not speak: power of speech gone, I forgot my lines: this double confusion occurred while I acted in a play by Jonson, given in Bewick, when we were on a summer's tour. How vividly I remember that smoky inn—the crowd, the torches. In Chester, my lines once more escaped me: utterly perturbed, I gaped at the audience standing and sitting in the August sun: I wiped away sweat: how they stamped and jeered. Confidence might have returned, after later successful performances, except for another lapse: memorizing lines for *Othello,* I began to speak them, alone in my London apartment: again there was nothing, no sound, no memory: I had been emptied, as a rapier can take care of a wine sack: only the sound of rainfall, as I stood in my apartment: in my writing, too, lapses sweated me: there was no one to help: I told no one: soon, I thought, I'll suckle fools and chronicle small beer.

How easily I memorized, as a youngster, swallowing the lines of a play in a night or two. Now I know that impotence can assume many forms, between the legs and between the eyes.

Henley Street
December 4, 1615

So the plays evolved, week by week, line by line, the crabbed scrawl, poem and song, comedy and tragedy; so the characters came into being: Agrippa, Iago, Ophelia, Troilus, Falstaff, King Henry, bearded and beardless, slut and angel, lady and commoner: they gawked across my sheets of paper: I see them here, about me, crowding my candle's niggard flame.

But *look*, they have become phantoms!

Never again, king or coward, never Romeo and Juliet, never a pair of lovers to kiss and die beside a tomb. It was the nightingale and not the lark that pierced the fearful hollow of my ear...

Phantoms.

Let me be taken, let me be put to death, and not wait here, await the hand of tyranny, the slow grasp of this town's sod. I am to lie inside the church. The bell will toll. They will carry me. On my grave they'll cut these words: I decree:

Good friend, for Jesus' sake forbear
To dig the dust enclosed here:
Blessed be the man that spares these stones
And cursed be he that moves my bones.

YOUTH—

Was there youth?

I sometimes think of the Avon that summer, thunderstorms booming, the river very high. Cousin Will was trying to yank a calf out of the water, when the river sucked him under. Kathlene Hamlett played at Ophelia—letting defeat suck her down. That was a summer of defeats for most of us, the loss of my father's property, theatres closed because of official disapproval, weeks of suffocating heat, the sun caught in the trees, frying our brains, flies buzzing...

Cousin Will was a cheery, responsible boy, with a pitiful limp. Good at lots of jobs, he was thinking of marrying. Fishing was his love...poaching too. Kathlene was good and capable but tried making love before she was old enough...

I miss their smiling faces.

Ben writes such an elegant hand: he has that Italian influence to perfection: his scripts are damnatory of my provincial scrawl, I who can't remember whether to write Willm, Will or William...thank God for copyists, those drones, our skull-down, penny-quill calligraphists. Too bad someone is not dotting this.

Stratford

Gossip hangs over me, leaving me naked as vulgar air: home gossip, precipitated by Ann, when Philip drops by, then Blanch, then Longworth, then Melun, then Peter, then Elinor, then Pembroke: Elinor has had a severe cold; Longworth has lost his mare; Melun's wife is down with pleurisy. Philip's face is so emaciated he can't carry a rose over his ear; Elinor has to be helped with a pick-up. "When is another doctor coming to practice here?" Pembroke asks. Ann knows—and tells. Ann thinks there's a possible rape of the church, no less. Blanch's face puckers in disgust. Longworth asks for a glass of water. Peter talks genealogy. Their arrows are carefully wrapped in leaves: all afternoon they talk in the shade, under the apple, trotting in and out of the house, moodily conferring in knots or pairs, then sauntering back to leafy conference. There is a consensus of opinion that the bridge over the Avon may be too poorly built... "it can't last... Sheriff Grimes has been appropriating tax money...he must go..."

Someone objects but when Ann objects he objects and she objects to his objection and the objections because I object are more objectionable and this objectionable quality leads to further objections...on a summer's afternoon.

Henley Street
December 7, 1615

Not long after Hamnet's death, Ann removed Judith from school, against my wishes. Though fond of school, Judith became slaved at home. Later—in a year or so—Ann needed Susanna, another home puppet. She further alienated us by this decision. I still say that ignorance, like horse piss, stinks, cankering the mind. Example: Ann.

I have had more visitors, five Stratford puritans, who attacked my play writing. I got very angry yet tried to conceal my anger; remembering the smallness of my town I said little to the women; as if in the wings I waited, remembering:

"How unworthy a thing you make of me! You would play on me; you would seem to know my stops; you'd pluck out the heart of my mystery; you'd sound me from my lowest notes to the top of my compass...there's music in this little organ and yet you can't make it speak. Why?"

I talked to them as best I could and then a fat wench bleated, jerking at her gloves:

"You talk in riddles, sir. Your plays ridicule us. You disesteem our monarchs, King Richard for one. Your plays attract the vulgar. You praise the rotten..."

By standing, I asked them to leave: perhaps they felt the pain I felt; then my sickness grew worse after their visit.

An apple tree shakes out a boy:
The boy, Linnus, performs acrobatics in the branches:
He's fourteen.
Laughter:
Then King Lear's voice:
"Never, never, never, never..."

Henley Street
Stratford

Linnus, whose gypsy father is an acrobat, visits me these days; with his father in jail he has to wait for his release. Dumpy, leather-skinned and wild-eyed, Linnus is fourteen, and has a four-year-old brother, Peter. Their mother is dead.

My old apple tree is Linnus' home, when he is here; I sit outside while he performs tricks he has learned from his father, tricks I have never seen. Peter yawns on the grass or stands between my legs or pods my lap, thrilled by his brother's arm and leg cleverness...the sun warms the three of us.

His tricks done, glad to rest, Linnus stretches on the ground, to incline me a little of his wanderings, the hunger, always the hunger: it's as if he never had a full meal. They are scourged out of town, thrown into jail, entertained at castles, fed on cakes and ale, left to starve on a farm. Linnus points to Peter, asleep on my lap.

"Why do you like him? He's ugly."

"He's ugly but he may change and grow to be handsome, perhaps become an explorer, like Drake." And I talk to Linnus about Drake and the Armada and as I talk it seems to me I'm talking to Hamnet, or is this Hamnet on my lap?

It doesn't matter.

Linnus and Peter matter, and after a while we rig fishing gear and go to the river and fish, dawdle all afternoon, Linnus croaking gypsy songs, Peter in and out of the water, dashing after magpies and crows, gabbling berries, every problem forgotten.

Home late, Linnus prepared supper for us (Ann away for a few days): he was quick and clever in the kitchen, reminding me of an actor familiar with his part.

Henley Street
Stratford
December 11, '15

Linnus described a play he saw last summer and I was reminded of the first play I saw, as a boy, performed by gypsies who told a tale of Scottish intrigue and murder that ended with the beautiful heroine's suicidal plunge into a loch. Those swarthy actors seldom left my mind for weeks, waking me, haunting school and play. I can yet see the sheriff torturing the girl accused of stealing: words have gone but not the actions.

That evening, Papa and I walked home together. He would not talk about the play. Mama disliked plays and never attended, damning them as "lucifers." I suppose the gypsy play was a "lucifer."

Henley Street
Stratford
December 12, 1615

One of my bitterest experiences was seeing Pericles killed by a sheep herder. On the outskirts of London, Pericles burst into joyous yappings and began to frolic and nip sheep, an immense herd, stretching for blocks. I saw him tangle with a black ram. The herder, rushing at Pericles, mistaking his fun, struck him with his crook and beat him to the street; then, before I could shove my way through the herd, flailed him over the head with the butt. Yelling, pushing, I knocked down the man but reached Pericles too late... I wanted to leave the city; I wanted to spit on mankind. I wish I could have my friend to talk to, eat meat from my hand: there's plenty of meat for you now, boy.

Midnight

What is it that has embittered me?

I felt the bitterness long before someone tried to kill Ellen. Did the bitterness come about through attempting the impossible in my acts of creation, losing life in work? A tree is tree now. Once it was wonderful. My spleen stems from the sleepwalker's for I am sleepwalker-without-taper, from Romeo to Shylock, king to clown, hero to villain. I can see distinctly: there's no mirage about cottage, family, friends, and Avon. Stratford is Act 5. I wait my cue! Go to, what are your lines, Yorik?

Caesar's battleground kept me from a sane life. Drinking stronger than ale I kept company with the bloody horde...rape in my heart...thief at hand...deceit as friend...murder as bed...

Someone beats on my door; that's Burbage: "Let's go, Will," he yells. "It's almost one o'clock; you have to be at the Globe in half an hour."

The hour, the play, the scene, the glass running out, faster, faster, faster!

Henley Street
Stratford
December 20, 1615 Evening – late

Most of all I shall miss a beautiful woman, her smile, the eyelids and features faintly powdered, the white of her hands and arms, the sense of longing, her voice's mystery, the carefully rounded breasts, their softness, her light gait, her voluptuary whispers making slave, the weight of her at night, her softness underneath in the morning...

So I never saw her again...writing was my coition...my fake living...no, I never saw her again; that was fate, or...to never see the wanted is that phenomenal blindness; to never have the beauty is pismire.

Our old friend sits on her throne, above marble steps, wearing blazoned robe, her crown straight—and neck straight, too, the lidded concern apt, antique scepter beside her: her awareness is aware of certainties, watching earl and captain, bawd and bugler.

We are to love her, do collective obeisance, beseech her favors. And she, with her rufescence, shall free us of every plague, down to smallest poverty, and, like Merlin, give us castles for cots, hope for despair, money for thought.

Sleeve lifts pontifical hand and blesses with its kissing ring. Rays of sun, through lozenged windows, fold leaded shadows over troubled brows.

Ah, Queen, your majesty is unparalleled, you are our patron of the arts, generous in every particular, particular to man's freedom, eschewing stock, pillory and scaffold.

As she rises, sequins and braid tremble, every motion capsuled in scarlet, the very velvet of confidence—the robe quite long, ruffs and ruffles fresh, the jewels paying their worth: she walks, our Queen walks: we remember her mother scaffolded for adultery.

Henley Street

Shylock was less persistent than I to own, fief vs. chattel, clown vs. crown, thoughts vs. dreams: with such a goal, a man stoops, a man batters, a man astonishes himself with crudities that some might call vitality: this is the sighing, buying, signing: and when I began to own more land and houses I owned less and less time: that was my mortgage, paid over and over by less writing.

Henley Street
December 24, 1615

Scene: Seashore

Lord Thomas	Was it yesterday?
Philo	No—it was the day before—at night.
Thomas	When...when was it?
Philo	Speak lower...they'll overhear us! Sssh!
Thomas	I didn't bury her the day before. No man buries

> love at night, only hate. You saw me carry her to her room—lay her down tenderly. You share the secrets of our lives...and now the secret of her death. 'Sblood, that is that remains for each of us, hide carefully, forgetting intrigue, forgetting Scotland...

But I can no longer write!

Snow beats on the windows and winter chills me, cold hands on my throat. Where are my faithful players? Where is Alleyn—speaking divinely? If I could talk to him I might be able to write again. If this storm did not batter this house so treacherously!

Green lozenges of light penetrate the oriel,
green drinking mugs,
green on table decanter,
Shakespeare and Jonson drinking.
Stratford streets in the late afternoon sun,
sounds of a carriage,
sounds of kids coming home from school.
Jonson quotes a line,
Shakespeare quotes a line.

Henley Street
January third, 1616

It does no good to rage at my impotence and yet I rage...come bird, come...come, heart, perform your art.

Yesterday, I was carried out of my private madness by Ben Jonson's visit: we drank and laughed, his thick cloak thrown off, his broad shoulders broader, voice kindly, eyes the eyes of one acting well-remembered lines, hands relaxed on his lap or gesturing easily.

"Now that the night begins with sable wings to overcloud the brightness of the sun, and that in darkness pleasures may be done...let us to the bower and pass a pleasant hour..."

He said those lines years ago, and that night Ellen came to me, and waited backstage, there, with the dusty props and dirt. Ah, her beauty: I saw it against the sticks and pricks of make-believe! I felt its warmth. I asked her how she was but she wanted kisses, not civilities.

(Vapid lines out of the *Spanish Tragedy* seemed foolish there backstage and could not matter less as Ellen and I drove to her apartment—in her red carriage, swaying through the rain.

Her fireplace was stacked with flame. Her servants withdrew and she leaned against her marble mantel, breast leaning forward, her dress low, shoulders and neck bare, such ivory.

Her cousin had accompanied us in the carriage; now we could talk:

"I hadn't expected you in London tonight," I said.

"I came from Dover, yesterday, late yesterday" she said.

"From your brother's place at St. Cloud?"

"Yes. A hard trip across the channel and hard to be away so long from you... My dear, this play's better than the last. How you make those Venetians live! They're like so many I've known... You must have known them too..."

"Darling, I like your hair this way. French? Your hairdresser really knows..."

"Will, tell me that you love me. I love you."

"Should I?"

"Your letters tell me but now, you tell me."

"With hands and mouth..."

It was like that—her gown letting me—but it was also fear, remembering that Ben had warned us that we had been followed by another carriage as we left the theatre...twice now.

Ellen and I hoped our purse of hope would lose all counterfeit coins...foreign exchange no...no cheating, no niggardly luck...could I foresee with gypsy insight?

Our goblets touched.)

But I prolonged Ben's New Year visit: we sat on chairs in the oriel, and talked and talked, and the talking of him brought out the talking in me, and there was no bothersome time: I suppose we ate by candlelight; I suppose we went to bed, but our talking was not bedded, and I hear it now in the sound of his retreating horses: I hear hope retreating, hoof on cobble, hoof on brain: for he will not come again. Or should I ask him, being thought-sick?

Twelfth Day

In the fall I went across the fields to the poplar trees under which Ann and I used to make love; I sat in the sun and let it drench me. The trees were nobler though limbs had fallen off; one tree was rotted at the top; another...but no matter.

I sat and remembered how it was before our twins were born, sat with elbows on my knees, gaping. I tried to see that pair of lovers loving on the grass. That love had never happened. No. The thing that was real was my gaping loneliness...

I walked home and took up a packet of her letters; this one was lying on top:

> Dear Red,
>
> I am glad that people like your play, that *Romeo and Juliet* play. That was the one we saw at the Globe, I think. The Capulets frightened me much. What is the name of your new play that you are writing at? I can't remember. Is it the *Merchant* play?
>
> You should write a play about your papa and his glovemaking. The twins are sick again. Hamnet is the worst, sick at night, and all that. Judith has a flushed face and she coughs and coughs, and I keep her in bed.

Write soon.

Love,

Ann

I try to forget the casualness and say it belongs to a buried past and then I say to myself, if this is dead then all life is equally dead, including myself.

I opened another letter and a dried flower fell out of the yellowed paper. I had to hold the sheet to the window before I could read it, meantime trying to harden myself, half remembering. My wits are diseased, I thought.

Dear Red,

> So you have made twenty-two pounds at the theatre from all the good attendance. That will help take care of the clothes we need, and winter right against us. What is this play they are playing at the Globe, the Othella thing? I have heard Mama talk about a woman like that—some foreign woman. Is Othella your leading person? Is she pretty? Is it true you fought a duel? That will not help you get ahead in London. You said that people talk.
>
> You should see Hamnet. How well he does with his school work, better than anyone at school, I hear. He takes after you, his master tells me.
>
> Our bedroom window was broken in the storm last week, but Tom has put in new glass, and leaded and puttied it nicely. It was the window by the good chair.

Love,

Ann

Like roses, red roses on a stalk, or was it, coral is far more red than her lips' red...love is my sin...my love is longing still!

I put away her letters and closed the shutters and lit the candles and the rush lamp, and, settling in my chair, I read of another past, to palliate myself, Virgil's.

Stratford

I have been thinking of Merlin and his magic ways, the thrall of his immense dabbling: this island should have been named Clas Myrddin: Merlin's Enclosure. Perhaps Gawain and Lancelot would have enclosed us and the grail might not have become the great illusion among illusions.

I am reading Spenser's *Amoretti* now: now I read what Raleigh read in prison; the coincidence is appropriate enough. There are not too many coincidences in life but there are many kinds of prisons. Perhaps the worst is the prison imprisoning the prisoner against his will; the other prison, self-germinated, self-maintained, can be as ascetic, as impassioned in its tortures, and yet it has its rush lamp for the outcast state:

Pour soul, the center of my sinful earth,
Thrall to these rebel powers that thee array.
Why dost thou pine...such a mistaken canister
Of words that I would not put them down once more.

January 15, 1616
Stratford—Henley Street

Viola bows rasped and recorders piped and rain hit the door and windows at Hall's, the quartet playing before his fireplace, the men sitting with their backs to the blaze, instruments fired.

"More ale?"

"How about canary?"

"Cake, eh, Will?"

Cakes and rain perpetually, the strings for a throat, garroting the night...the rain, it raineth every night. Admit no impediments, listen:

Never say that I was false of heart...the poison left her stunned, as if beneath an avalanche of men. Mad slanderers, no, Ann deserved the slander but what could slander accomplish? Like incessant rain, or that repeated low note on the fiddle, what good? A flooding melancholy, and Ann unchanged.

Love was my sin but now my sin is breathing. And tonight it is a multiple sin for I am listening, hoping these instruments and players have a message for my soul. The shattered rain on windows is everyman's storm, the gutter thief, the pimp, the king—all of us hunkered under pain.

The good Dr. Hall bends over me:

"Feeling better tonight, Will? I hope so."

I chuckle and say I am.

Put on your cloak and hurry, Hall. There's someone sicker than I who needs you. Eat a crocodile. I'll be going home soon. I should be there now, going over my accounts.

Music has unstopped my ears but no grapple of sound holds tonight, not with the scrofula of rain, the wink of time on cavernous faces beefed by the fire.

See that wizened face, that's Hall, tall and thin, and next to him my frump, belly puddinged, hair screwed at angles, lines and then more lines lining the half-open mouth, the missing teeth... Ann, dear Ann, was it to you I wrote the sonnet beginning? Ah, no, the errors snare us, bare us to the quick of lime. The arithmetic of memory multiplies fantasy.

Poetry, succor me in this hour of need, help me as you have: I have given you my life; now, you must lend argument to my folly. Dry the rain on my skull! Be youth: be Ellen, outcast, incast, what is your substance, whereof you are made, that millions of strange shadows on you tend? Is this *my* memory? Or do the lines remember me?

The notes of the quartet confuse the shadows, the fire's instrument, the tankards on the table, one for you, Marlowe...

I am to wait, though waiting be as hell—

And we walked home together through the rain, she who has never met Touchstone or Polonius or Othello...

And so to a cold bed.

–*S*–

On some of Dr. Hall's visits, he urged me to discontinue my journal, wanting me to rest. I told him that the language I used was hardly playwriting, requiring the barest effort on my part. I explained that I need something. He huffed and rumbled, with professional sincerity, like the good neighbor he is, and I understand now that my resurrected fears may, like a Greek chorus, pervade and annul. But what do they pervade and annul, this corner, precharnel, prepaid house in Hell? Am I to talk with trees? Am I to forget manhood? Am I to cheer old age? Infirmity? Hall is such a knotted creature I wonder my Susanna married him: such a sultry woman for such a cadaver! His contorted body, pinched here, pinched there, sewed here, unsewed there, his starvation face, with zealot eyes in bald skull, leaves me lacking in confidence; yet, I listen and he prescribes and we talk and play chess. I am his medical pawn, gulping doses for him, bleeding for him: is the final move his or mine?

Home
January 18, 1616

Dr. Hall, when you found your woman in my Susanna, you found bed-woman, kitchen wench and apothecary girl. Your shop, shelved, bottled, ointmented, reeks of balm and poison. Long before you married my Susanna, I got to know that smell when I came to you to help me battle pain. You were never too ill or busy to help me check pain's unkindness.

But underneath your skin you are another Timon, another hater of mankind, concocting health to make more health to make more pain to make money. Pestel in hand, you measure alleviants, the richer your patient, the cleverer your compound. How you worry on behalf of the young countess. How you thumb your books for the Lord Chamberlain's gout.

Drum bottles—

Beat shelves—

Smash glass—

See, his shingle in the wind, JOHN HALL – PHYSICIAN, weeps rain, and I sit waiting, with vapors, losses, pangs, venoms in my blood, anticipating prescriptions—or epitaph.

His face grimaces his thanks, his hand extended, his pox is to "rob one another. There's more gold! Cut throats...all that you meet are thieves!" All this is patiently and subtly withheld by the good doctor since frightening the patient frightens money. Only dear friends discover the true Timon...

Oh, God, how pain strangles me today! It paves my skull! I am on fire! Such useless misery! Pain is the greatest cheat. Pain, your friendship is much too covetous! Pain—you old prostitute—swallow your own hemlock for a change!

Henley Street, Stratford
January 20

I am too hard on friend Hall!

I've spent hours there, puttering, talking, laughing, entertained by his curious, Indian cow's tail, stones cut from men's bladders, uterine balls of hair, paw of a bear, and skeleton of a pigmy.

This year, he is publishing a treatise on the *Wounds of the Abdomen*. He's as clever with his scalpel as his concoctions of wormwood, rosarum and menthol. Around Stratford, he is best known for his treatment of dropsy.

Stratford
January 23, 1616

Logs burn in my fireplace and I have a book on my lap: I have a kingdom: a crown: crackling of wood becomes voices, stuff of dreams, friends, stages, plays, quarrels, hopes, changes, beginnings, endings, the pen scratching paper, pigeons chuckling, laughter, death, Hamnet's face, father's, the cloak, the whisper, the plague, the rain, fog, losses, waves against rocks: a log totters and the upended section spurts into a pennant...shake-scene!

I have no picture—no drawing—to help me remember Hamnet. Inago Jones could have done one. I should tear apart pieces of paper and fold them until they become his face, or, with scissors, cut out his silhouette. Damn the weak mind that makes such simple wishes impossible!

There was no artist in Stratford. Stratford had no skills to offer except death's skill...death for all of us along with that triumvirate, love, marriage, children; with fornication for pallbearer, adultery for sexton, rape for choirmaster...

How weary and stale and flat are the uses of this world. Bring hebenon for O...

Youth's falcon on his glove, Hamnet stands with his friends around him, most of them young, their well-groomed horses held by pages.

On the distant shore of a lake, a castle breaks through a grove of beech.

Hamnet is laughing at his unhooded bird.

"Have you unseeled him?" someone asks.

"He can fly," Hamnet says. "Now."

"See...he's looking for game!"

"Hamnet, is it true your father writes plays for our Queen? London plays?"

"You should see his *Macbeth*! That's a play for you! Duel and all! We'll go to London and see one of his plays. There's one at the Palace soon."

How I would like to rearrange life, bring happiness, bestow wealth, fix love, make well, foil crime, reverse ill luck. But only the stage can accomplish miracles and there custom stales the plot and disharmonies garble intention.

But, as evening galls, and candles go on, I hear Hamnet's footsteps...he wants new gloves, new hood, new leash...

What's past is prologue:

At Blackfriars, the chandeliers of candles are hugely lit and light streams upon Alleyn, who is speaking on stage; the boards are clean and shine; all actors are in their places; the seats are almost filled; I see a woman, in dark green velvet; accompanied by her maid, she takes a seat; rows of faces beseech the stage: oh kingdom, place of tempest and calm, engulf us again!

Henley Street
Stratford

Linnus, whose gypsy father is an acrobat, visits me these days; with his father in jail he has to wait for his release. Dumpy, leather-skinned and wild-eyed, Linnus is fourteen, and has a four-year-old brother, Peter. Their mother is dead.

My old apple tree is Linnus' home, when he is here; I sit outside while he performs tricks he has learned from his father, tricks I have never seen. Peter yawns on the grass or stands between my legs or pods my lap, thrilled by his brother's arm and leg cleverness...the sun warms the three of us.

His tricks done, glad to rest, Linnus stretches on the ground, to incline me a little of his wanderings, the hunger, always the hunger: it's as if he never had a full meal. They are scourged out of town, thrown into jail, entertained at castles, fed on cakes and ale, left to starve on a farm. Linnus points to Peter, asleep on my lap.

"Why do you like him? He's ugly."

"He's ugly but he may change and grow to be handsome, perhaps become an explorer, like Drake." And I talk to Linnus about Drake and the Armada and as I talk it seems to me I'm talking to Hamnet, or is this Hamnet on my lap?

It doesn't matter.

Linnus and Peter matter, and after a while we rig fishing gear and go to the river and fish, dawdle all afternoon, Linnus croaking gypsy songs, Peter in and out of the water, dashing after magpies and crows, gabbling berries, every problem forgotten.

Home late, Linnus prepared supper for us (Ann away for a few days): he was quick and clever in the kitchen, reminding me of an actor familiar with his part.

Henley Street
Stratford
December 11, '15

Linnus described a play he saw last summer and I was reminded of the first play I saw, as a boy, performed by gypsies who told a tale of Scottish intrigue and murder that ended with the beautiful heroine's suicidal plunge into a loch. Those swarthy actors seldom left my mind for weeks, waking me, haunting school and play. I can yet see the sheriff torturing the girl accused of stealing: words have gone but not the actions.

That evening, Papa and I walked home together. He would not talk about the play. Mama disliked plays and never attended, damning them as "lucifers." I suppose the gypsy play was a "lucifer."

Henley Street
Stratford
December 12, 1615

One of my bitterest experiences was seeing Pericles killed by a sheep herder. On the outskirts of London, Pericles burst into joyous yappings and began to frolic and nip sheep, an immense herd, stretching for blocks. I saw him tangle with a black ram. The herder, rushing at Pericles, mistaking his fun, struck him with his crook and beat him to the street; then, before I could shove my way through the herd, flailed him over the head with the butt. Yelling, pushing, I knocked down the man but reached Pericles too late... I wanted to leave the city; I wanted to spit on mankind. I wish I could have my friend to talk to, eat meat from my hand: there's plenty of meat for you now, boy.

Midnight

What is it that has embittered me?

I felt the bitterness long before someone tried to kill Ellen. Did the bitterness

Henley Street
Stratford
February 1

Suum—nun—nonny, the wind said, as my father and I worked in his glover's shop, quiet hours, among the many kinds of leather, sheepskin, goat, kid, lamb, pigskin, coltskin, doeskin, buckskin. In his tiers of drawers were the pontifical gloves, liturgical gloves, gloves for dignitaries, ladies' gloves, wedding gloves...

A bird sang in its cage by the door.

Between the opening and closing of the shop we talked pleasantly or waited on customers with consideration:

We talked of Rocco Bonetti, the great London fencing master, and his fencing school; we talked of the snail and how it shrinks in its house when hit, or sits in the shade of its shell; we chatted about spears and helmets and mottos like *Non Sanz Droict,* his favorite; we talked of great castles, like Kenilworth, and their ghosts; we talked of kings and how to catch larks with a mirror and scraps of red cloth...the buzz of our talk was a good buzz.

So, another memory!

Candlemas

I wrote *The Tempest* at Stratford, the only play I wrote at home. For the first time I had leisure to write, in my garden, the summer warm: this was an island for an island: time faded: I remembered *scenari* I had seen at the *commedia dell'arte:* I remembered the wreck of the *Sea Adventure* in Bermuda: a drunk sailor stopped me and described that grievous storm, described the bewitched island, and I began:

On ship at sea:

Captain: Boatswain!

Boatswain: Here, Master, what cheer?

Captain: Good fellow, talk to the sailors, warn them, fall to it quickly or we'll run aground!

Enter sailors:

Boatswain: Quickly, my fellows! Take in the topsail speedily! That's the captain's warning whistle!

Then the shipwreck followed.

It was pleasant to invent without pressure: I wanted a lively yet serene play, with a mixture of philosophy, humor and fantasy: I wanted a play to fit the new mode, free of symbolism.

I walked about my garden and my peace trees, and there, over there was Caliban, a savage slave; I took another turn, and there was Ariel; I heard the wind blow hollowly across an uninhabited island...

"Safely in harbor is the king's ship; in the deep nook where once you called me at midnight... Go, make yourself a nymph of the sea... Where should this music be? In the air, or the earth? Delicate Ariel, sea nymphs ring the knell...in the dark backward and abysm of time..."

Discs of spinning yellow, pink, lavender:
A hundred Kemps are jigging,
each in yellow clown suit,
grinning, clowning, enroute to the Globe.
Kemp jigs onto the stage:
Applause.

Home

So it went...

As I left the Globe, near the end of a play, I found Will Kemp, slumped on the steps, by the street, head on his arms, sobbing: he would never clown for us again: he said he was too old, that he embarrassed us, that times had changed: as I stood beside him, he glanced away.

I had watched him a hundred times and thought him better than Summers, or any clown: Kemp was legend, for jig and bawdy tale, for the laugh at the end of the play. Londoners flocked to see him—had flocked to see him for years.

His make-up streaked by the rain, his yellow suit soaked, he tottered to his feet, as if drunk. Last summer he had danced his way across country, from place to place, enthusiastically received by villagers and townsmen—carried aloft on their shoulders.

His wrinkled face was drunken-lined, shining in the rain. He yanked his hat lower: was he remembering his fustian scenes, hard-drinking, quarrelling? He was famous for his winnings at primero—stubby, rock-muscled, little, knotted—he wavered, seemed about to collapse.

The play was over and the theatre crowd vomited out and milled around Kemp, encircled him, caught him up, hoisted him and bore him, through the streets, howling, cheering: KEMP...KEMP...KEMP!

Home

A number of years before we dismissed Kemp at the Globe, I visited him at his Thames River home—a home in the Sir Walter style. Kemp's carriage brought me. I strolled about his extensive garden for a few luxurious moments, viewing the river below, thinking how well it paid to invest in land and play primero. His doormen showed me in, for I had been invited to dinner.

Mrs. Kemp, dressed in pale green, came toward me, to greet me, a charming young woman: like a clap of thunder, Kemp came at her, caned her, lashed her with fierce blows, and dragged her to her room. I didn't wait for an explanation of his violence...

I do my best on the pot and think of my sex and think I'll be rotting soon, and I hear pegs moving in the beams, and I hear old time and new time—outside the church bells strike. Outside of what?

Henley Street
Stratford
February 8, 1616

Why do I write?

All day Ann has sat by the windows, embroidering, soaking sun, her rheumatic fingers paining her, her silence and disdain evident.

Her stooped shoulders anger me because they remind me of my age, and I rant at time's disdain and irreparable devastations: a plague on time's house, a plague on mine—sickly wife and sickly husband.

Egypt—it is well you aren't here, to be contorted, cheated, frailed or paunched. To nourish an illusion is hard and grows harder through the years. The only wisdom is the quiet heart, born of the smile of heaven, seeking nature, not the wild sea of conscience.

But that is for the wise! Today, there is no Orpheus. The trees are not our sanctuary. The seas don't hang their heads; I hang mine. Where's the lute, the player? I travel round and round the dial, to Ellen and the cloak, the fog and loneliest of men. Time should cure all, they say. But time—as I see time—does not oblige.

My last will...my last walk...my last play. I never thought of a last play. *Henry VIII* was to have another and yet another...creeping on but creeping to be sure...other sonnets...other songs...to sleep, to die, to sleep...

O shit on death.

Home
February 10, '16

I used to wake with anticipation. I wake these mornings and know that I may not wake in another twenty days. When I lie down to sleep I think I may fall asleep and from that sleep never wake. I consider the worried faces about me and realize they will not have to endure me for long. Jonson visits me and I think this is his last visit.

Cheat, your door, as it swings open, opens onto a cave; no shepherd's note signals to watery star...cuckold...bastard...my tale will end and my small cubicle will be filled. Have I put down man's spirit with enough spirit? Beauteous youth, have I recorded you? I never wanted to write love's epitaph... Antony was my tongue in praise.

I am certain that love is the best, love that is closest to beauty and the kindest of affections. Sensation surpasses thought. Imagination is well enough but it is not love. Between earth and heaven, imagination compares with no warm arms and legs.

Feb. 11, '16

Stunned by poverty—how hard it was to write during those early years. Belly gnawing, I kept at it: I lay down, I got up, sat at the big table. Storms hunkered over the roof tops, the sun licked at the roofs, snow bundled them, and I was cold, cold. Smoke puffed from chimneys, bent in the icy mornings like hearse plumes. Chimneys—I never wanted to count them; broken, dying chimneys, strewed the city below me. One brick stack leaned far over, yet belched smoke.

Pimps lived on one side of me, prostitutes on the other; I could not move without paying my rent. My place was never warm: my hands cracked because of the cold. I kept my legs wound in rags, coughing.

Because of pleurisy I had to sell all of my books: Mary sold them for me, one by one, maybe two or three at a time. How old was Mary? Twenty? I was about twenty-five. It would take another twenty-five years to dim her memory: the stalk of her body, her restless, weightless feet. She bent a little to the left, as if injured, the arms also restless, the eyes inward. Did she ever laugh? Her smile always seemed something pushed into being, only a little jolt got it there.

She sold my books and bought my food and fed me, the hell of pleurisy riding me: tears in my eyes I attempted to eat: tears of many kinds crushed me. The roofs, the cold, the sorrow, how they come back to me! The anguish in my side went on for weeks but Mary never failed or complained: she fucked men at night and succored me during the day: sometimes she slept on the floor beside my bed or lay across the foot of the bed, a blanket around her. Her black hair might unpin itself and lie about her.

"Let's keep a bird, when it's Spring," I suggested.

"How can you feed it, w-w-without money?" she asked.

"My father is sending money."

"When? Soon?"

"Has someone written to him? You must see to it, Mary. Make someone write."

"I think s-s-s-so. I'll try again, ton-n-n-night."

I managed to eat more when the money came and Mary ate well: I ate for those who were poor, I ate for my father, for the starving waifs, for the sick, those in prison, fighting in wars. I ate because it would soon be Spring. I ate because I must write.

Wrens built a nest above my window. Day after day, they fluttered in and out; day after day it got warmer; I was able to take care of myself; Mary and I were planning to picnic beside the river; she never came; I waited and waited; I asked those who knew her; no one had seen her.

I asked for her many times. There was absolutely no trace of her. She simply disappeared. Some criminal? Some man? Death? I never knew.

Ave Maria!

Home

Over the years I have read Ellen's letters, hearing them almost. Those lines of hers, when I was dismal and lonely, shook off the curse of disillusionment. Even now, after these years, lines come to me:

> Surely the greatness of a play lies in its mystery: we are taken inside a private world that is tragic or amusing or sentimental; things that are a part of this world must be judiciously hinted at.
>
> Your plays take life apart because your poetry is so profound. It's the finest poetry I know. Knowing you gives your work added profundity...
>
> The theatre gives man breadth: it's his second life. A country without a theatre is a poor, barren country.
>
> Spring is the best part of the year...we decided: our lochs

take on a greenness that must originate in deep, moss-covered rock. I think that water has a definite temperament, a personality, if you like... I like to walk when the sting of spray mingles with fog and underfoot, like a blanket, are the tiny flowers... I want you...

My brother is fond of you. He laughs and asks what is it that makes me take to that man? You must come back to Scotland, Will. Write me seriously about a possible visit... Love finds a way...

I wish you could be here, the castle is so beautiful, springtime is so evident, so unlike Scotland, full of gay things, white lilies and pansies along the paths, tulips and agnus-castus, roses around our statues and ramblers on the arbors. Only the biggest roses are in full flower: you should see the yellow ones. You know, I think yellow is my favorite color, and it's because the sun is yellow, for what would this earth of ours be without the sun? We wouldn't even have love, would we? And I wouldn't even be able to dream of your kisses and your arms about me. And that's what the sun is for, for dreaming, springtime dreaming...and I wish for you, to walk with me, and love me. I will pick a pansy and wear it for you. I will pick a rose and put it in my room, for you. Will, when can we see each other? Can't you come here?...

Her letters were like that...

Stratford
February – 1616

Queen Elizabeth came on our stage at the Palace as I played the role of king, the afternoon stainglass bangling her jewels. I was shocked at seeing her galled face and yet had the guts to continue my lines, adding improvisations as well, to force her to wait. While she waited, she dropped her glove (playing her part), and as I arranged my robe, talking as I stood there, I picked up her glove and slowly faced the audience and said:

"Yet we stoop to pick up our Cousin's glove."

How that amused her. "Such propriety!" she said.

"Such folly," I wanted to say.

This is high class prostitution commonly called "purse penury," our coldest-oldest art. The art is especially susceptible to jewels and the brazenness of crowns. Men have been hung for their inability to kowtow, with poverty in the wings, snivelling or prancing jubilantly.

KING JAMES—

Now that you are our new friend, sceptering this Brittic island with careful gaze, ours is the homage! We see that your awareness is aware of considerations, a King James version of Sleeves and Ruff duly pressed. You surely press promises without guilt for gilt. Through narrow lozenged glass the sun administers your ceremonials.

Oh, king, your uniqueness Towers over us: you are our stiller of war, our buffer of hate, our unbiased protestant.

You rise—and London rises.

You walk—and London walks, for we are your guardians.

If your latest diamond is somewhat small, speak to us and it will be remembered in moors, fens, and locks. If your crown, coming from a woman's head, needs adjusting our adjusters are sure hands, toward continuity.

Henley Street
Stratford

When Susanna visited me in London we ate at the Swann: she loved the rich and badly seasoned food, the purpled windows and painted scripture walls. "Oh, Papa, this is a wonderful Inn... Oh, Papa, isn't that a beautiful house by the river? Think of living there! Those people must be awful rich! Will we get that rich?

...Papa, I've never seen such beautiful books... And look, look at the Thames in the sun; the sun seems squashed right into the water. And can we really ride in a boat again, down toward the ocean?"

Enthusiasm was her best quality. And very little perturbed her. Trash strewn in the street, a dead cat, brawling seamen...she drew back in disgust but soon found something exciting or beautiful. When I sleepwalked and stumbled against a table and broke the rush lamp, she was undisturbed. She kissed me, and we talked about what we'd do tomorrow. She was fifteen, then. Fifteen—what an age! She wanted to remain with me in London and I would have permitted it if I could have looked after her. There was no budging Ann to the city. Some thought Susanna a hussy.

Fun-loving, keen at games, she outplayed her friends. While she played I would be at my writing. In the midst of her fun, she might pop up and say: "Papa, you're working too hard: you never have fun." Her consideration brought me to my senses and I remembered growing up with six kids: none of them had her brightness. Of course the years changed her: her copper hair darkened: her enthusiasm faded: marriage ruined her figure: marriage made her a business woman: her hussiness became sexmate: Dr. Hall her all! How clearly I can remember today...a warning. And why do I write?

Shakespeare discovers Ellen's blue cloak
in a heap of theatre crud in his Stratford closet:
Puzzled, he sits on the floor, holds up the cloak,
checks the fabric, his face sickly:
Fog at the door of his house.

Henley Street
Stratford
February 24, 1616

Rummaging in my storeroom, I found forgotten things, things I had supposed lost or destroyed, a velvet jacket faced with grubby ermine, a pair of crimson trousers, a leather breastplate and brass helmet ornamented with a dragon's crest. It annoyed me that none of these things had deteriorated. For some unfathomable reason—Caesaria ego—I put on the breastplate and helmet and gaped at myself. How now, that sickly face and stupidity: my stupid room, some of it visible in the same glass: the odious German etchings Judith gave me, Papa's cracked leather chest, the unpolished table, seamed plaster and varnished beams.

Tossing breastplate and helmet into the storeroom, I noticed something. A cloak? Lifting it out of a box, unfolding it, I thought it was her blue theatre cloak. How could it be, after having disappeared years ago, in the street? But, holding it higher, I searched for the slash and the blood stains. Of course it had been cleverly cleaned and mended! I was too disturbed to go over it carefully. No...no...I dropped it and put out the light and went to bed.

Lying there, I watched sky, clouds floating, white over stars and then the stars dazzlingly near and then the cloud-cloak covering them once more, drowning.

Fear sifts through my fingers and mind.

What am I—a lie? Was she a lie? Was life? The cloak?

Why haven't I, if I am sure of myself, seen to it that my plays have been published? I leave nothing. Nothing! *Antony*, *Hamlet*, *Macbeth*, *Winter's Tale*, *Romeo*...not one. I must speak to Jonson and Alleyn. I must write to them at once!

Fog lay about in pieces like pieces of my life. Ground fog.

In the starlight I glared at my hands and saw that they were swollen, as they have often been lately.

Wasn't that snow falling, flakes of morning?

I tried to remember Ellen's face, tried to feel her presence.

When Ann brought me breakfast I could not look at her though she spoke to me kindly.

I write with costly effort—hands worse. I am cold. My mind staggers.

To the oriel—to look outside.

Thinking makes poverty.

Religion as we came to regard it in London was a glib and soiled art.

Eclipses of our mental sun and moon betray us; so I beseech you, brain, do not regress as time shows time's ending: old and reverend, think straight.

Eater of broken meats I seem to be: knave, rascal, ruffian. Reverence to self...

Perhaps this cold world will turn us all to fools and madmen...

Stratford

Why is it I grimace so much? Alone I mug, pull my beard, rub flat of hand over my eyes, crack knuckles, shrug, sigh. Is this my sane monologue with self? What's its purpose? Perhaps I must convince myself that I am alive and battling: grimace at the window, grimace on the pot, grimace at bed. Grimace is my hornbook. For the best of self-conviction I prefer knuckle cracking—such skeletal speech.

Stratford
February 26, 1616

So I'll never know who attacked Ellen?

Is it because I am sick that I care?

Could it be that someone stepped from his stage of bitterness and struck her that night the fog drowned her carriage? Did he resent my luck? The harder poverty knocked the keener he felt my good luck: was that how it was? Was hunger a knife in his belly? Did he run away from London afterward? His hungry, motherless kids asked him to kill for money? Was that how it was?

"Your brother Fred is here, bending over you..."

"Was that Ann, who said that yesterday? Or was it Hall, bending over me, who said that Fred had come by?"

Ellen, could you come? Or Hamlet? Othello? Marlowe?

Stratford
March 5, 1616

Years ago I wrote this:

Can honor set a leg? Or set an arm? Or take away the pain of a wound? What is honor? A word? What is that word? Air? What has it? The fellow who died on Wednesday, does he feel it? Does he hear it?

But I still hear it...honor lives for me, in my memories of my father, for all those who have worked before I came into being, for the cathedral spire, the ship, the cut gem, the book, the play, the figure standing in sun and snow...

13th

Very sick for three days. Dr. Hall. Others.

Pain.

Can't get to the oriel.

Wouldn't know a hawk from a handsaw.

15th

I go before my darling,
I go before...
Follow to the bower in the close alley,
There we will together sweetly kiss
And like two wantons, dally—dally—dally...

Sing it again—sing to me before I die—the candles are dying—the wind is dying—I suffocate in my room—I want to be with you—sing our song—oh, to dally once more—sing—

March 18, 1616

Judith married early because I felt I could not last much longer... Judith, will a hundred and fifty pounds help you, with that husband who doesn't want to work? A fine son-in-law...but...ah, the trouble I have caused. She could have waited...but, at that time...she thought... My will is insufficient...

Illness is such folly

I still remember names

Alleyn was here to see me...

Burbage won't come...the man you care most to see, cares less for thee.

March 19

My affection remains, blazes as it were: there were winnings: good things strive to help us: come unto the yellow sands for their beneficence: hark: a pox against pain: who has pain! No. Defy the monsters, prod the phoenix, bury pig-nuts, come forward magical, fecundate freedom, build, levy songs.

I need Raleigh's elixir! If men concoct an elixir of youth it is too late for me.

Then, that elixir of elixir of elixirs, hebenon!

Sprinkle it.

March 21, 1616

Now that I am sick, it seems so rare a thing I once climbed elms for rook's nest and slashed all afternoon, in the August sun, to scythe the timothy in rows. I was fifteen, I think it was. Larks flew and sang. I liked the click-a-click of my scythe as it bladed. Crickets chirped. Magpies and jackdaws took the air. There was a kingfisher diving.

I long to dive where I used to swim, at Gray's pool, alongside the burned mill; I used to strip and plunge off the sluice, after working in the field. Or we used to swim there—five or six of us—and test who could stay under longest, test—what was it I wanted to test?

Cowslips grew cap-a-pie on two sides of that pool and their cinque-spotted faces got trampled underfoot as we dashed nakedly about, lewdly knuckling each other's penis. Banks of violets were thick on the shady side of the mill, thickest among heaps of smashed and rotting shingles...her favorite flower! Hers!

Home
Suppertime

Getting ready to die is looking across a stage through semi-darkness; it is muffing one's lines; it is listening to incomprehensible promptings; it is taking the wrong exit. It is tampering with the plot, eliminating the star from the best scenes, substituting a beginner. Getting ready to die is watching the candle gutter, hearing the rooster before dawn, saying love's good-bye; it is the footstep on the stair, the reveled, sleeved and broken sword.

Getting ready to die is no man's business!

O, that this too, too solid flesh...

Home – Evening
March 27, 1616

For several days my eyesight has failed and I have been unable to write. I have less pain but I can not eat. They talk to me and I lie here, restless, hearing, hearing... I want to hear something like a promise, an echo of things hoped for.

That knocking at the door!
Rain over the house.
To sleep, to sleep...

March 28, 1616

When I was twenty, splendid, strong, I thought it would be noble to die in the Spring: ah, noble death I praised you childishly. This is springtime, and I see no signs of nobility.

Tired with all these, for restful death I cry—

how like a poem those lines read, and lie! At that time, when I wrote that sonnet, I was never more in love with life.

For days the rain has been falling over the town, fine rain, grey rain that is determined to shatter the last of my courage...for days.

Ann stands by my bedside, a plate of food in her hands, urging me to eat: "Take something...it will help you, Will."

Susanna sits by my side and sighs, "Papa, Papa."

Alleyn visits me, his voice warming my room, in the beaten way of friendship.

March 30, '16

Again I am reminded I must complete my will—and so I must.

Tomorrow I'll dictate...how will it go?

In the name of God, I, William Shakespeare, gentleman, in perfect health and memory, make and ordain this last will and testament...

How can I say perfect health and memory?

I commend my soul into the hands of God, hoping and believing to be made a partaker of life everlasting, and my body to the earth thereof it is made...

Custom...

Item: I bequeath to my daughter, Judith, a hundred and fifty pounds (shall I make it more?); in addition, I grant her my estate in Warr County—I like that place...

To Joan—I leave my clothes. Why?

To Elizabeth Hall, I leave my silverware...

To Thomas Combe, my sword. (I liked that sword...its inlaid hilt!)

To Richard Burbage (good friend), money for a ring.

For daughter, Susanna Hall, my home, barns, stables, orchards, gardens, lands, tenements...my new house in Blackfriars.

To Ben Jonson—fifty pounds and this journal. Short-changed again, Ben.

Item: to my wife, my second best bed and our furniture. (It should be more. What shall it be?)

To Dr. John Hall, all settlements after the payment of debts...there is no more...

I must remember to speak in a clear voice.

In two sepia rectangles, the renowned Droeshout portrait of Shakespeare and the famous Gerard bust...

The bust revolves slowly as a voice intones Shakespeare's last will.

The talking portrait speaks from the Stratford church wall: through the open door of the church a blue cloak half conceals the Non Sanz Droict *coat-of-arms.*

Lincoln's Journal

For Freedom

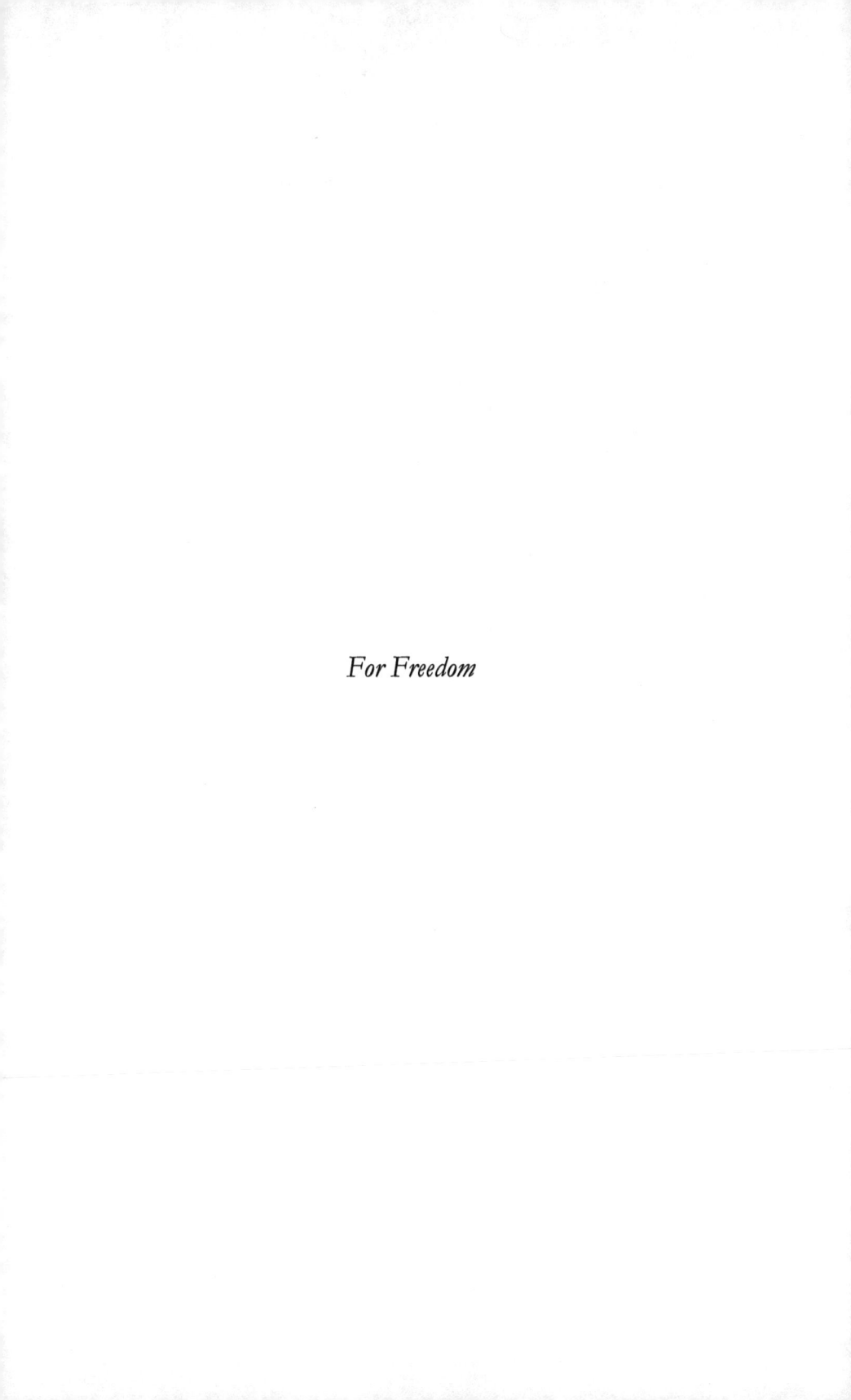

All of the quotations of Abraham Lincoln's writings are in the public domain:

Pages	
521	lines 9-10
522	entire page
523	lines 1-4 and 22-24
524	lines 2-5
528	lines 1-3
534	lines 11-12
537	lines 25-30
538	lines 1-26 and 30
539	lines 1-21 and 26-33
544	lines 10-14
548	lines 18-20
556	lines 29-30
557	lines 1-4
560	lines 3-11
563	line 15
568	lines 5-7 and 12-20
572	lines 14-17
575	lines 17-20
579	line 3
585	lines 18-25
586	lines 1-6
588	lines 22-29: Diary quotation, Doneway & Evans, *A Treasury of the World's Great Diaries*
589	lines 1-2: *ibid.*
591	lines 5-16: quotation from Ohn Quincy, President of Harvard, *Harvard Record*
591	lines 19-23
592	lines 1-2
598	line 26: song, "Tenting Tonight"
603	lines 15-23
605	lines 23-26
606	lines 9-15
607	lines 24-28
610	lines 15-19: Shiloh quotation, Doneway & Evans

1

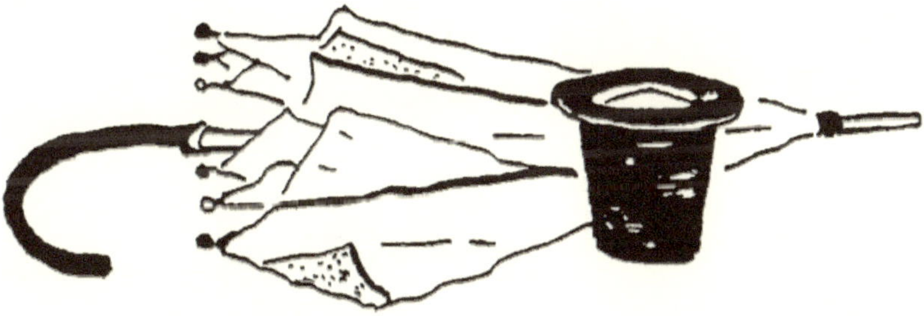

Executive Mansion
May 4, 1863

Not long after my inauguration I made a resolution to write something about my life. Writing, late at night, I hoped to escape the pressures of the war and go back into time.

April 12, 1861 — at 4:30 a.m., the war began.

Thirty-nine days after my inauguration!

When I called for 75,000 volunteers, I thought hostilities would end soon. I thought of many things in those trying days. There was the terrible summer of '82, when wheat fields were swept by gunfire, 20,000 Confederates died, the Union lost 16,000. Boys, mostly boys. Which General woke me during the night? Dark days, dark nights. The Army of the Potomac had 100,000 soldiers. Their losses and gains are part of me. Deserters, absentees, spies—each is part of me. The wounded, the sick, the dying, the dead—they are part of me.

Oh, Traveler, why did you bring this war?

And Wall Street remembers this war! Fears it!

There seemed to be panic in rooms of this building.

The two years I have been here have taught me a great deal about men and self.

Yet, now, now I will record my life though life surges around Washington, though each one of us is sorely tried; we have read anew life's "great tragic volume," as John Adams called it. The pages lie open as drums thud along the Potomac.

Executive Mansion
May 7, 1863

North versus South, we have a population of 18 million fighting a population of 5 million, folly vs. folly, brother vs. brother, Commander Lee vs. General Lee, Major Crittenden vs. General Crittenden.

Europeans assure me that my cause is a lost cause. They say I will never eradicate slavery. The South says I will never end slavery because it is an honorable way of life. Our Indian brothers have sided with the South. But it is the cause of the Union that gives us strength, gives us right.

Union forever...flags...they wave yet do not heal...they acclaim patriotism. But patriotism can blind us. It is a "whirlwind," as Emerson reminds us. For my part, it is my oath to preserve and protect this government of freedom for all men.

My convictions do not wane as cabinet members fail me. I am firmly convinced that tact can win against men who oppose, who are selfish or temporarily deaf. I believe the citizenry understands me as I understand them, as they pour into my office and talk with me.

May 19, 1863

I reaffirm myself.

I wish to tell that I was a man of the wilderness; I wish to write about my mother, about my village of New Salem, my home in Springfield with its maple trees. I see the sunlight in my office windows and it is also the sunlight of my boyhood and youth.

Tomorrow night, with my lamps lit and candles on my desk, I will begin to find out who I am.

I will begin to go back twenty years, thirty years, forty years. Snow storms will batter our log cabin. I will recall what it was to go hungry. I will try to fit together hours, days, nights. I'll open the prairie schooner of my brain.

I had requested the telegraph office: NO TELEGRAMS between one and 5 a.m.

To commence my diary I will use lines I wrote a few years ago for an Illinois newspaper.

May 20, 1863

I am six feet four inches tall and weigh one hundred and eighty pounds. I am lean, muscular, have dark skin, coarse black hair and grey eyes. My legs and arms are long; my hands are large; I wear a size 12 shoe.

I was put to work when I was about eight or nine—farmed out for 13 cents a day. I cut wood, mended fences, herded cattle, dug ditches. At home, I milked our cow, lugged pails of water, cleaned slop, fed the stove. Weather meant almost nothing to my family; we lived exactly like Indians in our 3-sided cabin. We ate like Indians—when we could. At times we said nothing to each other for days on end that could be in any way construed as interesting.

Executive Mansion
May 22, 1863

I was born February 12, 1809, in Hardin County, Kentucky. My parents were born in Virginia, of undistinguished families—second families, perhaps I should say. My mother, who died in my tenth year, was of a family of the name of Hanks...

My paternal grandfather, Abraham Lincoln, emigrated from Virginia to Kentucky about 1781, where a year or two later he was killed by Indians, not in battle, but by stealth, when he was laboring to open a farm in the forest.

My father, at the death of his father, was but six years of age, and he grew up literally without education. When I was eight he removed from Kentucky to Indiana; we reached our new home about the time the state came into the Union. It was a wild region, with many bears and other wild animals still in the woods...

My father settled in an unbroken forest, and the clearing away of surplus wood was the great task ahead. Though very young I had an ax put in my hands...and from that, till within my twenty-third year, I was constantly handling that useful instrument.

...A few days before the completion of my eighth year, in my father's absence, a flock of wild turkey approached our new log cabin. Standing inside, I shot through a crack and killed one of them. I have never since pulled a trigger on larger game.

I think that the aggregate of all my schooling did not amount to one year. I was never in a college or academy as a student, and never inside of a college or academy building till I had a law license. After I was twenty-three and had separated from my father, I studied English grammar. I have studied and nearly mastered the six books of Euclid since I became a member of Congress.

Executive Mansion
June 1, 1863

In the wilderness there were some schools, so called, but no qualification was ever required of a teacher beyond "readin', writin' and cipherin' " to the rule of three. If a straggler, supposed to understand Latin, happened to sojourn in the neighborhood, he was looked upon as a wizard. There was absolutely nothing to excite ambition for education. Of course, when I came of age I did not know much. Still, somehow, I could read, write, and cipher to the rule of three... The little advance I now have upon this store of education I have picked up from time to time under the pressure of necessity.

My father lived in Knob Creek, Kentucky; from this place he removed to Spencer County, Indiana, in the autumn of 1816; I was eight. The removal was partly on account of his resentment of slavery, but chiefly on account of the difficulty in acquiring legal land titles.

I became a sort of clerk in New Salem; I served as postmaster; then came the Black Hawk War; I was elected a Captain of volunteers, a success which gave me more freedom than any I have had since.

I went on the campaign, a campaign that led nowhere, except to the dead, that row of eleven men, lying in the sun, each head neatly scalped. I ran for legislature the same year (1832), and was beaten. It is the only time I ever have been beaten by the people. The next and three succeeding biennial elections I was elected to the state legislature.

As I rode horseback along the county roads something rode with me, an inner person. Beside the road, my horse browsing, I read a book. I remember sitting by a creek, listening to the frogs in the chill spring air; there was that person, that inner force.

I knew that there was little or no chance for advancement in this rural community unless it came through politics. So, politics had to shine my shoes and buy my trousers. I would prove that honesty was appreciated here. I would fit it into the crown of my hat.

June 5, 1863

It is a great piece of folly to attempt to make anything out of my early life. It can be all condensed into a simple sentence, and that sentence you will find in Grey's *Elegy:* "The short and simple annals of the poor."

And I add Grey's lines for myself :

Far from the madding crowd's ignoble strife
Their sober wishes never learned to stray;
Along the cool sequestered vale of life
They kept the noiseless tenor of their way.

One more thought:

My mother was the illegitimate daughter of Lucy Hawks, and a well-bred Virginia farmer. God bless her; all that I am or ever hope to be I owe to her. I believe that I inherited extra drive from her unfortunate background. That drive stands me in good stead.

Executive Mansion
June 10, 1863

I have experienced death many times. My aunt, my uncle, my brother's death. Then my mother's death of milk sickness. Such suffering. I whittled the pegs for her coffin. I can see her grave outside our cabin. I could see it each time we opened the door. In the spring and often during the summer I placed flowers on her grave. She loved lilacs and roses. Her kindness lingers on. Friends called her a woodland madonna.

Later, when my step-mother came, her love was felt by each one of us.

"Let me help you, Abe. Let me strain the milk tonight...you're tired. What a big stack of wood you've cut for us, son. That should last a while!"

She could handle an ax. She could lug a sack of flour. When wolves howled, she'd lean over me and say a few words or kiss my forehead. When my shoulders ached she rubbed them with bear grease.

"If I should die before I wake, I pray the Lord my soul to take," is a prayer she taught me.

Sometimes we planted pumpkin seeds together, on a nearby slope. She was faster than I. Again and again, she urged me to attend school. Each time we moved, she located the nearest schoolhouse. "You've got to go, Abe." I used to read to her.

She liked *Aesop's Fables* best. We'd sit in the evening sun and lean against the side of the cabin and I would read. We learned the fables quickly. Her favorite fable was "The Wolf and the Crane." In those days, my favorite was "The Snake and a File."

The White House
June 12, 1863

Often, when I am alone and tired, I remember the hot sun of the prairie summer, how it seems to hold down everything as far as the eye can see. I remember how it climbed almost every morning—like a wheel.

I remember the squeaking of leather as my horse pulled his plow; there was small corn growing nearby, in field after field. There were birds.

There is a biting sense of loss, looking into the past: we know this is something that can never take place again. We know, too, that we can resurrect ourselves, sometimes pleasurably. Today, I esteem those glimpses that reassure me, in spite of their passing. Without them I think life would be so overcome by the present it would be difficult to continue living.

The better life should be everyman's goal, a life that is not eaten up by toil, a life where there is freedom for thought, freedom for action. Men should be able to draw from the past; men should be able to construct for the present, a plan. Man should have time to evolve for himself and posterity—a heritage evoking pride leading to achievement that makes life worth living.

The White House
June 20, 1863

Some of my happy days were passed in East Salem, when I was an Illinois postmaster. Since the mail arrived only twice a week, I could peruse the *Louisville Journal* and the *Intelligencer*. I think there were about twenty-five families living in Salem in those days. I enjoyed delivering the mail personally; there was ample time to be friendly. So, I stuffed the letters inside my hat and walked from house to house. I got to know everybody that way. Summers were easy times. Remembering those summers they seem to stretch in a long line, with groves and fishing spots here and there.

I remember a huge boulder where I used to sit. Probably I had delivered my last letter. A rabbit liked to sit near me. I would shut my eyes and appreciate the greatness of life in the rabbit, in the trees around me, in the wind—the greatness that existed in my mother's life.

June 24, 1863

At the Burkes' home, not far from the post office, I rented a room. The Burkes, who are Quakers, a family of two, put themselves out for me, and gave me an upstairs room with a lamp. At night I got out needle and thread and mended my clothes, or, sitting in a leather chair, I read. Charles Burke and I fashioned that chair.

He lent me pen and ink, and I was able to practice penmanship—copying from a spelling book; it seemed great fun to me to spell out words, so much easier than working with an ax. Mrs. Burke's tabby, grey and fat, liked to keep me company, flipping a paw at the M's and L's.

In Salem I fell into debt.

When my partner died, my partner in the grocery business, I assumed his indebtedness—$1,000. It took me years to wipe out that sum, as huge as the national debt. I shucked corn, cradled wheat, chopped wood, ferryboated, clerked...$2.00 here, $5.00 here, $7.00 here. My debit column required all of my scheming. While I struggled to pay that thousand dollars I resolved to lay aside something as a cushion, but it was many years before I could carry out that resolution. Those were pinching times.

Executive Mansion
June 25, 1863

At Number 4, Hoffman's Row, we had our law office, second floor, a narrow room with a pair of elegant brass spittoons, a Pennsylvania wood burning stove. High on the wall, above my desk, hung an engraving of Benjamin Franklin. Our rough center table was usually overloaded with documents—like some outlandish mule. Legal books and newspapers filled shelves. A narrow window faced the street; another window let in sunlight. The elements washed them. The floor was bare oak but we had a fine assortment of chairs. There was a lounge near the sunny window and I liked to stretch out there, on the shaggy buffalo hide.

Billy Herndon and I had that shingle, good natured Billy. Here we talked business, cockfights, women, and horse races. For sixteen years we kept at it, learning, unlearning. For every stick of wood we burned in that Pennsylvania stove we had an ardent opinion.

Billy and I earned about $3,000 or $4,000, good for a town that already had eleven lawyers. Springfield, in those days, offered better legal services than sidewalks. Pigs in the streets, mud on our boots—so it went. We offered our services at all hours of the day. Often I never walked home for lunch. When I rode circuit, Billy kept house. The wren that lived in a box outside our door had a neater establishment than ours, but, she was not a member of the state legislature.

The White House
July 3rd, 1863

During my political career, I have striven to be astute where slavery is concerned. The issue of slavery has been a sensitive one, always difficult. Anti-slavery sentiment has been in existence no matter where I lived, usually undercover. The Baptist preacher I listened to as a boy was anti-slavery. I believed him. I saw blacks in chains, men and women. I soon learned about the cruelty that menaced their lives, destroyed their lives; I felt that I could, if I lived long enough, thwart slavery, perhaps abolish it, make our great nation a free nation. Patience, I repeated again and again to myself. I knew about Linda Mae. She was bound to William Wison for ninety-nine years. She was nineteen when that legal document was signed. When she reached 118 years she would be free. Patience?

Slavery was an old institution in Illinois, winked at in the 30's and 40's. The first governor of the state possessed slaves. I have seen human beings herded and treated like animals. Our family moved from Kentucky, troubled by the ways of slavery. My black clients sometimes confided in me, described, underlined, the devious trickeries of the whites. Billy, my Springfield barber, had tales to tell. I have heard them as he shaved me or trimmed my hair.

I am slow to learn, and slow to forget. My mind is like a piece of steel—very hard to scratch anything on it, and almost impossible after you get it there to rub it out.

Memories...it wasn't so long ago I tramped at the head of the ox team, as we moved from one place to another, one beginning that had not really ended, to another beginning that might not end. The oxen were faithful. They meant much to me. I will not forget. They ate from my hands, they blew their breaths on my fingers, they regarded me intently. It rained on us. The sun shone on us.

July 11, 1863

Was it twenty or thirty years ago, we drifted down the Mississippi, three of us on a loaded flatboat? She was well overloaded because all of us wanted to get rich quick. The second or third day on the river, a tornado-like storm struck us; I thought we would lose more than our cargo. Down went the stern, down went the bow. I thought lightning would strike us. My friends, John H___ and John J___ , were experienced river men. With luck we made it. In New Orleans, we sold both cargo and flatboat, and returned home by sternwheeler.

Memories—one of the most vivid is the New Orleans' slave auction: men and women for the highest bidder. How much is my mother worth? I asked myself. How much is my father? My Uncle James? Two women were sold while I watched at the corner of a busy street. Two women, then three men were sold. Were they friends, relatives? Did they speak our language? Where were they taken? One of the men in New Orleans left the auction stand in handcuffs. The women rode away in fancy buggies—faces haggard.

I have never had to summon a jury in defense of freedom. No court can defend slavery if men are honorable.

Tuesday evening
Late

As the months pass, as troubles increase, I hunt for moments from yesterday, moments that may strengthen me, moments that may prove I was once young.

There is my Ann Rutledge. I see her auburn hair, blue eyes and delicate face—more than ephemera. My love for her is real, apart, unrelated to the man I am, yet remembered—a contradiction. Although it is a lie I feel that Ann is alive.

I allowed my burden of debts to turn me away from marriage. I believed that frontier hardships were to remain my lot; I could not see harnessing her to a life of animal drudgery. Debts...they were like bars in a gate; I peered through those bars at her beautiful face.

We buried her among currant bushes, in the wind, in the sun. I left the cemetery to wander through hungry woodlands, woodlands I never saw again, that extended...I don't know how far they extended. Hunger and sorrow...they were mine.

All that remains of our brief relationship is the memory of her voice, as she spoke, as she sang. She loved to sing hymns and frontier songs—her voice so feminine.

The touch of her hand, the touch of her voice...in the midst of war, under desperate commitments.

Evening

We were to enroll. Ann was to enroll at Jacksonville Academy. I was to enroll at Illinois College.

That year I called on her at the Rutledge farm, several times. We worked together in the fields. When she worked at Jim Short's farm, I rode over to be with her. I helped her with the chores. Swampy place.

August came, hot, dry August. Corn was stunted that year. Few martins and swallows were around. But malaria was around and put me down, a day, two days, three. I sipped Peruvian bark—jalap. Late that month, her father sent for me.

Valued brother, come, Ann is very ill.

D. H. Rutledge.

I still have that message.

She lay on her bed, feverish; the log house seemed to be claiming her; she put her small hands in mine; her corn silk hair was around her face. In two days she was gone. We buried her in Concord, seven miles away, seven miles to walk behind her coffin.

It was many weeks, many weeks and miles of walking, before I recovered, out of that grey mystery.

I still write to her family. I want to know how the Rutledges are faring.

White House

In wagons, on foot, on horseback, they stream west, for the gold rush, for the promises. Ours is a migratory urge. Flux of men, women, children, reapers, sowers, which comes first? Which the most important? We Americans expropriate, accomplish, destroy. The rough rock becomes polished by time, but do we? Can such migrations achieve a true union?

I realize there is a power larger than self, more powerful than leadership. It is this mysterious power that causes this human wave. It is not destiny. It is an interchange of ideas, a wave or waves of emotion, a desire for betterment—and beyond that! The pioneer has this in his mind, as he hacks at timber, removes stumps, sprouts corn. Deep inside me, like a blue pool, I am in accord with these frontiersmen.

White House
window wide open
August 1st, 1863

In Springfield, when problems got under my skin, I sometimes woke at night, puzzled, thinking where am I? I'd find myself sitting up in bed, gesturing, talking to myself. Alarmed, I would dress and lay a fire and sit by it the remainder of the night, sit by the stove or go out into the backyard, if it was summer or autumn.

Melancholia has always dogged me. It seems to sit inside of me and peer out. It catches me, involves me, at the most unexpected moments. Melancholy influences my decisions, legal decisions or those at home, even while I am playing with the children. Like any physical handicap I try to live with it, minimize it.

Springfield problems were largely legal problems, problems for Billy and me, problems about horse thieves, mortgage foreclosures, defaults in payment, land titles. I lost a manslaughter case but won my defense of the nine women involved in rioting. I had a bevy of widows trail after me when I won the case of the man accused of robbing the mail of $15,000.

Such problems create a backwash over the years; I see now that on my circuit I avoided home very frequently, staying away two or three weeks at a time. Marital bliss and melancholia are known to be mates.

Executive Mansion
8/9/63

For years I was haunted by a great number of things. First, it was essential to learn to read. Then to write. To find work that would support me. I wished to help others. I felt that there was more to life than brute labor. I found friends. Honesty appealed. I was not impressed by rowdies. Serving as Captain in the Black Hawk War taught me that causes are not always good causes. Scalped men are not helpful men.

I can not forget those men lying in the bush, lying in a row, red sunlight on them.

My father was a slave to ignorance.

My mother was a slave to the wilderness.

I longed to abolish all kinds of slavery.

Some of my black friends were slaves; I wanted to abolish their kind of slavery. There is the slavery of poverty. Men and women eating potatoes day after day.

So, I was haunted.

Could I become man's benefactor?

Lying in my attic, on my bed of corn shocks, I confronted log walls—- strong log walls.

August 9, 1863

On my circuit rides, when weather favored, when there was enough time, I stopped at a grove, dismounted, walked to a tree deep in the grove, a tree I had blazed when county surveying; I walked on to the second blaze that marked a green pool. It was a small shallow pool rimmed with short grass. Dragonflies came there. Crickets lived near there. Standing there, sitting there, I found meaning, a meaning I still respect.

Tell me, ye winged winds
That round my pathway roar,
Do ye not know some spot
Where mortals weep no more?

The White House
August 12, 1863

I suppose I may as well confess: I have always envied my partner his marital luck: Billy Herndon married Nancy Maxcy, back in '40, a quiet beauty, a gentle beauty, blonde as corn silk, ready with dreamy smiles. She gave Billy rare personal happiness, made it easier for him after annoying legal squabbles, after long circuit rides. She gave him six healthy children. She was a giver in so many ways—alms for all. Theirs has been a continual romance.

The mind does tricks. I am back in my boyhood cabin. A prairie schooner stands outside. A man and woman have unhitched their oxen team, their little girl is made to feel at home by my mother. She is eight; I am eight or nine, I can't remember. I remember that she was pretty. We played together all day. Then, came sunup, the ox team hauled away the schooner...my love was gone. I dreamed about her for weeks, happy dreams; in one of those repeated dreams we eloped, we went to California, we built a beautiful home...

My love for her has never gone away.

August 14, 1863

Many times Jenny plodded my rural circuit.

Usually, I gave her the reins. Every stopping place, store, tavern, church, saloon, school, was fixed in her brain. If I had to check her it was for some washout, new ruts in the road, a downhill run, a flooded creek. As we plodded along I read my law books or played the harmonica. June, July, August...January and February, we rocked in that black buggy with its scarlet spokes. I kept it in good shape but I never did eliminate the squeaks in the right rear spring.

In those days prosperity was slow in arriving. I settled my cases under trees, in churches, in schools and stores—for barter and for cash.

Mary never neglected my food hamper; always something tasty, with an apple or a carrot or two tossed in for Jenny. We would stop in a patch of woods on a hot day; I would yank off my boots and rest my corns. Thunderstorms often fell on us; at the nearest stable I would rub Jenny until she was dry, and she would look and look at me as I rubbed her.

Willie liked to accompany me on our summer jaunts; he got to know the lone dead pine; the maple grove at Dobson's Creek; he knew the roosting place of the red hawk, the place of the squirrels. We often saw fox and deer. I might read Fennimore Cooper to him as we rode along.

"...Papa, look at those pigeons...a whole cloud of them."

Willie's favorite topic was the railroad, the locomotives. He knew every type of engine, their speed, their horsepower. "Wonder horses," he called them.

"All aboard," he would shout, as we got into our buggy. "Let's go...the Indians are comin'."

Who owns Jenny now?

Where is she?

She's about eleven years old.

The White House
August 29, 1863

Glancing through a Greek history, I found something Euripides said in one of his plays:

Slavery, that thing of evil, by its nature evil,
forcing submission from man to what no man should yield to.

To set men free—that is the greatest goal any man could achieve.

But slavery is part of our issue. This is essentially a people's contest. On the side of the Union is a struggle for maintaining in the world that form and substance of government whose leading object is to elevate the condition of men; to lift artificial weights from all shoulders; to clear the paths of laudable pursuit for all; to afford all an unfettered start and a fair chance in the race of life.

Tuesday

I like to forget East Salem's juvenility, sparring, boxing, wrestling. Pranks could be alarmingly stupid. There was Ike and his pony. He was fool enough to try to ride his piebald through a bonfire of shavings and cornstalks—to settle a bet. He raced across a field toward the blaze; just as he reached it, the pony bucked and pitched Ike into the fire. The onlookers stomped and roared and whistled. I was angry and took Ike to Dr. Samuel's office, where the doctor shaved his head and salved his scorched face and hands.

I saw no profit, no form of progress in Salem's rowdies. I preferred the simple things in life, a job, a long walk, hills, sun. As county surveyor I communicated through transit and tapes, through timberland acreage. They arranged life in useable proportions. This was a function beyond the village. To measure land was to measure the future. Precision spelled confidence.

September 1, 1863

To give the victory to the right, not through bloody bullets but through peaceful ballots—this is essential. Our constitution proves that the ballot can rule. Right-thinking men shall go to the polls, without fear or prejudice.

I think these thoughts, I write these words, as men attack, counterattack, retreat, die. Hate and bitterness are in control. I raise my spyglass and look through my window. A small sailboat moves along the Potomac. It is possible for a man to provision a boat, set sail, disappear. It is possible for a man to work with other men and achieve.

September 2, 1863

A drum corps passes the White House.

I listen.

I must ask myself some questions this evening: must civilization be influenced by greedy politicians, connivers, self-promoters, toadies? Is there such a thing as common sense where the bulk of mankind is concerned? Is Christianity a bulwark to be counted on, or is it cleverly concocted pretension? Must tragedy dog man's footsteps? Does a lie have a more lasting influence than the truth? Do the echoes of John Brown end? Is the Dred Scott case on trial, decade after decade?

These and other questions flog my mind.

Men say I am moody, they say I am a man of mystery. If I am mysterious at times it is because I seek answers. I demand answers. Only fools accept the face of things. Men weary of my tales and my humor as I hunt for enlightenment for this troubled country. It is my duty to care more than anyone, and humor and satire have an influence not to be scorned.

The White House
September 15, 1863

If I were home my fat Filibuster would shove his whiskers into my face and meow. He loved to be scratched...he was Robert's pet but when I lay on the floor of the parlor to read he would stretch out beside me. I'd scratch him and try to go on with my reading.

I would like to have supper tonight in my shirt sleeves, and answer the doorbell in my carpet slippers.

I would like to hear Mary scolding the iceman, as he tries, once more, to overcharge her.

How well she managed our house, penny-wise always. How well she attended the children. She found time to help the poor; was never too busy to chat with a neighbor.

"Let's see a play tonight. There's that new one, *A Fortune to Share*. Shall we go?"

I see myself puttering in the yard. There was time to prune the trees, to cut wood, plant flowers. The horse and cow were part of our lives. I was another man then.

I wonder what happened to my grey hat; it had a wide band inside, fine for stuffing letters and checks. Maybe Billy has it, hanging on the tree, at the back of our office.

The White House
Evening

Throughout that long, dry summer, Stephen Douglas and I battled our verbal battles. There was a noble pertinacity in the "Little Giant." I called him a "slanderer" and a "sneak." He dubbed me a "fraud," and alluded to pro-slavery conspiracies. He attacked my "house divided" stand... I insisted that a nation could not endure half-free, half-slave.

Douglas had his private car, bannered and flagged. A handsome brass cannon boomed from a flatcar coupled to his train, boomed his entry into every town and city. Often our debates were veritable picnics, fireworks, bands. I rode on a Conestoga drawn by six white horses...bunting... flowers...pretty girls. Sometimes a secretary recorded our speeches.

As the summer wore on, I began to stress the moral issues with great emphasis. I had little hope that I would win the senate seat; my voice, pitched higher than his, also lacked accomplished delivery. The silent artillery of time was firing at us. I heard the country's slaves crying out. I remembered that John Randolph said that slavery was "a volcano in full eruption."

Votes...but it is not altogether a matter of votes.

Yet the day of reckoning arrived.

Douglas – 54. Lincoln – 46.

So I lost.

It will be hard to die and leave the country no better than if I had never lived.

September 29th, 1863
My Desk

I may remark that having in my life heard many arguments—or strings of words meant to pass for arguments—intended to show that the negro ought to be a slave—if he shall now fight in the Confederate Army to keep himself a slave, it will be a far better argument why he should remain a slave than I have ever heard before.

Perhaps he ought to be a slave if he desires it ardently enough to fight for it.

Or, if one out of four will, for his own freedom, fight to keep the other three in slavery, he ought to be a slaver for his selfish meanness.

I have always thought that all men should be free; but if any should be slaves, it should be first those who desire it for themselves, and secondly those who desire it for others. Whenever I hear anyone arguing for slavery, I feel a strong impulse to see it tried on him personally.

Once again, we ask: what is freedom?

Individually, it is a chance to worship or not worship, it is a chance to earn a living, to raise a family, examine the past, improve one's intellect, guard one's health. It is also an opportunity to perfect national and international law. Certainly, freedom should not be a code but should emphasize, in every respect, human values. Millions in our land lack freedom. This condition must not continue. Education is the sure route toward freedom.

Thursday
My Desk

If A can prove, however conclusively, that he may, of right, enslave B, why may not B snatch the same argument and prove equally, that he may enslave A? You say A is white and B is black. It is *color* then; the lighter, having the right to enslave the darker? Take care. By this rule you are to be a slave to the first man you meet with a fairer skin than your own.

You do not mean *color* exactly? You mean the whites are *intellectually* the superiors of the blacks, and, therefore have the right to enslave them? Take care again. By this rule you are to be the slave to the first man you meet with an intellect superior to your own. But, say you, it is a question of *interest;* and if you can make it your *interest,* you have the right to enslave another. Very well. And if he can make it his interest, he has the right to enslave you.

I hear rifle fire in the night.

October 4, 1863

This rainy evening I take up my pen again.

There are no accidents in my philosophy. Every effect must have its cause.

The past is the cause of the present, and the present will be the cause of the future. All these are links in the endless chain stretching from the infinite to the finite.

Probably it is to be my lot to go on in a twilight, feeling and reasoning my way through life, as questioning, doubting Thomas did. But in my poor, maimed, withered way bear with me as I go on seeking for a faith that was with him of olden times, who exclaimed "Help thou my unbelief."

I do not see that I am more astray—though perhaps in a different direction—than others whose points of view differ widely from each other in the sectarian denominations. They all claim to be Christians, and interpret their several creeds as infallible ones. I doubt the possibility, or propriety, of settling the religion of Jesus Christ in the models of man-man creeds and dogmas.

It was a spirit in the life that He laid stress on and taught, if I read aright. I know I see it to be so with me... The fundamental truths reported in the four Gospels as from the lips of Jesus, and that I first heard from the lips of my mother, are settled and fixed moral precepts with me. I have concluded to dismiss from my mind the debatable wrangles that once perplexed me with distractions that stirred up but never absolutely settled anything. I have tossed them aside with the doubtful differences which divide denominations. I have ceased to follow such discussions or be interested in them. I cannot without mental reservations assent to long and complicated creeds and catechisms.

The White House

I had a visitor this morning who needed to be reassured. He is a trembling old man from Arkansas, a local politician. After spelling out some good news for his benefit I told him this anecdote... I think it worked very well...

An eccentric old bachelor lived in the Hoosier state and was famous for seeing big bugaboos in everything. He lived with an elder brother and one day went out hunting. His brother heard him firing back in the cornfield and went out to see what was the matter. He found him loading and firing into the top of a tree. Not being able to discover anything in the tree, he asked his brother what he was firing at. "A squirrel," the man said, and kept on firing. His brother thought there was some humbug about the matter and looked him over carefully and found a big louse crawling about on one of his eyelashes.

Executive Mansion
October 12, 1863

After my nomination Springfield filled with ox carts, wagons, buggies, horsemen, trainloads of folk. Fifty-thousand poured into my little town. Hordes jammed the street in front of my house, yelling "Speech...speech!"

I greeted them, said a few words, joked.

Reporters swarmed around me. Friends came and went. I forgot to stable the horse, forgot to milk the cow. Mary scolded me for forgetting my supper.

Tad got lost in the crowd.

Wind blew, dust blew.

It seems very amusing to me now. Unreal.

Streets were lit with burning tar barrels and torches. People sang, paraded the streets.

"Ole Abe Lincoln came out of the wilderness,
Out of the wilderness, out of the wilderness..."

I turned in mighty late that night, yet singers were still singing, singing "Gentle Annie" and other favorites.

October 13, 1863

Before leaving for Washington, I went to my office to say good-bye to Billy Herndon. It wasn't easy climbing that stair. It was difficult to say good-bye to my old partner and friend. I gathered up some books and papers and laid them on the big table. I stretched out on the old couch, with the buffalo robe under me.

"How long have we been working together, Billy?"

"Over sixteen years," he replied.

"We've never had a cross word all that time, have we?"

He nodded.

"That's right."

I asked him to retain our old shingle, on its rusty hinges.

"If I live, I'll be coming back, and then we'll go on as if nothing had ever happened."

At the bottom of the stairs, we shook hands.

In keeping with my philosophy I felt certain that I would never return to Springfield.

October 21, 1863
White House
Library

The unfinished dome on the White House continues to trouble me. The incompletion has become a symbol. I peer through its maw and it seems a war wound. When will it be finished? And when it has been completed will the union of the North and South begin? A carpenter tips his hat: "Good morning, Mr. President." Throughout the morning I have heard hammers and saws. Patience, I tell myself. A wise man invented patience. The emancipation of man will require great patience.

It is pleasant writing in the library. I will return again.

Here is a book, on my desk, entitled *Sparta.* I believe that the Spartans were often respected for their courage.

What is it men fear most? Death?

Ten men will have ten answers.

From the days of the Spartans men have floundered over freedom—spelling it a hundred different ways! The Iroquois had their idea of freedom. The Pilgrim had his. The blacks. The list can go on and on.

Freedom and death... I see they have an ugly affinity.

Nov 1st – 63
The Library

As far back as I can remember I have always watched over my dollars. In Springfield I knew what each month's expenses amounted to. During my sixteen-year partnership with Billy Herndon, our agreement was fifty-fifty. There never were any problems. Though it is miles to Springfield, I can summon figures. Our last year together, Billy and I earned $2,300 each. We had 63 cases at

$10.00 each; we had 20 at $15.00 each, etc. Twenty or twenty-five brought in $5.00. Apart from these combined earnings I added about $1,200 on my prairie circuits. This is a singular improvement over 31¢ a day at farm labor. As farm hand I earned about $100.00 a year, eliminating thunder and lightning, hail, sore muscles, broken ax handles, corns, a chronic failure on the part of farmers to pay their promised payments. City lamplighters do better.

Few in this capitol have ever enjoyed the intimacy old Jenny and I shared, buggy-sharing, spelled out with faithful grunts, special ear signals and soft nuzzlings. No, it wasn't always money-concern for me. Another asset was Billy's library—his Kant, Locke, Spencer, Volney, and Emerson.

Another virtue, one that is very difficult to spell out, Billy kept my inkwell full.

November 12, 1863
Evening

Today has been a day of war problems. Telegrams contradict telegrams. In my bedroom I opened my Shakespeare to *Julius Caesar:*

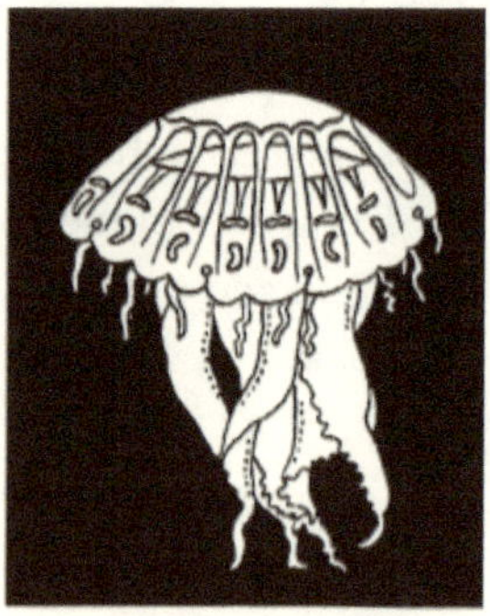

There is a tide in the affairs of men
Which taken at the flood leads on to fortune;
Omitted, all the voyage of their life
Is bound in shallows and in miseries.
On such a full sea are we now afloat,
And we must take the current when it serves,
Or lose our ventures.

Where is there finer counsel for me?

Foremost in my mind is the termination of this war, the abolishing of black servitude, the welding of our statehood. A triple goal!

Saturday

I used to wash in an iron keeler, scrubbing hard after plowing or splitting rails. Saturday was scrub night.

Here, at the Executive Mansion, the pretentious bathrooms trouble me. There are thousands of neglected, hungry folk. It is a president's obligation to assist those in need.

For all concerned there have been more favored times; as a people we are trapped between violence and the mending of that violence; in spite of our bewilderment we reach out.

I can not say grace any longer. I have tried. I stumble. I can not express my thanks for food when men are hungry. When whole communities are hungry, when death stalks our nation. If I am fortunate I may be fortunate at another's expense, another's disadvantage.

Tomorrow, I will saddle Old Abe. I will shove my new Wordsworth book into my saddlebag and ride into the country, along the Potomac. I will eat dry corn bread. I will lie in deep grass and read, all day.

Nov 20, '63
Early

I prefer art that pictures a Niagara or a lofty mountain range at sunset or a tall vase full of flowers. I don't go for the painting of faces—portraits. The painting done by Francis Carpenter troubles me; for one thing I wish he would remove it from the dining room where he has excellent chandelier light. Of course I can not find time to sit for him during the day. And all those faces on his canvas are so dull, such solemn faces; seven dull men surround me as I sign the Emancipation Proclamation. People, looking at those men, will think ill of us. At dinner, if the painting is still in the dining room, I face away from it. Carpenter says he will take the picture on a national tour. I believe that is an error.

Monday evening
Fireplace fire

Where are sexual malpractices focused?

Let me indicate:

In 1850 there were 405,523 mulattoes. Very few of these are the offspring of white and free blacks; nearly all have sprung from black slaves and white masters. In the same year, there were 56,649 mulattoes in the free states; but for the most part they were not born there—they came from the slave states. During this year, the slave states had 348,847 mulattoes, all of home production.

The White House

Since no man is born president of his country, he must cross a difficult bridge between home and capitol. Crossing it, he is involved in national issues and problems he could not anticipate. About him is a sea of new faces; he must remember each; he must remember names; he must define personalities as quickly and as intelligently as possible.

Following my inauguration, Fort Sumter, at Charleston, was bombarded; within six weeks state secession had begun. "Secession is revolution," I reminded my dissatisfied fellow countrymen. Grim cabinet meetings took place; telegram followed telegram; I soon realized that months of decision and indecision lay ahead. I saw it would be months before I could control my own house.

Needing friends, I reached out and found a few; needing wisdom, I made mistakes. My office window showed me an alien river; there were more than thirty rooms in the White House, rooms and sounds. And the sounds were more often drum beats, slow beats, suggesting caution, intimating death.

FORT SUMTER FALLEN. Commander Anderson Surrenders. *April 14, 1861, Fort Sumter, located in the harbor of Charleston, S. C., surrendered yesterday, after 34 hours of Confederate bombardment. The 100 survivors, without food and ammunition... 75,000 Union men called up...*

I have lost that newspaper clipping but I can repeat the tragic news word-for-word, words that shocked our entire country! That left us embattled! Now, I can not, will not, review in detail the war's progress. Must each battle fought on the battlefield be fought again here? I want this diary more man than history. If that is possible.

W. H.
November 29, 1863

Last year, on May second, I began the banishment of international slave trade. Congress appropriated the sum of $900,000 to aid in its suppression. Five ships have been captured at sea and the slaves on board those vessels have been returned to Liberia.

Now, an American ship, the *Erie*, out of Portland, has been captured off the West African coast, and 893 slaves have been liberated. Captain Gordon has been hung for his crime. To bring even greater pressure and afford greater success, my Secretary of State has negotiated a successful Anti-Slave Treaty with England. On April 24th, 1862, this treaty was ratified by the Senate. It was a distinct pleasure to have the Secretary congratulate me warmly. Our eradication of slave trade has been a marked success.

Henceforth, the blackbirders will find slave trade dangerous and unprosperous, with both the United States and England patrolling the seas.

If I accomplish nothing more than this, my White House term will be worthwhile. Although it is 2 a.m. and chilly—I must celebrate. I have rung the kitchen for a bowl of soup and some crackers.

November 30
Late

It has been difficult to find a few hours alone. To sit in my chair by the fireplace...that privilege comes only now and then. I think I will write an item for the papers, to increase morale, to lessen the influence of detractors. I will begin it...

Let us have faith that right makes might, and in that faith dare to do our duty...

White House
December 5

Tonight I wish I could eat an apple but there does not seem to be one in the White House. Peaches and apples—they are my favorites, eaten in front of a fireplace. What an appetite I used to have. I used to think that the best food in the world was bread and honey—honey in the comb on plain bread.

I rang the kitchen for a bowl of popcorn.

Pretty soon that Greek goddess of the Potomac, little Miss Rosie, who is the perfect mulatto, traipsed in, holding the green bowl she loves, balancing it on a silver tray, the tray she thinks belonged to George Washington.

"Heah you is, Mistaaaa President...popcohnnnn, wid plenty a fresh-churned buttaaaah."

Miss Rosie did a curtsy and smiled and that smile of hers made me happier than the popcorn because it told me that before long the war would be over and people like Rosie would be treated like any white woman.

Sunday
1863

A president is not permitted to have smallpox but I have a mild case, nonetheless. Bed is a poor spot to keep up a diary. What can I say, this Wednesday? That I have been reading Shakespeare? I have not. That I have read the newspapers? I have not. During bouts of fever I let myself return to other days; I see a woman in a log cabin bending over an open fire. I smell bacon frying. Deep in the night I hear a hermit thrush. Its sorrowful sound assumes great beauty. I have a feeling I am in the wilderness, that wilderness almost Christ-like, beneficent.

December 12, '63
Desk

Documents. My pigeonholes are bulging.

In a few days I will feel all right.

I miss our green-shuttered house in Springfield. It seems much farther than 1700 miles away, and it seems more than nineteen years since we bought it—back in '44. We Lincolns were proud of that home. I liked the fireplace in the parlor on snowy nights. I liked the comfortable rockers and the black hair settee. Mary worked hard to sew and tailor the drapes. Her touches were everywhere. Yet, when we moved to Washington, she ruled out everything that was personal.

"Leave things...till we return." Then we rented our place. What will it be when we do return?

And she threw away a pair of my old boots.

Willie, Bob and Ted packed their toys, kites, drums, bats. How Willie stormed when he was told he could not take every single toy.

When Mary and I married, I had three words engraved on her wedding rings: *Love is Eternal.*

I had not reckoned with death.

Evening

I would like to have opportunities for meditation. Surely the bettering of life has to come from within. I would like to steal an hour or two every day. The only time I can steal is at night, when the White House is wrapped in memories. Then, candle or lamp beside, a fire in the fireplace, I hunt for inner balance. Perhaps the candles go out. Perhaps the fire goes out. I wait for connections, maybe wilderness connections or connections with the prairie, connections with perceptions that can become new. I may be able to use those perceptions in my day-to-day.

Library

This evening I have re-read some Volney, that old French scholar and traveler; this analysis strikes me forcibly:

> *Man in his blindness has riveted his own chains, and surrendered himself forever, without defense, to the sport of his ignorance and passions. To dissolve such fatal chains, a miraculous concurrence of happy circumstances would be necessary: a whole nation, cured of the delirium of superstition, must be inaccessible to the impulse of fanaticism...this people should be courageous and prudent...*

Sound advice for these times! When are we prudent? What, beside the passage of time, years of peace, will evolve prudence? Is war a kind of superstition? I have thought so. Certainly it is a delirium.

I see the Library has a copy of Volney's *Travels in Syria and Egypt.* I have asked for a copy.

Evening

In this sad world of ours, sorrow comes to all; and, to the young, it comes with bitterest agony, because it takes them unawares. The older have learned to ever expect it.

The Anns and the boys with their Bibles.

The White House

As I study the office wall map of the war zones I am afflicted by partial blindness. The name Fredericksburg blurs. I hear myself saying: I have made a covent to free the slaves. I hear General McClellan say: "We must declare a truce to bury our dead." Alexandria, Fairfax, Sharpsburg, Harper's Ferry, Spotsylvania. That peculiar blindness continues, focuses now on faces I have loved, her face, the face of a friend in Springfield, the stairway leading to my law office, my children playing on the street in front of my home, riding in their little red wagon...

I am not a cartographer of war; however I surpass some of my gallant military officers. Their logistics have led to useless slaughter. Hellish bungling, I call it. But that blindness intrudes: I am surveying a piece of property near Salem, it seems.

What if this was a map of the entire world? What if I were in command? What then?

I hear my mother speak to me:
"Abe, shall we go out now and plant those squash seeds?"

W.H.

How are we to establish labor relations in the North and in the South? I am glad to see that a system of labor prevails under which laborers can strike when they want to, where they are not obliged to work under all circumstances, and are not tied down and obliged to labor whether you pay them or not! I like the system which lets a man quit when he wants to, and wish it might prevail everywhere. In mill and cottonfield there has to be a leveling, hours, pay, conditions. We have to regulate a work week.

The White House
December 16, 1863

Thomas Jefferson was a great man, but no great American keeps slaves, and Jefferson had two hundred. Call it custom, excuse it as custom; yet not every wealthy man kept slaves.

I admire the Adams family: their racial integrity stands out, their intelligent diplomacy. The relationship with foreign nations is often a delicate one; the Adams succeeded—their statesmanship stands out.

Recently men have asked me to comment about George Washington. I declined. I sympathize with his problems but I can not get deeper into the man. History does not always afford us ample means for fair judgment.

Thirty-three states oppose eleven states in this conflict. If I were to ask a citizen of Europe which entity he might support I think the answer would be the state group with the largest population and greatest wealth, surmising that these advantages would bring about a definite resolution. However, in this conflict, the gamble is also a moral gamble. With this moral issue in mind we must pursue a sane course of action for everyone in this country, a course of action that must embody prolonged patience.

The White House
December 29, '63

I met Harriet Beecher Stowe the other day, and liked her. We sat in front of my white fireplace and she said she loved a fireplace, and I said I liked one too—that we had a couple of them at home. She said she wrote a lot of her *Uncle Tom* in front of her fireplace; then she asked me friendly questions about Springfield, the people, the town.

I shared my conviction that writing has a lasting influence. I tried to make her realize what books have meant to me. I am afraid I reminisced too much about what I had read. She nodded very pleasantly and did not say much; wrapped in a blue shawl she seemed more like a tired housewife than a person dedicated to writing and the rights of man.

I told her how I used to do my three r's before our cabin fireplace. Silence came between us. In spite of myself I forgot my guest; I could see a long road in summertime; I was walking along that road; I had borrowed Weems and stopped to read; I sat down on a culvert; a frog appeared; there were trees, fields of grass, yet I was in the midst of history.

When she rose to say "good-bye" I was startled.

2

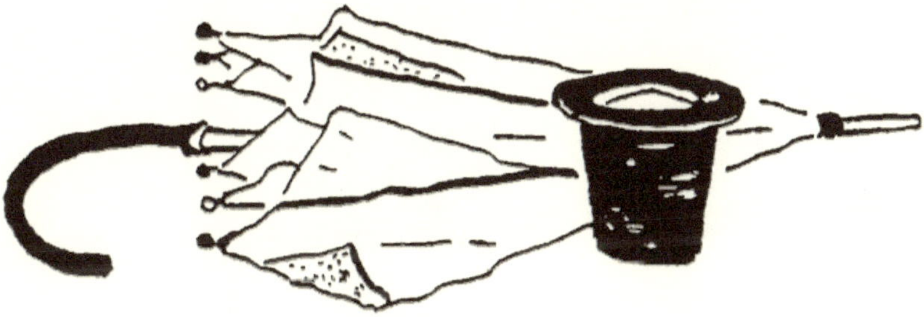

January 4th, 1864

Today I visited the stables and talked to Old Abe. As usual, he was pleased to see me. I offered him a handful of oats, and he bobbed his head. The sun was warm in the stall. I stood by, as Abe munched. I could believe that he knew I was thanking him for my escape yesterday.

My hat is lying on my bed—a bullet hole right through the crown. A good hat. If Abe hadn't bolted someone might have shot again. We were lucky it was growing dark, Abe and I.

I offered him more oats.

Stablemen were arriving. Bill Slade appeared.

"Good mawnin', Mistah President. How is you this mawnin'?"

A fine person, Bill Slade—from Kentucky.

I must give away that telltale hat. It cost me eight dollars. Certainly, Mary must never find it; that would mean severe hysteria.

I have been considering the purchase of a taller horse. No, Old Abe will serve me. I must shorten the stirrups. I appreciate his easy gaits. Gentleness—something hard to come by these days.

Desk

William Seward—I wanted to call him Will, wanted to bridge the gap that exists between us, a gap some three years wide. As my Secretary of State he has assisted the government through his foreign diplomacy; as an ardent anti-slave man he has successfully blocked the Confederacy through foreign influence. As governor of New York he left an enviable record; as senator he is above reproach. With his friendly Irish spirit, he has favored Irish immigration. With his eye on the presidency he has not spared me.

As friend of Jefferson Davis and his wife, I have had to work to allay suspicions, suspicions that have proved ungrounded. Seward's eye on the presidency will continue beyond my stay in the White House. He has an intense desire to improve our nation, to push on; I admire his faith in tomorrow. Unfortunately, he has not always manifested political balance. When he suggested an all-out war with Europe, to force an amalgamation of North and South, I was utterly nonplussed.

Trainer of Arabian horses, owner of Arabian horses, breeder of Arabians, Seward is many things. He is sixty, has white hair, slouches, swears, smokes cigars. When asked by an hysterical officer, when Washington was threatened with invasion at the time I took office, "What shall I fire at?," Seward responded coolly: "Fire at the crisis!"

One winter's afternoon, Louis Agassiz drove up to the White House, with his brilliant wife, Elizabeth. A Swiss-American, he speaks English with a marked but distinguished accent. We three had a long walk through the December garden and our conservatory, and he emphasized the value of studying from nature. Bustling to his carriage, parked on the driveway, he returned with his four-volume study, *Natural History of the United States.* He was pleased to present it to me—and inscribed the first volume. Elizabeth did her best to enlighten me on scientific points since I have never studied the sciences, a brief elementary course, I might call it. I found the two remarkable. When I can, I dip into his *History.*

Later, he sent his *Recherches sur les poissons fossiles,* this study in French. I have bequeathed it to the Library.

The visit of this pair has shown me depths that lie in Europe—depths I must explore.

Executive Mansion
1/14/64

I reviewed my Emancipation Proclamation to the best of my ability. Lights were on, the house quiet. Rain streaked the windows. I wanted to re-test each word, wholly for myself. In these troubled times I must rescue something for myself.

Thus:

> *...I, Abraham Lincoln, President of the United States, order and declare that all persons held as slaves are forever free. The Executive*

> *Government, including the military and naval authority, will recognize and maintain the freedom of such persons...*
>
> *I enjoin all people to abstain from violence. I evoke the considerate judgment of mankind...*

Forever free.

Those words still ring in my mind.

As I signed, I remembered slaves, slaves in a slave depot, slaves on a barge, slaves on a Kentucky plantation; I remembered the dead and the dying, brother against brother; I thought about pillaged homes, families in rags. I saw. I stared at the Proclamation and saw.

Now, as I sit at my desk, it seems to me that I have been guided by experience. My presidency has been justified. It seems to me, in all calmness, in objectivity, I have placed a permanent seal on the ages.

Later

In Boston there have been two mammoth celebrations. Longfellow, Whittier, Emerson and politicos attended. Harriet Beecher Stowe came. Beethoven's *Fifth Symphony* was played.

Throughout the nation, in small towns and hamlets there were schoolhouse ceremonies, church ceremonies, to honor the Proclamation. Hymns and prayers.

In Norfolk, two thousand former slaves paraded.

I have gone through many newspapers to read of the rejoicing.

A black is quoted:

"Freedom are an unbroke filly...but I gwine to mount her."

Hundreds of thousands of copies of my Emancipation have been printed and distributed.

To preserve the union.

Office

Surrounded by war I try to remember what Washington was like when I first came here about eighteen years ago. What a bedraggled place it was! I stayed at

Brown's Hotel. And Washington is again a bedraggled place, in a different way now, with tents, troops, cavalry, guns, death.

In '47, I leased my house in Springfield for $90.00 a year. This time I have leased it for double. My tenants were neglectful in '47; I expect neglect again.

In the wilderness each Christmas was a day for sober thoughts. Easter was a day of inner conflict. When was time both gentle and kind? Underneath the stars on a summer's night? Perhaps. Even then we might hear a wildcat scream. Wildcats were more numerous than books.

There was that winter when the cold and the snow killed many of us, us and our livestock. Drifts hung lean-tos on our cabin. Papa shot a deer. Wolves used the crust to raid cattle. We cut wood, lugged frozen water. A fire burned day and night.

I lived ten years in that cabin.

One day, in town, I met a man who offered to sell me a barrel for 50¢. I bought it. In the bottom, buried under straw, I found a book: *Blackstone's Commentaries.* 1753. It was warm at the blacksmith's and I began to study the commentaries there.

It is very late, perhaps two or three in the morning. I forgot to wind my watch. I hear men on the street, men and horses; this city never rests; there is weather here but I do not think of weather. The climate of dread has assumed a reality beyond all else. When you control men and control armies you lack inner core.

White House
January 15, 1864

In spite of myself, I recall the meals I had as a boy, the meals when there was nothing to eat but potatoes. There were better times, when we had perch or catfish, wild pig, grouse, or venison. But, eating potatoes, here in the White House, brings to mind that struggle. Memory. How constant, how untrustworthy, how valuable. Here, my Shakespearean-aside, will, like a juggler, toss up thoughts, three or four at a time, potatoes.

In those Illinois days I was lucky when I earned 30 cents a day, working on a farm. Walk to the farm, walk home. At dark I climbed my peg ladder to the cabin loft and slept on corn husks, my grizzly bear rug not always warm enough. Lying among the husks and the squeaky mice I puzzled, knowing that soon I must leave. I determined I must get away. Living there I lived like an Indian, an Illinois Indian, barefooted all summer, moccasined during the winter. Like an Indian, I knew the meaning of silence, the dread of silence and its comfort. My father taught me to work but he never taught me to love drudgery.

Some of those pioneers used to say:

"Don't see all you see; don't hear all you hear."

That is sound advice. It applies here in Washington. Many aspects of my life have assumed ridiculous proportions among these people. The fact that I was a wrestler affronts some; that I could plow with oxen annoys others. My humor shocks many. My lizard joke, that I thought very amusing, is now in bad taste. If I said: "Spit against the wind and you spit in your own face" ...well, certain politicians might understand and appreciate that.

I see people and more people. My office is often crowded. I am criticized for the amount of time I devote to the public. My secretaries try to restrain me.

I'll do the very best I can, the very best I know how. And I mean to keep doing so to the end. If the end brings me out all right what is said against me won't amount to anything. If the end brings me out wrong, ten angels swearing I was right would make no difference.

People have asked me how it feels to be president, and I sometimes say, if there is an appropriate moment:

You have heard about the man tarred and feathered and ridden out of town on a rail? A man in the crowd asked him how he liked it, and his reply was that if it wasn't for the honor of the thing, he would much rather walk.

W. H.
January 20

The other night I had a dream and in that dream I observed myself in a huge mirror; my face had two distinct images, one more or less superimposed on the other, the underneath face much paler than the upper face. The dream has perplexed me; something about it, its shadowiness maybe, seems part of my wilderness life, the shadowiness of those star-roofed nights. Mary was disturbed by my dream. She interpreted it, saying that it meant that I would be re-elected for a second term. The pale image meant I would not finish that term. As she talked about the dream I remembered how emphatically I felt that I would never return to Springfield, an emotion that nearly overwhelmed me as I waved from the train.

W. H.
1864

It was only a few years ago that John Quincy Adams was swimming in the Potomac with his son. Adams used to rise at five, to read the Bible, Commentary, and then read the newspapers. He was about fifty-seven when he was President. I recall his vivid description of abolitionist Lovejoy's printing press tragedy, in Alton, in '37, how the mob destroyed the man's press and murdered him, such a fate for a truly conscientious man! A martyr to the cause of freedom! Adams recounts preacher Joseph Cartwright's plea for money, for $450 to buy the freedom of his own three grandchildren. What a meaningful exemplification of slavery!

JQA—fine President!

White House
January 24, '64

Job seekers have besieged me. It must be the new year that sends so many. They come from every part of our nation, even the deep South. Some of the job seekers feel they have every right to storm my office; some are pitifully humble. Some bring recommendations; some have prepared a little speech; some have no credentials. Yesterday an elderly woman burst into tears as she pled for a job. I helped her to sit down. I offered her a drink of water. I did my best to console her. In her case there seemed to be no job available; I asked her to return in a few days; I had to ask my secretary to show her out. I am resolved to permit my countrymen access to my office. I can understand my country through these seekers. If some are loath to leave, I can sit up later over my important documents. Of course there are not enough oats for all these hosses.

February 2, '64

The howitzers and the rifles and the bayonets and the ammunition and the sandbags are gone from our public buildings. The invasion crisis is forgotten. Some say that 10,000 men guard Washington, perhaps 8,000; I am wary of statistics today.

There is a hint of spring in the air today.

I stand on the steps of the White House and shout for a boy to bring me the morning paper.

How do I obtain accurate information?

I learn that two million dollars have disappeared from our national treasury.

I learn that General Grant is seriously ill.

I learn that the Confederate forces plan to invade Wilmington tomorrow at noon.

I learn that I have assumed dictatorial powers.

I read that the Confederacy has 220,000 men under arms.

Tomorrow the Cabinet meets... I will point out some of these items to my Secretary of War, my Secretary of State, my Secretary of the Treasury.

February 5, 1864

I think that my strength as wrestler, ox driver, and rail splitter helps me. I channel it into my cabinet meetings, office hours, discussions, late hours. Chase, Sumner, Seward, Trumbul, Usher—each receives some of that energy. I repeat that the dogmas of the quiet past are inadequate for the stormy present. I re-affirm that we must act anew. We must continually disenthrall ourselves.

Fellow citizens...we of this Congress...ours is a mutual concern at this time...

And at all times there is someone who wishes to enter by the back door, who has a special message or a letter of prime importance...

Some of my friends predict a final cataclysm; some believe that by wheedling we can conquer; some voice the old voice of the abolitionists; some offer a packet of new tricks; theirs is a jack-in-the-box credibility.

White House
February 8th, 1864

This morning, early, I heard a low rap-rap on my office door. S. O. S.

The Morse code... S. O. S.

Tad, still in his nightgown, climbed onto my lap.

Together, we figured out how many bales of hay we should order for his pony, and Willie's pony. How many bushels of grain. We decided that the pony's halter should be re-adjusted, a new strap over the nose, or a new buckle. We also puzzled over what should be done about the small hole in the new red saddle.

If these were not matters of state, we made them as important—until I showed Tad my pile of correspondence; then, with a wild kiss, he rushed off, banging the door.

February 18, 1864

I suppose that Willie and Tad—although strictly forbidden—will rig another toy cannon on the roof of the White House. That flat roof is an ideal playground for those scoundrels. With their cannon in place the boys fire invisible bullets at invisible enemy ships and troops.

How I laughed when Tad gobbled all the fresh strawberries intended for a state dinner last June. Pranks such as that annoy the kitchen staff—and I am blamed. They cannot possibly understand that when my boys go berserk I am relieved of war anxiety for the moment. When Willie and Tad ambush me in some room or corridor, that tumbled mass of arms and legs and heads is my medal for the day. As we tumble, Jip growls and barks and joins in.

Their doll, Jack, a long-legged, blue-jacketed Zouave, has been put on trial recently. Because he fell asleep while on picket duty the boys sentenced him to death, and he was to be buried under a bush in the garden.

"Jack is pardoned. By order of the President," I wrote, and signed my name.

However, if I am away, Jack may be accused again and they may destroy him.

Tad's Birthday

Tad received a pair of snow-white kittens, toys, a wooden box of stick candy, and then a boat ride on the Potomac. The spring afternoon was calm and beautiful. Tad loved every moment—especially when the skipper allowed him to steer the sloop. He dashed about the cabin, hung over the bow, waved a flag at the stern. His grinning face is unforgettable.

Back in the White House, he became the devoted master of his kittens. With them lying on his bed, he stuck each toy in front of a nose, saying :

"Isn't that a nice one! Look at this little frog, kitty!"

Tad met a woman in the hall, a woman in homespun. She told Tad that her girls and boys were hungry and sick, because their father was in prison in

Washington. Tad believed her; taking in every word she said he ran to me. I was at my desk; I had been hearing bad news of deserters; deserters present a grave problem; often there are complications that make judgment difficult.

Tad's tear-streaked face shocked me, and, little by little, as he sat on my lap, as I cuddled him, we put together the woman's story. He kissed me and clasped me around the neck and begged me to intercede. I promised I would.

Dashing into the hall, he knelt by the woman, and cried that she was to have her husband back, that her children were going to have something to eat.

"Papa promised," I heard him say. "Papa promised."

March 3rd

Many object to Tad, to his vivacity, his dashing into my office, throwing his arms around me, staying or dashing off. There are those who think I, in my office, my high office, should be above love. Some of those same people object to my rural humor.

I carry Tad to his bed. I tell him stories. I linger, linger until he falls asleep. Young as he is he knows that death is around the city. I ask his fate: shall he experience an early death, live to be old and wise, remembering some of these days in Washington, some of the war stories? A father can ask questions.

Make a noise, Tad, dash into my office tomorrow, jump on me, kiss me.

I remember the presidential chair vilified, pilloried. I see the grim cartoons lampooning me. A child offsets those.

Tuesday evening

This morning I visited one of the hospitals, a tent hospital by the river. Rain was everywhere. The wounded felt it, that was easy to see. I went among them, shaking hands, enquiring; this was not my first visit; I knew some of the men by name.

"Abraham," I heard a man whisper to his cot mate.

Can a name influence a life?

Abraham—"father of a multitude."

Through the centuries, thousands of infants have been christened Abraham.

What has it meant? And what kind of father am I? In the deep of the night, or during a cabinet meeting, or while playing with my sons, I ask. Which of the wounded, which of the dead, was my responsibility?

Now and then the candle beside my bed does not want to go out.

Mid-afternoon
Rain

In Springfield, Billy de Fleurville's barbershop was my favorite barbershop. We were friends, Billy and I. Billy is a Haitian. His English is a remarkable mixture of soft, sometimes incomprehensible sounds. A stable person, he has raised a family and has been a civic influence for fifteen years or more. He initiated a committee that brought about a school for blacks. He loves his rabbit paws and his jokes; while he shaves you or trims your hair, he entertains. Since Billy loves gumbo and fricasseed chicken I saw to it that he had more than his share through the years.

At the depot, as the train pulled out for Washington, he was there, handing me a farewell note, to read on the train.

He writes me that tenants are taking proper care of my house and yard.

"Filibuster has kittens," he adds, in a postscript. "One brown, two yellows."

Evening
Desk

I treasure a letter from a child named Grace Bedell. Grace wrote me :

"I have four brothers and part of them will vote for you anyway, and if you let your whiskers grow, I will try and get the rest of them to vote for you. You would look a great deal better, for your face is so thin."

Grace's suggestion amused me...and I might glean those two votes! So, I let my beard grow, and Billy de Fleurville trimmed it for my inaugural. In Westfield, at the depot, my train was on a siding. While it was there I asked the crowd:

"Is Grace Bedell here?"

She came running to the train, and I was able to hug and kiss her.

The White House
Sunday

They were good days in Springfield, our children growing, bursting with energy, up to antics day in and day out. They helped and hindered boisterously, helped pitch-fork the cow's stall, water the horse, carry in the wood for the stove; they hindered by being unreliable, off somewhere when needed.

I liked pulling the little ones in their red wagon, up and down our street, the kids yelping or fussing happily. It would be pleasant to be in Springfield, but not the same, with Robert away at school. But, I would stretch my legs onto a footstool and lie back on the old horsehair sofa.

No, a thousand slaves are throwing up fortifications in Richmond, in Charleston, in Atlanta....fortifications to enslave more enslavement.

Someone, in the south, has written me:

"I warn you... I will kill you before long. You are destroying the nation. You have no right to be President..."

March 24th, 1864

Here is another anonymous letter:

"Dear Mr. President—

"In addressing you, I am prompted by the kindest motives. I wish to warn you of the peril you are facing if you remain in office. The South has strong motives for desiring your death and has resolved to take your life in the event of your not relinquishing your office. The blacks are disillusioned by your presidency. The whites can not, without endangering more lives, allow you to remain in the seat of government..."

So another letter, with "kindest motives," has reached me. How many have, though both secretaries screen my mail. There is no doubt that anonymity makes a man courageous.

April 2, 1864
Evening

The North commits atrocities. The South commits atrocities. War is, without the shadow of a doubt, a form of insanity. As Commander-in-Chief I can order troops to attack; with the cessation of military activities I can not order 50,000 men to reconstruct a devastated area. The legality of such an order has never been questioned, as far as I know, by any victorious power. Perhaps, during my second term in office, I can weigh the consequences of such an official directive.

Think of Libby Prison, consider Andersonville. They are collective atrocities.

Was it two years ago a man handed me two red apples at a depot in Ohio, bowing, and wishing me well?

I insist that the United States form a strictly federal community, that the states are essential to its welfare as is the central government, and North must never dominate the South or the South dominate the North. I also insist that the Chief Executive remain as center of the government. If the President uses his power justly, the people will justify him; if he abuses it, he is in their hands to be dealt with by all the modes they have reserved to themselves under the constitution. This is essentially a people's contest, I repeat. On the side of the Union it is a struggle for maintaining in the world that form and substance of government where the leading object is to elevate the condition of man...can I repeat this too often?

The White House
Library

There is room enough for all of us to be free, and that it not only does not wrong the white man that the negro should be free, but it positively wrongs the mass of the white man that the negro should be enslaved.

Here among a heap of newspapers I pause...

April 6th
White House
(windows open)

When brought to my final reckoning, may I have to answer for robbing no man of his goods; yet, more tolerable even this, than for robbing one of himself and all that was his. When, a year or two ago, professedly holy men of the South met in the semblance of prayer and devotion, and, in the name of Him who said, "As ye would all men should do unto you, do ye even so unto them," appealed to the Christian world to aid them in doing to a whole race of men as they would have no man do unto themselves, to my thinking they contemned and insulted God and His church...but let me forebear, remembering it is also written, "Judge not lest ye be judged."

My words, my record, this diary, seem obtuse at times; I attempt to write down what I think and the writing evolves another way.

In pensive mood I realize that President Jefferson Davis sits at his desk in his White House. I sit at my desk in my White House. He orders his army to move across the chessboard of war. I order my army to move across the same chessboard. His men fight for their homeland. My men fight for a nation. It seems to me that this is an ancient form of puppetry, a puppetry that came into being in days before the time of Christ. It is obvious, then, that we have gained nothing in the realm of diplomacy.

The cause of slavery has little to do with puppetry; it has much to do with man's future. The nation must have freedom as its base, a living freedom, a worker's freedom, a thinker's freedom.

Executive Mansion
Desk
April 16, 1864

Some folk still call me "Old Abe," "Honest Abe," "The Backwoodsman," "Rail Splitter." I like those names; they come out of my wilderness; they can be warm. They helped me through those stormy debate days and still help me in this prolonged struggle to save our country.

Lincoln: 1,866,452 votes
Douglas: 1,376,957 votes

Those numbers are printed in my mind's eye. I am proud that I beat Stephen Douglas, a great man, who, often impartial, said good things about me as we contested, as we debated. How was he able to carry on so valiantly? A sick man—I've seen him stagger from fatigue. I've seen him fall asleep, on the platform, after final arguments. Yet, next day he was on his feet again:

1,866,452

I saw those figures as I walked along Pennsylvania Avenue after the inauguration ceremony, as I walked through the White House garden. That was my lucky number, my lottery number. Destiny, hard work, luck, time—they dovetail.

I felt the loss keenly, when Douglas died in '61. He wore himself out in his effort to save the union.

The White House
April 24, 1864

At the outset of this war, we had a military force of about 16,000 men. Few of these men could be classed as professionals. After the loss of Fort Sumter, I called for 75,000 volunteers. Moving into combat, in those early days, men fought with antiquated guns and poor equipment; however, our artillery, at least, was superior.

Our soldiers were fortunate to have field tents. They bivouacked in mule yards. Uniforms were issued willy-nilly. Hats had to be stuffed with newspapers. Some men had to survive on desiccated vegetables—cakes of them. On the march their knapsacks fell apart.

I see that war is fought on folly. I half-believe there were sane men who could have steered us without conflict. Day after day, hour after hour, I walk through this tragedy. I question my judgment and the judgment of others. I study a war map and realize I am studying a map of corpses, men, women, and children.

I wake in the middle of the night. There's a bell, a drum.

The White House

We have 3,200,000 slaves in our country.

What man would not want to set them free?

Among them there must be many a man and woman who is among the finest. Among them there must be inventors, lawyers, doctors, preachers, teachers—men who never had a chance. It is my duty, my dedication, to liberate them as soon as possible. The world can not be a better place until they are freed.

Three million men and women and children, bound in irons, what a world! I will do my best to strike those irons, take away every shackle, so these people can look at the sun and say: *this is my world to make something of, it is my chance to get something out of life.*

The White House
Desk
May 1, 1864

Three or four times I have hidden (incognito?), in the wings of a theatre to hear an opera. *Tales of Hoffman* was performed last week, and I sat in a red leather chair behind the curtains. Back home I used to watch magic lantern shows; they were fine antidotes to melancholy; the *Tales of Hoffman* minimized the Washington volcano.

I escape some of our war tragedy by reading Spencer. In my bedroom I read till sunup. Every man must skin his own skunk and I skin mine through books. At sunup I can lay down my book and sleep, until someone wakes me.

Tonight I would like to bowl at Caspari's but bowling, because of the war, is off-limits for me. Somebody's afraid a strike might make me laugh. I had a few good strikes before the war.

The White House is asleep. Perhaps I should find a ruler and compass and attempt to square the circle.

And so to bed...

My wife is one of the loneliest women in Washington. Her hospitality, her lavish entertainments, have bred enemies and have engendered no rewarding friendships. Because Mary exceeded her Congressional allotment for essential White House expenditures, the press has attacked her. I have volunteered to pay the bills out of my salary. I have cautioned her against ostentation: "War is no time for preening."

Elizabeth Keckley, her seamstress, a former slave, is her confidante. With three brothers fighting in the Confederate army there are those who accuse Mary of treason. Injustice can strike. And the sad face, the sad thoughts continue. Poor Mary. Sharing intimate emotions with Elizabeth Keckley is a mistake. I do not dare reproach her.

Today's cabinet meeting was a bitter one.

Yes, it is true Mary has relatives fighting for the Southern cause. So has General Grant and other officers. Does this imply some form of subterfuge? I am well aware of my wife's integrity. I respect her family sympathies. To impugn the loyalty of my spouse is tantamount to accusing me of treason.

When I learned that a secret committee had been formed to investigate the loyalty of my wife I made a point of appearing dramatically, by a seldom used door to the committee room. I stepped inside without a word—hat in hand.

A dozen men were sitting around a long table. Rain was streaking the windows. No one spoke. I waited. I stared at first one and then the other, searching the faces. I knew most of the men well.

I said:

"I, Abraham Lincoln, President of the United States, appear of my own volition before this Senate Committee to say that I, of my own knowledge, know that it is untrue that any member of my family holds treasonable communication with the enemy."

I walked out.

I have heard no more from that committee or any other; however, my resentment lingers, sticks in my craw. Who could forget such calumny?

I have attended lectures at the Smithsonian Institute, where Horace Greeley has been outspoken on the abuse of slavery in our nation. His influence, through his lectures and his associates, through his editorials in the *New York Tribune,* is an influence I intend to curry.

At the Smithsonian he drew me aside and thought it important to inform me that he is a vegetarian, a teetotaler—that he would never stoop to smoking a cigar. He seemed to be sounding me out by cataloging his qualities. Grasping my arm, he grinned and said: "I want to share this one...since you like stories. I have loaned considerable sums to the son of Commodore Vanderbilt. Last week the Commodore burst into my office and rapped on my desk with his cane. When I glanced up, he said: 'I will not be responsible for my son's borrowing money from you.' I said to the Commodore: 'Who the Hell asked you to.' "

At another Smithsonian lecture, I met George Bancroft, our distinguished elder historian. Obviously disgruntled and tired, he wanted to know: Why is General McClellan living in an aristocratic style in an aristocratic mansion? Is it true that John Jacob Aster pays his salary?

When I introduced Bancroft to McClellan, he questioned Mac about the condition of the cavalry: Is it true that half the horses purchased for the army are unfit for service? Was it true that in the District of Columbia, horses have been chained to trees, where they gnawed bark, leaves and branches until they died?

McClellan was not happy with Bancroft. I was not happy with Bancroft and McClellan. Since the General has become known in Washington as the "general most gifted at masterly inactivity," I am seriously considering taking to the field as Commander-in-Chief. My qualification: integrity.

I can not sleep.

In Chicago, one windy night, I attended my first symphony concert. I was in the city working on the McCormick lawsuit. The concert was all Italian. Verdi. I recognized, as I listened to the rich outpouring, how much I had missed during my prairie years. There were no available seats in the theatre, but that was unimportant; I leaned against a wall, in the foyer, hat in hand. Mama would have rejoiced over such music! Why must so many die young and deprived?

Drums passing.

The White House
Library
May 5th, 1864

De Tocqueville wrote that there are few calm spots in this country for meditation; yet, in this library, there is a spot. This afternoon it seems to me that these ancient books, with their ancient wisdom, ask what is freedom? Is it something nailed in pain against the morning sky? I think not. Surely freedom is not to limit mankind; it is to share life's values. I remember these lines, learned as a boy, "What avail the plow or sail, or land or life, if freedom fail?" It is our duty to know and analyze freedom, however illusive. I hear it is a flame. Then, if that is true, we must keep it burning in our minds. The altar of freedom is an expression that illustrates how sacred freedom is. Freedom, if we can say it briefly, is the dignity of man.

White House
May 9

Can a truly religious person support war, I query?

I am my brother's keeper, I am instructed.

In the core of night, knowing that my countrymen are waging fratricidal carnage, I perceive that I have been nurtured on violence: I countenance war.

As Commander of the military forces, whose intention is victory, I am beginning to see that war is a form of slavery. Generals Grant and Sherman, Generals Johnson and Lee confirm this. So, we, the people, with our armies, fight slavery with slavery.

No doubt others have mulled over these or similar tenets. But I return to the cost, the human cost, the countless lives lost, the shattered families, shattered homes. Our lintels are hung with crepe.

The White House
Desk

Surely, I should kneel in prayer each night, but for years I have not been able to pray, not even the simple prayers my mother taught me. Now, with the war pressing down on mind and country, prayer is needed. But this war, this tragedy and my part in that tragedy, controls me.

Mary has taught Tad to pray. His little prayers, as he lies in bed or kneels beside it, trouble me because of my lacks.

Dear God —

The White House
Office
May 14th, '64

He, too, has to die.

I see an old man and this thought occurs. I see a child playing: he, too, has to die. I see a beautiful woman, and I hear the same words. We are doomed. Let us be brothers.

In times like the present, men should utter nothing for which they would not willingly be responsible through time and eternity. Nobody has ever expected me to be president. In my poor, lean lank face nobody has ever seen that cabbages were sprouting.

Executive Mansion
June 1, 1864

It has been a couple of weeks since I have written here. No matter. Some of the things I write are as thin as the homoeopathic soup that was made by boiling the shadow of a pigeon that had been starved to death.

Tonight the ticking of my watch is audible—it is meaningful following a long day listening to men and women express their desires. As I sit in my bedroom, my watch my companion, I feel that time is not on my side. Time is slow at bringing the war to an end. Time cares nothing for us. In the garden I have studied the sundial on sunny and cloudy days. We are also time pieces.

For years I wished to own a watch and chain, a gold one with a gold chain. It is time to pick up the key and wind my watch again.

Willie's Birthday

In our dining room our dining table was festive—for Willie. His friend, Charlie Mathers, was special guest, Charlie, so splendid in his freckles and red hair. Both boys were dressed in their Sunday togs.

I gave Willie a Zeiss field glass, an antique ship's compass from Italy, I believe; also a red handkerchief and books.

Mary gave him a British belt buckle with lion and unicorn, a set of brushes and tubes of pigment...

Charlie brought a box of candy.

Willie, at the head of the table, opened his gifts sedately, barely commenting, shy, rather like a little prince, not a kid from Illinois.

Tad pleased him with a checker set, board and pieces handmade.

(Today's war casualties are shocking.)

The White House
June 21, '64

During the last year I have had several consultations with White House and Washington physicians. They are encouraging about Tad. They believe that he may be able to speak normally as he grows older, that he may be able to learn to read and write, that his frenzied actions may diminish as he matures. I had a White House doctor observe Tad for over a month; he is quite optimistic.

Dear Tad—Mary and I love you.

When I hold him in my arms he has no defects. I think his ponies and goats and dogs and cats have helped him. He is always kind to his little friends. The soldiers love him. He's their Illinois Lieutenant. The blacks, too, are fond of him.

Mary loves to cradle him in her arms, in the peace of her bedroom. Sometimes he sleeps with me. Of course we spoil him. We spoil Willie too. When I am in conference and Tad dashes in it is amazing how intolerant some people can be over his effusiveness.

Well...when I am with Tad I forget the war.

July 20, 1864
Office

What does my old freckle-faced pastor think of me, now that I am in Washington? He never writes. Does he think I have forgotten Springfield?

He forgave Tad for whittling on a pew; he tolerated my long absences when I rode circuit; he preached directly, discreetly from the Bible, eager to please his congregation. Today he is probably sermonizing from Job: the war must weigh on him because he is a just and careful man. I imagine he remembers that Thomas Jefferson kept slaves. Does he know that there are some 200,000 blacks serving in our army? I would like to sound him out. How does he feel about the importance of a country united? If I could drop by...listen...if I could ride circuit for a fortnight I would learn much.

I notice that I have not written here for about a month. Pressures. Here, as I write, I seem to coordinate myself.

July 24, 1864
Executive Mansion
—office—

I believe it was arson.

Someone set fire to the White House stables. I rushed out when I saw the flames and heard men shouting. Our fire engine crew arrived too late. Willie's pony died. Tad's pony died. Four horses died, three survived, among them Old Abe. The fire occurred at night, while Willie and Tad slept. How much more disastrous it would have been if they had been awake. A number of us worked for five or six hours, to calm the surviving horses, to drag away the ponies on a sledge, for later burial. In the morning it was a very hard task to inform the boys.

With Tad sprawled on the bedroom floor, and Willie slumped in a chair, Mary and I attempted to comfort them. They were not to be comforted. We promised replacement ponies. They wailed and cringed at "replacements." The day was lost.

Arson, yes, everyone thinks it was arson. Some of the stable hands feel that the fire was set to bring me to the stables at night—a possible assassination attempt.

The White House
The Library

I have sought sanctuary in the library.

Willie is dead.

He was thirteen, handsome, intelligent, gentle, fond of each of us. For two weeks he battled for survival, his doctors helping little or not at all. When his doctor left him, when I was alone with him, I felt his cold face and held his cold hands. I thought, he's not really dead. It must be an error. He isn't dead because I feel his presence in the room, hear his voice.

Typhoid killed him.

Mary, hysterical, suffered grave headaches at his death. She is unable to comfort Tad. She is unable to speak coherently. She sometimes fancies that he is not dead: she wants to go into the bedroom and speak to him. She says she hopes to communicate with him through a séance. Only I have a chance at comforting Tad. Sitting on my lap, his head against my shoulder, he sleeps. Certainly he knows the sleeve of care, the worn sleeve.

Today we buried our Willie. Mary and Robert and Tad and I stood side by side at the grave.

It was like burying a part of my own body... I felt the earth strike my hands, my arms, my face, my mouth.

Cabinet members attended, military men, friends, White House staff. Tad held Jip in his arms. It rained some.

I'm a tired man. Sometimes I'm the tiredest man on earth.

August '64

Mary has passed days in her darkened bedroom, wracked by headaches, scarcely able to communicate, hardly able to eat. Her faithful Mrs. Keckley looks after her. There is little or no response when I attempt to comfort her. God, she claims, has deserted her.

I return to my office.

Now the war is my distraction. There is a hellish healing power in the roll of drums, the rumble of caissons, the tramp of a regiment. Washington's armed camp is always on the move.

Willie...

Maybe he is fortunate. At least he has been spared the confrontation of brother against brother.

I return to Mary's bedroom.

I offer coffee. She declines.

Robert came and knelt by her. He will go back to Harvard next week. Tad lay asleep at the foot of Mary's bed. Sometimes, when the four of us are in the bedroom I feel that grief is fourfold.

I retreated.

Jip comes.

August

After Willie's death I received a warm and understanding letter from Billy Herndon, my Billy. Each word weighed carefully.

Through the years he was much more patient than I; when I read aloud, back in the back of the office, he overlooked the nuisance. He tolerated my kids when they burst in on me. They sometimes wrecked havoc. He never brought his kids, never permitted them to come to the office...or if he did, they were no problem.

Billy could prepare his cases faster than I.

"Abe, are you still lingerin' over that Moffit suit?"

When he stood before a jury he was accurate and his accuracy taught me to prepare my cases with care.

Billy liked Willie. Well, he liked all my children.

How often we spread ourselves in my parlor and talked. Billy is like a cedar post, deeply imbedded.

Maybe he misses the buffalo stampede of my kids.

Summer

Personal tragedy strikes most of us. At this time personal loss is the fabric of this country.

What does a man do, does he sit in his chair, in the middle of a room, and wait?

I have not adjusted to Willie's death. Just a few days ago he was alive, riding on his pony; then, then the four of us stood around his grave.

The night he died I sat up all night; I worked with letters, documents, senate papers, proposals for a rail west, telegrams reporting the war. Someone brought me coffee.

Jip came in, and sat on my lap.

It is one thing to encounter personal loss in the theatre, another to read a tragedy; certainly it is another emotion to face it yourself, to realize that no power can reinstate.

The disciples had their hands full when their Lord and Master was crucified. I do not measure my little boy as any kind of lord but he was my son, a promise.

The father in me does not go away.

I go, now, to curry Old Abe.

I would like to chop wood a while.

White House
Summer

Again I am besieged by office seekers. I can name a hundred: Whitney, Schurz, Collaman, Blair, Wallace. They seek posts as consuls, envoys, inspectors, paymasters, commissioners, postmasters. Although I now have fixed hours, they intrude. Favors, all wish favors! I am accused of nepotism by the press, by staff and cabinet members. How would they shuffle the cards? Responsible positions are wrestled over by Vermonters and New Yorkers vying with Missourians and Ohioans.

Note:

Speak to Capt. Dobson about balloon observations. Work out telegraphic communication with the balloon observer.

August 20th

I woke early. It is already hot. No breeze.

I look out of the windows at the tents of the wounded. Behind the tents is the river, flattened by the heat. I have been inside of each tent several times. I have seen inside some of those men; I listen; I wait and listen. There are men with letters from home, men with Bibles beside them. Men or boys. Perhaps there is no essential difference when one is wounded. Man or boy is lost. There is no catching up for him. His trip home will show him a different world; if he goes home in a coffin—his homecoming makes that home unreal forever. One boy shows me a *minié* ball extracted from his leg. One man tells me how much we need a balloon corps. Another grasps my hand but can't say a word. At the very back of the tent someone is playing a harmonica, the "Camp Town Races"...or so it was yesterday.

The White House
Summer

Today I have been able to pardon two boys accused of dereliction of duty, Company K, while on guard near Washington. Regardless of reports I feel that they had carried the Union on their bayonets. Cramer and Phillips will have a second chance.

The heat of the afternoon has been oppressive; to cool me off, my mulatto brought me a cool drink on her famous tray; then a chaplain and a private spun stories of regimental pets. Once again I heard of the eagle in the 8th Wisconsin Volunteers. He is still alive after being in battles in seven states. His six-and-a-half-foot wingspread has been crippled by bullets; they say he screams when his Corps sees action.

A Minnesota unit manages to keep a half-grown bear; they swear he is the best picket-duty man. A black and white dog, named Jacko, has been dubbed a "brave soldier dog," because he has been wounded twice, while his men were in action.

I have also learned that there are gamecocks, a coon, and several badgers in the field. Mascots all.

Militiamen, who visit me, talk a language I understand: jaggers, hardtack, barbed wire, pup tents, canteens, bivouacs, sutlers, coffee...

There are stories about dysentery: one boy said, "I jus' cut out the bottom of my trousers!"

The Library
Summer

Mary's kindness resumes. She visits the hospitals, the injured, taking flowers, food. The men are delighted to have her. People bring her newspapers and magazines, and she distributes them...she has made a little friend of a one-armed boy; sitting beside him, she becomes his mother.

Last week she brought about the abolishment of a death sentence. Due to her perseverance there will be no firing squad for Richard Miller, a youngster who fell asleep on duty. My "Lady President" obtained a reprieve from General McClellan.

The Press wars against Mary. Reporters ridicule her when she goes shopping in New York or Philadelphia, in her attempts to refurbish the White Rouse. If she visits Robert at Harvard, that too is criticized. Her letters to relatives are sometimes confiscated. I am aware that there are spies in the White House, but not Mary!

Is this why I assumed the Presidency! It is very difficult to curb my resentment.

Tonight, I will be spending a while with Frank Carpenter, watching him paint his Emancipation scene. He is a quiet, serious fellow, and I enjoy his company. I appreciate his skill, as he slowly brings his figures to life. He is still working in the dining room. He'll bring me a rocker and I will stretch out.

The White House
—My desk—

I have little admiration for Napoleon; I have less for my little Napoleons who believe or half-believe this is a war of conquest. Again and again I remind them of emancipation. They nod. The negro? The slave? Can it be that there is a moral issue? It is possible that our government can wipe out slavery and free thousands of blacks? A few are astute enough to understand the potential here. A few are astute enough to project themselves in time, asking how are we to repair the devastation caused by General Grant and General Sherman. How long did it take for our men to burn Atlanta? How long does a city burn? Some say that Rome is still burning.

Andersonville—a prison... Libby—a prison. Thousands of men are incarcerated. Who pays for these criminal acts? All of us pay. We pay as though we were buying sugar at $12.00 a pound. A man weighs about 160 pounds. If he loses weight while he is imprisoned do we pay less?

Summer

With my watch lying on the desk, the seconds seem to move all too swiftly. Nine, ten, twelve...each second a life around Washington...cabinet members...family...friends. Here at 9:58 is Willie's birth; here at 4:00 is Tad's birth. A few more seconds pass and I am delivering my inaugural address. The war is threatening, the war has overcome us.

I put away the watch.

When Billy Herndon presented me with that watch I thought I would spend the rest of my life in Springfield. I thought our partnership would go on and on. I was lying on the old sofa, tired after a circuit ride.

Billy handed me the watch; I opened its box; then he said :

"We've been working together for ten years."

He brushed his fingers through his shaggy beard and sat down at his desk.

A gold watch —

Executive Mansion
September 1st, 1864

"This is a beautiful country," said John Brown, as the hangman hung him.

He was no black Christ: no gentle Uncle Tom; yet, he is becoming a black Christ as we continue this civil war, as we become more and more harassed by casualties. We will need black Christs if we are to free the negro. *Uncle Tom's Cabin* must add space—room by room, year by year.

All the powers of earth seem to be combining against the chattel slave. Mammon is after him, ambition follows, philosophy follows, and the theology of the day is joining the cry. They have him in his prison house; they have searched his person, and left no prying instrument with him. One after another they have closed the heavy iron doors upon him; and now they have him, as it were, bolted in with a lock of every key—the keys in the hands of a hundred different men, and they scattered to a hundred different and distance places; and they stand musing as to what invention, in all the dominions of mind and matter, can be produced to make the impossibility of his escape more complete than it is.

This evening I heard negroes singing, as I worked at my desk, the windows open. I heard that song in New Orleans on my first visit; I heard it later when on the Mississippi, when we were on our cargo-raft, when we tied up at a wharf. That was quite a scrap. The blacks almost threw us off our raft.

Oh, was you ev – er in Mo – bile Bay,
Low – lands, low – lands, A – way, –
My John, – A – screw – ing cot – ton –
By the day, My dol – lar and a half a day.

Poverty...those days were poverty days.

And after this war is over we will have greater poverty in the South. Poverty will be a pestilence in the South. It will require years of work to wipe it out. Poverty will breed treachery and crime. What police force will be able to contend with it? I will urge Congress to pass an aid bill. I will propose groups of citizenry who can advise.

The White House
Saturday evening

Here are some interesting figures I encountered:

Less than one-half a day's cost of this war could pay for the slaves in the State of Delaware, at $400 per person.

All slaves by 1860 census:	1,798
Cost of these slaves:	$719,200
One day's cost of the war:	$2,000,000

Less than 87 days' cost of this war could, at the same $400 figure, pay for the slaves in the States of Delaware, Maryland, District of Columbia, Kentucky, and Missouri:

Cost of the slaves:	$173,048,800
87 days of war:	$174,000,000

Would compensation to all the slave owners satisfy them? Of course not. Their honor is at stake. If we do not make common cause to save the good old ship of the Union on this voyage, nobody will have a chance to pilot her on another voyage.

Note:

Write General Grant regarding the improvement of all military telegraph service. Suggest a military Telegraphic Corps.

The White House
September 8, 1864

When I reviewed the Army of the Potomac, when the greatest cavalry in the world rode past, I felt no pride, only sorrow, for the military pomp. To those of pensive turn, the military implies death, men in uniform are death-men, dealers and receivers. They work in the counting house of death.

Tad rode with the cavalry, his little shoulders wrapped in a grey cloak.

Dear Tad, what do you know of pain? You will sit on my lap and babble and then ride horseback, and imagine yourself a great general.

There are no great generals, Tad.

I salute the officers but take off my hat to the men in the ranks. They are the great men. There are no victors—not if there is heart and memory among men, consideration for the maimed, the widows, the orphans, the deceased.

Some men war for glory. No...peace is the glory.

There is only one cause: the country, its flag, a united people from coast to coast. I know that of thousands of men, chosen from the ranks, there would be a thousand reasons why they fought. Perhaps that is not quite right.

The men in review, the thousands who rode and walked past, were soon to retreat. Mishandled by General Hooker, 20,000 were killed, died in a wilderness of trees and thickets.

Wilderness of trees and thickets...so is much of my concept of this war, due largely to inadequate reports or reports that arrive too late to be of any use.

My colored pins, on the fields of battle, designate more than battle lines, regiments, infantry, artillery, cavalry, fortifications...those pins are men, my men, my country.

I understand that some of the New Englanders dumped their Bibles on their long marches—their knapsacks too heavy. I can see those Bibles, dropped beside a fence post, left underneath a tree, regretfully placed on the side of a corncrib.

For my dear Son, Charles—

love, Mother

I read most of my mother's Bible. It was a solace and a threat; it was a puzzlement because I could not disentangle legend from fact.

Was there such a city as Zidon?

Was there a Goliath?

My mother's Bible had a few maps—they led me to travel by camelback, through Egypt and Assyria. At night, in my attic, I imagined the sacred tabernacle, the pyramids. I repeated some of the *Song of Songs*.

September 20, 1864
The Library

To a great extent, this war is capitalism versus a kind of feudalism. On one hand we have free labor and on the other slave labor. The North boasts more millionaires than the South, in normal times. New York City probably has more millionaires than the entire South. John J. Astor is an example of an individual who has amassed wealth by canny manipulations—his kind is unseen in the South. As I understand it, Northern labor practices are questionable at times, shackling the workers; this must be leveled out in years to come.

Strange, seeing beggars on Northern streets; yet none in the South.

As the war continues I learn that Southern railroad cars lack windows for lack of factory labor. House glass can not be replaced; conventional glassware for the table can not be replaced. If a man wishes a prescription filled he must furnish his own bottle or packet. Needles, pins, scissors, knives are smuggled in and sold on the black market. Drugs have vanished from pharmacopoeia.

The White House
October, 1864

Tonight my watch lies on my chest of drawers. Ah yes, the seconds are passing, the minutes are passing. Jim Maitland is dead. Colonel James Maitland, Massachusetts man. His handsome face, his humor, leadership, bravery, gone. I thought him my protégé and friend. I was to grant him a Major's commission.

The seconds, the minutes, ran out too quickly for Maitland. As I stare down at the second hand, in its small circle, I see his face; I see him dressed in his Zouave uniform.

Tad will miss him.

For a moment he held the enemy flag in his hands, then a shotgun blast.

Executive Mansion
October 2, 1864

An officer has given me a war diary kept by a Southern soldier, Fred Parker, corporal. Rain has soaked its pages; pages are missing. Here are four entries, written during the Wilderness Campaign:

> *May 6, 1864. Face-to-face fighting all day. Rifles. Pistols. No help from our cavalry or artillery. Pine woods surround. Trees close together. Weather poor. Fred died beside me at midday. Jeffrey has had his leg shot at the knee; knee shattered; men carried him away. We hide, shoot, duck, lie down.*
>
> *May 7. Not much to eat. Awful hungry. Rifle fire constant.*
>
> *May 8. Grant's forces surround us. 120,000 men.*
>
> *May 9. Dead and wounded everywhere, behind trees, under bushes. I*

see pieces of a sweater. Shoes. Boots. A hat. Bayonets. Broken musket. A brass belt buckle.

The diary tells me that life must be more than a belt buckle.

Executive Mansion
October 15, 1864

Hamlet's thoughts, his moods, fit the conflict that assails our country.

> *...We defy augury; there is special providence in the fall of a sparrow. If it be now, 'tis not to come; if it be not to come, it will be now; if it be not now, yet it will come; the readiness is all; since no man has aught of what he leaves what is it to leave betimes? Let be.*

Let be. Do we?

Little Tad heard Mary speaking about Maitland's shotgun death; he climbed onto Mary's bed and talked about our friend's funeral—tearful details about the White House ceremony, details bitter for childish emphasis.

Perhaps it is repugnant to write here when men are dying. Perhaps my diary should not have been written; perhaps I should have been attending the wounded in the hospitals. But that confusion, that confusion of pain and sorrow, would not, could not, carry me forward.

Executive Mansion
October 21st, '64
My desk

How vividly I summon up the hundreds of exhausted soldiers in the streets of Washington.

I watched them from the White House, a stream of muddy, rain-soaked men, walking through a downpour, going nowhere. Men without guns, without knapsacks; some men covered with blankets. Some staggered. Some fell, lay on the street. Women brought coffee. There were Michigan men, New York men,

Minnesota men—defeated, defeated at Bull Run. The broken regiments struggled all along Pennsylvania Avenue. Victims of panic—defeat. Not a drum sounded. All took place in rain-washed silence. Men without shoes, men leaning on one another.

I ordered the White House staff and military guard to provide coffee, food, blankets, shelter.

Hundreds passed...all day long.

For a long while after this there were conferences, men realizing that Washington could be attacked. A long time before the city was protected.

Defeat, I am told, is a particular kind of crucifixion. I know. I have thought—

October 24, '64

I wish I could go bowling, swap yarns.

When I bowl I really never care whether I win. When I make a good score it is luck. It is talk I enjoy. It gives me an uplift. It's an exchange, maybe, if I relate one of my circuit stories.

I can not go bowling when men are dying. There is no escape. I should not look for an escape. I want cessation of conflict. Enduring peace. I wish to command a strong nation, a great nation that can stand before the world as an example of what men can achieve.

A sadness pervades our White House gardens, a more than autumn sadness.

Mary and I tried to make a haven of our garden whenever possible. Sunsets have been Potomac sunsets, wilderness and prairie sunsets. Nevertheless, that great stillness intrudes as we walk and talk about our family and obligations. Flowers lie in Mary's lap, as we sit on a bench. She smiles.

Now four years have come and gone.

We measure those years, wanting to understand. We no longer speculate about the future, our future. Life, for the moment, is held in balance like an upraised oar.

Was it yesterday, after the rain, with a faint rainbow, that the sentries paced along the far side of the gardens, and a white duck waddled toward us?

The White House
November 3rd, 1864

"We have seen our courthouse in chains, two battalions of dragoons, eight companies of artillery, twelve companies of infantry, the whole constabulary force of the city police, the entire disposable marine of the United States, with its artillery loaded for action, all marching in support of a Praetorian band, consisting of 120 friends and associates of the United States Marshall, with loaded pistols and drawn swords, and in military costume and array—for what purpose? To escort and conduct a poor trembling slave from a Boston courthouse to the fetters and lash of his master! This display of military force the mayor of this city officially declared to be necessary," so wrote our Harvard University friend, old Josiah Quincy. He also added, that summer in '54, "Slaveholders have multiplied

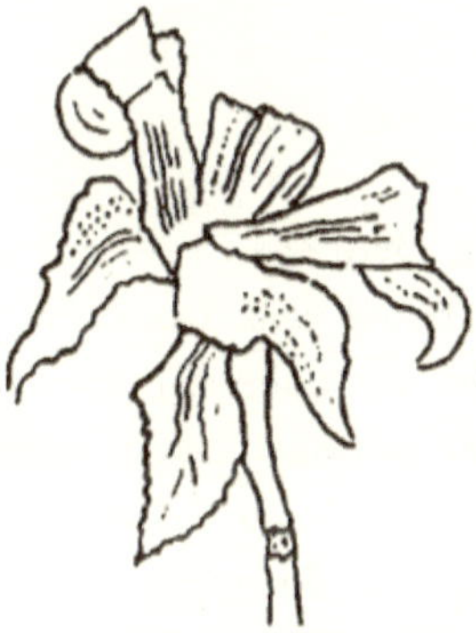

their black cattle by the million; and are every day increasing their numbers, and extending their cattle field into the wilderness..."

I respond to those impressive words with mine, since the slave issue dies hard.

The ant who has toiled and dragged a crumb to his nest will furiously defend the fruit of his labor against whatever robber assails him. So plain that the most dumb and stupid slave that ever toiled for a master does constantly know that he is wronged. So plain that no one, high or low, ever does mistake it, except in a plainly selfish way; for although volume after volume is written to prove slavery a very good thing, we never hear of the man who wishes to take the good of it by being a slave himself.

Certainly, though a man may escape death and injury in the front lines, changes brought about by the war may alienate him at home, after he leaves the army, if he still has a home. The black who has fought for the North may find his Southern neighbors have become enemies. The black who has found a measure of recognition while serving will find a lack of recognition after the war.

We have made little or no provision for the wounded. Our hospitals are inadequate. Southerners will return to their farms with little more than the horse that saw combat. Custom dictates that he reject the negro.

As a nation, we are in a maelstrom of change. It is my hope that the church may help democratize. As I study the Washington archive I learn essential facts, but these facts are not disseminated. How are we to coordinate these state laws? Missouri hardly comprehends the laws of Massachusetts.

Justice—many strive for justice. Efforts must be doubled. I hope it may be said that I was just.

There are nights when I can not sleep. I get up and pace the floor of my bedroom or go into my office.

Many continue to threaten my life; so I do not walk the streets of Washington. If I were home again I could walk freely. In Springfield, it is pleasant to imagine, I would shake off the war trauma. I think old skies would reassure me. But days in Springfield will not return. I have lost more than half my life here—but it was not the ax that cut me down. What was it, in all truth? Craving for glory? For power? I accept those weaknesses but above them is my desire to help my country, to balance the welfare of our people.

The White House
—cold, rainy—

Very often my commanding officers prove to be inadequate and I have to substitute one for another. Most officers, I find, shun advice or suggestions.

Grant and Sherman are the best listeners. Ours is a mutual respect. Grant has the essential military skill to control the entire armed force. He also has ample courage for his job (it takes courage to fling men into battle; I also send men to death).

Sleep continues to be difficult to come by...peace is difficult to come by we know by now...hope is hard to come by.

It is curious and amusing to look at life across time: man knows his detours: it is incredible how he has fumbled his way through the centuries. In spite of the fumbling, I believe in mankind.

Executive Mansion
Christmas

CHRISTMAS—1864.
Mary and Robert and I have exchanged gifts.
We have given many presents to Tad.
Late in the afternoon, we placed a wreath on Willie's grave.

This evening I received this telegram from General Sherman:

"I beg to present you, as a Christmas gift, the City of Savannah.

– William T. Sherman"

Wintry

Rain beats on the White House, rain mixed with snow.

Old newspaper clippings remind me that six thousand soldiers died in an hour at the battle of Cold Harbor.

Another clipping reminds me of Gettysburg.

Another...

I have been reading the fifth chapter of Isaiah. It does not help. It seems there are days when nothing helps.

If re-elected, how shall I live through a second term? But I must; there is work to be done; I am the best to carry out honesty for all. I want no recriminations.

Perhaps I can find peace, someday, in Europe. My son, Robert, is ill-disposed toward me. There is Tad, poor little wounded Tad.

Mary is ill, seriously ill.

Now, I shall open the Bible once more.

3

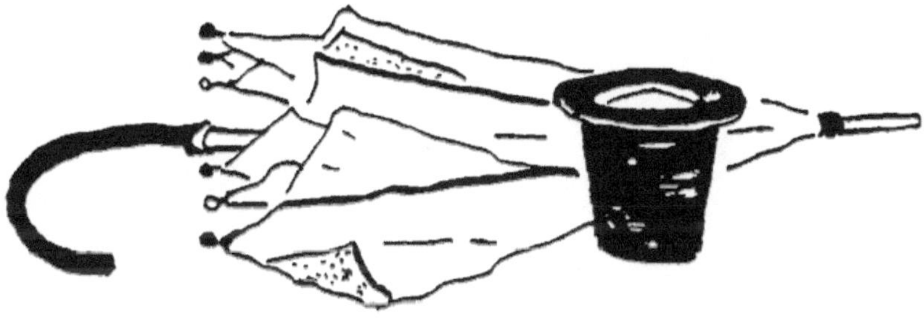

Late

Since many of our soldiers are fifteen or sixteen years old, I am aware that discipline is wanting, both discipline and stamina. Yet they fight furiously, build bridges, lay rails. They fight with their muzzle-loaders, cannon, mortar, bayonet. Most of them had never heard a gun fired except while out hunting. In a grim sense we are witnessing a youth crusade against injustice. For $13.00 a month they are fighting a man's war. And dying is a man's job. Poor children, crawling out of some entrenchment, they fraternize during a lull—swap tobacco for coffee. They soon learn that our hospitals are dangerous places. Tents. Barns. Churches. Sheds.

We accepted this war for a worthy objective, and the war will end when that goal has been attained. We must succeed. This war has taken four years! It was begun or accepted to restore national authority over the whole national domain. Yes, we must succeed.

The White House
Office

The pigeonholes of my desk contain reports of disgraced militiamen, unfortunate prisoners of war, civilian and military spies, reports that demand that ultimate yes or no. I study these reports, I weigh each one carefully; some two thousand reach me every month. Across the Potomac River, as I write, I hear gunfire, Virginia gunfire. Perhaps this is Butcher Day—our men are facing a Confederate firing squad.

I am reprimanded. Officers protest I weaken army morale when I commute a death sentence. Yesterday I pardoned William Scott, Vermonter, Company L, who fell asleep while on sentinel duty at a Potomac bridge. Nineteen years old, a farm boy, he was undoubtedly accustomed to going to bed at dusk. I rode to the Potomac River Camp and found Scott handcuffed in his tent.

"Boy," I said, "I'm going to send you back to Company L."

Boys can do us more good above ground. If a man had more than one life to live, I believe a little hanging would not hurt him too much...but he has one life.

Nothing exhausts me more than death sentences, death warrants, death. Young life is priceless. There are thirty million people involved in this war. Youth must be considered, if we are to survive.

I want to write something about my old friend, the Virginian, Ward Hill Lamon, of Danville days. Hill is my volunteer guardian, spy, Rabelaisian crony, scribe. Time and again he bundles up and sleeps all night in the hall outside my bedroom door, a derringer at hand. He is constantly alarmed I may be assassinated. He upbraids me when I ride alone in the White House carriage.

"That stupid coachman can't look after you... I want a dozen or half-dozen cavalrymen to attend you."

Evenings, Hill may appear and size me up, and sing a sad little song or a bobtail-nag melody, thrumming his banjo. Husky, courageous, he befriends me every day. Breakfasting together, he has a kernel of advice for me, I'm sure.

I have borrowed his hat, borrowed his cloak, but not his boots.

"As President, it is incumbent on you to look after your own boots and your own umbrellas," he says.

As warden he has problems with both North and South; it aggravates him when he has to confer with me; he wants to be the little eagle. On our frequent visits to the hospitals he is always sympathetic. "Somebody's Wallace," he says, remembering one of my stories. Playing his banjo he will sing "Picayune Butler," his southern accent warm and beautiful, delighting the sick and wounded.

Often, late at night, we talk of Danville, circuit friends, horses; he is adept at driving off my melancholia.

"The war is going to end soon," he prophesizes. "It has to end soon...it's hard to get hold of new banjo strings."

The White House
January 5, 1865

So, another year has come into being.

"Many are the hearts that are weary tonight, waiting for the war to cease..."

For days I have been remembering that song. Yesterday, as I rode in the barouche, the melody kept time to the trotting of the horses.

Wind and sun helped, as we rode.

Alone, I was able to commune with nature, able to consider the Potomac, the trees along its banks, the finished dome of the capitol, the monument to George

Washington. For a while I was able to survey the property, measure it, plan a city layout.

The barouche horses are bays, a young pair, well-trained, handsomely harnessed. My driver is a stalwart from Rhode Island; he says he used to work in a cotton mill; now, he looks forward to a job in a warmer climate.

We talk about the chestnuts and the oaks; for a mill worker he is well-informed about trees; suddenly, our drive is over.

Late

Nightmares occur.

I sit up in bed and recall in vivid detail scenes I have never witnessed, men dying under artillery and rifle fire, tent amputations, men struggling across a muddy, swollen river, a firing squad where men are shot down as I sit in a rocking chair.

I say nothing to anyone about these dreams but they are a weight to my world.

Lately, it is difficult to eat; I forget or refuse my lunch on its tray; coffee helps. I long to get away for a week or ten days.

Sunday
—windy and cool—

A heavy hog to hold, this war.

Sometimes people in Kentucky are loyal to the Union; sometimes not; it depends on whether General Lee has lost or won a battle.

Men find me lacking as the nation's attorney. Some demand that I plot the future. I remember that the pilots on our western rivers steer from point to point—as they call it—setting the course of the boat no farther than they can see. That is how I propose to handle some of the problems set before me.

I seldom forget that it is a momentous thing to be the instrument for the liberation of a race.

I look out of the window, at the statue of Thomas Jefferson on the lawn; it puts me in mind of that lonely bronze figure atop the White House dome, a woman, symbol of liberty, visible for miles—cast by slave labor.

Was Jefferson's statue cast by slaves?

Monday
—windy and cool—

There are something like a thousand deserters every month, Northern men and Southern men. I see them being marched through the city, all kinds, bareheaded, with caps, hats, with bandaged heads, with bandanas, handsome fellows, sickly fellows, wounded men, dirty, most of them in worn-out uniforms—miles of men mixed with leather, steel, horses, guns, wagons, riders, guards.

450,000 widows and mothers have lost their men.

White House
January 10, 1865

How well some officers understand one another, with a hem and a haw, with a nod or lifted hand. They are masters of military deception, just as politicians are masters of ambiguity. The colonels have their lingo; the majors have theirs.

I confront them with a plan of action. They bow over a map. Immediately, I sense that their secret codes are in operation. They guess that I am suspicious; I see that when a lieutenant touches the general's knee. I decline the general's offer of a cigar; he has forgotten I do not smoke. The men light up. Smoke hovers over the map. Brady appears. He wants to take some photographs. Some men sit, some stand. All the time the subtle deceptions continue. It is my job, as Commander-in-Chief, to ferret out honesty and promote it.

Troops are marching by.

Drums.

There is no room for humor.

The White House
January 12, 1865

Behind a hospital, the other day, I saw a wheelbarrow filled with amputated hands, arms, and legs.

I walked up close to the barrow, uncertain what I saw there. A hand reached out for my hand.

I held that hand. The stiff fingers were those of a farmer—a man from Tennessee or Illinois, a corn-husker's hand.

I saw a boy's hand next to the farmer's.

I wanted to put those amputated pieces back in their proper world. All those pieces, the hands, legs, feet, wanted to return to the woods, the prairie, the barns, the canoes, the plantations.

As I write down these words my hands are not steady.

The White House
January 20, 1865

A month or so ago, I wrote General Grant on behalf of Robert. Now that Robert has graduated from Harvard, he insists on joining the army. I agree. Grant has replied and has given him a captain's commission, and he is to become a member of Grant's personal staff. Robert has not written me; perhaps he had learned of his mother's parental concern and has included me as an obstructionist. Now he is less likely to be bayoneted or blown to shreds while on the General's staff.

Another of Mary's brothers has been killed in action. Her fears for Robert are understandable.

I must impress her that fewer White House levees are in order. I realize it was proper to honor Prince Napoleon but there are few such obligations. I shun ostentation. We have no right to ostentation these war times. That money that goes into ostentation can go into blankets for the soldiers.

A calm evening
Late

"Devoutly to be wished"...to have a woman, enjoy her physically; yet preserve essential private values.

A helpmeet, yes, but it has been my misfortune to never encounter such a woman who was also a woman.

Early in life, at East Salem, I learned about the unhappiness of others.

Misguided lives are powerful guideposts.

In the wilderness I found something mystic, something out of self for self. It taught me to be legally self.

In Springfield, I studied its citizens, its girls and women; I found that being an outsider was wise.

My wisdom is indeed my misfortune.

The White House
2/15/65

Yesterday a woman came to me, crying, sobbing, pleading for the release of one of her sons from service, since her husband and three sons were in the army.

I wrote a discharge for one of her sons and gave her instructions where to go and what to say, to get her lad released.

She found the military camp, regiment, company; she found her son wounded, dying in a nearby hospital. After his death she begged:

"Mr. President, will you give me the next one of my boys?" Again she produced official papers.

"I have just lost a son... I have another," I managed to say. As she stood beside my chair I wrote a release; as I wrote she placed her hand on my head and smoothed my hair with a mother's touch.

When I gave her the document she ran sobbing, crying her thanks.

The White House
2/18/65

Again I admit that dreams have perplexed me. I also think them significant if we can interpret them properly.

Last week I had a dream that has haunted me ever since. After it occurred I opened the Bible. Strange as it may seem, it was at the 28th chapter of *Genesis*, which relates the wonderful dream of Jacob. I turned to other passages... I seemed to encounter a vision wherever I looked.

I should not have related the dream to Mary but the thing got possession of me, and, like Banquo's ghost, it would not down.

As I told her I felt something grabbing at my throat.

About ten days ago I went to bed late. I had been waiting for important dispatches from the front. I was very weary and fell asleep as soon as I lay down. Then I began to dream.

There seemed to be a death-like stillness about me; then I heard subdued sobs, as if a number of people were weeping. I thought I left my bed and wandered downstairs. There the silence was broken by the same sobbing, but any mourners were invisible. I walked from room to room; every object was familiar. I was puzzled, alarmed. I kept on until I arrived at the East Room. There I met a sickening surprise.

Before me was a catafalque, on which rested a corpse, in funeral vestments. Around it were stationed soldiers acting as guards. Beyond the soldiers was a crowd.

"Who is dead in the White House?" I asked one of the soldiers.

"The President," he replied. "He was killed by an assassin."

An outburst of grief came from the crowd.

I woke...

Mary was very disturbed by my dream; I gained nothing by telling her; in tears she threw herself on her bed.

"Don't repeat your dream to anyone," she said.

2/21/65

How blustery, more like December or January; it will be raining soon.

This morning, when it was more pleasant, I visited the Potomac Book Shop where Willie and I used to buy books. Here and there were a few soldiers. I was pleased, especially when one of them asked me if I would recommend a book of poetry.

On my last visit I bought Pope's *Essay on Man.* I noticed a British copy bound in morocco. At the Potomac I have acquired some Emerson, Wordsworth, Longfellow. I picked up a copy of *Leaves of Grass*, but it did not appeal to me. The shop reminds me of one in Boston; I told the owner; he laughed: "The shop you mention belongs to my brother... I furnished this one with Boston pieces."

I hope I can get Tad to take an interest in learning to read. Willie's enthusiasm did not rub off on him.

Returning to the White House, one of our horses threw a shoe.

February 27, '65

Hill tells me we have imprisoned a Confederate citizen who was delivering a £40,000 draft to the Southern forces. He also jailed a M. Louis de Bedian, who had letters of credit ($39,000), for the Confederate army. He has apprehended Charles Kopperl, Washington resident, who boasts that he killed Union soldiers. Obviously, Washington has strange, determined men.

Some countrymen objected to Hill's political imprisonments, and I am criticized, in turn. Again nepotism ghosts.

Billy Herndon has walked into my office. Our get-together seemed as though we were in Springfield, in the old office. I threw out questions about friends; he had the answers. The weather favored us as we rambled around Washington, in the presidential coach. Together we explored the White House—Billy's high-point. We had dinner, with Tad at our table.

Billy gave Tad a hand-carved pony express rider, in walnut. My books interested Billy. He thought my walnut bed a world's wonder. "Is it really nine feet long!" The carvings on the headboard amused him, and the wooden nest with its walnut eggs, under my side table. We parted reluctantly.

I wish I had ten men of his caliber to work with here. He went away quite shaken by the cost of the war. "How could it be...$2,000,000 every single day... Can our country recover such an outlay?"

March 9th
The Library

We can not escape history. We, of this administration, will be remembered in spite of ourselves. No personal significance or insignificance can spare one or another of us. The fiery trial through which we pass, will light us down, in honor or dishonor, to the last generation.

The great books in this room confirm this. The sun in the windows has promise.

Spring is with us along the Potomac. Through my open windows I hear it.

I wish I could place a sprig of lilacs on my mother's grave.

Tomorrow we will visit Willie's grave, but we will leave Tad with friends. His new pony is coming in a day or two; that will make him happy. I bought a Shetland, brown and white.

Mallards mix with small craft. There's not a breath of air moving; life is making a turn.

Wednesday

After reviewing troops on Monday I had that dream. I was staring at myself in a mirror, a full length mirror. I was seeing myself double—double vision. This time I seemed to perceive myself as traitor. Traitor to what?

Reviewing troops is an experience that shatters satisfaction. How can a man, a thoughtful man, watch men on parade and minimize the fact that some or all of those men will soon be dead or wounded? Or will maim or kill other men?

Last Monday the troops slogged past in heavy rain.

White House
Monday morning

The signs look better. Peace does not appear so distant as it did. I hope it will come soon, and come to stay; and so come as to be worth keeping in all future time. It will then have been proved that among free men there can be no successful appeal from the ballot to the bullet, and that they who take such appeal are sure to lose their case to pay the cost.

And then there will be some black men who can remember that with silent tongue, and clenched teeth, and steady eye, and well-poised bayonet, they have helped mankind on to this great consummation, while I fear there will be some white ones unable to forget that with malignant heart and deceitful speech they strove to hinder it.

The White House
Saturday

Again I have visited the Patent Office, this time in the evening, after a tedious meeting. I was accompanied by my escort, cavalrymen with rattling sabers, spirited horses. At the Office I was struck by a vivid recollection of how it used to be, before the war, the rows of cabinets and cases, each containing models of inventions.

Now cases and cabinets have been pushed aside or removed. Flush along the walls are row after row of wounded, as many as four rows deep, the wounded and their beds and cots reflected in dull glass doors.

Lamps and candles gleamed and smoked among the soldiers. I shook hands, passing from row to row. I talked, sat down. Here were signs of resignation, flashes of courage and hope.

Patent Office, I thought, you have a patent on suffering and death. As I stood, talking with doctors and nurses, they carried a man away.

"There's such a shortage of medical supplies," a beautiful nurse exclaimed. "Isn't there something you can do to help? Did you know there are 12,000 wounded in and around the city?"

Note—

Check telegrams at T. Office. See Seward and Blain.

The White House
March 20, '65

With malice toward none; with charity for all; with firmness in the right as God gives us to see the right, let us strive on to finish the work we are in; to bind up the nation's wounds; to care for him who shall have borne the battle, and for his widow, and his orphan...to do all which may achieve and cherish a just and lasting peace, among ourselves, and with all nations.

That is my prayer.

Something resembling peace came as I wrote.

7 a.m.
Office

A lieutenant visited my office one afternoon last week, a thin ghost of a man. Sitting in a chair alongside my desk, he seemed to totter, to lean toward the sun coming in the window.

He showed me pieces of bone that had been removed from a shoulder wound, laying them on my desk, in the sun.

I talked with him for about an hour, questioning about his army experiences, his home...he is mustered out. Back to Albany.

A soldier bumped into me on the White House grounds, swearing because he had not been able to get his pay; his crutch poked at the ground, his leg-stump jerked, as he talked to me.

"Let me see your papers? Remember, I've been a lawyer and maybe I can help."

Jip is dead.

March 28th, '65

Someone is singing outside my office, singing that old favorite, "Massa's in de cole, cole ground."

Memories.

I see the newspaper heading:

> 5,000 COTTON BALES BURNED.
>
> Baton Rouge, last week bales were piled in the Commons, soaked with alcohol, and burned. At this date, bales are valued at $100.00 per bale.

Another item, by the same reporter:

> Two flatboats, loaded with cotton bales, were floated down the

> Mississippi, at New Orleans. Soaked with alcohol, they were set afire...

My little mulatto brings me my lunch; she bows and says:
"Good day, mistaaaaa President...cawnbread...thais cawnbread on my tray..."

March 29th

I have gone through my desk today, weeding out.

I have had a pigeonhole marked: A.

That's for assassination.

I think there were about eighty 'nonymous threats in that pigeonhole. I have thrown them into the fireplace. I should have done this long ago. Some of the threats were made by persons who had never been to Washington, whose geographical knowledge would have led them to the stables rather than the White House. Some seemed to think I resided in the Washington monument. One person proposed that he assassinate me on the Presidential yacht. No doubt he felt that would please the press and general public.

It is uncommonly chilly this afternoon; I think I will have a fire in the fireplace. We can have some oak logs to burn up the ashes of the assassins.

General Grant and I have been on friendly terms for a long while. He likes to talk about his farming days in Missouri. He used to haul wood ten or twelve miles into St. Louis. $10.00 a cord. He is proud of his log cabin, which he designed and built, a two-story.

At his HQ we sat under a tent flap and talked. He unfolded a letter from his wife and showed me his baby's smudge print. Wife and son are two thousand miles away.

I talked about my courtship days, and Grant said:

"...Let me tell you how I got hitched. We were buggy riding and had to cross a flooded creek. As the buggy sank into the water and the water poured in, she yelled: 'I'm gonna hold onto you no matter what happens.' After we crossed I asked her: 'Would you like to cling to me the rest of your life?' Or something like that."

We got to talking horses. I described some of my nags and some of my faithfuls. He talked about his West Point horses, thoroughbreds... Wilma could outhurdle any other...six foot six inches...then he talked about Mexican horses and Mexican saddles...you should see the one I got as booty...silver ornaments...

It was good to get away from Washington.

When I reviewed Grant's troops, I rode his Cincinnati, a huge bay. The soldiers are always pleased by my visits. I remove my hat and bow. Men clamor around me, huzzahing. They stroke Cincinnati. They kiss my hand: these are the blacks who are willing to fight for the union. Grant singled out a corps: recently, they had captured six cannons, under fire all the time.

Cincinnati whuffs and bobs his splendid head, as Grant and I ride along, a woodland around us.

After lunch in his tent, he gave me a lieutenant's diary, written at Shiloh.

> *Our General Grant sat on his horse and watched the enemy try to capture a hill. Men fought from tree to tree. A man near me has been shot while aiming his rifle, one eye is closed, one eye is still open. A corporal has been disemboweled by a cannon ball. Riderless horses are running wild. Trees are plugged with lead bullets. I counted sixty bullets in a small tree.*

I plan to collect personal accounts of the war; men must know.

Mary Mitchell, a volunteer nurse, has written:

> *The wounded filled every building and overflowed into the country around, into farm houses, barns, corncribs, cabins. Six churches were full, the Odd Fellows' Hall, the Freemasons', the Town Council room, the school. I saw men with cloths about their heads, about their feet, men with arms in slings, men without arms, men in ambulances, carts, wheelbarrows.*
>
> *At the center of this autumn harvest stood the little white Dunker church, where the teaching on Sundays was that war is a sin. There the dead lay in gray and blue. In the fields lay thousands. Corn leaves over some of them were spattered with blood.*

Grant and I ride. There is mud on the horses. His officers crowd round. Grant helps me dismount. We talk. Grant speaks favorably of yesterday's battle, speaks with a rasping voice, hand to his throat. Behind his chair lies a muddy saddle. It is cloudy, cold. A private brings a dispatch. Grant reads it and nods. I respect this man.

Cabinet members reveal their excitement. Rumors. But the rumors may have solid foundations. Grant, they say. Sherman, he left to rejoin his army. His army will move. My secretaries believe in the rumors. Seward is optimistic. Hill waves his arms. Of course. At the telegraph office the men say "yes." It is a kind of yes that could mean almost anything. The newspapers are reporting this same news.

Mary has spent $2,000 for a gown. She has spent $3,000 for earrings. $5,000 for a lace shawl.

She thinks I do not know about these extravagances. My previous efforts at control produce hysteria, hysteria that lasted for days.

I remember Ann Rutledge.

I order the brougham and drive.

The April weather is fine.

As the war draws to a close I remember that four million people have been involved in this struggle.

I have heard from Robert but he reports that his mother's letters are unbalanced. He has offered to bring them to the White House when he has leave. He says that her letters have been distraught for months. He is deeply concerned over her condition.

Evening
Desk

Details are coming in.

General William T. Sherman, with his 60,000 men, has cut a swath across insurgent territory, a swath twenty to forty miles wide, and three hundred miles long.

All day the news comes.

All items confirm the success of his march.

Sherman's men have foraged off the country; their devastation of property has been extreme; miles of railroad track have been ripped up; rolling stock has been captured; his forces advanced ten or twelve miles a day. The Confederate press refers to his march as a scourge.

Savannah—that was Sherman's gift on Christmas.

Now, across the nation, a million and a half slaves have been freed.

Wednesday we went to Richmond by boat, a party of us, the day clear. Most of Richmond is gutted. Smoke is rising from burned buildings, buildings burned by the retreating Southern army. I walked a main street, holding Tad's hand, our escort with us. Along both sides of the street were derelict people, blacks and whites, hungry people, uncertain what our presence meant to them.

I walked into the capitol building, sat hesitantly at the desk of President Jefferson Davis. Sitting there, the escort nearby, I remembered a pubic statement made by Davis, that blacks are children, that slavery is their training school.

In the streets we were met by cheering blacks; they wished to crowd around, realizing we meant no harm.

I sent men to that hellhole, Libby Prison, where thousands of our men have died of starvation and disease and torture; they are to be freed from that tobacco warehouse cesspool.

Riding in a carriage we saw the devastation of the city, ashes and memories. Five years ago today there were three million slaves.

Palm Sunday
1865

In the salon of the *River Queen* I met with my guests as we sailed up the Potomac, the river calm and the air fresh. We talked of the ruins of Richmond, the looters, the burned buildings, the wounded in tent hospitals. I saw a general feeling of sympathy.

During the afternoon, a military band played for us—the "Marseillaise" for my special guest, the Marquis de Chambrun; we had "Dixie" and Foster melodies for the congressmen and their wives.

As we sailed by Mount Vernon someone asked me about Springfield: did I think of returning after my second term? I thought it proper to say that my home was no Mount Vernon but I looked forward to returning.

The meals on our flagship were excellent. Tad was always hungry. Mary did not relish the food, or enjoy some of the guests. All of us know the war is winding down. General Lee has lost 19,000 men, as prisoners to Grant.

I can't remember when I have felt so encouraged.

As I lay in my bunk I could see in my mind a tree that reminded me of great trees I saw as a boy, trees with great shadows. It is worth a man's time to hold communion with trees. The trunk of this tree, seen on the river bank, supported layers of outgoing branches.

Next morning I read to guests in the salon. I read from *Macbeth.* I always find it relaxing to read aloud, though my glasses sometimes bother me. I explained how Macbeth suffered mentally after becoming king. I helped my listeners visualize the murderer. I read from the quarto, graciously given me by Dr. Bancroft.

With Tad sitting at my feet, I read:

...After life's fitful fever he sleeps well;
Treason has done his worst; nor steel, nor poison,
Malice domestic, foreign levy, nothing
Can touch him further.

The White House
Library

Here I attempt to find sanctuary, among the poets.

Now I realize that Mary is going insane.

Only imbalance could bring about such reactions; no one can forget her insults to Grant, to officers and friends at his headquarters. All this distress centered on an innocent pretty woman.

For years I have detected imbalance in Mary. It has come into focus following Willie's death. Hysteria, illnesses, doctors.

I am puzzled why I have persisted in this diary. For a time it seemed fitting to write it for my sons; for a while I considered Mary. As President, I thought of posterity. However posterity should have a solid record, objective, and this record, written at odd moments, emotional, leaves much to be desired.

While with Grant at the front lines, seeing men dead in the field, a man without hands dying, after seeing lifeless boys in the woods, I asked and I ask again, why do I add to these pages?

For a while it seemed to me I was learning about myself and others through these jottings. With Mary's decline I find more question marks here, question marks beyond war's great question marks; these question marks began with Ann Rutledge, resumed in East Salem, continued along the Mississippi and on my legal circuits. For years they lay dormant in Springfield, in the Lincoln house with the green shutters.

Executive Mansion
April 4, 1865

The capitol is decorated from dome to portico.

Victory!

Flags are everywhere.

The weather is fine.

The Treasury building has a huge bond picked out in lights. Cooke's Bank has GLORY TO GOD spelled out in golden stars. Hotels, shops, restaurants are festive, I am told. Bands play "Dixie" and "Yankee Doodle," Irish tunes, Foster's songs. Fireworks and rockets explode over the Potomac. Cannon boom.

Horsemen, carriages, wagons, buggies, pedestrians...there isn't a quiet corner in Washington!

This morning, General Grant shook my hand sadly, hardly a victory gesture. I did not try to penetrate his mood.

Tomorrow I am to speak to a crowd in front of the White House. I will try to envision a sane future. Rain is forecast. It will not matter, nothing is going to diminish the enthusiasm.

Robert is due here tomorrow.

Mary remains in her bedroom.

General Lee has surrendered his forces at the McLean House, at Appomattox. Grant has permitted Lee and his men to return to their homes; they may retain their mounts. Lee pointed out that his army was holding a thousand Union prisoners, prisoners who have nothing to eat but parched corn. His own men amply supplied, Grant has turned over 25,000 rations to Lee's men and fed the Union prisoners.

As I write, fire engines roar, whistles blow, church bells ring.

This morning there was a salute of a hundred guns.

I spoke to a throng in front of the White House. The newspapers will carry my words but I also add them here, thinking to improve the text.

Mary is ill...all very unreal.

An end like a beginning can have a bitter edge.

Let us think as brothers. The great rebellion, which we have endured together, must be forgotten. Now, starting at once, each state must be granted full privileges of the Union as soon as state governments can organize and as soon as 10% of its citizens have taken the oath of allegiance. It is our national goal to offer clemency and pardon as we attain peace, peace for our democracy. I will at once lift the naval blockade. I will urge Congress to appropriate $400,000,000 to assist the South in its economic recovery. Ours is no longer a nation within a nation; ours is a victory for all mankind.

April 10, 1865
Evening
Beautiful sunset

Now that the war is over, Grant thinks we can reduce army expenditures by at least a half a million per day. We can reduce navy costs at the same time; this will bring down our national debt to something like normal proportions.

I am cheered by such prospects.

Peace is ahead and I will be exploring its possibilities intensively. It will be a pleasure to convene a cabinet meeting, to discuss economic changes, foreign relations, amnesty, rail expansion, and state laws. I find a new amicability in senate and house.

In another two or three months it may be possible to have a week or so in the Adirondacks, the three of us.

The White House
Sunday—late

Many have come to congratulate me on the cessation of the war, warm praise now that the union is preserved. Telegrams flood the telegraph office. Boys are always seeking me out, with their hands full of messages. I read newspapers with pleasure. Letters are piling up on my desk; my secretaries are complaining happily.

Everyone in Washington is celebrating. There are parties in homes, in churches, schools, hospitals and public buildings. The White House has scheduled a gala. I am happier than I have been in years.

I look forward to attending a play at Ford's Theatre. I am told that it is a play full of puns. I am in a mood for something light.

I am also told that we are having corn bread at supper.

Note—

Estimates:	North – 360,000 killed in action South — 260,000 killed in action

The White House
April 14, 1865
—rain—

Mary invited Laura Keene, the British actress, to tea. She is in her forties—rather pretty. Dressed in dark green velvet she suggested something of quality in the theatre. She has her own playhouse in New York City. Her talk was mostly about her acting days in London where she produced and acted in foreign and American plays.

She said that she is a friend of Taylor, the author of *Our American Cousin.* "He has written over a hundred plays," she told us.

I spun a frontier story or two; she listened rather absently, her hands in her lap; Mary queried her about forthcoming New York productions; very abruptly Miss Keene exclaimed that she hated war; she said that slavery could have been abolished without destroying lives.

When Tad bounced in she made over him. He took to her, laughing hilariously over her British accent as she asked him to solve a riddle.

"Say it again, pretty lady," he urged her.

"I've heard good things about *Our American Cousin,*" I said. "I guess you already know that we'll be seeing the play tomorrow night."

I

About the Author

Paul Alexander Bartlett (1909-1990) was a writer and artist, born in Moberly, Missouri, and educated at Oberlin College, the University of Arizona, the Academia de San Carlos in Mexico City, and the Instituto de Bellas Artes in Guadalajara. His work can be divided into three categories: He is the author of many novels, short stories, and poems; second, as a fine artist, his drawings, illustrations, and paintings have been exhibited in more than forty one-man shows in leading galleries, including the Los Angeles County Museum, the Atlanta Art Museum, the Bancroft Library, the Richmond Art Institute, the Brooks Museum, the Instituto-Mexicano-Norteamericano in Mexico City, and many other galleries; and, third, he devoted much of his life to the most comprehensive study of the haciendas of Mexico that has been undertaken. More than 350 of his pen-and-ink illustrations of the

haciendas and more than one thousand hacienda photographs make up the Paul Alexander Bartlett Collection held by the Nettie Lee Benson Latin American Collection of the University of Texas, and form part of a second diversified collection held by the American Heritage Center of the University of Wyoming, which also includes an archive of Bartlett's literary work, fine art, and letters.

Paul Alexander Bartlett's fiction has been commended by many authors, among them Pearl Buck, Ford Madox Ford, John Dos Passos, James Michener, Upton Sinclair, Evelyn Eaton, and many others. He was the recipient of many grants, awards, and fellowships, from such organizations as the Leopold Schepp Foundation, the Edward MacDowell Association, the New School for Social Research, the Huntington Hartford Foundation, the Montalvo Foundation, and the Carnegie Foundation.

His wife, Elizabeth Bartlett, a widely published poet, is the author of seventeen published books of poetry, numerous poems, short stories, and essays published in leading literary quarterlies and anthologies, and, as the founder of Literary Olympics, Inc., is the editor of a series of multi-language volumes of international poetry that honor the work of outstanding contemporary poets.

Paul and Elizabeth's son, Steven, edited and designed this volume.

Voices from the Past

was set in Garamond type by Autograph Editions. The typeface is named after Claude Garamond (c. 1480-1561), a French type designer and publisher and the world's first commercial typefounder. Garamond's contribution to the history of typesetting was substantial. He perfected the design of Roman type: The fonts that he cut beginning in 1531 were recognized as possessing a superior grace and clarity, so much so that Garamond's fonts influenced European printing for the next century and a half.

It is interesting to note that Garamond type is the evolutionary ancestor of the type used to print the first official copies of the Declaration of Independence. In the 1730s, Englishman William Caslon refined Garamond's version of Aldine roman, the well-balanced typeface became popular, and was introduced to the American colonies by Benjamin Franklin.

Despite his considerable contribution to the evolution of typography, Garamond was not a successful businessman and he died in poverty.

During the past five centuries, so many variations of Garamond's type designs have been created that the phrase 'Garamond type' has come to be used loosely, with little memory remaining of its history.

www.ingramcontent.com/pod-product-compliance
Lightning Source LLC
Chambersburg PA
CBHW020241030726
47499CB00001B/23
9780615141206